JUSTICE DIED AT DAWN

JUSTICE DOES NOT ALWAYS COME IN TIME...
BUT DAWN ALWAYS COMES

VIKTOR UJKIC

Paperback ISBN: 978-1-967828-69-2

Hardcover ISBN: 978-1-967828-65-4

Published by:
Pine Book Writing
www.PineBookWriting.com
R-10225 Yonge St Suite #250, Richmond Hill, ON L4C 3B2,
Canada.

Printed in the United States of America

DEDICATION

I dedicated my first book to all of those who fight for justice, for what they deserve instead of what they get...

For all of us who fight for freedom, family and friends.

Doing good by others but never by us...

For all of those who never surrender...

To what they believe...

ACKNOWLEDGEMENT

This book was written during quiet nights, difficult days, and in moments of doubt. I want to thank my family for standing by me, even when I drifted into fictional worlds. To the ones who love me and I love them, who never stopped asking, "How's the book?"—thank you for reminding me it mattered. And to everyone who believed in me before I believed in myself. I want to thank My Mother, brother and my biggest supporters: Tanisha Mullings, Viktor Camović, Daniel Ujkić, Đoko Pajović, and Momčilo Lakićević, my biggest supporters since I started writing. A special thanks goes to my publishers, Pine Book Writing Inc., especially Steve Hayes, Rex Brown and Sara Lane.

Happy reading!

AUTHOR'S NOTE

It began on an ordinary afternoon—April 9th, 2025—when a quiet thought planted itself in my mind: what if I wrote a book? I didn't plan the world. I didn't outline chapters. I simply imagined a single character, gave him a name, a purpose, and placed him into a time long past. From there, everything else came to life. Castles, betrayal, whispers in candlelit halls—none of it was forced. It felt like the story had already existed somewhere, waiting for me to listen.

Writing this novel became more than storytelling. It was an escape. It was discipline. It was the only thing I looked forward to on the longest days and the latest nights. There were moments I nearly gave up; moments I felt like the story didn't matter. But I kept going—because something about it wouldn't let me stop.

This book is a piece of my solitude and my curiosity. It's fiction, yes—but like all fiction, it carries truths in disguise. About longing. About justice. About how we carry pain, love, guilt, and hope through time. If you're reading this now, thank you for stepping into the world I found. I hope it speaks to something inside you the way it spoke to something inside me.

—V. U

EPIGRAPH

They say he vanished before dawn.

But the blood on the stones said otherwise.

Contents

Introduction

The story takes place in the Medieval era in Europe, in Germany, Austria and Romania. During the reign of the Holly Roman Empire that used to dominate at that time.

The protagonist of the story is a boy, Victor, born in Bavaria in 1444, from a poor and struggling family, especially at that time of crisis and desperation in every possible way, his mother, Lara, and his father, Thomas, were hard-working people. His father was a farmer; his entire land was covered with wheat crops. On the other hand, Lara was a tailor, a hard-working lady with precise sewing skills and innovative thinking; however, it did not pay working day and night, due to the domination of the black hearted thorns and high rank society the rest were just poor and hardly coping with the life at that time. Lara and Thomas gave up on believing in God and were mocked by society for not going to the Sunday mass, due to that, they lost what they had, starting with Thomas not selling the wheat and Lara losing her customers. One long winter night of December in 1452, while all were having dinner, Thomas thought that he could maybe borrow 500 Golden coins from a trader in order to move with his family to France to seek a better life. His wife did not agree and just wanted to remain there and try something else instead, maybe going back to church. Thomas was raging; he just threw the chair.

"God does not exist and does not help, once poor, always poor," he bellowed, hoping that God himself would hear.

Lara remained calm for Victor, reassuring him, "Everything will be all right."

On the morning of the next day, Thomas went to ask for the loan, not knowing what he was getting himself and his family into. He knocked on the door of Michael D. Schneider, who was a high-ranking trader working for the black hearted thorns and the order of the wicked ones. Thomas did not know any of that. He was welcomed in the most beautiful manner and with high hospitality, he thought to himself, "Michael must be a nice fellow." - He was wrong.

Michael and his Wife, Emiliana, invited him for lunch that day, inviting Lara and Victor as well.

And there they went, hoping in themselves that God was looking down to them and that there is hope after all. Michael opened the doors of his Castle, and they went inside, after eating and chatting about the usual life, Michael asked Thomas, "So, what do you need the money for?"

Chapter One: A Chaos Before a Dream Could Start

Thomas beamed at the opportunity to discuss his plans for the future. "I want to move with my family to France. I'd love to start a business there; Lara could open a small shop in Paris. She's always dreamt of her designs being worn by the high society ladies of France, haven't you darling?"

Lara nodded enthusiastically, looking from Thomas to Michael, smiling.

Michael agreed and gave him the money, without further questions, but along with money, there was an envelope that explained the due date for the return of the loan and further information.

Upon arriving home, Thomas opened the envelope and started reading. It was stated that the money belongs to a black hearted thorn who was willing to lend it to him on one condition, and that was to attend the church and become a member of the order of the wicked ones.

On the other hand, if refused, the loan cannot be paid back, but both Thomas and Lara would be eliminated by the order of the wicked ones.

Reading this, Thomas was raging and desperate and in disbelief, shouting and swearing and kicking the table, losing control. He got outside the house, mounted his horse and went back to Michael's house to return the golden coins; however, Michael did not open the door. Thomas left the sack of golden coins in front of the Castle's door, hoping that he owes nothing to the black hearted thorn and to the order of the wicked ones as well.

Upon returning home, he tried to remain calm and to hope that all was over, but what he read in the letter kept haunting him. Lara did not know this; she was in the town that day, hoping to sell some of her handmade dresses, but did not succeed.

The next day, Thomas was preparing to work on the land to clean the grass around the crops. He noticed a black carriage driven by a black hearted thorn who was gazing at his and his house. Thomas did not feel pleased with this, he tried to approach, but the carriage by then drove off. Lara was preparing to go to the town again to try once more, not knowing that Thomas returned the golden coins.

Victor was left with his father that day. He played on the front porch of the house with wooden sticks and was beating the fences with them, imagining that they were the black hearted thorns. Thomas was sitting on a chair, thinking about what to do next…

Days passed and weeks, and the black carriage was in front of their house every Sunday at 14:00. Driving them mad and questioning their

4

existence, only Thomas knew this; he tried to protect his family by remaining silent, but that did not end up as he thought it would.

While people were returning from church that day, nobody greeted Thomas and his family that day due to the fear of the black carriage, but one lady called Samantha approached their house. "Thomas - the day is near," she warned, before turning back to the town and leaving.

He understood at that moment what was going to happen, so he did not hesitate to tell Lara to take Victor and to run as far as possible, but that just worsened the situation and alarmed the area. Upon trying to escape through the narrow streets full of mud and dirt, the horses grew tired and began to slow down. Thomas told Lara, "Leave me. Take Victor and go," - he wanted to give his life in order to save them. But at that moment, the black carriage showed up, and two the black hearted thorns were standing in front of them, one was tall and had a beard, and the other one was shorter and had a moustache. Both had brown hair and looked alike.

Thomas approached them and told them that he had "I have returned the money to Michael. Please, I implore you, spare the lives of my wife and son."

Thomas sank to his knees, begging for their lives.

The one with the moustache smirked as he hissed, "The order of the wicked ones does not agree."

At that moment, Thomas offered his farm and the house and everything they had in order to spare his family, but at that moment, rain started, and the tall black hearted thorn explained coldly, "The order of the wicked ones has commanded that we eliminate you both."

Panic struck Thomas's heart like a bolt of lightning.

He shrieked, "Lara! Take Victor, run! Do not look back!" frantic with concern for them.

At that moment, Thomas was eliminated, shortly after they caught up with Lara and eliminated her as well, leaving Victor to see his dead parents. The black hearted thorns drove off and left a mark on their chests in the symbol of the cross. The rain was pouring, and the thunder was raging. The sky was darker than death itself for the poor kid Victor, he was crying and shaking, yelling and shaking their bodies in hope for any kind of response, nobody wanted to help him or to even consider talking to him.

His world was shattered into pieces, his hope was gone, and in front of him was a desperation of existence and a memory to linger forever, he didn't know what to do next or from whom to seek help, it took him five days and nights to dig the graves for his parents and to bury them.

After finishing the burial he fell asleep on the front porch of the house on the same chair that Thomas used to sit, he had a dream that he was kidnapped by the black hearted thorns and that he was the last from the order of the wicked ones for that family, in his dream he was one of them helping the rich to become more richer and the poor to become more poor, in his dream the black hearted thorns who eliminated his parents showed up and told him that it had to be like that, he was trying to fight them in a dream, but he was just a kid.

He was woken up by a raven who got his wing hurt. The raven was a baby raven. Victor fed him and took care of him for weeks, becoming friends with the Raven, and he named him Oni.

Oni followed him everywhere until something changed the entire path of his life, leading to another chaotic situation on a morning in May.

Poor Victor was hungry and devastated, broken from life and what had happened; he did not need another heartbreaking situation. That morning, he was approached by another black hearted thorn whose name was Mark. He was the head of the leading organization to take the orphanages to the training center led by the Church in association with the order of the wicked ones. He offered him two choices: to train in the Church to become a trader, or to become a black hearted thorn. He chose the training center; he was taken there and had his hair cut, was given a uniform and a set of rules to follow. Basically, he was in prison there for six long years.

He was trained by the Nuns and Priests, taught to write and learn, taught to pray and obey!

That organization and the Church was led by Father John and the leading Nun Nora; both were evil and enjoyed torturing the kids. One night, they beat up Victor for saying that God is bad; they beat him so hard that for the upcoming four weeks, he could not move out of the bed. In that Church, there was a boy named Chris, his parents were eliminated by the black hearted thorns as well, in some stranger settings. Chris, one day, was attending mass but saw Victor and asked him to join him at the lunch table. The nun Lora split them, and since then, months passed, and they did not see each other. However, one day in October, Chris snuck into Victor's room.

"Is there any way that we can talk?"

Victor whispered anxiously, "It's dangerous... we might get caught."

A sound from the corridor was heard, it was Father John walking, so Chris hid in the drawer until John passed. They talked about what to do next and how to plan the escape but there was no way out for them at that time.

Since all the doors were locked and the keys for the ground floor were held by John, while the keys for the gates were held by Lora, Chris suggested to Victor to try and steal the keys while everybody was asleep; however, Victor hesitated, thinking that it would cause more trouble if the plan failed.

The flame of the candle was flickering in Chris's eyes as he plotted, "First, we must steal John's keys and then Lora's keys. We must sneak and remain as silent as possible."

But another problem was the guards, how to bypass them… Victor had a brainwave: "We should lure another member into this."

The next Morning Victor and Chris were separate but could see each other from the distance at the dining table in the hall of the church, Chris was signaling Victor to look to the left at the ninth table from the row, pointing at Otto another kid who was popular for being a revolutionary in the church and got beaten up very often by the nun, priests and guards.

Victor wrote a letter to Otto saying, "Meet me and Chris at room 26 at midnight." Victor stood up, holding his plate and started walking towards Otto's table, he dropped the letter unnoticed by the other kids or guards.

Chris snuck up once again to Victor's room, and both waited thirty-five minutes for Otto to show up. That night, Otto could not make it.

The next week, on Thursday at mass, Otto whispered to Chris, his eyes darting around the room to ensure he wasn't caught, "I was caught by the guards and beaten. Perhaps we should try tonight."

Once again, Chris snuck up to Victor's room, and both waited for Otto, and he arrived right at midnight. They suggested that Chris should steal John's keys, Victor should steal Lora's' keys, and Otto would look out for guards and signal first to Chris and then to Victor until all of them reach the front gate.

They continued with the plan and on the next night arranged an escape at midnight. Chris was the one to take the silent steps towards John's room, walking silently and in every step he took was cautious and ready to get the signals from Otto, to look up for guards. At the end of the corridor was a guard who was heading right, but he was tired and took a chair to sit, Chris waited to see what would happen next. The guard sat on the chair, and his head started to fall down, indicating that he was about to go to sleep. Chris took even lighter steps in order to pass the corridor. Upon arriving at John's door, the keys were hanging too high so he could not reach them, he was way too scared to make noise in order to move and object and climb into. So, Chris had another plan to reach them with another object, with the sword of John. He tried once, twice and then once more until he reached the keys. Chris nearly closed the door of John's room to remain calm, and silent he had to bypass the guard once again to reach the gate and to signal Otto that Victor had to make the next move and to steal Lora's keys, so he went slowly by walking through the dining room and then going left to towards the nuns rooms, and to reach the end of the hall to Lora's room, but the guard was awake so was Lora.

Otto signaled him to wait, so Victor waited for a full two hours until the guard finally fell asleep, but what Victor did not know was that Lora was not asleep.

He was walking silently towards Lora's room, and he noticed that the door was not completely shut, at that moment, Victor was on one side happy, thinking that it would be an easy task to steal the keys, but on the other side, Victor was fearing that she might not be alone. He pushed the door a bit and heard strange noises from Lora's room, apparently, she was having sex with a priest. Victor was in disbelief seeing such a scene for the first time in his life, but he thought this is my chance to steal the keys which were on the table from his right side. He was approaching the table, and Lora was reaching her climax, so Victor was more scared but managed to grab the keys he left the room, but the noise from the old door upon opening alarmed Lora and the priest. Luckily, Victor managed to hide in the cabinet ten meters from Lora's room.

He was not discovered by the priest. The priest grabbed at Lora's waist, trying to tempt her back to bed as he whispered into her ear, "Nobody is there; maybe they were just noises from another room." Apparently, the priest did not have any in a long time…

Victor's task was to meet Chris and Otto at the gate. It was late, so everyone was asleep. Chris had arrived first and was waiting for Victor, and Otto appeared sometime later, but Victor was late. Upon waiting, they saw a strange light in the sky. Otto's mouth widened into a toothy grin, and his eyes were bright as he exclaimed to Chris, "It's a sign from the sky!"

"Perhaps it is a sign from the sky… But we can talk about it once we escape this hell." Chris replied, still apprehensive that they may be caught.

While chatting Victor arrived and they managed to escape the Church, hungry and thirsty they walked three weeks through the woods and were scared by various wildlife but managed to reach the town, upon arriving the plan was to steal three horses and to ride off to Austria, aiming to arrive in Vienna and hoping to start new life for all three of them.

At dawn on June 15th, all three planned to steal horses along with the weapons from a local shop near the black hearted thorn's house, which was located west of Bavaria. Victor prepared the plan and was ready to share the details with Otto and Chris.

That morning, Otto was the one who was obligated to steal the horses, Chris to steal the weapons, and Victor to distract the shop owner; however, the plans all changed when the drunk black hearted thorn was roaming around the streets yelling and cursing the current situation that he was in. Victor wanted to lure the black hearted thorn to the cornfield and to beat him up; they all gathered up and talked about this, but this plan was successful after stealing the horses and weapons.

12

Stealing The Horses and Weapons

As they went according to the plan, Victor promised Chris and Otto that they would make it to Austria, but they just had to have faith in themselves. Chris was a bit scared in the beginning, but managed to gather the courage and move on. Victor got inside the shop and was chatting with the shop owner while Chris was stealing five swords and four knives along with three axes; however, some of them were dull and in need of repair. The shields were broken, and he could not find the bow, but some arrows were found too, all this at the house of the shop owner. On the other side Otto was having a hard time stealing the horses at the barn of the shop owner just a few meters away from his house, due to the fact that the horses were scared and did not recognize Chris, but he managed to calm them down by brushing and petting them, along with slowly tapping their neck. Chris had a strange vision at that moment that all of them were chased, but the vision was not so clear, so who chased them remains to be revealed.

Victor was still inside the shop and was waiting for the signal to get out. When he got out, right before him was a drunk black hearted thorn singing and drinking rum from a bottle. Victor had an urge to lure him to the cornfield, where Chris and Otto were patiently waiting for Victor to come back.

Hatred got the better of Victor; he smiled sweetly at the black hearted thorn as he said, "Come with me, I have more rum for you, sir."

He got lured easily and followed him there. Otto and Chris did not understand what was going on, but as Victor was walking with the black hearted thorn behind him, a little girl showed up out of nowhere.

With worry in her voice as she ran to him, "Papa, Papa, why are you drunk?"

At that moment, the world froze in front of Victor's eyes, and his heart was filled with rage; his heart was on fire, and all the memories came back to that moment, his heart was beating fast, and his face grew pale. Chris understood what the plan was. Otto was staying still and looking at that situation, Chris grabbed the girl and took her to the playground, where other kids were playing.

"Your father will be here soon," he reassured as he patted her head.

Meanwhile, Victor tempted the black hearted thorn, "Just a little bit closer, and I will give you more rum."

As they both got to the cornfield, the black hearted thorn explained, "The new order will arrive by the head of the order of the wicked ones."

Victor's voice was full of spite. "Not for you…"

14

At that moment Victor saw the weapons and grabbed the swords and eliminated the black hearted thorn he felt how it is to eliminate for the first time; he felt so much pain and desperation after that so that he could not sleep for a week and also grew distant and somehow silent but not talking and not eating their entire journey to Vienna was just cold after eliminating the black hearted thorn.

One day, whilst they were resting, Chris glanced from Victor, who was sitting on a rock at the riverbank, to Otto.

"He needs more time to recover. He's not who he was before…"

Otto eyed Victor cautiously as he whispered, "His entire perception has changed… He wants justice for his parents, no matter what obstacles are standing in front of him."

Could this make him a step closer to becoming something else? Time will tell.

On the evening of July 8th, upon arriving in Vienna, their plan was to steal enough for new wardrobes, food and other supplies since they had nothing but stealing did not come easily since they had no previous experience. Otto was the one who was pickpocketing and learned it fast; also, he could easily tell who was rich, judging by their look.

Chris was the one who stole wardrobes from shops by sneaking in and out, and Victor was the one who stole gold from houses when nobody was inside by breaking in through the windows and leaving no tracks.

Months continued like that until they got on their feet and got what they wanted in the first place, until one day, when Otto was caught pickpocketing by an old man called Frank, who saw him stealing. Otto was chased by the royal guards through the streets until he hid under the carriage of a rich trader in town.

Investigating The Crime Scene

The next morning, after all the fuss with Otto, there was an elimination, the entire place was alarmed, so all three of them wanted to know what was happening there. The wife of the Austrian trader was murdered she was found dead on the floor, upon arriving and sneaking in Chris found out that on her right hand there was a note in which was written TEMPLE OF JUSTICE, he showed the note to Victor.

Chris stared at the note, "It might be some sort of organization."

However, Victor was skeptical about that and chose to ignore the presumption.

On the other hand, Otto found out that she had been killed by suggesting that "Only a professional could make something like this."

Again, Victor was intrigued at that moment; they could not find footprints or any other visible traces for the striker and up until that moment, it remained a mystery.

They continued to talk about it and brainstorm after leaving the scene, that evening, while a thunderstorm was growing bigger and bigger outside, scaring the entire town deeply.

That evening Chris had a dream that they went to a temple underground and that there they met some strange people who spoke a different language and were praying to some force, somehow, they managed to get to the front and each and every one of them was missing an ear but the dream was blurry and was not clear in some other details.

Upon waking up, Chris told Victor and Otto about this, at which they both laughed at that part, missing an ear.

Victor chuckled as he joked, "They had one extra, didn't they?"

Chris went outside a bit nervous but upon stepping foot outside he thought that he saw one of them in the distance and when he started to chase him, he ran away. He felt strange and a little scared due to the fact that everything was so strange and an enigma.

Preparation To Rob the Stage Couch

In order to have some gain, all three decided to rob a stagecoach that was transporting gold from the local bank. As they gathered around the table to draw the plan, Otto had an idea to leave no trace; however, things did not go as planned.

Victor strategized with the targets in mind, "We must be calm and not make a scene. We only need to gain more funds in order to move closer to the black hearted thorn."

Chris agreed, and they all sat and drew the plan.

Otto was the one who had to act dead in front of the road in order to make the stagecoach stop and to make the driver leave the position thus, that makes it easier for Victor to pick the lock from behind while Chris was the one who had to knock down the other one and after that Otto had to knock down the driver. The plan is so simple, Victor concluded.

Robbing The Stagecoach

As they all gathered at the destination area before the bridge, Otto was already lying on the ground waiting, Victor was hidden behind the trees, and Chris was hidden behind the barn.

When the driver noticed that there was somebody on the ground, he did not care much. Otto was nearly run over; the driver must have known that it was a trick. Victor signaled Chris by hand signal to move forward and to ambush them, while Otto hardly got out alive, he got up after rolling and escaping death and aimed to beat the hell out of the driver, while Victor and Chris did the same to the other one, after leaving both of them on the ground unconsciousness. Vic went to pick the lock after succeeding, and upon opening the safe, guess what? The safe was empty. They all got mad and furious, as it seems the transport of the gold was the other way around.

"Where did they want to take the gold from the bank?" Chris asked, brows furrowed, and he tried to work it out.

Upon closer inspection, there was another layer on that couch. Otto saw it when he kicked the rear end; those two hid the gold on purpose and wanted to escape with it.

Vic was happy like never, Otto was shouting to both of them, bragging about the fact that he nearly died.

Chris sat there, his eyes glinting from all of the gold that surrounded him as he asked, "Wow, we made it, what now?"

As days passed, they all had their moments of fame and spending. There was a lack of focus on the black hearted thorn, a temporarily forgotten aim, as it seems. They all lived for today for several months, settling down and completing side missions for traders and for local people while spending in the evenings purchasing horses, weapons, equipment and such.

They developed a circle of drinking, gambling and living the wild life until things took another turn. Otto became obsessed with finding out the mystery of the order of the wicked ones and who is their leader.

Chris, on the other hand, wanted to master witchcraft, and Victor wanted to bury the past, but the past haunted him in his dreams and visions, such as seeing his parents often, like a reminder of having to get back on track.

One night, after leaving the bar drunk while walking, they heard a noise from a distance. Lured to get there was a lady who was crying and screaming while she was sitting next to her dead husband. Upon asking, she explained that he was eliminated by a man with a long jacket. They got it immediately and realized that there was an organization of the Temple of Justice.

Now, all that they wanted was to catch one of them and find out where the location of the Temple of Justice was. Not knowing that upon finding it, their lives would change forever - so much for being naive…

In the morning of the next day, at the window of Vic's room, Oni was standing and moving his wings. When Vic woke up and saw him, he was so happy that he screamed "Oni!" which scared him off. After that, Oni returned, and he spent the entire day with Oni. Chris and Otto were just in disbelief. How is this possible?

"How can he be this close with a raven?" they asked each other, completely perplexed.

In the evening, Vic explained to them the entire story of Oni and the Raven, sticking with the story to the end from then on…

Rescue The Lady from The Robbers

After chopping the wood and preparing for the winter, while Vic was loading the horses and leading them on foot to the house, he stumbled upon an unusual situation. There was a hill nearby, and next to it was a huge tree; everybody called that tree the Compass because it was the main orientation of the area if you didn't have a compass. A lady named Sarah was robbed and tied to a tree. She explained to Vic what was going on, and he asked her to direct him to her horse so he could follow the robbers, but he did not untie her.

"When I return, I will untie you."

"Why not untie me now?!" She asked, her eyes pleading for freedom.

Vic replied coldly, "You might steal my wood and horses…"

He then left the lady tied up and carried on riding in order to find the robbers, following the tracks of the horses. Vic came upon an old house in the countryside. The house seemed abandoned and long left, but there the traces ended. He then heard some noises from inside; it sounded like some objects were dropped. Upon closer inspection, there they were, hiding the stolen goods.

They were talking about some of their plans to steal the Relic of the King. Vic then wanted to approach and to hear more, but the floor was sensitive and it broke down under his right foot, scaring them. He then ran after them and interrogated them after a bit of a fight. He found out that they were only simple thieves and that the relic story might be made up. He picked up the goods stolen from the lady. On his way out of the door, he told them smugly, "I've got to go, the lady is waiting tied up to the tree…"

Upon arriving back, the lady was waiting and when she saw Vic was shouting desperately from a distance, "You came back, untie me!"

After he did so, she thanked him and told him next time untie me first, they both laughed and went their separate ways…

Steal The Ancient Books Containing the Strikers in Them

Upon arriving home and gathering to prepare the next step, Vic suggested that they should steal the books that contained the Strikers and any kind of info that could get them closer to the Temple of Justice.

As they began to plan, Chris told Otto, "We should look at the black hearted thorn's houses since they are the ones who are always at war with them."

Vic agreed but added, "Do not exclude the church as the searching point as well."

The plan was simple: Don't get killed, and if you get caught, RUN!

Since it is a high difficulty Mission, and this is where Oni was doing its best.

As they all separated and went to steal the books, they saw that it's impossible to sneak in alone in three locations, so they all came back to the house and gathered again, concluding that sometimes in life we have to stick together... as they did so.

This time they used disguises and uniforms to blend in with the guards at one location and as priests at the second one, and as the black hearted thorn at the third one.

The black hearted thorn's door could not be broken into; it could be opened only by a special key.

The key had to be stolen, and that black hearted thorn was dead, so his grave had to be found and opened...

At sunset the next day, they all gathered together to go on the first life-risking mission.

They all swore an oath dedicated to reprisal: "If any of us does not make it, the rest must continue in fulfilling the aim of vengeance and finding the two strikers."

Chris took the lead by walking in front of the church disguised as a priest full of self-confidence and full of belief that it can be done on the other hand Otto was the one who figured out that the black hearted thorn's location was at that same church but in the second-floor room at the end of the corridor. Upon arriving at the church Chris was blending in and it looked like he was trying to look as though he was praying, and saw Otto by looking up to the left, he signaled him to wait by raising both hands up. Victor was sneaking in from the underground entrance and had knocked down three guards. He was looking for the grave of the black hearted thorn. It was hard to make it alone, so he waited for Otto to find what he could at the black hearted thorn's room and to join Victor, as well as for Chris after he had managed to steal the key.

Chris took the lead by approaching the altar to take the Body of Jesus at the end of mass and silently stealing the key from the bishop, he was almost caught.

When mass was over, Chris dropped the key through the canal and signaled Oni to make the noise in order for Victor to get the signal that the key is in the position. Victor went to take the key but heard from the distance that somebody was entering the area, upon closer inspection, while staying hidden behind the wall, there were two nuns approaching the area. He waited until they passed through that area and went to climb up in order to take the key. Meanwhile, Chris was heading to the underground location and Otto was trying to find the books Victor took the key and opened the door of the catacombs and started searching for the grave that contained the black hearted thorn's tomb, one by one and row by row the area filled with rats, spiders and some snakes it was not easy to get by especially in that kind of settings. Victor was determined to find the grave, in the meantime, Otto found some books and arrived in front of the entrance, guarding and waiting for Victor to get out and Otto to move in.

Time passed and Vic managed to find the Grave but could not move the stone alone, upon trying four times the fifth time he gather all his strength in order to push the grave and managed to push it but he felt that some kind of force in him had helped him to push it after that a headache started to occur along with dizziness, his sight grew blurry and teary he did not understand what was going on, his legs started to shake and he felt he lost control of himself and something was happening. Chris grew impatient by then and decided to step in, while he was walking he felt some sort of dark energy in the area and his heart was pounding, however when he saw Vic from the distance he ran towards him all worried and in disbelief of what was going on, he then took the books and carried Vic to the surface area, at that moment Otto was heading to the entrance area, when Chris managed to put Vic on the carriage and ride off. Otto arrived and upon entering he saw that nobody was inside again, signaling Oni seeking for help to reveal their location, Otto climbed the roof and started running from roof to roof as he was feeling some strange but good force inside in order to follow the Raven and find Vic and Chris.

Chris carried Vic next to the fire and was trying to help, but he did not regain any strength or give any signs of movement.

At that moment, books were in the carriage, nobody was even thinking of them, and then Otto arrived and took the books and opened the door, not knowing what was happening, and when he saw them, he understood what was going on.

Both of them did not know what to do at that particular moment

After a few moments of thinking had passed, Otto said with certainty, "We must call the local doctor."

Chris raised his hand to Otto, his gaze never leaving Victor. "Wait… Give him some time."

In front of the fireplace, while outside a storm had started Victor had a vision of all of his future in front of his eyes, everything that was going to happen as if like he was in a future realm and seeing his future, his eyes filled with tears that rolled down, his soul filled with rage and his heart with vengeance. What else he had to lose…

After some time, he started to move his fingers and regained the cognitive functions of the body and laid down to sleep. He slept for half a day and woke up the next day confused and tired.

In the meantime, Chris and Otto were reading the books and discovered the Location of the Temple of Justice and their system of norms and regulations, as well as the origin. They decided that it was not time yet to let Vic know about all that, so after some time that day they all went for a hike in the mountains just to pass sometime in the nature and to be with nature, to smell the fresh air and to hear the birds, gazing at the trees and feeling the grass.

After reaching a good distance of hiking, they arrived at the lake. Vic wanted to dive in the water to feel the power of the water.

Chris was uneasy. "Are you sure that you can do it?"

"Did you regain all your energy?" Otto asked, equally as concerned for Vic.

"I feel like there must be something in the water," Vic replied, certain that it was something that he must do.

As he jumped in the water, all the birds took off, and the sound of wolves howling was heard from the distance. While diving deeper and deeper, he saw something that appeared like a ghost, a transparent-looking creature of a lady that was moving slowly, but it appeared that the ghost was not moving at all, and when he reached to touch it with his hands, the creature disappeared. Perplexed, he asked himself, "Am I dreaming all of this? What is going on? Where is all this leading to and why?"

Upon coming back to the surface, he climbed on a rock and sat there for hours, trying to meditate, but could not reach the focus.

Otto and Chris decided that it would be best to leave Vic with some time on his own.

He slept that night near the lake, and when he woke up, he felt strange, as if that ghost had done something.

He started to walk to reach the house but was confused and tired so he called Oni to help him go home, instead of Oni just leading the way he landed on his arm, but Vic being without the leather protection on his arm Oni scratched his skin which started to bleed. At that moment Oni took off and lead him home bleeding and dying inside, upon reaching home he saw that Chris was sleeping and Otto was reading, Vic started to drink and one after one he got drunk, got out on the streets and started to yell "OH BLACK HEARTED THORNS, PRIESTS, KINGS AND QUEENS - face me at once!" The area was alarmed, and chaos was about to start, but at that moment, he was kidnapped by a striker who was watching all that from the roof of the Monastery.

He was taken to the striker's home and given a potion that made him talk about everything that he had in mind. He explained to the striker why he was desperate and what was going on with his life at that current moment, as well as what was the cause that led him to that state of mind and soul.

"Find us when you are ready." The striker said as he handed Vic a medallion.

Vic left and got home. Upon arriving, Otto and Chris grew impatient and started to question him.

Vic told them firmly, "I need more time. Time is all I have."

So, they planned the next mission.

<u>Entering The Inner Self</u>

Victor looked up to meet Chris and Otto's eyes.

"I plan on visiting the witch. I have some questions…"

Loyal as ever, Otto almost instantly agreed to go.

Ever the pessimist, Chris warned, "You may ask questions that you don't like the answers to, you know that, right?"

However, he did not quit.

Right at midnight Vic went to the witch's place alone, while he was walking he saw the full moon and felt some kind of power in his heart, the power could not be described with words it felt like some sort of force pushing him to move on and to achieve his goals, as well as his happy moment, maybe one day he will get the true happiness in life, or is he doomed to die in agony while living it. …we will find out…

While he was walking, trillions of thoughts occupied his brain, about everything that was happening and about what was going to happen. At the end of that storm, one question remained in his brain, and that was: Why did it have to be like this?

Upon arriving at the witch's house, he saw that the door was not closed.

He called out, "Anybody home?" as he opened the door and scanned the room for signs of life.

The wind carried the witch's shrill tones through the house. "Yes, come on in."

Her house was filled with symbols, stones of various shapes and sizes, colors, Voodoo dolls. In a big dish, something was cooking, and she was saying some magical words in strange languages… everything was so strange, as well as her millions of books and strange items.

The witch studied Vic as he sat down in a chair opposite her.

"What do you wish to know?"

He sat there for some time frozen, not knowing what to answer and what to think or what words to utter his brain froze, after that she began some ritual while she was touching the glass ball at her table Vic was still frozen, as the ritual was ongoing some strange voices were heard around, out of nowhere the wind was starting to shake the house a strange force was in the air consuming it, she knew all that and yet she continued even more to push it to the limit, the glasses were breaking outside and the noises grew louder and louder, black smoke started to come out of the ball of glass, Vic was still frozen…

She started to see into his future, and after some moments, she grew pale and her powers weakened. When calm after the storm fell, from her right eye a tear fell, and Vic came to his senses.

30

The witch whispered her prophecy like the low wind sighs.

"You will make it, the storms will shake the mountains, and from the sky will rain blood, never give up and never give in! Everything else is not mine to say or to tell you, it's yours to decide and to feel it."

When Vic heard that, he knew that there was hope and that not everything was lost. He then left her house and reached home.

That night, he could not sleep for a second; again, his thoughts started to occupy his mind like an empire that occupies countries and territories. He started to think about his existence in this life, as well as about the point of life itself. He forgot that the witch had told him that he will make it. Making or not making it, that was not the focus that night of his thoughts.

He felt like he had been possessed or that something was not right, due to the previous situations, or is this all some kind of progressing disease or curse, because blessing it cannot be.

At dawn, he stood up and went outside. Chris and Otto did not disturb him at all; they let him be. Vic mounted his horse and decided to go to the top of the mountain to try to meditate and clear his mind he spent nine hours just sitting and clearing his mind, in the end he managed to reach the point of meditation, when he cut the cord by coming back into reality his life changed drastically, he mounted the horse and rushed back to Chris and Otto.

Vic burst through the door, startling Chris and Otto. "I am back, let's go!"

Otto grinned as he asked, "Where shall we go, Captain?"

Vic's face curled into a smile, too. "Haha, very funny, let's go and continue what we started."

Save The Accused Lady of Being a Witch

As the day was about to start on an early October, Vic was sleeping, but the screaming of an old man woke him up. A lady was seen making some smoke rise in the air with her hand, and the old man believed that she was a witch. He started to scream and go crazy about it, waking people in the area up and letting them know that she was a witch. Upon accusing her, the guards rushed to take her to burn her at the stake.

Vic and the others woke up, immediately grabbing their weapons and rushing to save her from being burned alive. She was taken to the edge of the street, and the crowd decided that she would be burned; they all believed him that she had some superpowers, according to what the old man saw.

Vic was standing behind the crowd while Chris and Otto were ready to strike from the sides.

Eliminate The Guards Save The Lady

Vic was sneaking slowly through the crowd while Chris was ready to take the first guard down. Slowly, without being noticed, he eliminated the guard and hid him behind the wall, while Otto did the same, but on the other side. Vic was the one who had to eliminate the third one, who was holding the torch. Vic saw that it was seconds apart from him, laying down the torch, so he rapidly moved faster and kicked the torch with his left foot and instantly eliminating the guard with his sword. Then he rescued the lady and took her by the hand and escaped the area. Otto and Chris left too.

The lady scanned the area for any danger, but once she knew the coast was clear, the fear in her eyes became gratitude within the blink of an eye. "I can't thank you enough, you must allow me to reward you for rescuing me!"

While accompanying her home they talked about the injustice in society and what is happening, they shared some of their life stories and experiences. When they arrived the lady whose name we don't know rewarded Vic with an ancient bow from Japan that she held close and inherited from her grandmother.

Vic thanked her and was very happy to receive such a precious reward. So, the next moment he went to the craftsman nearby to purchase twenty arrows, which he did so, after that he rushed back home to start practicing and was admired by Otto, how happy he was with shooting arrows while Oni was playing fetch with Chris.

As Otto watched, he turned to Vic. "It runs in your blood, doesn't it?"

As Vic loaded another arrow, he shot off a quick glance and replied, "It seems it does."

"So, what now? Are you going to practice for days, or do we have a plan?" Otto asked as he stared at the tree, which had become Vic's practice target.

Once he had landed his shot, Vic lowered the bow. "Maybe we should visit the Temple of Justice that we were offered to join, what do you say?"

"Chris, come here, man," Otto shouted over to the back porch

Chris snapped, "In a moment!" irritated that he had been interrupted, but calmed as he commanded the raven, "Wait, Oni, stay still. I will be back."

He scampered over. "What is going on? I was playing with Oni."

"We want to go to the Temple of Justice, are you with us?" Vic asked him, unfazed by his annoyance.

This proposal calmed Chris as he had assumed he had been interrupted for something trivial. "Yes, let's go. Why not? We have nothing to lose."

Here it begins…

The Hidden Justice

Motivated and excited to begin their journey, Vic wanted Otto and Chris to share his optimism as he declared, "Everything has a beginning, but not everything has an end. When you are at the worst, you always do your best. Now here we are, after everything we went through and everything that we may go through. We are ready for the next step further, as we were never alone until now, we shall never be from now. Unity - all for one and one for all! Right until the end of time. As brothers, we live and as brothers, we will die, let's go!"

Solve the puzzle of the Temple of Justice and get into the Temple of Justice.

The next morning, as they gathered up for this mission it started to rain heavily, thunder was striking all around and there was nobody to be seen outside. Their horses were scared but without the horses it would be a really long journey to take. However, waiting for the storm to pass would just be a waste of time.

They decided to go on foot anyway it would take them several hours; they went together on foot through the storm, though the mountains and then following the Danube River with no stopping or looking back. On their journey, they met an old man called Richard.

Their optimism about encountering the Temple of Justice concerned him greatly. Gravely, he warned, "Do not go to the Temple of Justice. Your lives will change forever… You could end up dead or worse."

Though he appreciated the elder's wisdom, Vic replied with all of the ignorance of youth, "Richard, do not worry about us. We have nothing left to lose, and thus we want to do this no matter the results."

They continued this journey, and after meeting the locals of the village and telling them where they were about to go, everyone was scared and just left with no words. But that did not stop them.

Vic saw the signs where the organization might be, and as it seems, they were not very far from the location. There were drawings of signs in the stones, with the symbols of guidance, but none of them understood those symbols.

Chris saw a stone, and there was something written on it, but they had to solve that puzzle and find more clues about where it was leading them.

On the stone, it was written: "I am the Sun, at dawn, and I show only at night. What am I?

I am the moon at the sunset; at night, I shine. What am I?

I am the stone that is hidden, I am heavy and round, what am I?"

They were all thinking about these clues and concluded that at some point of the day or night, there should be a stone in the form of a circle, and they should all try to move it in order to reveal the hidden passage.

While they were searching around and patiently waiting for the right moment for the stone to show up, Oni flew up to help them to find more clues. He was lacking focus due to the heavy wind, rain and thunder, but mainly due to the dark and gloomy sky.

At that moment, Oni came back down and stayed with them all along.

At midnight, when the eclipse was about to happen and the storm stopped, there was a stone visible in twenty meters distance from them, the stone was surrounded with olive trees, and it was right there all the time, but the power of time did its own thing.

They all gathered around the stone and started pushing it, but it wouldn't move as it appeared it could not be lifted because it was too heavy; it could not be pushed either, because no matter which side they were trying to push from, it would not move.

At that moment, Vic remembered that he was given a medallion.

"Maybe this will move the stone," Vic said as he took out the medallion and placed it on the stone, but nothing happened.

As Chris glanced at the moon, a lightbulb lit up in his head.

"Maybe it should face the moon and not vice versa…"

Vic tried it, and here it was, the stone started to shake at first, and after that it started to move, opening the hidden entrance of the Temple of Justice.

They had made it; they all entered and were slowly walking through the tunnels that led to the Temple of Justice.

The walls were tight, and there was no light; they all lit the torches and started to move even slower. At the end of the tunnel, there was an entrance, a high door with their logo on it.

Two crossed blades, one red and one black. The black one was broken, and only in the red one had horizontal carvings on it, "Temple of Justice," and at the door, the medallion was once again required in order for the door to open. Vic put the medallion in the hole of the door, and it fit right in.

The door was opened, and finally they were inside.

Inside, there were enormous double staircases, the interior was decorated with pictures of the Members of the Temple of Justice since it was formed, as well as with their iconic blades and other weapons during the history of mankind.

Vic was stunned, as well as Chris and Otto; they had no idea where they had entered or what was waiting for them.

Chapter Two: Awakening

Making the permanent decision and facing the Temple of Justice.

After climbing the stairs, they all continued to walk and go on towards the main meeting room.

In the corridor, there was a member of them that greeted them.

"Welcome this way, please," he said as he began leading them through the halls.

They continued to follow the member while feeling somehow strange and not knowing what was about to happen.

At that moment when the doors were opening, Vic instantly recognized the striker that previously kidnapped him and that had given him the medallion.

And at that moment, he felt it in his heart what was about to happen, and that he was closer to the vengeance that he wanted.

The striker's name is Eddie; somebody had called him from another room. While they were walking towards the meeting room, Chris felt pain in his chest, and he told himself this cannot be a good sign, but let's go, and whatever happens, it is supposed to happen.

Upon arriving, they were stunned because of how the room was decorated and detailed to perfection in every way possible. They saw every detail and looked into every detail in depth. From the art on the walls up until the details in weapons and other equipment.

At that moment, another door opened, and there were three empty chairs, the chairs were those types of chairs that Kings had handmade from wood, top-tier leather and tons of other details.

After half an hour, three old men arrived and greeted Vic, Chris and Otto, each saying, "Welcome to the Temple of Justice, where 'We fight the unseen to keep hope alive.'"

At that moment, the curtains opened, and three empty chairs were discovered. The heads of the Temple of Justice, Jakob, Anthony and Peter, asked them what brought them here.

Vic explained that Eddie had given him the medallion, and he explained his part of the story, starting from where his parents were eliminated. Chris continued, and after him, Otto proceeded by saying that I am here because of Vic and Chris, we are all for one and one for all.

The heads of the Temple of Justice were impressed by the Unity of the three.

At that moment, Jakob suggested we shall proceed with the next step

Which was the oath he asked them all: "Are you ready for a change?

They looked from one another and back to Jakob and stated, "We are."

"Are you willing to serve Justice?"

"We are."

"Are you aware of the consequences?" said Jakob.

As Chris and Otto opened their mouths, ready to respond with "We are," Vic interrupted the sequence.

"What if I want to give up one day?" asked Vic with narrowed eyes.

Instantly, there was a reaction of rage from the Head of the Temple of Justice as well as from the members around them. They started to comment.

"How could he!"

"This is absurd."

"How is this possible?"

"This never happened before!"

Then Jakob was referring to everyone by asking for silence and trying to calm down the crowd.

Jakob stood up from his chair and answered: "Victor, my dear, from all of my years of experience, I never encountered such a question and such bravery; it seems like you understand the deeper picture of this all. In that case, when the Members compromise you or your missions, you either tell us or you fight them; the choice is yours. When you let us know, we take it from there. But when you fight them alone, you are no longer a member of ours, even though you have the title. We do not hunt each other or kill each other; we are all members of one organization, and we die for it. We die for justice, and we serve to bring justice. Now, shall we proceed?"

"Yes, we shall," Vic replied confidently.

As Jakob sat, he continued with the ceremony.

"Now, my children, you will receive the iconic item, which is the sword-"

As Jakob spoke, three members approached each of the trio, handing them each an identical, ancient-looking sword.

"Before wearing it, you have one more oath to swear - May it never be used for those who do not deserve it."

As they were wearing the gadget, it felt unreal and powerful. This feeling rushed the heart to beat faster, and it gave the sensation of hope.

After settling down and officially becoming members of the Temple of Justice, Anthony asked them to join him in another room for the discussion of their first mission.

Anthony explained, "The mission is not as easy as it seems... Proceed with caution because the area has alarming animals all around, and if triggered, more guards could join. Go silently and preferably to bypass at least five of the alarming animals."

Vic proclaimed confidently, "We are ready. It's time for the mission to begin."

Now it had officially started.

The power of Justice

Save the children from the warehouse and eliminate their boss.

As their glasses clinked, Victor toasted, "New day, new chapter, new life! Now we are three Strikers who joined the Temple of Justice - brothers! From now on, we seek the justice of what was done to us. We push the limits of reality and everything unjust that has been done to us and to everyone around us, even in the streets, we make it right. Officially, we are heading to our first mission as Strikers. Let's make a toast. Cheers!" It was a cold November night in the streets of Vienna in the year of 1453. The city was covered in snow; the wind was pushing its speed up to unbearable and intolerable levels. Imagine kids working at the warehouse in those conditions, imagine where we as humans went without any kind of mercy, seeking only wealth.

As the snow was piling up and the wind was hitting them right in the faces, when the shivers from the snow started to kick in, the body was in pain, but the mind was set to finish this. Thus, this was only the beginning, and here it has begun…

As they reached the warehouse, Chris snickered, "Only two guards, this will be light work."

Otto shot him a look of annoyance. "Well, I suppose they'll be for you two then."

Chris met his glance with a smug grin. "Don't worry, inside there will be plenty."

Vic directed, "Hey, you take out those two I will go from the side entrance."

Chris and Otto made their first kills with the blade and were hungry for more; meanwhile, Vic took out the guard from the side entrance and climbed the ladder to take a better view from up high. When he reached the top he saw that there were in total nine guards he could have taken out three of them and the other four was up to Chris and Otto, but this time Vic decided to make a decision of his own and do the first elimination from above like that, which he did and that gave him more courage to do more, so in that mission while Chris and Otto were waiting for his signal Vic eliminated all nine guards by himself. Chris and Otto were confused and were given the signal to eliminate the boss of the labor kids. They first made him look for them by whistling and playing hide and seek, and in one moment, when they grew bored of playing, Otto, in stealth mode, was walking silently behind the boss and whistled when he turned. He switched the blade and eliminated him in the chest.

"This is for the injustice." Otto's words were like a thunderclap of vengeance.

After that, all the kids were given food and clothing and taken home to their parents in the late-night hours. All the parents showed gratitude and thanked the three heroes, and rich parents of one kid even gifted all three with throwing knives and new swords.

"Continue your good work, since this world is not getting any better." Said the father as he handed them the weapons.

"Thank you for this. These blades will be of great use to us. This act will never be forgotten." Replied Victor, grateful that their act had been recognized.

After leaving the house of the rich family, they decided that it was time to be heading home.

When they all reached home, they decided to rest, and the first thing in the morning was to visit the Temple of Justice and let them know that the first mission was successful.

Upon arriving home, Chris suggested that they should celebrate this first mission: "Let us raise a glass or two!"

Vic and Otto agreed that they should all drink, but drink after drink, they all ended up being drunk and losing it. When the imbalance kicked in, they couldn't remember what they said or what they did that night.

When the morning came, they were asleep. That day passed for them as they slept until the evening. When they woke up, they all had the hangover sensation, and there was no memory of what happened last night whatsoever.

Chris had taken a pause from groaning and clutching his head to suggest, "We should visit the Temple of Justice and let them know."

Vic and Otto were frustrated about that and started to rush to get ready to go to the Temple of Justice, as they were all in a rush and looking like the world had fallen on them. In that state of mind and in that condition, they arrived at the Temple of Justice.

When the door opened, one of the members saw them before greeting them; he just smirked and said, "It must have been fun last night, right..." as he flashed them a wink.

As they rushed, climbing the stairs and rushing to meet the leaders of the Temple of Justice, Eddie saw them and commented, "How is that drinking going? Headache huh? At least you celebrated your first mission."

Upon arriving at the main room, their world was spinning in their heads, and they were thirsty like never before in their lives.

Anthony suggested that they should go home and rest, and leave it for tomorrow to discuss the next mission.

Chris was irritated that he'd dragged himself in with this dreadful hangover and interrupted the conversation, asking, "Can we at least get the summary of the mission so that we can go first thing tomorrow?"

Peter asserted, "The next mission takes more time and focus; it's not that simple. The main thing is to rest, and tomorrow we can discuss the details."

Vic stood firm with Chris, not wanting to have wasted a journey.

"We will not be able to sleep tonight. We request the mission details now, and we will take our time tonight at home to plan the strategy."

After some negotiations, they decided that the mission details should be revealed, so be it.

"The mission is to find and steal Mark's writings. Mark is an evil priest - the Temple of Justice wants to find out who is he working for and what evil plans he has. Mark has a beloved rabbit that he loves more than life, and it's optional to steal it too, so that you could drag him to find it. It will be easier for us to gather the intel that we want from him personally after we find out about his writings."

The elimination of Mark is a failure of a mission.

Stealing Mark's writing, steal his rabbit

In the evening of the next day, Vic turned to Chris and Otto.

"I am going alone on this mission. It is nothing personal, it's just the way that I feel about this mission." Vic declared solemnly.

Chris eyed Victor. "It could be dangerous, Vic…"

Victor smirked, "Don't be ridiculous, what could happen? The priests could kill me?"

Chris raised his eyebrows. "Well, actually, they could."

Vic grabbed his jacket and headed towards the door.

"See you in a couple of hours," he said over his shoulder as he closed the door.

Vic was thinking while he was heading there, maybe it would be better to send Oni first to gather more info, as Oni was in the sky, nothing was revealed whatsoever. After that, Vic decided that it would be the best option to use opportunities such as a disguise or a hidden passage, but he had no clue where the writings could be.

He decided to use the disguise of a server of the church, climbed up to the second floor and picked the lock of Mark's room, inside there was no writing or clues.

"So now what?" he muttered to himself.

In that moment, he heard somebody talking from next door, and there were two nuns talking about something, but Vic had to get closer in order to overhear what they were talking about.

"Have you heard about the hidden passage in Mark's room?"

"Hidden passage? What hidden passage?"

"Oh, Mark is full of secrets! He even has a secret door that he uses to indulge his fetishes with the nuns!"

Vic decided to search for that room, knowing that he could gather info there.

He went back to Mark 's room and searched everywhere for the hidden room for a long time. At one moment, he was very tired and sat on the chair and felt that the chair was unusual somehow. Upon closer inspection, the switch was on one of the chair's legs, so he had to spin it clockwise, and after that, something from the was just popped out. Vic pulled the handle, and the door opened. He did not close it on purpose because he was thinking of how to open it again after.

When he got inside, he did not want to stay there for long, so he grabbed Mark's writings and inspected the area and the other room, but there was no important evidence whatsoever.

Before leaving, he heard some movement of something small, and at that moment, he remembered about the rabbit, and it was scared at the corner of the room. Vic approached silently and reached to get closer, but guess what, imagine it took all the world to catch a rabbit.

After all that work, Vic finally managed to steal the rabbit and was heading home, trying to get there as soon as possible.

When Vic got home, he could not wait to start analyzing Mark's writings, but after hours and hours of close inspection and trying to interpret the writings, he could not find more than two clues, the first one was that Mark was working for an old man whose nickname is: the Eyes and the second clue is that he does his dirty work every Sunday evening. Vic decided to take the writings to the Temple of Justice, and then maybe some of the leaders of the Temple of Justice could help him figure out this enigma. At that moment, Vic took the writings along with the rabbit and mounted on his horse and went to the Temple of Justice.

When he arrived, he told the leaders about this issue, and Eddie joined them. After several hours, they all concluded that the Eyes is a highly marked Target, thus finding him would not be an easy task and even if found, the mission will not be easy at all due to high security level.

"Perhaps asking people won't be a bad idea to gather information about the Eyes' location or even somebody else who works for him. Interrogating Mark would be a bad move due to the fact that you've stolen his writings and his rabbit. You must lie low for some time." Peter advised.

The next day, after Vic decided to let some time pass before engaging in that mission, he decided that he should find a side mission to help some people that had some kind of trouble in their lives. At that moment, he went out and mounted his horse and went for a journey without a destination. For his journey, he saw an old lady struggling to carry her vegetables, and she was very sad.

"My income was stolen by some thieves in black dresses several hours ago…" she sighed.

"Wait there," Vic whispered before vanishing.

He went to find the thieves following the footsteps that led to a small cottage east of the town. At that cottage there were three of them dressed in black and he did not eliminate them even though he could but decided to teach them a lesson by beating them very good and telling them that if they steal again from the innocent there would be different outcome of the situation, Vic then retrieved the old lady's income, brought it back to her and helped her to get back home.

After some time, Vic went to the Craftsman to invest in his weapon upgrade and equipment. He upgraded his swords and his axes, even bought new types of arrows that are lit with flames and can be used to set things on fire, even the enemies.

Vic was very happy and decided to go home and get some rest. In his dreams he saw Mark and discovered his location, after waking up he decided that in the morning it was time to pay him a visit, but the Temple of Justice will know that after some days, due to the fact that he did not want to go against the Temple of Justice's wishes and commands not for now, later we shall see…

In the morning, Vic decided to go to the place that he saw in his dreams, and even though it was scary and a dangerous mission, Vic decided that he did not want Chris and Otto to be involved in this mission.

The location was a tunnel under the River Danube, a hidden passage that led to Mark's hidden point. The place was highly secured. That's why Vic decided to use a disguise again in order to bypass the guards.

Upon arriving, he jumped into the river and dove to locate the hidden passage. The door was heavy to push due to the water pressure, but after trying several times, he succeeded. After that, the tunnel led to a catacomb. In front of the entrance, there were two guards, and in order to remain silent, Vic decided to lure them further from the entrance and to knock them out or eliminate them, it was up to him. After whistling, he got the guard's attention, and they started to walk toward him. He eliminated both of them and took the uniform of one of them, and started to go deeper in the catacombs.

In the meantime, he did not make himself look suspicious and did not engage in a fight with the guards and the servants there, but went straight to the objective to find Mark's hidden place and interrogate him. But he could not ask for the location due to the fact that it would be obvious why he was asking, and could get in trouble.

But from his right side, there was a room that was heavily guarded, and Vic thought for a moment this could be it. He heard the voices of a male yelling and asking where his rabbit was.

At that moment, Vic knew that it was Mark, but since the room was highly secure, Vic decided to wait for Mark to get out and to follow him to a place that he could grab him to interrogate him. Vic waited several hours until Mark was finally out, frustrated and angry about his rabbit. He followed him along with two guards in front of him and did not engage until he was sure that he will not raise an alarm. After some time, the guards stopped, and Mark got into another room. Vic took the risk of getting close to the guards so that he could close-combat eliminate them, and after doing so, he opened the door. Inside, Mark was alone and facing the wall. He was praying to find his Rabbit. Vic decided to be silent and approach him from behind. After grabbing Mark, Vic held on the grip and started to interrogate him.

Vic began, "Who do you work for?"

Mark, of course, did not give in that easily, even after some punches.

Vic snarled, "I have your rabbit, you know…"

Mark immediate got sensitive and started to beg.

Mark whimpered, "Please, please don't hurt my rabbit!"

Vic slammed his hand against the wall in frustration as he roared, "I will not hurt the rabbit, but I will hurt you if you don't start talking!"

Mark did not hesitate to talk. As he started talking, he also started mumbling, and at first, Vic did not understand what he was talking about.

"For all this, don't blame me; they call her The Black Sorrow. She has grey hair." Mark managed to choke.

"I need more intel."

"She stays hidden during the day and operates during the night."

Vic raised an eyebrow. "Does she now?"

"She is, and she is very dangerous and very strong," added Mark

"What is her location?"

Mark's voice was trembling now, the fear of repercussions gripping him.

"She is often seen doing rituals at the graveyards in the north-west village of Währing."

Vic then let go of Mark; it was optional to eliminate him or to let him go, and Vic decided to leave the area as soon as possible.

After leaving the area and upon arriving home, Vic reported to Chris and Otto, and they were very surprised. First of all, how did Vic manage to succeed in this mission alone? They decided to report to the Temple of Justice. After reporting, they were instructed to eliminate the Black Sorrow and to end her life for good.

Eliminate the Sorrow, and leave the area

The next night, around midnight, they arrived at the village and were searching for the graveyard. Oni was in the sky and reveled at the location. The Sorrow was alone, and they felt insecure because of how strong she could be if she were alone.

Little did they know, she was not alone; she had a small army of ghosts fighting for her. When Chris decided to throw the spear, thinking that it could end her life, he was wrong. When the spear got closer to her, it ended up being shattered into pieces. This left them all shocked.

Vic decided that maybe all together should fight her and aim for the weak points, joints in the legs and then in the end through the heart. But it was harder than it seemed.

Otto was shooting arrows, but it was useless. Then they all decided that she should be distracted by one and attacked by the other two.

Chris attacked her from behind while Vic decided to get a chance to stab her through the heart, but it was not easy at all; they all struggled for a while to end her life.

Upon ending her life with a throwing spear that Otto managed to do to, strange voices and screams were heard in that area, as if like the place was cursed or she was cursed herself.

When they arrived home, none of them were able to sleep or rest for a few days. It seems like something was haunting them from the elimination of Sorrow; they could not forget the screams and all that energy from that night, along with the full moon and everything else that had happened so far.

That evening, Victor started to question his own existence, and something deep inside himself had awoken. At that moment, he stood up.

"What is the point of life that we live, for what do we fight all these bad people, all these evil people? We put lives at risk every day, more and more. How desperate we must be to follow this path. Why don't we feel anything after eliminating these people? I know, I know, don't tell me that they are evil and the world is better off without them. I know, but do we know that we live like a tool of somebody else? Do we know that we are nobody to them? We are nobody to everybody else, and eventually, we could end up dead at any given time. Why don't people just understand that? Why don't we understand that? We will never be at peace, not even after death; we will run all of our lives."

At that moment Vic just lost the balance and started growing pale and helpless like before, it seems like he is developing a deadly disease that is taking his life slow, Chris and Otto were silent again deciding to let it go and to let him face his own daemons alone, a few moments after that Vic felt in a deep sleep and went into a deeper dream. In his dream, he was a kid in the blooming spring near the river, just like when he was a kid.

Playing and enjoying life like every kid should, gazing at the sky and embracing the moment of the beauty that nature has to offer.

In the morning when he woke up, he decided to escape from reality and to go in the middle of nowhere just to get drunk and forget about anything and everything for a couple of days.

He went on his journey up in the mountains it took him a couple of days to reach the destination that was out of the society through the woods and up in the mountains alps of Austria, there he did travel with this thought and everything he carried in his soul and in his shoulders surrounded by the sounds of the nature birds from above and howling of the wolves from around, roaring of bears and much more. Vic did not feel any pain during this journey; he was connected to nature.

Yet he did not want to talk to anyone, about anything; all he wanted was to be alone and to make all the terrible feelings that were haunting him go away, at least temporary for a couple of days.

When he reached the top of the mountain, he looked down and underneath was the deep lake. In that moment, he felt the urge to jump to feel the joy and to feel the falling. He did not hesitate to do so, and at that moment, he spread his arms and jumped. At that moment, upon touching the water and diving deep, he felt like all that trouble had gone away magically. Does the water really cure, or is it just an old myth?

Moments after that, he started to walk back in his thoughts. He had only one aim, and that it to become better and better every day in every way possible.

When he arrived in the city, he felt that it was time to move on and to pursue the next mission, and right after that, he decided to go to the Temple of Justice and consult with them about what would be the next mission.

Upon arriving, he was greeted like always and went to the main room.

There, Peter advised, "You should investigate the Cathedral. Rumors have been spread that an item of great value is there, and it's hidden between the books on the west side of the library. It is believed that the item holds a power to detect dark energy and people, and it changes color when it reacts from silver to black. The Temple of Justice wants to have the item for its use in order to discover the traitors inside the organization."

Vic did like that idea very much and asked for permission to try it himself in the Temple of Justice, but his request was denied.

After the denial, he felt like they were hiding something from him, and something did not feel right, as if something should be discovered, but maybe it was not the right time. And in the depth of the soul, as if he was able to predict the future, he saw in his mind that the item will reveal deep secrets, and upon revealing those secrets step by step, everything will make sense in the end.

Then he just left in silence and was heading to start the mission.

Steal the magical item in the cathedral

Vic was a bit confused on his way to the cathedral, and his thoughts were all over the place, but knew that he had to focus on the mission. When he arrived, a priest was in front of the door.

The priest beamed, "Welcome, my son, to the house of God and may the blessing be upon you!"

"Thank you, to you too."

"My son, what is that attached to your shoulder?"

Vic smiled, "It's a gift from a friend."

The priest drew back a little.

"It looks like a weapon to me; it has a sharp edge."

Vic's smile spread even wider to reveal his teeth "It's a gift like I said."

The priest began to close the door, his voice trembling.

"This is the temple of God; here you don't need any weapons, it's against God's will!"

Vic's foot blocked the door from its latch.

"Oh, is it now? I told you it's a gift. So please, I need to get in."

The priest spluttered, "My child, God has plans for you, and for us all; he does not like such items in his holy temple!"

Vic's eyes were dark "Was his plan as well for my parents to be eliminated when I was a child?"

The priest was speechless as Vic shoved the door open with the force of Thor himself.

"Say hello to him when you see him. Now I have to get inside."

When Vic entered the cathedral, he did not feel anything, any kind of connection with the place or any kind of peace, just like when we were kids as well. He recalled all the situations in which his parents were pushed around because they did not practice religion, and at that moment, that feeling filled him with rage.

He then closed his eyes and called Oni to be his vision from above. Oni located the Chests to be opened that Vic liked very much, because of the fact that their loot, of course and stealing makes life more interesting. Oni then was focused on looking for the Item in the library. It was in the top shelf and it was not easy to reach, but Vic had to come up with a plan, otherwise the mission would become a failure.

Vic then stood up and looked around for the best entry point to the top floor his first objectives were the chests, he used his disguise as a priest and walked slowly towards the stairs, upon arriving at the first room to open the chest a nun was sleeping and heavily snoring he got irritated while listening to her snore while he was pick locking the chest but after managing to pick lock the chest and upon opening and seeing five big chunks of gold, on his face you could see huge smile of course.

He then continued to open the remaining two on the next floor, and he realized that his inventory was full and had room for only one item, so he needed to make himself a bigger leather bag.

At that moment, Vic was almost caught red-handed by a nun that came into the room and did not knock at all.

"Excuse me, Father, is everything all right?"

Vic grinned from ear to ear.

"It has never been better!"

The nun's eyes narrowed "Any reason in particular for that joy?"

"Of Course, God gifted me today with big presents!" he beamed.

"What kind of presents, if I may ask?"

"Shining holy spirit!"

The nun's mouth widened into a smile "Amen to that, Father! God is Good!"

"Amen, he is good indeed! Now I have an arranged confession to make, if you will excuse me."

Vic, with a sarcastic smile and evil expression on his face, went to the library, but there he stood up for several minutes trying to figure out how to get to the top. He then started to climb up, and it felt good, almost like having a superpower.

Upon reaching the top, he then pulled the book that the relic was supposed to be behind, but the relic was not there and as it seems he has pulled the wrong book from the wrong side of the library. He climbed down and called Oni again.

He brushed Oni's head gently "Friend, this time show me where the book is - or did you too start to drink?"

After locating the item, Vic climbed again and pulled the right book this time, stole the relic and climbed down. Now it was time to leave the cathedral.

Vic then left the area and was headed home. Shortly after his arrival, Chris and Otto were practicing archery.

"Hey, Vic, where have you been?" Chris called over as he spotted him.

Otto chimed in, "Yeah, man, where have you been all this time? You don't need us anymore, huh?"

Vic grabbed a bow and lined the arrow up with its rest "Calm down, guys, I was on a mission alone."

Chris looked from Vic to Otto with raised eyebrows "All right then, maybe he hides something from us, what do you think, Otto?"

Otto looked at the target as he lined up the shot.

"Nah, man, he does not; he just needs time for himself. You know, going around and completing missions."

Chris glared at Vic, "It seems like we are under his level…"

Vic's face crumbled into a frown as he hung his head "Maybe you two are right, maybe I left you aside and I was selfish."

Chris placed his hand on Vic's shoulder "It's okay, just keep it together and don't keep breaking down."

Vic met Chris's gaze as his face softened again. "All right, Chris. I need you to go and find a person named Mile, he is the best craftsman in Europe, they say. I also heard that he is a good person but a bit moody."

Otto's eyes lit up "I heard about him too, but I never had a chance to meet him. Can I go with Chris?"

Vic shut it down immediately "No."

"Where can I find him? And what do you want me to do?" Chris asked, eager to get started.

Vic instructed, "For now, just purchase the latest Sword and don't ask too many questions. He is at the marketplace, he is short, and his workshop shines from a distance due to a high amount of silver. And don't steal anything, we need him."

Meet Mile and purchase the latest sword

Don't steal anything

Don't get into a conflict

Chris mounted his horse, took the golden coins from Vic and left off for the mission. While he was riding his horse, he was thinking of the fact that Vic sent him on a mission, and there must be a reason behind that, or maybe he was overthinking this situation. And got a bit confused, but continued on his path with a high level of self-confidence and an aim to bring the best results. He arrives at the marketplace and sees all kinds of traders and shops there, people gathering, people arguing about the prices, kids running around and playing.

And shortly after, he saw a shiny shop and figured this could be Miles' shop.

"Good day to you, are you Mr. Mile?" Chris asked as he strolled in.

"Don't call me mister. I am Mile indeed."

Chris smiled, "It's a pleasure to meet you. I heard that you are the best craftsmen in Europe."

"If they say so, then I must be," replied Mile, his face expressionless as if he hadn't just been paid a compliment.

"I am here to purchase the latest sword that you made."

"Alright, I made several; you can choose your style"

Mile laid the collection on the counter.

"I think the Black and Red one would do," Chris concluded once he had looked at all of the swords.

Mile lifted Chris's selection.

As he did so, light danced across the blade.

"This one is called the Bloodshed sword of a Warrior; it costs nine hundred and fifty gold coins."

Chris hesitated before handing over the money.

"It's a bit expensive... but I will take it."

Mile began counting the cash "Next time you purchase from me, I will give you a discount."

"Thank you, goodbye, Mile."

Chris then took the sword and left the area with a smile on his face feeling that he had done something good and that from now this sword will be an iconic piece to possess, he mounts on his horse and rides back home, while he was riding he stumbled upon three riders who stood on his way as it seems they were bandits and required from him all the money or they will kill him.

Chris stood calm before them.

He looked each of them dead in the eye.

"Think twice before you make this decision. The fact that there are three of you means nothing," he warned.

Chris then calmly dismounted his horse and started to test the new sword swiftly and fast, cutting the first one's left arm and kicking him in the chest with his leg. After that, he slew the two remaining ones in a matter of seconds in combat.

He immediately felt the power of the sword, but was still unaware of what was going to happen.

Chris mounted his horse and rode back home. Upon arriving, Victor was in front of the house drinking beer and talking to Otto about the elimination of sorrow.

"I got the sword, it's amazing! I will show you." Chris explained as he dismounted his horse.

Vic scoffed, "Hello, how are we? Are we doing good? Thank you, yes, of course, we are good."

Chris began to pull the sword from its sheath.

"Sorry, guys, I am impressed by the quality of the sword! I bought it for you, Vic, you will love it."

"For me, who told you it was for me?"

Chris looked from Vic to Otto and back again.

"Then for whom is it? For Otto?"

Vic smiled, "Chris, it's your sword. It's a present from me to you."

Chris threw his arms around Vic "Oh, really, I can't believe that it's for me! Thank you, I am so happy I can't explain it with words! I stumbled upon three bandits on my way home, and I slayed them. It's an amazing sword."

Chris released Victor, only to hold his shoulders as he looked at him.

"Thank you, Victor. I will remember this for the rest of my life."

Vic grinned as he placed a hand on Chris's arm "It's okay, remember it until you get the better one."

Chris chucked.

"Haha, very funny."

That day, all three together celebrated by drinking and singing all night. When the villagers heard them singing and celebrating, they decided to join and to bring gifts such as food, leather, wood, a new wardrobe and such.

They all had a great night and experienced a successful experience so far, with ups and downs as in every relation between humans. The next day in the morning, they were woken up by a messenger who knocked on the door, and Otto was the first one who wake up and was told by the messenger that they were required to go to the Temple of Justice for an urgent Mission.

They all got ready in a hurry and mounted their horses and went to the Temple of Justice. Upon arriving, they were greeted as always and were told to go have a meeting with Jakob and Peter.

Since Anthony was not there, they all sat down and started to get the brief of the next mission.

Peter looked from each of the trio to the next as he began, "Welcome and thank you for coming in time when required to. This mission is of high importance for the Temple of Justice; hence, it is not an easy one, and it requires patience and skills that I believe that you have. I need you to go to Germany to find a traitor of the Temple of Justice. Her name is Ellie. She fled to a small Village called Cochem, near the Moselle River. There up the hill is her house, but beware, it's highly guarded."

Vic sat forward "Do you want us to kidnap her or to eliminate her?"

Peter considered this before answering.

"It would be best the kidnap her and bring her here for punishment and interrogation. But if you could find out for whom she works, then you can eliminate her. I am informed that she joined a cult called 'The Children of the Stars.' The organization hunts strikers and wants to bring us down. There are around two hundred of them who joined the cult, so one by one, we will take them all down."

"This is very complicated and way too much work to do. Could we divide and finish several missions, or do we need to find Ellie first and then the rest?" Chris asked as he rubbed his forehead.

Peter thought once more.

"Good point. Chris, you can go and gather information about the cult in Germany in a cave called Unicorn, which is located in Lower Saxony in Germany. Meanwhile, Otto remains here with us to do the research and Vic, you go, and you choose how you want to handle the mission about Ellie. Good luck."

Kidnap Ellie and find out more info about the cult (Victor)

Infiltrate the ritual in the cave and eliminate at least five of the members (Chris)

The next day at dawn, Vic collected the needed resources, sharpened his axes and swords, mounted his horse and went on a mission. He travelled for an entire day, passing through mountains, lakes, villages, and rivers, until the evening of the next day, when he and his horse grew tired and had to make a stop for the night. On an abandoned house in the mountains, since it was cold and the snow had been falling for days, Vic had to make a fire and was looking for a way to do it. He started to search for flammables. He decided to start burning wood and making a fireplace. Got some rest in the windy and snowy night until the morning, when he continued his journey. It took him four more days to get to the destination. And when he arrived, he gathered info when he called Oni to give him details about the guards and the location of Ellie in the House up high near the river. Oni saw that there were twelve guards, and all were located in different locations. Ellie was sleeping in her room with a stranger by her side.

Vic took the first step by approaching the house, and in front of the gate, two guards were standing. Vic climbed a tree and whistled to lure them further from the gate, and upon their approaching, he then eliminated them.

After that, he went further, and there were two guards, one was moving constantly, and the other was sitting on a chair in front of the entrance door. He shot the moving one in the head and the other one in the stomach with arrows. The entrance door was locked, and his picklocks were no longer in use since the pins were broken; he had to find another way, perhaps through the window. He managed to get inside through the window on the second floor. There was a chest, and he, of course, opened it. Two guards upstairs, both drunk, Vic decided to knock them down instead of eliminating them. On the second floor, there was Ellie with three guards. He had no other choice then to react quick and wound two of them and close combat attack the other while and knock down Ellie too.

After that, Vic decided to tie down Ellie, to wait until he became anonymous and to start interrogating her.

"Wake up, little princess." Vic spat as he slapped Ellie to bring her to.

The pain made Ellie's cheek prickle, and she hissed, "Who are you? What do you want from me? Guards!"

Vic snarled, "I am your worst nightmare, that you will never forget. Your guards are dead and gone.

The color drained from Ellie's face.

"Please let me go. I have gold, take all of it. Just let me go!"

"Oh, I will take it all, don't worry… You better start talking. Who is behind the cult?"

Ellie cackled, "The cult will take you down and all you strikers, Ha-Ha, you will see."

Vic glared, "Will they now?"

He lunged and stabbed her knee.

"Now talk bitch!"

"Urghhhhh, it hurts, please stop!" Ellie screamed.

Vic shook his head, "Just talk already…"

"I don't know who is behind the cult, I swear! I just know what they do, their aim is to destroy the black hearted thorns and to kill the strikers in order to bring down the Temple of Justice. I was a striker too," she explained frantically.

Vic rolled his eyes "I know all of this already. I need more info."

Ellie searched her mind for what she thought might be new information for the striker.

"All I know - Simon is the one who gives us orders, and he attends the cult's ritual once a month. He is tall and scary. Please let me go."

"Can he be found in the same cave, or do you lunatics spread this nonsense everywhere?"

"At the unicorn cave, yes, how did you know that?"

"It's a private business, called none of your business. Now you have two choices: die here and now, or I'll leave you here to die alone."

Ellie began to sob uncontrollably.

"Please let me go, I told you everything, please, I beg you."

Vic headed towards the door "Let's leave you die alone, sometimes it's the best way like that."

Victor gathered the info and did leave the area, but did not choose to go back to the Temple of Justice all that way back; instead, he chose to go to the cave's entrance and to wait for Chris, because he did not want to leave him alone in that mission.

It was sunset, and Vic decided to find some berries in the woods due to the hunger that he felt. From the distance, he saw Chris and started to run towards him and started whistling to get his attention. When Chris saw him, he was surprised and did not know what was happening.

"Vic, why are you here? You were told to find Ellie. What's wrong?" Chris asked with wide eyes.

Vic's gaze was fixed on the cave "That mission is completed. Nothing is wrong, let's do this mission together."

Chris's face hardened "But the Temple of justice?"

Vic glanced at him briefly "It's okay, some things are meant to stay hidden."

"Alright. So, what is the plan?"

"We infiltrate the cave. We use the disguise like them and find out when the so-called Simon attends the ritual."

"Who is Simon?"

"It's somebody who gives them orders, apparently high rank."

"We eliminate him?"

Vic turned to Chris and grinned, "Hell yeah, we do!"

They both entered the cave, there was a fireplace in the middle of the cave, and all were gathered around the fireplace holding hands and forming a moving circle, there were all dressed in red, and their faces were covered; however, there were those dressed in white too with golden marks those were members due to the respect they received by the rest. Vic and Chris had to find out more info about Simon and preferably to take down at least five of the ones dressed in white.

Vic thought for a moment what would be the best approach, perhaps to act like he was part of the cult and Chris would just follow, maybe just a small talk would be a good start with the simple questions, acting like we are new members.

Vic decided to approach one of the members, and while he was walking, he overheard that they greet each other with the term "Stars upon us" and that it could be useful to use it since we want to gather info. A lady was distanced from the crowd and gazing at the flames burning. Vic thought that this could be the perfect opportunity.

"Stars upon us, sister. I am a new member. Could you spare a couple of minutes with me?" Vic asked as he approached.

She turned to him, smiling.

"Stars upon you, too, brother. Of course, I don't see why not. What do you want to know?"

"I would like to know more about the rituals since I am new here."

"We practice God's will that only the chosen ones like us are to remain. As you know, our aim is to destroy the black hearted thorns and the strikers, but until one of our leaders arrives, we cannot take any kind of action."

"I understand. When does he usually arrive?"

"Well, he attends the ritual once in every month. Today is our lucky day, he is expected here anytime soon."

A smile spread across Vic's face.

"Perfect, that was a surprise, it's our first time here, you know, me and my friend there. Can you tell me what is that in the center, that every member brings a piece of something?"

Childlike excitement danced in her eyes as she explained.

"That is our God, it's called the Star Above All Stars, and we bring him our precious carved golden pieces in the complete the entire pyramid of gold. Our Leader will be the last one to put the last piece of the puzzle."

"How does one earn respect here?"

"By obeying rules and by eliminating our enemies, did you eliminate the black hearted thorns and strikers by any chance?"

"Of course I did, lots of them. I do it every day."

"Oh, really? Well then, maybe we should introduce you to the leader when he arrives."

Vic grinned, "It would be my pleasure! One more thing, I think I have found a place where eleven strikers live, so maybe you could call some of the members and join me and my friend to take them down after the ritual. What do you say?"

"It would be my pleasure, and of course, we will come."

"Perfect then, let's wait for the leader."

After the conversation, Vic thought for a moment that this was the perfect chance to perhaps seal all this gold; it must be worth a fortune, but let's focus on the mission first.

While they were all praying and going around the fire, suddenly a cold breeze was present in the cave, heavy footsteps like a beast were heard, and everybody present started to panic and rushed to get into the position to form an army-like formation. There he was, Simon. He was tall and heavy, almost looked like a giant, Vic thought at that moment, "Well, good luck eliminating this guy" he stood in front of them all, and everybody at one sound said: Stars upon you.

He then sat in his majestic chair and was served only by those members dressed in white. He drank the finest wine and ate the rarest foods. When he was done, the ones dressed in white ate what he left and what they left was for the ones dressed in red.

He then stood up and asked Whoever killed more than fifty, the black hearted thorns, raise your hand, Vic thought for a moment, *what should I do, because I don't know what to say.* And then, for a moment, hesitated and raised his hand.

After that, Simon asked him to approach him

"Stars upon you, you are a new face I see."

"Stars upon you, too, yes, I am a new member"

Simon eyed Vic cautiously "Why did you eliminate fifty of the black hearted thorns?"

Vic smirked, "Every day practice, numbers rise…"

"Brothers and Sisters, we have a funny one here," Simon announced as he looked around the sea of faces.

The crowd laughed.

Vic's smile faded, and his face grew solemn.

"As a kid, I wanted to bring hope and joy to the people. I always wanted to bring justice, no matter how hard it was and how impossible it seemed every time. Every day, more and more. I never gave up, so when I got the chance to make my first elimination, I did not stop there. So maybe it's not funny after all."

Simon's jaw dropped in awe.

"I am impressed with the speech. Let's see how well you can handle combat. If you make me fall in combat, I will grant you the rank of my assistant from tonight."

Vic considered the challenge for a moment. This could be the chance to eliminate him. If not, he could play along, and if he made Simon fall, then he could eliminate him whenever he wanted.

Vic finally cried, "Yes, deal - let's fight!"

Chapter Three: Becoming What He Never Wanted To

Simon gave Vic a sword, a small knife, and then they faced each other, and everybody else was gathering to see the fight. Simon started to attack, but was slow and heavy with his movements. If it hits, it's over. But if Vic could dodge his attacks, then maybe he has a chance.

Vic let him strike around twenty times until he got tired and was running around in circles to make it harder to keep track of him. At some point, Vic attacked Simon first in the left knee and then in the right one with a perfect aim to the chest with the small knife, and Simon felt it at that same moment.

Everyone in the crowd was surprised and was cheering him up, but that upset Simon very much, and he started to attack with no mercy. Vic, at that moment, knew that it was the perfect chance to eliminate him and since nobody else had weapons, maybe to eliminate all the other members as well.

Vic used the same strategy as before to let him use all of his energy and stamina first and then to attack, but this time maybe it's better to aim for the head, as Simon was unleashing his fury he hit Vic in the stomach with his hammer, but at that moment Vic somehow managed to grab the hammer and to jump reaching his chest while in the midair he attacked right in the neck bringing an end to one of the leaders of the cult.

At that moment, Chris did not know where to look; he looked at Vic and rushed there instantly, grabbing Vic's Sword. While on the other hand, Vic used Simon's hammer. It was time to take down the rest, but since there was a big fire there, Chris thought that maybe it could become bigger by throwing lit torches in it and making it bigger so that all of those evil people could be burned in that cave. And just like that, it was from fire to ashes.

As they left the area and ran out of the cave, directly into the river to cool off, they both swam, and when they reached the shore after some time, they decided to steal the ship so that they could get home faster.

Vic looked around with childlike wonder.

"Chris, how amazing it is to be having a ship, look ahead, loot!"

Chris giggled at Vic.

"You and your stealing, how much richer are you looking to get?"

"Haha, Chris, very funny. You know I love looting." Vic said with a grin.

"This ship is amazing, Vic. Raise the sails, we will move faster."

As Vic raised the sails, the sea breeze flowed through his hair.

"Here she goes! Now we have more opportunities for our future, let's take into consideration to get ourselves a crew."

Chris nodded in agreement.

"Of course, so that we can seek adventures."

"And fight pirates as well, oh yeah!"

Chris shook his head, smiling.

"Step by step, Vic, step by step."

Vic urged, "Where is your sense of adventure, Chris?"

Chris looked out onto the horizon.

"It's hidden somewhere. I will let you know when I find it."

Vic rolled his eyes.

"Well, you better find it, otherwise you will end up being boring if you continue like this."

Chris's face snapped back to face Vic.

"Shame on you, friend, I was never boring…"

"Sometimes you are…" Vic trailed off, bored of the argument before it had even begun.

Chris's gaze drifted back to the open ocean.

"As you say, as you say."

When they arrived home, they decided to visit the Temple of Justice and to let them know that both missions are completed and were very eager to find out what is coming up next, little that they know the next mission was beyond their imagination.

When they reached the Temple of Justice, they sensed that something strange was going on since all the members were waiting for them as if they knew they would be there at that exact moment.

Both Vic and Chris felt strange and somehow deeply confused, not knowing why such behavior, as if it were the first time entering the Organization.

As it seemed, they both were about to witness something out of the ordinary when they arrived at the main room, all three leaders were standing and welcoming them.

"Welcome, we were expecting you," Peter said as he smiled at each of them.

Vic studied Peter's face.

"Thank you, all this seems strange today"

Before Peter could respond, Anthony began.

"Today is the day that both you and Otto, too, will be given a mission like never before. I want you all to rescue my son, who is being held captive by the black hearted thorn called Freddie. We have no further info; my son is sixteen years old. His name is Oliver; he is tall and skinny with blonde hair. He was kidnapped three days ago."

In that moment, Vic felt a flashback of how much he wanted his parents to be saved, how he wished he had that power that he has now, back then. Tears roll down his face, and his heart beats like crazy. It seems like the most sensitive topic has been brought to the table, but Vic still deeply in his heart, believes that one day he will avenge his parents and that he will find peace and die peacefully. He just wished that he had not been that weak back then, but after all, he was just a hopeless child who had to witness what he did.

Vic snapped back to reality.

"I am sorry, Anthony and everybody, sometimes these visions captivate me out of the blue."

Anthony placed a hand on Vic's shoulder.

"It's all right, take your time."

"We can proceed," Vic confirmed after taking one final deep breath to compose himself.

Anthony continued.

"We believe that Freddie is a member of the cult, and secretly, he acts like he is a black hearted thorn. Now it's up to you to find out. You can ask the locals where they are located, but be cautious not to be obvious when it comes to sharing information because the locals are always scared of those in power."

Vic needed to clarify.

"So, what is the plan? Find out information and do what we must to save Oliver. Anything else?"

"You can proceed in any way that you wish with the mission, but the main objective is to bring my son alive and well," Anthony explained, the pain he was feeling evident only in his voice.

"I meant to ask, can we eliminate Freddie?"

"If you think it will be easy to do so, don't hesitate," Anthony replied ruthlessly.

As they left the Temple of Justice, they decided to get to the point immediately and to start searching for clues, as the day was turning to night, and sunset was at its peak. The only thing that they could do was to ask strangers about Freddie, which they did, but that night, with no success at all. In the morning, the clouds were grey and it was about to start raining, but that could not stop them from pursuing their aim when all the people were seeking shelter. Vic, Chris, and Otto started to go from stranger to stranger and to keep asking until Vic managed to crack the surface of this case. In the dialogue with a man called Eric.

"Good day to you, I have some questions for you, Eric."

Eric looked Vic up and down.

"Go on, but if it's about Freddie, that will cost you fifty golden coins."

Vic scowled.

"Fifty, no way on earth I will pay you that much!"

"No way I will talk then."

"Listen, Eric, it's for the good of us all that you start talking. I will pay you five golden coins, or you will end up hurt, and you will talk, and you will get nothing out of this. You got that!" Vic roared.

"I got nothing to lose, even if I get hurt for five coins, I will not talk," Eric replied cooly.

"Then I will burn your home and beat you up badly."

"Go on, as I told you, I have nothing to lose."

Vic paused for a moment and considered how to proceed because his threats were not budging Eric.

He calmly asked, "What do you need fifty golden coins for?"

Eric looked off into the distant longingly.

"I want to go as far away as possible from here and start a new life."

"Well, if it's like that, I may consider your request here, and may you find what you are looking for, now talk," Vic replied, tossing the bag of coins to Eric.

Eric counted every single coin before he would talk, paranoid that this may be a cruel trick.

"Freddie is the kind of person who is also known for his technique of torturing people with snakes; he puts them in a wooden coffin and lets them suffer in agony until they pass away - he has a great collection of snakes in his castle."

Vic's mouth fell open at what he had just heard.

"That's some wicked man… Useful info, I can burn all of those snakes, I hope."

"He holds something very dear and valuable for himself, and he guards it with his life. It's a book of broken spells. Freddie also is known for missing his index finger in his right hand, and I heard rumors that he has a sweet tooth, so maybe you can manage to poison him."

"Also, useful info, but can you tell me where is he located?"

"That I do not know, but I heard that he lives in a castle for sure. Which one I cannot say for sure, one thing I know is that the castle is not an ordinary one. Look for clues near the Danube River in the east, that's where people say they saw him. Also, his horse is enormous and black. After killing him, you should get his horse; it will do you good."

"Anything else you can tell me, after all I gave you fifty golden coins, didn't I?"

"Of course, don't worry, I will tell you everything that I know. A sailor told me some moons ago that he has a daughter who is a prostitute at the gambling place they call the Dragon's sons. It's in the suburbs of the city. She hates him, and she would gladly provide you with more information. Oh, and one more thing - he has an army of trained guards, and they will not hesitate to attack on site; everyone is equipped with poisoned arrows. Freddie himself wears the most protective gear in the town, so good luck."

"Thank you, I will need it, good luck to you too."

After the conversation, Vic decided to visit the gambling place; the best option was to join the game and act like he was there only to play and have fun. He decided to dress casually and to act like he knew nothing about Freddie's daughter. When he entered the place, he saw that they were drunk and heavily abusing alcohol; a lot of things were broken on the floor it was a chaotic state. Vic then joined the table for playing dice and drinking mead. He decided to bet with twenty golden coins. Everyone was surprised at that point due to the fact that they only had one or two coins at the playing table. Freddie's daughter was surprised to see twenty golden coins and offered Vic a drink; he accepted. After that, Vic managed to win five golden coins from the game, and upon seeing them all fight and ready to kill for coins, he decided to give back those five coins and decided just to drink and have a chat with her. She offered him a private room, and he did not hesitate to take the offer, which cost two coins. They went to the room and she started to undress. At that moment, Vic told her, 'No need for that. I will give you three more coins if you just answer some of the questions that I have.' She agreed without hesitation.

Vic turned his back to allow her the privacy to fully dress and glanced out of the window at the moon.

"It may be inappropriate in this way and in those settings to ask you this, but I would like to know where Freddie's location is."

"My father…" When she spat this, Vic could almost see venom fly.

She continued, "I hate him because of his greedy personality and his evil traits. I think he lives in a castle near the river. It's a big castle and it has an enormous gate in front of it. People say it's called the Snakes' pit castle. Maybe this will help you locate it."

"Can you tell me if there is any way to enter as a guest or a trader in there, without attacking at sight and being obvious?"

She thought for a moment.

"Freddie like mysteries. You could dress as a wizard and make up a story about some spells. That way, you can get inside and have a meeting with him."

Vic turned from the window and looked from the woman to the door.

"That is a clever idea, thank you. I must leave now."

After that Vic went home to have a conversation with Chris and Otto about the mission details, he was thinking the entire way home about this mission and all the opportunities that come along with it, so he decided to take another step forward and before going home he felt like he had to meet Mile the craftsman and purchase the newest sword and upgrade the arrows since this mission was difficult to complete. Mile was working in his shop; he was making an axe that looked extraordinary and was for heavy combat.

"Good day to you, Mile. We haven't met yet, but my friend purchased a sword from you; people say you are the best craftsman in Europe."

Mile surprised Vic when he looked up, and a smile spread from ear to ear.

"Good day, my friend. Welcome! I heard rumors about you. They say you are a hero; you save children and take down bad people around here and beyond. Is it true, Victor?"

"Well, they haven't lied so far. Yes, it's true," Vic replied as he smiled back.

"Then it's my pleasure to be at your service then Victor. How can I help you?"

"I am looking to purchase that axe that you are working on, along with the latest sword that you've made and to upgrade my gear and arrows. Perhaps you can offer me the latest bow that you worked on."

"Friend, when it comes to the axe, you will have to wait another hour until it cools off, and I will sell it to you for ten coins since you are a hero. The latest sword I made it's a special one. Crafted from the unique steel that the traders import from far away. I call it the Revenge sword since it cuts with no mercy. It costs fifty coins, and I assure you it will last a lifetime. The gear I will upgrade for free, and I can offer you the bow of the white snake skin along with the arrows that cut through walls for twenty coins, what do you say?"

Vic reached out and shook Mile's hand firmly with enthusiasm.

"I agree, and it's my pleasure to work with you."

"The pleasure is all mine. Here you go. Come again, and until then, take care."

Victor left the Mile's shop with a happy feeling and a great sensation of accomplishment, as if he had achieved something big in his life, since those upgrades made him feel more powerful and fierce like the true warrior he is.

He arrived home and put the newly purchased items on the table, at which point Chris and Otto were not surprised since they saw it coming. Vic then sat on the chair and started to make the plans for the mission.

"Now we should talk about this mission and how we shall proceed with it. Any ideas?"

Chris leant into the centre of the table, eager to share his strategy.

"I think that the best approach would be if you chose a disguise and proceeded like that in order to get the meeting with Freddie. Since you can't take any weapons except the small blade, maybe I could smuggle your weapons. We could choose a meeting point after you take him down and proceed with other objectives of the mission."

"I agree with you there, Chris. I was thinking I should take the role of a wizard since he loves mysteries and magic. I could get his attention, but it won't be that easy, and hell, I hate snakes, so let's try not to leave any snake alive."

Otto shuddered at the mere thought of them.

"We all hate snakes. I was thinking maybe I could take down the guards and then sneak in to look for his precious book of broken spells, taking down some snakes on the way."

Vic shook his head.

"I disagree with you there because you will raise an alarm, so that's not a good idea; we must remember that they are highly ranked for combat."

"What do you suggest I do then?" Otto asked, visibly irritated.

"You should find a hidden passage with Oni's help and look for Oliver. If you find the kid, then rescue him and silently leave the area. Me and Chris will do the rest. If we need you or if we get in trouble, I will send Oni to let you know that we need you.

Otto's face softened.

"You have yourself a deal then."

"What about me?" Chris asked.

"Chris, you should wait outside the castle from the north side and guard my back. After I give you the signal that I took Freddie down, you can start taking down the guards by my side."

"Let's do it then," Chris said, pushing his chair away from the table to get up.

They all stepped outside, mounted their horses, and Chris took Vic's weapons, and they were heading to look for the castle of the snake's pit. As they were travelling following the river they came across several castles and when they reached the one that they suspected it was that one Vic sent Oni in the sky to confirm, as oni was spreading his wings and was observing the area there were a lot of guards and wooden cages with hostages inside, the castle looked strange and gloomy along with the spikes around it so at that moment it was confirmed that it was the castle that they were looking for. However, they decided to wait for the nightfall since the wizard's disguise could have better chances at passing through the guards at night. They remained hidden not far from the castle until it was time to go in. After three hours of meditating, Vic decided to go.

Vic knocked on the door, and it opened a creak to reveal a guard's face.

"Good evening, I am the wizard of the darkest dreams. I'm here to meet Freddie. We have crossed paths several times, I want to offer him the book of broken spells," explained Vic before he began to speak in a made-up language.

The guard stared at him warily.

"Good evening, first we must check you for any weapons…" he said as he patted him down for any sign of a weapon "And to make sure that you are a wizard, we need to see some magic."

As the guard stepped back, satisfied that Vic didn't have any weapons, Vic moved his hands around, trying to conjure the guise of a sorcerer.

"Go on, my weapon is my magic! Now look at the sky and close your eyes for a bit… Now open, did you see how fast I changed the color of your sword?

The guard's eyes were wide with shock and confusion.

"How is that possible! I will go to inform Freddie that you are here."

"Go on."

"Wait there…" he held the door so that Vic could not see inside, but unbeknownst to the guard, Vic could hear everything.

"Master, I am sorry for disturbing you. There is a wizard by the name of Wizard of Broken Dreams who wants to talk with you about a book of broken spells. He did some magic for us to convince us he is a wizard."

Vic could hear Freddie's voice echoing through the castle.

"A wizard, ask him what is the broken spell for greed. If he answers, 'never is enough,' let him in; if he answers something else, kill him."

"I understand, Master."

The door swung open again, and the guard asked, "Wizard, what is the spell for greed?"

"For greed, the spell is 'it is never enough,'" Vic explained without hesitation.

The guard held the door open and gestured for Vic to enter.

"Come, follow me this way."

While he was walking and upon entering the castle, Vic started to feel uncomfortable seeing the first snake in the hall, and many more since he has a deeply rooted phobia for snakes, but managed not to show the obvious that he is feeling. In that castle, besides snakes and all the evil things, there were war supplies that had to be burned and chests to be opened. Vic saw the people dying in agony, just like Eric had told him. What a disaster. In this place, everything was wicked.

The guard led Vic to Freddie's guest room.

Freddie was petting his cobra lovingly.

"Welcome, wizard. I heard you are a real one. Do you know how many of them tried to dress like a wizard and come here trying to get things? To steal from me or to try to take me down."

Vic did his best to not let his gaze slip from Freddie to the cobra.

"Thank you, Master, I am very aware of that as well are the mercenaries and strikers and such, but I assure you that I am a wizard. I am here to talk about the book of broken spells and to tell you that you have a hidden enemy."

Freddie glowered at him, "Do you think that I am a greedy wizard?"

"We all are at some point; you have plenty of everything, which is obvious, so why not want more?"

Freddie's face eased a little.

"Hm, good point, an enemy you say?"

"Yes, I saw in my visions that you have a very dangerous enemy coming to haunt you, and I wanted to tell you in person, but shall we proceed with the book of broken spells?"

Freddie looked around thoughtfully.

"Who might be that enemy? I am thinking maybe someone I know?"

Vic turned to the fire to hide the smirk that was spreading across his face.

"I think that you do not, Master."

The cobra glided down from Eddie's lap and was getting closer to Vic.

Vic's lip curled in repulsion.

"Your pet, Master, is it ill? It crawls without a pattern."

"NO! What are you talking about? That cannot be, my beloved friend can't be ill."

Freddie bounded from his chair and gently lifted the cobra to his chest, stroking it gently.

Vic slowly approached.

"May I take a look, Master?"

While the cobra's head was nestled into Freddie's chest, he seized the opportunity to take them both down with one strike of the small blade.

The cobra's limp body fell from Freddie's hand as he clutched his chest.

"Oh, you, a Striker? I did not see it coming, you fooled me there!"

Vic moved towards the window.

"I did what I had to do."

Vic immediately signals Chris to start taking down the guards, while he steals the book of broken spells. Chris signals Otto to call oni and to look for a hidden passage and to look for Oliver. Vic stole the book and managed to kill the other snakes in the guest room, but he took Freddie's weapons as well, since they could come in handy until Chris brings Vic's weapons.

Chris did take down four guards with some effort, even though it was not easy. At that moment, Vic and Chris met and fought together against the guards and the snakes as well. While Otto managed to find a hidden passage with the help of Oni, and was looking for Oliver after Vic and Chris took down all the guards and burned all the war supplies, they decided after finding Oliver, they should put the entire castle on fire.

They both found the hidden passage, too, and found Otto in a locked cage. He warned them to leave, but there was no chance that they could leave; the real danger was waiting for them that they could not even imagine. From the darkness of the night there could be heard heavy footsteps that were slow and they were shaking the ground, Otto was frightened Chris wanted to hurry up and release Otto so that all of them could fight the coming danger together, while Chris was working on the process of picking the lock Vic was holding tight the grip of his newly purchased axe, Chris managed to pick the lock just at that moment where the giant guard arrived, he was two and a half meters tall and one and a half meter wide he looked like a living monster with the oversized head and a sword that five people together could not carry, Otto was free and all of them decided to leave the area and lure him outside planning to burn him Chris started shooting arrows on fire at him but that made him more angry and wild, at that moment Vic decided to use the fixed heavy crossbow while Otto was throwing torches at him waiting for the right opportunity to set him on fire, Vic was taking an aim and hoping to get the shot at his knees in order to make him immobile, at that moment the giant felt and for the final move Vic lid the arrow on fire at aimed for the giants head they succeeded in setting him on fire and finally taking him down.

It was time to look for Oliver since all the guards were taken down, Chris took the lead and searched on the second floor of the castle, Otto searched where he had started and Vic searched for Oliver in the ground floor, however Oliver was never to be found they were all exhausted from the fight but did not give up to finding the poor kid Oliver, Vic decided to send Oni in the sky since it was the only hope left, Oni spotted a farm behind the castle it looked like a place where the black hearted thorns use it to torture the enemies at a small cottage Oni spotted a cage.

They all ran to the farm, which was deserted and forgotten. The grass was burned, and it looked like a post-apocalyptic scene when they arrived and opened the door of the cottage. There was Oliver, who was nearly dead from starvation, and it seems like he has not eaten in weeks. They opened the cage, but he was scared to come out.

Vic held out his hand.

"It's okay, kid! Anthony, your father sends us to find you. We will not hurt you."

"Water, please..." Oliver croaked.

Chris filled a cup and handed it to him.

"Here, kid, easy! Sip by sip, slowly"

Otto handed him a loaf of bread, "Here, kid. Don't rush to eat."

Vic's hand was on his head in disbelief at how weak the child was.

"The kid cannot walk; we will carry him until we reach the horses."

"Poor kid, what did they do to him?" Chris asked through a frown.

"Anthony will be very happy to see him," exclaimed Otto.

Vic lifted the boy to carry him.

"Aren't we all! Now let's move."

They walked a pretty long distance without any breaks and reached the horses. Their horses were, however, tired and thirsty, so one of them had to go to bring them water. Chris was the one who went to bring water while the others took some time to rest and catch their breath. It took some time for Chris to arrive due to the heavy weight on both sides, but he managed to come before dawn. They all rested along with the horses, but did not have any shut eye at all.

They started to travel to the Temple of justice a little before noon, passing all that distance again, and hoping that nobody and nothing will trouble them on their way, but luck was not on their side this time, while they were passing through the muddy waters a grizzly bear was hungry just like them all, out of energy and stamina they decided to separate and make the bear run for only one of them. Otto was the one who took this sacrifice and told them not to wait for him and to move on. Chris and Vic did not want to let go, but it was the only option. Vic told him to let them know that he managed to escape or take down the bear by sending Oni to signal them.

They continued the journey and arrived before the sunset at the Temple of Justice. They opened the door and went to the main room. Anthony was waiting there along with Peter, and Jakob was asleep in his room.

Anthony fell from his chair to his knees at the sight of them.

"Oliver, my son, you brought him back to me! Thank you, I cannot describe how my heart is filled with joy and how my eyes are filled with tears. My heart thanks you all, I will be thankful for this for as long as I live and beyond!"

Vic smiled warmly.

"It's our pleasure to bring the kid back, alive and well, to his father."

Anthony flung his arms around the boy and pulled back to look at him.

"My son, you are so skinny, what have they done to you?"

Tears filled Oliver's eyes.

"Father, they put me through hell. I would not survive another day if they hadn't rescued me."

Anthony held his face.

"I know my boy, go rest and thank our friends for bringing you home safe."

Oliver looked over at Vic and Chris.

"Thank you for saving my life."

He hugged them tightly.

"It is our pleasure, kid," Chris said with a genuine smile.

Anthony looked around.

"Boys, where is Otto?"

"We had several incidents on our way, so we had to separate when a bear attacked us," Vic explained.

Oni signaled from the distance.

Vic let out a sigh of relief.

"Otto is fine."

Chris looked out of the window and into the distance where the house was.

"He must be exhausted."

"For sure, after all, we cannot imagine what he has gone through."

"Rest up, boys and meet us in a couple of hours at the hall. I want to throw a feast in a thankful gesture for my son's rescue." Anthony explained cheerily.

"Thank you, we appreciate it," Vic said as he and Chris headed towards the door.

Vic decided to get a good sleep, while Chris decided to go and eat and then rest. This was a long-needed rest for them; however, Vic had a dream that would haunt him until the realization of the meaning of that dream. His dream took place at the never-ending loop, a dark place full of mist and blurry vision. There was a girl in his dream, and she was constantly running away from him. He had been woken up in another dimension of the far away realm in his dreams. The air was heavy to breathe, and the gravity was zero; everything was floating the air. He woke up in the middle of nowhere, it nearly absolute darkness there. He started to walk and realized that he started to float, totally aware of being in a dream. He started to run but could not manage to after starting to walk, it felt like never ending maze and that he was moving in a circle of a time loop scenario. In his dream it felt like an eternity and that every second that passes it felt like a year, after some time from distance he saw a girl and in that moment he knew that in his dream he was not alone, then he started to move towards her and to even try to say something but he could not utter a single word, she started to run away from him until she disappeared in the horizon. The same scenario went down for about dozens of times until Chris woke him up after several hours.

Chris shook Vic impatiently.

"Wake up, Victor, wake up! It's about time you slept enough; you will miss the feast."

"Chris, is that you? What is happening to me? I feel strange. I was in another realm. It felt so real, it felt like I was dead or something." Vic gasped.

"It's just a dream, forget about it. Let's join the feast now and try to relax after resting."

Vic sat with his hand on his head, recalling the dream.

"In my dream, a girl was running away from me, and I'd never seen her in my life. I don't remember how she looks, Chris. The dream must mean something."

"It means that if you don't join the feast, all the girls will run away, come on, get up now!" Chris jeered.

"You don't understand me, Chris. It was as if she wanted to tell me something or to warn me." Vic cried.

Chris chortled.

"Yes, to get out of bed and to start to have fun right now!"

Vic threw the duvet away from him.

"Let's go, I can tell that you are not taking this seriously, but never mind…"

As they were walking down the corridor and going to join the feast at the hall for the events, everything was decorated and pretty organized as if it was the event of the millennium. Songs and drinking contests were very popular among the guests, as well as the scoring games in archery and knife throwing. Chris was absolutely having fun and hitting on girls and ladies who were guests, even the female co-members. He started to drink early, and among the first ones to get drunk, he got drunk with a blonde and ended up both sleeping while hugging the stairs. Vic did not react and let it just be the way it is. He just let his friend do it his way while having a bit too much fun. Vic did drink as well, of course, but was not in the mood to cross the limit. He chose not to participate in any kind of games; instead, he was looking at the crowd from a distance, still thinking about that dream that he could not get it out of his mind. From the crowd, a lady called Luna, who was from a royal family, approached him.

"Excuse me, young man, have you seen my dog? She is dressed like a little princess?" she asked, her voice as delicate as a flower.

Vic laughed.

"Princess, you say? I think she went that way to meet her prince," he explained as he pointed at the balcony.

Luna smiled to reveal pearly white teeth.

"Oh, my Lord, thank you so much, young man," she said, before running off to find her dog.

Vic broke out into song.

"Hey, all you people of the royal family, how come you can never see

Hey, all of you, that gold shines in your room, why can't you see your doom

Hey, hey, all of you who have nothing wise to say, why are your lives so grey…"

Luna returned with eyes as pleading as a puppy dog.

"I could not find my dog, young man. Are you sure she went that way?

Vic swung around.

"Yes, I told you, she went to that balcony to meet her prince, and they both met their maker."

Luna's nose wrinkled.

"Maker, what are you saying? I don't understand your point?"

Vic rolled his eyes and smirked.

"I know you don't, that's the point…"

Luna's brows furrowed. "Are you playing around with me? Do you know who I am and whose daughter I am?"

Vic laughed.

"I do not. Haven't your parents told you who your parents are?"

Luna began shrieking like a banshee, stamping her feet and looking from Vic to everyone else in the room, expecting someone to deal with him.

Vic continued to sing, shaking his head in disappointment.

"You are a fool, do you know that? I cannot believe that you have no respect!" she screamed.

"Respect is earned; you cannot buy it at the market." Vic's voice was calm as the sea in the summer.

Luna's tone became shriller.

"I can buy whatever I want, I am beyond rich, and I am just getting richer."

Vic turned his back on her and ignored her.

After Luna left, Vic continued to gaze at the crowd and kept asking himself why the society had no understanding for some crucial segments in life; perhaps they only want to satisfy their needs, and nothing matters after that. The scenes where Anthony was happy and was having a wide sincere smile because of Oliver got his attention and it brought a sense of nostalgia in his soul, reminiscing how happy he was with his parents and how much he misses them, and that now everything has changed in his life, he was roaming from place to place stealing, killing, kidnaping, burning and doing everything for the cold hearted man that he created like a shield around him to make the inner one feel more secure and not showing the real emotions at all.

After the majority of the guests ended up drunk and the feast was nearly over, Vic heard Oni from a distance. He knew that something was about Otto. At that moment, there he was, entering the feast all injured and bleeding; he was hardly walking and barely staying on his feet.

At that moment, Vic and Chris rushed towards him to take him to another room to bed in order to start treating his wounds. They all spent that night at the Temple of Justice Organization, and in the morning, were headed home. They were told by Anthony to lie low for a couple of days, and after that, Vic was supposed to get back and discuss the next mission's details.

The next day Chris stayed home with Otto to help him recover, however Vic decided to go the town for supplies since they were all tired of looting and fighting after all that has been happening the night before, while he was walking, he could not take out of his mind the dream and was constantly trying to shift his thoughts and to try to let it go for at least some time.

In the market, there was a busy Saturday, and Vic, after purchasing the needed supplies, was heading home, but something got in his way that could not be ignored.

An old woman in black approached him and told him "You will be betrayed and you will destroy all your enemies in ten years' time, nothing is real" after that she disappeared into the thin air, and it seems as he was hallucinating, he decided to ignore it for a while but he started seeing her and again she was gone as if she was haunting him. Again, Vic could not fight something that was not real, but it seemed real. He was very tired from everything and decided to ignore her and continue his path home.

Upon arriving he thought that finally that imagination or whatever may be called, it was over but that was only the start of it, when he sat down by the fire the entire home started to shake and her voice was louder than the thunder itself Chris was in disbelief and Otto was hurt while Vic stood ready for whatever was going to happen, as the scream grew stronger he grabbed his sword and tried to confront her but every time he would reach to fight her, she would disappear.

Vic gasped, dropping his sword to the ground.

"Who are you and what do you want from me?

"I want to let you know who your enemies are," she hissed.

The hairs on the back of Vic's neck stood on end.

"You don't sound so friendly either.

"I am not alive; it's my ghost haunting you to open your eyes. Don't trust anyone."

"I won't, now leave. Can you?"

"No, not until I get what I want…"

"What is it that you want?"

"I want you to close your eyes and focus on my voice."

Vic obeyed and closed his eyes.

"All right, let's do it."

Her eyes fixed on Vic as she concentrated.

"Now I will show you in your mind what I mean."

Vic focused on the images flooding his mind.

After a short time, the screams went away and the situation was stable it seemed like the ghost left the area, Chris came up to Vic and asked if he is okay, he did not respond but just nodded signaling that he was but what he saw moments before will change everything to the core, he decided to remain silent and keep it for himself and act normal like nothing has happened.

Along with the dream to bury this as well deep inside his mind and thoughts, with a decision not to talk about it to anyone until both reveal itself when the time come, the next morning since Otto was injured and Chris was the one who was taking care of him, Vic decided to go for a morning walk and to clear of his mind in nature, while he was walking he decided to make a stop at the river and to feel the water right after that why not a deep cold dive, which lead to finding a chest he took the chest from the bottom of the river at the shore and decided to open it, after opening it he found seven golden coins and a map, the map led to Leobendorf at the castle of Kreuzenstein. He figured since it was on the lower side of Austria, he should take this side quest and see where it leads. At that moment, an old man was trying to get some water, but Vic decided to help him, and by accident, the old man saw the map and immediately recognized it and from there, all the details were revealed.

The old man tsked at the sight of it.

"Many have tried my son, and many have failed. There are rumors about the Teutonic order that still haunts the castle; gold will not do you any good there."

"How do you know that? Tell me more. What else is there?"

"It is said that ghosts of the fallen ones in that castle still roam the place and will not welcome any guests; you are to be doomed if you go there, and everything you touch, it touches your back."

Vic's eyes narrowed as he met the old man's gaze.

"What do you mean it touches you back?"

"It gets under your skin, like a crawling spider in the night."

Vic shivered a little.

"How do I break the curse?"

"If you want to set them free, you need to find out where the grave of the last king is. Open it, take his sword and set it on fire. Then the enormous black smoke will come out of the fire, and all the souls will be free."

Vic paused and pursed his lips.

"And what if all you are saying is not free?"

"What if it is?" the old man replied with a hint of a smile on his face.

"What are you getting out of this? You are old, what do you need the gold for?"

The old man shrugged.

"I am old, but I have a family too."

"Tell me more, and I will reward you when I get back; consider this a favor."

The old man thought for a moment.

"There are traps in the castle, in the tunnels underneath. Traps have been set to guard the relic of the Thunder."

"Relic of the Thunder, does it give you power?" Vic asked, intrigued by the relic.

"People say that it has the power of Thor itself. Upon acquiring it and if it is in the right hands, one can gain the power of a hundred warriors."

"Is that so? So, if it does not work, then it's not in the right hands."

"Yes, exactly!"

"Anything else hidden there?"

"There is one more thing, the writing hidden there could give you more clues and unlock more mysteries. I do not know what, but I heard about it from a friend a long time ago."

Vic stood back from the well.

"I should get going then, let's hope for the best results. If I don't return, then my friends will pay you; they will find you."

The old man shook his hand.

"I know you will get back."

Vic whistled to call his horse and went on this journey out of curiosity. While he was riding, he was intrigued to see for himself if it was true all that the old man had told him. He continued his journey and something unexpected has happened on his way, he was attacked by a mercenary who was hunting him down for a bounty, Vic was surprised to experience this since for that to happen somebody must have had spied along the way, He became wild and started to fight back slashing the mercenary with his sword and interrogating him like never before but in that case not even death could make him talk, so he decided to leave him like that crippled in hope that one day everything will be revealed, he took the mercenaries blade to ask Mile about it, since he is the best craftsmen, maybe he knows something. In the evening, Vic arrived at the castle and decided to go directly in with a torch, but as it seems he was not alone, looking for the relic voice could be heard from the outside, where they ghost or actual people, maybe both.

As he was moving slowly, not to make any noise, he was overhearing a conversation between a leader of the group and his men. The leader was giving them orders to search everywhere for gold and whatever they can find. From what Vic could hear, they were only thieves and were not aware of the relic.

Since Vic could not wait anymore and waste more time, he decided to approach them in a friendly manner to convince them to work together, since he could lure them into traps and save himself the trouble of gambling with their fate.

"Excuse me, gentlemen. I could not help but overhear your conversation. Maybe we could split the loot if you help me after all. Do you happen to have a map in your possession?"

Their leader spun around.

"Where did you come from? Wait, what map?" he asked.

Vic held up the map, which had been rolled into a scroll.

"Well, I have a map. On this map, there are three places that we should go. The first one is to break the curse, and after that, we become rich. What do you all say to that?"

The leader studied him.

"How can we trust you? Maybe you are leading us to trouble?"

"You need my help, I need your help, we both win. If I wanted trouble, you would all be dead by now."

The leader laughed heartily.

"Haha, dead, you say? But we outnumber you!"

"Sometimes number is not a measure of strength. So shall we proceed...?" Vic asked.

The leader hesitated but eventually decided.

"Let's go!"

Vic shows them where to go to break the curse and explains everything in detail, what to do and what not to do; hence, knowing them to be only greedy, they did not pay too much attention.

At that moment one of the men decided to touch the wall and slowly his arm became black like he had caught a disease of a strange kind right away, Vic remembered what the old men said "whatever you touch it touches you back" at that moment he warned everyone not to touch anything until we break the curse, as they continued to walk through the tunnel's underneath the arrived at a graveyard but Vic did not know which grave should open and which sword had to be thrown in the fire. He decided to investigate the area for clues while touching everything only with a stick, not with bare hands.

They did not listen so half of them ended up dead, Vic investigated the graves decided to open the one with the symbol of the pentagram in it since it was a sign of something he decided to use the axe along with the help of the leader of the group who decided to use gloves in order not to get infected by the force in that area. Upon opening the grave, they could immediately recognize that it was a grave of a king, and they hoped that it was the right one the leader took the sword of the grave and while Vic was making a big fire and the leader dropped the sword on the flames, at that moment a black smoke was visible and became more and more in volume and size, the understood that the curse was broken and they now were available to take anything without worrying that something might happen.

It was time to pay back the group, and Vic decided to let them take the gold from the graves of the kings so that they could now help Vic to find the relic of the thunder. The leader called the remaining four men and told them that they all became rich, but one thing was left: to search for the relic. They all split up and started to search while Vic took another task in finding traps and bypassing them. It was not an easy task, but it was not impossible either.

Since the traps were visible but deadly, Vic saw a trap that had spikes. Upon taking the wrong step, the tiles were black and red; the red ones were deadly, while the black ones were safe. After crossing, he found a letter that contained the riddle that could lead to the relic. It was about the three stones, and if the correct one was moved, a door in the tunnel would be opened.

One stone contained a picture of rain, the other one had a picture of fire, and the last one had a picture of smoke.

Vic thought for a moment, since the fire burned the sword and freed all the trapped spirits here that was not the one, smoke came out of the sword, but rain has a connection with thunder, then he called the leader and his men so that all together could push the stone after the moved the stone a door was revealed that came out of the ground at it was obvious that it was an old mechanism but the question raised who build it and why? Perhaps millions of years ago.

The relic of the thunder was glowing and shining like a star. Vic took it and immediate felt the force that it has and the power that it gives, not that he had another level of power, and this was a great step ahead for his future and for his destiny, along with the main aim of avenging his parents. The leader and his men wished him luck and thanked him, but Vic told them there was one more thing. He asked the leader to give the old men forty golden coins since he was the one who introduced all this to him, and the leader agreed since they were all rich now. They went on separate ways while Vic was heading home and was about to tell Chris and Otto about this big upgrade in his strength, even though it was not tested yet. When Vic arrived, he saw Otto and Chris practicing archery together, which made him very happy first because of the fact that Otto was recovered and second how well they had become real, true friends.

Vic bounded over.

"Hello there, friends. Otto, I can see that you recovered. How are you feeling?"

Otto lowered his bow and turned to Vic.

"Welcome, Victor. Yes, I am doing pretty well and feeling even better than you should. Should we proceed with the next mission?"

Vic lowered his voice and looked around.

"We will go to the Temple of Justice in an hour, but I have something to tell you guys."

Chris's eye did not falter from the target.

"We know, no need to explain."

Vic's eyes widened as he looked from Otto to Chris

"What! How do you know?"

Chris lowered his bow and turned to Vic.

"You think you are the only one with a sense of intuition? We know about the relic of thunder and that you are stronger now."

Otto began to snigger.

"He is messing with you, Vic, we know because the old man told us that you were heading to find it."

Vic looked to Otto with a perplexed expression

"How did he find you guys?"

"He did not find us; we found him. Oni showed us the way," he explained as he glanced over at Oni.

Vic's glance also drifted to Oni.

"That sly bird has started to reveal my movements…"

"It's our legendary Raven; we all love him!" Chris beamed, admiring the bird on his perch.

"Sure, we do! Now let's go to the Temple of Justice to see what awaits us." Vic replied as he set off across the grass to mount his horse.

Chris and Otto looked at each other before racing after Vic.

"Let's go!"

They all went to the Temple of Justice and were greeted as always. The leaders were all there, and analyzing some maps and writings at that moment, Eddie showed up from another direction of the main room and greeted them. He seemed somehow stressed out about something.

It seems like there was something big going on with the Temple of Justice. Peter was the one who was the most worried of them all. Vic tried to approach and talk to them, but Anthony told him to wait with a hand gesture since they were not ready yet to talk about the mission details. After an hour of them analyzing and not talking at all, just looking at the maps and the writings, the mission brief started.

Peter eventually broke the silence.

"Dear members of the Temple of Justice, I want to talk with you. We received a threatening letter after you brought Oliver home. The letters contained knowledge of someone who is aware of us and our actions. Luckily, they are not aware yet of our location. I suggest that Victor and Eddie go on this mission."

"This is about someone who either is a traitor or somebody that we do not know yet." Eddie gasped as he stared intently at Peter, and tense silence followed.

Anthony broke the silence.

"As I could see on the maps, the location is near the lake of Gousausee. Perhaps the bird will give you more details about the area."

"What exactly are we looking for? Vic asked, looking up from the map to find Peter watching him.

The fine lines in Peter's forehead deepened.

"I want you to find this person who is threatening us and to bring him or her here for further investigation. Be careful because there could be ambushes. I assume there may be many of them. You should find their leader."

"From all their writings and letters, I gathered up info about a very dangerous enemy of ours. You should do your best to take down all the others and bring the leader here." Anthony continued.

Eddie scoffed.

"This is a mission that we do not know much about… but we will find out in the process."

"Should we get going then?" Vic asked, eyeing the door.

Peter nodded.

"You should, good luck!"

They both left the room and were headed to the lake, but they had a lot of time ahead of them due to the distance of travelling, passing through the mountains and crossing through the cliffs that were sharp like a sword, followed by rain, thunderstorm and heavy snow in some areas. They managed to continue for hours. Until one moment, Eddie started a conversation.

"What is the reason for all this going up and down, searching for people? Don't you ever feel like a tool that has been used since you started all this?" he asked.

Vic laughed weakly.

"Sometimes I feel more like a fool, but the aim still stands stronger above all."

"I know, but there is perhaps more to it in this life and the next."

"We shall find out…"

"What have you been up to lately, or the usual same old?" Eddie asked, desperately trying to fill the empty air for his own sanity.

"There have been days of glory and there have been days of despair as well," Vic replied earnestly.

"Have you ever thought of disappearing and leaving all behind?"

Vic's parents' faces flashed through his mind.

"After I avenge my parents… of course I've thought about it…"

" I often think that something in my dreams keeps telling me something…"

Vic's face whipped round to look at Eddie's, his eyes full of wonder.

"Dreams, you say, I have the same problem."

 Eddie turned to smile at him.

"If you want, we can talk about it."

Vic turned to face what was ahead.

"I would rather prefer not to."

Chapter Four: Revealing the Hidden Faces

Upon arriving at the lake, it was visible that it was a piece of art that nature had created. They both stood in disbelief and were impressed by the looks of it, how it looked like it was clearly unreal. At first glance, it looked like there was nobody and nothing there, but when Oni was called, they were given a clue that revealed something hidden. The hidden passage was under the lake, which led to a cave. Their entry point was from the bottom of the lake through the water tunnels up until the entry of the cave. They both dived deep in and went through. When they arrived at the cave, everything seemed to be calm and empty. Perhaps it was a trap or a setup. Oni could not help them anymore since they were under. Eddie looked around and could not find anything useful or any kind of hidden passages; on the other hand, Vic was looking at a huge piece of ice that looked like a mirror, but did not decide to break it yet, since he wanted to be sure that that was the only way. They searched everywhere in the cave, there was another but smaller piece of ice, like a mirror, but they were confused which was could be the right one to break.

They both decided to break the small one, because the big one could be a trap and behind it could be only water or worse. They broke the small one, and another passage was revealed that passage was leading to another cave that was three times bigger, and it was not empty.

When they arrived, they could feel the presence of something, but it was not clear what it was. In the middle of the cave, there was a beast that left them speechless. It was huge in size, terrifying and dangerous. It was something that they had never seen before. They had to take it down in order to move to the next stage, but how? That was the question. Like everybody and anything else, the beast must have a weakness. Their only advantage was that it could not move fast due to its size. Eddie suggested that with arrows, they could find its weak point. On the other hand, Vic suggested that Eddie should distract it while Vic climbs up somehow to its head and stabs its eyes with his swords so that it could be easier to take it down.

"Now you go and I will distract it, I will find a weak point," Eddie instructed, his eyes fixed on the beast as he reached for his bow.

"Here I come, beastie, here I come!" he whispered before taking a breath and running straight into the eye of the storm.

"Vic, look, the tail is faster than the rest of the body, don't hang onto it!" Eddie shouted over to him

"I can see that, it's not helping at all!" he cried, leaping backwards, narrowly missing its swing.

"Good! Climb onto its leg - I shot it in the head, but it doesn't react. I think I just made it angrier."

Vic bounded up the creature's leg and clung to its scaly skin, his fingertips struggling to latch on securely.

"I can't hold on; it's going to put me down again!"

"Just hang on tight, you are halfway there, Vic!"

"Shoot it in the chest, let's see if it falls even for a bit." Vic cried, clumsily trying to clamber higher.

Eddie yelled angrily.

"I can't close the shot for its chest; it's blocked with its huge arms," he growled.

"Well, get another angle then, man!" Vic bellowed, his eyes wide as he held on for dear life while the beast thrashed around.

"I am trying, but I haven't landed the shot so far! Throw some arrows, I am short."

"Here catch…" Vic called, throwing arrows at Eddie.

"And aim this time!" he added sardonically.

Eddie aimed, and the arrow pierced the beast's vast chest, slowing it down.

"There! Now climb as fast as you can, make it blind."

Vic climbed with the expertise of an ape. He reached the creature's head and thrust his blade into its eye. He reached for his axe and struck its head with the force of a thousand men. Meanwhile, Eddie's arrow punctured its right eye. The beast lost orientation and moved without direction.

"Now is the change, charge at it, both of us!" Eddie cried.

Vic struggled to cling to the beast and dropped onto its shoulder as it thrashed around.

"We are, but this thing can't seem to feel a thing; we made it angrier."

He held on to its shoulder as he dangled and thrust his blade into its chest.

"Let's try until we defeat it. Look, it's falling down."

"It's falling because I stabbed its heart…" Vic explained, the adrenaline turning to sorrow.

"Shame on you, how could you!" Eddie screamed scornfully.

"I feel sorry too, I won't forgive myself…"

"Now let's move, who knows what waits for us next?"

"Nothing but trouble, I assume…" Vic replied as he jumped from the beast's shoulder to the ground.

As they moved on the road, it was leading to a deeper place. It seemed like this place had no ending. Everything was engraved with strange symbols and terrifying scenes. Eddie did not watch his steps, so he fell into a trap, causing him to injure his leg and lose a lot of blood. It was too late to go back. Vic could not believe what was happening and started carrying him, it felt like an eternity until the arrived at the end, in front of them it was a door, it was not completely shut Vic pushed it and when they entered inside it was a lady facing the wall, she was tied with chains, the room had traces of blood and tools that only in hells could exist. Vic could not carry Eddie anymore, so he put him down and started to take a step further in the room. When he looked to his right, he saw a person dressed in black, but the face was hidden, and the person did not look friendly at all. Vic tried to remain as calm as possible, but Eddie was in so much pain.

"Welcome to my room, where demons are gathered to get their sacrifice…" he called from the shadows of his hood.

"I did not mean to interrupt your sacrifice. We are looking for somebody who represents a problem for us and for our friends. I was hoping to settle this in peace since we had trouble taking down one of your beasts. To be honest, we are tired, and my friend here is injured, as you can see. He is in so much pain, and I don't think that he can hold on much longer." Vic explained, not breaking his gaze with the dark figure.

The cloaked figure cackled.

"Ha-Ha-Ha, do I look like a joke to you? Since you set foot in this room, you are both doomed for eternity, and there is no going back!"

"Doomed, you say? Is that so? It's a pity we did not get the chance to introduce ourselves properly, but since you are directly into fighting there, we go." Vic grimaced.

"I will chop off your head and feed it to the dogs." The man in black spat.

"At least mine would be eaten by the dogs, yours wouldn't!" Vic shrieked.

The man in black started to pray in some strange ancient language and he started to lift from the ground his body grew twice its size and his hands turned into claws of the bear, Vic drew his sword and was ready for the combat, as he attacked the man in black Vic felt that it was not an easy target, but when he joined forces with Eddie they took him down by attacking simultaneously at least until they could tie him up and bring him back to the surface, Vic aimed for the arms to make him weaker and to leave him with no physical weapon, while Eddie unwillingly chopped out his right leg. They tied him up and carried him all the way back. It was time to travel back to the Temple of Justice and to bring him in front of the leaders. While they were travelling, the man in black tried to bribe them with gold and with superhuman powers, as well as with promises that he knew the way to living forever and so on. They got tired of him talking all the time, so Vic decided that they should shut him up by tying up a piece of cloth around his mouth. Even after doing so, he could not stop mumbling, so Eddie decided to hit him in his head until he stopped. Upon arriving at the Temple of Justice, the man in black was unconsciousness, and they brought him to the main room, and Peter was the one to wake him up with a bucket of cold water.

"Rise and shine, time to talk. I think we introduced ourselves two decades ago. How have you been?" Peter asked with a smirk

Anthony's jaw dropped.

"Impossible, I thought he had died in the battle when master Striker Daniel brought his sword and said that he had died. This is unbelievable!"

"I always knew he was a tricky one," Jakob added.

"We could not shut him down. He mentioned something about living forever. Does anybody here present know about that?" Vic asked.

Peter placed a hand on Vic's shoulder.

"Victor, you should take some time to rest; you are very tired, I assume."

"I'm fine, I just get the feeling that something is hidden here," Vic replied weakly.

"Nothing is hidden. This man was our member a long time ago. His name is Francis, he was one of our best, like you are." Peter explained.

Vic smiled weakly.

"Thank you. I guess we should let him talk then."

"That would be between me and him, if you all agree," Peter stated, looking around at the Temple of Justice.

Vic shook his head.

"I do not because you said earlier that there is nothing to hide, I want to listen to what he has to say."

"Alright, Eddie, take the cloth out of his mouth and let him speak."

Francis was in a frenzy.

"Peter, Peter, sick bastard, long time no see! Anthony, I still want to take revenge for when you eliminated my sister, and you, Jakob, when you let me bleed and disappeared, you will meet your maker sooner or later - I was loyal to you all, and you stabbed me in the back, how could you!" he hissed, looking each of them in the eyes intensely.

"The death of Anna was an order that we could not ignore or not follow, you know very well what she did!" Peter spats viciously.

"This is getting interesting…" Vic muttered to himself.

Francis's eyes were fixed on Vic.

"This new guy Victor looks like a nice guy, but unfortunately, he works for you. One day, he will become a legend, I can see that."

Anthony rolled his eyes.

"You're speaking more nonsense, Francis... You don't understand that we have existed for centuries, and we are one for all and all for one."

"I used to believe in that until you let me down in the cold," Francis murmured, staring at Anthony.

"We had no choice..." Peter sighed.

Francis's face snapped round to point his snarl at him.

"Ana was the one who killed the traitor in this Temple of Justice. You made her pay for that, even though the traitor was your brother Peter. Remember, nothing could stop us; we were ready for every enemy, including our closest ones."

"How do we settle this? Or this conversation will last for days..." Jakob interjected, wanting the arguments to end.

"Wait, wait... so if he is telling the truth, you let him down, all of you. Why would you hunt him down and make up a story that he is a threat to the Temple of Justice?" Victor asked, his brow furrowed and his gaze drifting from Jakob to Peter to Anthony.

"Victor, please, stay out of it! You do not know what happened; you were a kid then." Peter snapped

Francis glanced at Victor

"A kid who remembers..."

"Remembers what? Who?" Vic asked, his eyes narrowed as he tried to search for the hidden answers.

Out of nowhere, Anthony thrust the small blade through Francis's throat.

"No! Why did you do that? What is going on here?" Vic screamed

Peter shook his head.

"This madness, there was no need to kill him!"

"There was, his case was no turning back. Always was and always will be." Anthony replied, shooting Peter a look of pure indignation.

"I am left without answers. I assume now that he is dead, you three owe me an explanation..." Vic snarled.

Peter placed a hand on Vic's shoulder.

"Victor, my dear. I love you like my son, you know that."

"Love has nothing to do with this. Francis knew something about when I was a kid. What the hell is going on here?" Vic asked as he shrugged Peter's hand from his shoulder.

Anthony sighed and looked to Vic.

"He was the one to send the letter to your parents. Since you remember the man in black in front of your house, we never wanted to bring back your memories, but since you are stubborn as hell, there you go."

A lone tear rolled down Vic's face as he stood there in shock, unable to speak.

"We should have taken this differently," Jakob mumbled.

"He wanted to listen to what Francis had to say." Peter shrugged as he frowned.

Vic nodded as he bit his lip to distract himself from the sorrow.

"I should go. When I feel ready, I will come to talk about the next mission."

When he left the Temple of justice he could not stop recalling that moment when he was a kid and saw a person In black, his soul was filled with sorrow and his heart with pain he could not believe that after all these years such a flashback could feel so real, without hesitation his aim was to climb to the top of the mountain nearby which he did so while recalling every second of his childhood until the first time he saw the man in black.

"Oh, I wish I knew it was him. I would have killed him in the most brutal way," Vic murmured to himself.

Vic continued to climb with a wound in his heart that could not seem to heal at all. Now the wound was completely open, and there was no way to even think about anything else at all. The moment that he arrived at the top of the mountain, he just looked up in the sky, and another tear from his right eye fell down his cheek.

"Forgive me, for I cannot avenge you…" He whispered.

There was only one last thing to do, he thought, just to jump to make an end to this agony and suffering. As he was slowly taking a small step forward, his left foot started to feel the small stones slipping under. Everything was pointless at that point.

His mind was made up to jump, at that moment he decided to do it, but was stopped by a thunder out of the blue, the thunder was soon followed by heavy rain, and the grey sky.

Since a kid Victor had a weakness for the rain, it made him feel somehow calm just like diving but after all he decided to jump, while he was falling he was hoping for a painless death, but destiny had different plans, instead of falling in the ground he felt in the water, a deep water that is called the eye of the mountain, at that moment when he touched the water and started to dive deeper in, he realized that It must be a sign from the universe and that planting the seed of a suicidal though, was clearly a mistake, after feeling the depth of the water he swam back to the surface and decide to take some time for himself to think about the next move.

But little did he know, since he had jumped in the water and after sitting for a while and thinking out loud, he was not alone.

There was a girl in her late twenties that did the same some hours before him and that was standing behind a stone somewhere around ten meters behind him, she was spying on him and was eager to know how come they ended up in the same destiny the same day, perhaps similar reasons, she decided to approach him slowly from behind, but since Vic was being cautious and hated when people approach him from behind out of the instinct he drew he sword frightening the girl.

"Who are you? What do you want from me? One second, if I didn't look, I would have killed you. I hate when people approach me from behind." Vic explained with his back to her, his voice full of spite.

"I am, I am sorry! I jumped before you - I wanted to end my life, I ended up in water instead," she spluttered.

"What did the world do to you?" Vic asked skeptically as he gripped his sword tighter.

Sorrow filled her eyes.

"My husband was murdered, and our house was set on fire. I could not live anymore, so I came here. What happened to you?"

"I'd rather not say…"

The girl looked to the ground.

"I understand, I will get going now. I am sorry to interrupt."

Vic returned his sword to its sheath as he turned to face her.

"Wait, I am sorry for being arrogant earlier. I found out something about my past, and it terrified me, so I wanted to jump and end it all, but I guess we had the same destiny."

She turned back to face him.

"It's all right, I understand, no more jumping then for us again, I assume," she replied with a slight smile.

Vic approached her.

"Definitely not with this purpose, I would say. By the way, we did not introduce ourselves. My name is Victor, and you are?" he asked with his hand outstretched.

"Good then, it's a deal. Nice to meet you, Victor. I am Agnes," she replied and shook his hand warmly.

" I'd better get going now, Agnes, see you around and take care." Vic smiled as he turned to leave.

"Wait, could we go at least to have a drink or two to celebrate our survival?" Agnes asked.

Vic turned back and grinned.

"Hm… Good idea! Let's go, I will take you to a place that I used to go with my friends, it's not far from here," he replied, motioning with his head for Agnes to follow.

They arrived, and Victor raised his hand to indicate that he wanted service.

"Let's go, I want to drink until I cannot walk anymore!" Agnes explained as she took a seat at a table.

"Oh, such bravery all of a sudden, well done." Vic laughed.

"I mean, we will drink together, won't we?" Agnes asked doe-eyed.

The innkeeper arrived with two flagons of ale.

"Here we are, of course, together. Nobody alone. Here's to a long life; Cheers!"

"Together we drink, divided we fall ha-ha-ha, cheers!" Agnes replied.

Vic took a big gulp and sighed contentedly.

"Well, that was a good one. So, Agnes, tell me what do you do except for falling from the mountains?"

"I work as a sculptor, that's my profession."

"Hm… you are an artist, then I could say?"

"Yes, you could say that. What do you do?"

"I am just a regular guy, nothing special about me," Vic explained nonchalantly as he looked around.

"Ah, come on, man, you can't fool me! You are no ordinary guy." Agnes replied with raised eyebrows.

"I work for an organization, I complete contracts…"

"I see, what kind of contracts do you do?"

"Like find missing items, rescue people, sometimes to fight them and such…"

"I think I get the idea. I assume you are well paid."

"I can't complain about that."

"So, what is your life story? What happened in the past that you mentioned?" Agnes asked as she gazed at Victor.

Vic winced slightly.

"Perhaps another time we could talk about that. Now, cheers to our future!"

"Cheers! We could maybe go to my place later…" Agnes proposed.

Vic cleared his throat.

"We just met, I don't feel very comfortable. Maybe another time."

Agnes's cheeks flushed, and she avoided meeting Vic's eyes.

"I understand, sorry for mentioning it."

"It's okay, we can be friends with the same destiny."

"No doubt in that."

Vic smiled as he asked, "What part?"

"Both of them"

Vic finished his last mouthful of beer.

"I think I should get going now. We go apart now, don't follow me like a shadow."

"Ha-ha-ha, you really know how to put words into motion." Agnes chuckled.

"One of my special abilities. See you around," Vic replied as he waved and headed for the door.

"See you," Agnes called after him.

Vic got out and was headed home, but being drunk and lacking the focus was not an easy task for him to get home, but after several times of falling in the muddy floors and kicking the walls and doors with his head he managed to finally get home, upon opening the door Chris saw him how drunk he was and decided to help him go to the bed, Vic recognized Chris and told him that he jumped from the mountain and met a girl, Chris smiled and told him sweet dreams friend.

While his eyes were shut and he was entering the REM phase of sleep, another dimension in his dream opened. In his dream, he was sailing the seas alone on a gigantic ship. He was struggling to control the wheel due to its size and the force required to move it. The ocean was raging with waves smashing on the ship's hull, and the wind was pushing him back and forth through the captain's position. The sea became more aggressive and without mercy, at some point the ship could not hold it anymore and the sails began to fall, Vic did not care so much he thought it would take him somewhere, but shortly after the ship started to sink, so did he as well at that point he drowned in the depths of the sea before his last breath he woke up.

Tired and full of sweat, not a word to anyone, just out the door, and he was headed to the Temple of Justice. When he arrived, he was greeted, but did not respond at all in the main room, and the leaders were there.

Peter was startled at the sight of Vic.

"Welcome, how are you? Are you feeling better? We did not expect you so soon."

"Tell me what the mission is," Vic replied, his face unmoving.

"I think you should take a week or two off to rest after everything," Anthony replied.

"Just tell me, what's the mission, damn it!" Vic cried as he smacked the table with his fist.

Anthony and Peter stood in stunned silence, staring at Vic.

Jakob cleared his throat, and Vic focused on him.

"There is a riot in front of the Kings Frederick the third Castle, it seems like the society wants break free of the dominance of the holly empire, the religion is killing them and the poverty is raising in the lower class, the main mission is to find a way to open the Castle's gate so that the people could get it, in that way you will create a concern in the entire country and beyond, it will not be easy since the Castle is heavily guarded and the lower class society use their tools as a weapon, it is up to you if you want to engage in the combat, the second objective of the mission is to steal Kings signed documents for the rule of Witchcraft so that from then he could not be able to perform burning of the innocent women.

And lastly, you are free to steal as much gold as you can carry, but you are not allowed to participate in any kind of conflict with the King or get near to the King's room; if you do so, you will be kicked out of the organization. Oni will help you to find the document locations; it's not in the King's room."

"Understood, I will get going," Vic replied as he headed towards the door without even a second glance at any of the three elders.

Vic got out in a calm manner, and before that he was headed to the King's castle he decided to go to Mile's workshop to purchase the latest weapon that he had made, upon arriving they did not talk much, Vic asked him about the latest weapon and Mile offered him the double edge sword, the price was a bit high but Vic did not wanted to negotiated, he purchased and continued on his way. When he arrived in front of the castle there were too many people so he could not get through the crowd instead he decides to approach by climbing the walls and using the rooftops, When he got closer to the gate he saw that instead of ropes the gate was closed with thick steal chains, thus the only way to open the gate was from inside, it was a difficult task to do, he decided to sneak inside and find a way to pull the levers without being noticed but the guards and the warriors were everywhere, Vic could not risk taking calling Oni anywhere near that area due to the high risk of getting shot, the best option would be to cause a fire he though. Vic went to the east side of the Castle to cause a great fire by burning the cornfield that were food supplies for the horses. It would take the attention of the majority of the guards, and then he ran towards the gate, pulled the left lever and then the right one. He was caught by a guard, and without hesitation, he knocked him down. Afterwards Vic decided to climb the walls and let the crowd get inside, by looking at them from above it was such a scenario to watch them do such damage and chaos while the guards were busy with fire, an alarm was raised and Vic decided to call for Oni since nobody would be concerned about a raven in the sky while they were busy in the fight, Oni revealed that the documents were placed in the gallery hidden behind a big painting of the cross, Vic sprinted in the direction on the gallery and broke through the window, inside there was a plenty amount of gold that he did steal later perhaps to compensate the price of the newly purchased sword, he stole the documents and burned another cornfield and then vanished, Leaving a mess behind.

He mounted his horse and next destination the Temple of Justice. Upon arrival, he was greeted like always, but he did not respond this time either. In the main room, only Peter.

"Well done! That was faster than I expected!"

"Here are the documents," Vic replied as he thrust the documents into Peter's hands.

As Peter flicked through the documents, growing concern was evident on his face.

"I am afraid that a war will break out soon. I will send some members into the fields. We will be at war with the kingdom of France. If you want to participate, let me know."

"I will do it, I will be here tomorrow morning alone, leave my friends out of this."

"I understand. If you don't want, you don't have to."

"I want to, as I said, I will be here tomorrow morning," Vic replied as he turned to leave, not giving Peter the opportunity to respond.

As he was leaving the Temple of justice Vic went home and decided not to talk about it at all not a word to Chris and Otto, he remained calm and collected acted like nothing has happened he knew that it will be a sleepless night, with no further explanation he decided to wait for the dawn in front of the house gazing at the sky and hoping that after everything that is going to happen he will make it back alive, as the dawn as minutes away Vic gathered his weapons in silence, mounted his horse and went to prepare for the war, the warriors along with some civilians who volunteered were preparing for to go the field Vic was greeted from some of the members who were fellow strikers and were sent by the Temple of justice to protect their motherland, moments after they all began their marching singing songs of the freedom and hoping that they will all make it to Victory having in mind that for some of them it could be the last day of being alive, Vic remained silent and as the enemy was in front of them approximately one kilometer all gathered the courage and were ready to strike, The fist to go were the Horsemen warriors who carried long spears as the horsemen of the enemy were to fist to strike the others began to follow Seeing this Vic began to feel the terror of the war and while the rest engaged in combat Vic did too, striking into enemy fields with no mercy taking down the French warriors with sword and throwing axes at them as well, but at one moment one of the members was wounded and was laying down on the ground holding tight to its would in the stomach, Vic decided to carry him and put him out of the conflict field, as he got back in the field he continued to fight until both sides could not fight anymore and it resulted in retreating, Vic could barely stand on his foot looking at the dead bodies around him from both sides while the rest were begging to die since they were in extreme pain, this affected his mind very deeply and began to ask himself why do people make such wars and what is the point of all this.

While the King's army went back to the castle, the rest remained there carrying with them the wounded ones that could be saved, Vic decided to do so as well so they all went back to where they all came from, Devasted and tired they knew that tomorrow would be the same until there would be Victory or defeat, Vic fought for another seven months in a row every day until he was the last one of the members to remain in the battle, the war continued for seven years until 23 December 1482 where the both sides signed the treaty of Arras.

After seven months Vic decided to go back to the Temple of justice and tell them everything that he saw and what he had felt in the battlefield but the Temple of justice members told him, that life is sometimes cruel and the society cannot do anything about it, since the King's decision affects the entire country and people should understand that and live with it, Vic could not hold back and remain silent so decided to speak what he was feeling In a bit more hard way.

Vic stormed in like a bat out of hell.

"Do you understand the terror that people felt during these seven months in a row? Do you have any idea what a bloodbath it was out there in the field, while you all of you were having the best time of your life here, sitting and talking and living like kings? Why did you join us? Why were none of you out there? And what did you think would happen that after all this, I would come back here and act like nothing happened?"

Peter stood and held out his hands.

"Calm down Victor we understand how you feel it must have been hard, but as I told you it was not up to us everywhere war can begin anywhere in the world, it was our contribute to send some of the members to help the country but only you made it out alive, we are glad for your success and we decided that you should rest for a while until we continue with cleaning up the mess in this place in trying to make it a better place to live for all of us."

"Did you not hear me well, or did you not want to hear me at all? I asked you where you were, where we were killing each other on the battlefield?" Vic bellowed as the walls themselves seemed to shake.

"Victor, my dear friend -" Jakob began.

"I am not your friend!" Victor screeched, cutting Jakob off completely.

Anthony slammed his hand on the table and stood.

"What do you want from us, old men? We lead the Temple of justice, we make this place a better place to live, by eliminating the ones who spread the poison on this country, whoever that it.

"We try our best to maintain the balance where we fight the unseen to keep hope alive." Vic scoffed and shook his head.

"What the hell? Did it bring us any better so far? Where is the justice that I was promised?"

"The justice does not come after several years or by the blink of an eye, the justice is served cold in the end, we did not force you to become a member, you, with your friends, came here to us asking for our help, if you remember?" Peter screamed.

"How can I forget it? It was one of the best days of my life to decide to be a member. It brought me so much happiness," Vic replied, rolling his eyes and looking around at the Temple of Justice.

"Here we go again with your sarcasm, bravo, you should be very proud of yourself, where does it lead you?" Jakob asked as he stood.

"To a fucking sleepless night and deep agony since nothing is as it should be, I will go now. I haven't seen my friend in a while. They must be worried, unlike you."

As Vic stormed through the halls, he stumbled across Eddie, who tried to stand upon seeing him.

"Victor, long time no see, as I could hear from the balcony, you are making such a revolution here in this room, man."

Vic's face dropped in horror.

"Eddie, you are missing a leg. What happened to you?"

"While you were participating in a war, I was doing the same, but somewhere else, my leg. Oh, I lost it in the battle, though I made it alive, glad that you are in one piece."

"I am sorry, Eddie, to see that you are crippled," Vic explained, clutching his head in disbelief.

"Ha-ha, good one, there is perhaps a better way of saying it, but you don't seem to care."

"Oh, I care more that you think, it's just a defense mechanism."

A door opened, and Peter stepped out into the hallway and approached the pair.

"The Temple of Justice decided to reward both of you with the medal and the rank of Master strikers, since both of you sacrificed a lot and made such an extraordinary progress during all these years. We are thankful and proud of you."

"Thank you for such a gesture. I will do my best to serve the Temple of Justice for as long as I live, even though I am crippled." Eddie beamed as he stared at the medal, the gold glinting in the light.

Vic sniggered.

"A medal a magical one I hope that will make me go back in time and fix everything that was broken, thank you see you in a couple of days as I said I want to go to see my friends now, instead of giving medals you should see for yourselves the bloodshed in the battlefield since it's not over yet, see you all in a couple of days I am sure that there must a plan to stop the war."

Vic left the Temple of justice at that moment with a sad expression in his face followed by a deep disappointment in his heart, but could not continue the never-ending conversation since nobody seemed to care what he felt and saw during those seven months in a battle, while he opened the door and mounted on his horse in his mind flashbacks of the war came like a storm creating a chaos and bringing back all the memories of the people killing each other and how everybody was fighting for what for a piece of land, that nobody will take it to the grave with them. Vic continued until he could not take it anymore and dismounted from the horse and started to yell," Leave me alone, I cannot take this anymore." His voice was heard from far away, as it seems one of the survivors heard him and decided to yell back, "They haunt me, too." Vic decided to follow the voice and to see for himself who it was. He ran towards the way that the voice was heard and arrived, seeing a small cottage and a man missing both his legs and his right arm was sitting there shaken from the terror.

"I saw you in the battlefield, you were with civilians, God, you lost half of your body, man, I am Victor, the one who was sent by the Temple of Justice," Vic explained, approaching the man slowly.

The civilian's eyes lit up as he remembered Vic's face.

"I remember you Victor you fought like a beast, with no mercy until you began to feel the terror of the war and you were questioning the entire point of the war, my name is Hans and I made it alive but I wish I was dead, those memories can't leave my mind I feel like they are killing me slowly," he groaned.

"Hans, man, I am so sorry to see this like you. It was a chaos, that's for sure, but at least you made it. At some point, the memories will fade, perhaps after the war. Thank you, I did what I could, but I would not see any point in fighting for just a piece of land."

"People fought for higher stupidest that we are not aware of, trust me," Hans replied plainly.

"Oh, I am very aware of that, trust me, but sometimes I can't help but rage or yell when the emotions cut like a sword in my entire body and soul," Vic said, and as he recalled, he could feel the memories of adrenaline faintly pumping through his veins.

"That is when you know that you are alive and you have a kind heart. Promise me something, Victor."

"Thank you, promise you what?" Vic asked.

"That you will not stop fighting for justice until the end."

"I can promise you that I will continue to fight for justice, and maybe one day the world will be a better place to live for all of us," Vic replied sincerely.

"That is what I wanted to hear. Here, take my bow, it's one of a kind since I cannot use it anymore. I want you to use it, and may every arrow end up where it should," Hans requested as he handed Vic the bow.

"Thank you very much, this I will never forget, it will stay by my side until the end. Is there anything I can do that could help you?" Vic asked courteously.

"It is my pleasure that you accepted it. I am, as you can see, crippled. I cannot do much, but I will manage to live like this and accept my fate. There is nothing that could help me more than one day living in peace, all of us," Hans explained as he looked at the sky, hoping for a better future.

"We will all hope for that day to come. If we fight for justice, we will bring justice, but we all should unite if we want to see a better day," Vic enthused as he joined Hans in gazing at the sky.

"Unification may be for a thousand years when we destroy everything and anything, when there is nothing left."

"Don't say that Hans people won't do that, I hope that would be too much," Vic pleaded, not only with Hans but with the cogs of the universe which were in motion.

"As if it's not too much already…" Hans drifted off with nothing more to say.

"It is but…"

Hans sat silently, exhausted by Vic's faith in humanity.

"I should go now; I haven't seen my friend for seven months. Take care of yourself, and I promise that I will come to see you whenever I get the chance. I will send food and supplies to you. One of my friends will bring it to you by the end of this day. Stay safe and thank you."

"Go in peace and thank you, too, Victor," Hans replied absently.

Vic greeted Hans and whistled to call his horse, he was finally heading home to meet Chris and Otto, passing through the village and seeing the depression of the civilians faces, the cottages burned to ashes and people starving, it broke his heart and it made him feel even more unhappy but the hope inside his heart would never die, he knew that he will never give up not matter what when he was approaching the town, there was no major changes it seems like the lower class of the society was the one who suffered the most as they always do, when he was getting near to his house he saw Chris outside treating the wounds of the warriors and Otto feeding the ones who lost their arms in a battle, while Oni was stealing food from God knows when a bringing it to the wounded soldiers, His heart was filled with joy and his eyes were teary upon seeing his friends doing such a good deeds to help the ones in need, he decided to approach calmly since seeing them made him forget all the worries that he had.

"Hello there, my friends, it seems like you are keeping busy."

Vic's voice was like music to Otto and Chris's ears.

"Victor, you came back. We were worried about you, man. Where were you?" Chris cried as he ran and pulled Vic into a hug.

Otto ran to join their embrace.

"Welcome, finally, we thought we lost you?" Otto exclaimed.

"I was where the ones you are taking care of came from; it's a pleasure to see you both, of course, but a higher pleasure to see you are helping people," Viv explained.

Chris pulled away and held Vic by the shoulders, studying his face suspiciously.

"You were at war, really? Why?" Chris asked.

"The Temple of Justice needed members to send to war in order to help push the enemy lines," Vic explained.

"Why did you not tell us?" Otto asked.

Vic held both of their faces and looked at each of them.

"Because I wanted you to be protected, not to lose your lives on the battlefield."

Chris slapped his hand away.

"How generous of you, you always knew how to love others before yourself. We are proud of you, but angry with you as well - hold onto the world tight, I will be with you shortly," Chris explained before calling out to a wounded warrior.

"Why angry?" Vic asked.

"Because you disappeared for nearly eight months, without a trace, we were worried for you.

"We even asked around about you, but nobody knew where you went? Tell us more about what happened?" Otto pressed, eager for details.

"There is nothing much to say, except for the fact that I saw the terror that the war left behind, and it is still leaving today," Vic explained as memories of the trauma flashed before his eyes.

"I see, but how come you never contacted us?" Chris asked.

"I lost track of time, I nearly lost my mind, but somehow, I managed to survive, as you can see…"

"What now, you will be silent and you will leave us again, huh?" Otto frowned and questioned.

"Life is unexpected, as you know, after all, I may not wake up tomorrow, so what?" Vic replied as he looked away, unable to meet either of their expectant gazes.

"Always with your style of putting the words in the coldest manner, if we didn't know you, we would think that you are cold-hearted and don't care for a thing in this world." Chris scoffed.

"Even the coldest iceberg could melt seeing you two doing good deeds," Vic explained as he looked at Chris and smiled weakly.

Otto rolled his eyes and huffed.

"Now you are being sarcastic, you think we love that part of you, don't you?"

"I meant what I said, not get back to work and let's help the ones in need together, won't we?"

"Let's do it!" Chris and Otto cried in unison.

And as the heart was filled with joy, Vic continued for days and nights with just a little sleep to support the warriors and to stay by their side, he remembered that Hans needed help and asked Chris if he could go to him and provide him with food and supplies. Chris accepted it with no hesitation. While Otto and Vic were focused on helping the ones in need, Chris took what his horse could carry to Hans and told him that Victor sent him. Hans was more than thankful, and his eyes were filled with tears of joy. But he did not let Chris go back empty-handed as well. He gave him the Axe that he had inherited it for generations and told him to continue to be a good man and to do good deeds, and he asked him to use the axe only for good purposes, as Chris promised him so and mounted his horse to go back, Hans told him to send regards to Victor, Chris took off and came back home to continue helping the wounded one of them recognized Victor but lost his voice due to being hurt by an arrow in his throat, Vic was devastated to see him and not being able to get what he would like to say, he asked the wounded one to write on paper what he wanted to say, but the poor guy was illiterate. Victor felt very bad but there was nothing that he could do, they did not stop on helping the wounded ones they were faced with all kind of injuries some could be saved, some could not be saved and there was nothing that they could do, As new arrivals kept coming in every evening they did not give up on helping but Victor felt the need to go to the Temple of justice so that he could hear the next missions brief, maybe there was something that he could do in contributing to the society in a higher level in order to put an end to this misery, he told Chris and Otto that he has to go and that he promised to send Oni back to them to let them know that he is alive and doing well, he told that that he must go because if he stays there the only thing he can to is to help the soldiers and warriors but he was aiming for something higher than that, they both respected his decision and told him to take care and stay well, as he was ready to mount on his horse and to go to the Temple of justice, with a sad expression on his face because he is leaving them and with a sad feeling in his heart because innocent people are losing their lives because of war, so once again he was filled with sorrow and among all that sorrow and sadness there was hope for a better tomorrow and that one day people will have peace and learn to value it, since all that has happened there were more bad than good not in his life only but in general as well, He held tightly to that hope and with that high hope he opened the doors of the Temple of justice, he was greeted like aways and arrived at the main room, where only Peter was present.

Peter looked up from the scroll that he was working on.

"Welcome back, Victor. How have you been after the heated arguments that we had last time? Are you feeling any better? I sense hope in you. Am I right?"

"Greeting, Master Peter, I did good, actually. Finally, I saw my friends, and my heart is filled with joy since I saw them helping the wounded warriors and soldiers that have been injured on the battlefield that I was, yes, you are right, I have high hopes to make things right, and by God, I will."

"I am very pleased and happy to hear that you meet your friends, but happier that you are talking about hope with such determination, so by God you will!" Peter grinned.

"I think that things could be better than they are for the good of all of us and of those we will leave behind."

"I could not agree more with you there, my dear," Peter replied, tsking.

Vic smirked.

"Thank you, so tell me, Master Peter, what is the mission brief?"

"The Temple of justice decided to send you to Enemies reservations, and to infiltrate their areas during the night, if you have to eliminate the guards but your main objective is to burn and destroy all of their supplies and please do not leave anything behind, there are nine locations to complete, that is the first step to bring this was to and end before it's time, after you do that take down the leaders of all the nine locations and come back here for the next mission. And beware that the enemy is highly guarded and dangerous, but you always seem to find a way."

"I understand," I shout. "Get going right now, then see you when I finish the mission."

"Good luck, see you, of course."

Victor went straight out, and as it was sunset, he knew that he could engage in the mission soon. His mind was set on this, and there was no turning back. He mounted on his horse and called Oni to reveal his first location, which was nearby.

He then stood for a moment and was thinking about the fact that he should bear in mind that he bypass the alarming animals in the area not to cause unnecessary attention.

Determined that he could do this alone, he started at the first location by sneaking through the grass and finding a way in between fences. Since the main objective was to burn the war supplies, he did not feel that it was necessary to engage in combat if he could manage to finish all nine locations in stealth mode without being noticed.

As he stood and looked from above in the first location, he saw that from where he was, he could burn all three war supplies in those location by setting arrows on fire and aiming good for the explosive torches nearby or even shooting at the wooden box that the supplies were held into.

He started doing that, which resulted in success; however, the guards were alarmed, but there was nothing that they could do whatsoever. Nobody knew who shot the arrows and where did they come from.

After finishing the first location, he continued to send Oni in the sky to reveal the next location and the number of wooden supplies. They continued doing this until the fifth location was on the row, the war supplies were deeply hidden in the caves, and Vic decided to try to remain silent and not engage in the combat, as he was ready to enter the cave. One guard was in front of the entrance, Vic decided to whistle in order to get his attention and enter inside unnoticed. However, inside the cave, he could not escape engaging in combat since the place was crowded with workers, guards and warriors.

Seeing this, Vic thought, *"If I use a disguise as a guard, maybe I could burn the war supplies and escape."* He did so, but upon igniting the last one, he was caught by one worker nearby who spied to the guard.

At that moment, the only thing to do in order not to get killed was to run, due to being outnumbered. He ran and escaped, but the alarm was set; he had to lie low for a couple of hours to continue for the remaining four locations.

He climbed up the cliff not far from the cave, while being connected with the nature with the location and looked at the alarmed ones from above. After four hours, he went to the next location, and as it seems, he was faced with more difficulties, such as wild animals attack, getting shot in the right leg by an arrow and getting set on fire by the guard who shot the torch next to him at the sixth location. But, despite all of that, he managed to burn down the war supplies and escape.

Vic had to take care of the wound on his leg afterwards, all alone, and recover from the small burns. Thankfully, the old medicine against infections did its job.

The next day, after a rough sleep, he continued to the seventh location and managed to burn the entire row of war supplies by throwing twenty arrows on fire one by one.

The eighth location was more delicate since there were civilians nearby, and the last thing that he would want was to hurt someone innocent. Again, he used the disguise approach and managed to burn the three sets of war supplies. He continued until he had to engage in the last ninth location, but when he sent Oni in the sky, it got scared and flew back on his right arm.

In that moment, Vic knew that this was going to be the hardest one of them all. The entire castle was protected with ten-meter metal spikes, with at least fifty guards on towers all around that castle, and who knows how many guards outside and inside.

Since Oni was of no use in that part, Vic had to find all the war supplies alone. He used the hidden spots, grass, fences, walls shadows, sleeping guards, everything that could cover his tracks and somehow after four days in that castle, he managed to burn the war supplies up until the last one when he was shot again in the other leg and was faced with a challenge of fighting the highly skilled mercenary who goes by the name of Leo.

His moves in combat were too fast to escape, and ended up with a cut horizontally on the stomach when Leo attacked Vic and thought that he had him by holding the sword to his neck, and mocking him.

Vic took the opportunity to eliminate Leo with a sword through his forehead. Wounded, he hardly managed to escape the castle while the arrows were flying all around, but not hitting him. He spent that day next to the river, tending to his new wounds and whistled for his horse since he could not stand anymore.

At one point, he wanted to go home to see his friends and to let them know that he is alive, but instead, he called Oni and put a small letter in its claw, and in that moment, Oni knew where to take it.

In the letter he wrote, "Dear friends, I am alive and well. I cannot come to see you; I must continue this path of trying to stop this war. Your friend, Victor."

Shortly after, he decided to go to the Temple of Justice and talk about the next mission since there was no time to waste, and everything had to be done as soon as possible in order to achieve the main goal.

He arrived at the Temple of Justice and was greeted as always. When he arrived at the main room, he found Jakob and Anthony waiting.

Jakob rushed to Vic's side.

"Victor, my dear, you look like you've been through hell. What happened?"

"Hell is a small word for what is going on, and what I have been through, what happened, it's a bit of a long story. Where is Peter? Why the hell did he send me alone? I was outnumbered!" Victor spat venomously.

"We did not know about that. We thought that they would keep the supplies with a small number of guards. As for Peter, I do not know; he was here earlier," Anthony explained.

"Well, you thought the same so many times before, and the results seem to be very different, don't they?"

"Victor, I am fed up with your arrogance, sarcasm, your attitude and blaming us for everything. If you don't like it, just please leave and quit."

Vic began roaring with laughter and slapping his leg.

"Oh, spare me your diplomatic approaches and your ways of trying to make me feel more connected to the Temple of Justice than I am. If I wanted to quit, I would have done it a long time ago, and you are deeply aware of your mistakes. If you want, I can list them for you. Where is your respect? What has gotten into you?"

Anthony stood and marched from the room without another word.

"Victor, my dear, bear in mind that we did not tell you that. Anthony's wife is sick and dying, that's why he got angry. Please try to understand that we all have our moments of rage in life, and something else does affect us for the things we say sometimes. I am very well aware that this is hard for you, but trust me, in the end, all will make sense," Jakob reasoned.

Vic looked to his feet, ashamed at how he had approached Anthony.

"I am sorry to hear that. My apologies to you all, since sometimes I react in a very bad way due to the anger that I hold inside for various reasons. Can we discuss the next move now?"

"Absolutely, we can discuss it, and you are forgiven, my dear," Jakob replied as he led Vic to take a seat.

"Thank you."

"We live in times that we are all ruled by the church, and those who lead the church do not always have to mean that are all good people. Some of them are evil beyond our imagination, some of them are greedy, while some of them live to see the others suffer and suffocate until the end. My point is that we gathered info that the one who set this on motion is not a King. Neither ours nor the ones from the enemy's side, but as it seems, it is a Black hearted thorn who goes by nickname of 'Lizard.' Some say he became a thorn just for the rank, while we are sure that he is one of the most important members of the cult. According to this, he might be the key to the children of the stars. But do not worry, since you will manage to get the info out of him."

"I understand. What do you suggest I do? And how the hell can he be on both sides since they hate each other?" Vic asked.

"A lizard…"

"Very obvious."

"Another thing you should know is that he loves to collect tools for torturing prisoners. Perhaps you could purchase some or find some. And when you find out how to approach him, you should come up as somebody who idealizes him and wants to give them to him as a present."

"Another reason that he is a sick bastard, let's get to the point, where is he located, and what should I be aware of?"

"His location is Aichelberg Castle, he prefers to live alone, so you should not be aware of guards. In this case, you should be aware of his beloved wolves that guard him day and night."

"In that case, I suppose there is a big pack of them, so I might get eaten alive."

"There is always a catch. When he leaves the castle, some follow him, and the rest guard the entrance. He is known to leave at three after midnight. Who knows where he goes, and you can find your way in anywhere but not from the front entrance, but since the wolves have a high sense of hearing, try to be as silent as possible."

"Since I would be breaking in, there is no point in bringing him presents, just to interrogate him and leave, or should I take him down afterwards?" Vic asked.

"It's not going to be a problem when entering, the main problem is, he controls the wolves. You can take him as a hostage after you beat him up really good, and while you use him as a hostage, try to steal his carriage and escape, take him down if you want before escaping. However, he has to go down at some point. Right now, the most important thing that we want from him is information about who is the leader. When we find that out, we will gather info about how to approach and how to make him sign the treaty, but we are not close to that anytime soon."

"Good suggestion, in that case, I will not spare him at all. Before I leave, is there anything of high value in that castle? If you know what I mean…"

Jakob chuckled heartily.

"Ha-ha, Victor, you always had a special way of putting in a good humor"

"I mean… thank you."

"Whatever you find, steal it; however, if he possesses the so-called "Golden armor", you can use it for yourself or sell it, the choice is yours."

"I would never wear it, imagine me all shiny, I should go now until the next time."

"Take care and be careful!"

Victor left the Temple of Justice and did not rush to go to the castle since it was only afternoon. The gentle breeze was refreshing the soul. While he was riding his horse, he stopped near the river to rest and drink water and to let the horse feed and drink water as well.

At that moment, he told the horse, "Thank you, with you I have been all over the mountains and all these fields, all these conflicts rage and heartbreaking moments. Thank you, I mean it." The horse nodded as if he understood.

Shortly after that, Vic decided to go on foot to the castle and to leave the horse for that night since there was a high danger from the wolves. As he was walking through the woods, the foot dived deep in the grass and he was not looking where he was stepping.

All of a sudden, he stepped on a snake, and it bit him in the leg. But, to all his luck, there was an old sage whose name was Leonard, nearby just minding his own business, who saw the snake and Victor. He offered to help as if he was meant to be there to save Vic's life.

"Oh, heavens above us, that is a very dangerous snake that bit you, young man. You are far away from help; I can offer you the potion to drink. It will save your life," Leonard explained as he rushed over to Vic.

"And what do you want in return?" Vic asked as he studied Leonard's face.

"Have you lost your faith in society, my boy? Does a man need a reason to help another man in need? What kind of a man would I be to leave you here to die?"

"Then, if you put it like that, give me the potion."

Leonard handed Vic the potion.

"Here."

Vic pulled the cork from the bottle and drank the potion.

"Thank you!"

"If you need any kind of wizard help, you can count on me. I can control animals."

Vic thought for a moment about Leonard's offer.

"I am headed on a mission. I could use your help if you are good with wolves."

"Any kind of animal, don't worry."

"Then we have a deal, I will whistle three times and you keep the wolves calm when you hear me."

"Agreed!"

Vic continued to walk and left Leonard in the nearby area, but the air was different somehow, very tight to breath, as if in that area near the castle there was a curse of some kind.

As he was walking, he noticed a huge tree and climbed into it so he could see what the lizard would do while he had the chance to spy from above. As he watched, nothing happened at first. Two hours passed before the lizard was seen torturing a woman with a whip. Vic wasn't sure if she was a girl or a lady, but either way, it was a disturbing scene. The lizard enjoyed torturing people and making them beg for mercy.

When he grew tired of using the whip, he pulled out a metal tool. Not knowing its purpose, Vic decided to wait, though his patience was wearing thin. The lizard used the tool to pull out her teeth one by one until none were left. The woman screamed so loudly in pain that even the wolves gathered together into a pack.

At one point, Vic wanted to shoot the lizard with an arrow, but then he thought about the wolves. A new idea came to him. Since all the wolves were gathered on the right side of the castle, he decided to approach from the front while the woman's screams distracted them. He slipped inside through a window, unaware that the place was filled with wolf pups. One wrong step could ruin everything. His fear of stepping on a pup grew stronger with every move, so he decided to shoot the lizard right then.

He aimed for the shoulder, but missed, and the arrow struck the woman instead. In an instant, he drew another arrow, aimed again, and shot the lizard in the right shoulder. The lizard tried to run downstairs to open the door for the wolves, but Vic tackled him before he could. The lizard fell to the floor. Vic figured the best option was to knock him out and tie him up until he could think of a way to keep the wolves away. The woman, though badly hurt, was no longer in immediate danger, so she could wait.

Since wolves fear fire, Vic considered using it to distract them, but he thought it wasn't the best idea. Instead, he grabbed one of the pups and pretended he would throw it out the window. At that moment, Vic whistled three times, and Leonard's soft melody echoed through the air, calming the wolves.

Vic began moving the pups from the second floor to the first, carrying as many as he could each trip. He ran up and down who knows how many times, determined to secure the second floor until no pups were left upstairs. He didn't have a plan, but a plan seemed to find him.

Since the lizard had enjoyed torturing people, Vic decided he wanted to return the favor. But before that, he remembered the poor, toothless woman. He untied her, apologized for shooting her, and helped her climb from the second-floor window into the tree. He told her to run home and stay safe. She fled, and Vic hoped she made it to safety.

At that moment, Vic felt relieved: the wolves were calm, the woman was rescued, and now it was time to deal with the lizard.

Vic slapped Lizard round the face, and he woke in shock.

"Mr Lizard, I think it's about time you woke up."

"Who are you? What do you want? Untie me, you don't know who I am. If you just touch me, they will find you and feed you to the dogs," Lizard cried.

"I thought you preferred wolves, but however, that is not of any importance now. Who I am? Oh, I am your worst nightmare ever. What do I want? Come on, man, I haven't even started," Vic explained.

" Listen, we can make a deal. I have plenty of gold, and I have other precious items. I can give you everything, take it all, just let me go, and I won't tell a soul that you came, I promise," Lizard pleaded.

"First of all, you can't fool me, you are a lizard, that's obvious, and you can try to fool somebody else, and second of all, man, I will steal it all, trust me, after I am done with you here."

"What do you want then? I can make it happen. Just ask," Lizard begged with desperation in his eyes.

Vic stroked his bow, which was lying on its side on the table.

"I think we should start softly by playing a little game here. I have an idea! Lizard, what if I blindfold myself and shoot an arrow at you? Let's play. I am in a very good mood right now."

"No, please, spare me, I beg you, I will do anything."

Vic tied a blindfold around Lizard's eyes tightly.

"Not so though now, huh, Lizard?" Vic aimed and fired, the arrow narrowly missing Lizard.

Lizard began to sob uncontrollably.

"Please don't kill me, I am begging you!"

"Since I missed what a pity. Now, I should pull a tooth, I am feeling good right now," Vic said as he picked up some pliers.

Vic lunged at him and pried his mouth open, tearing out one of his teeth.

"How do you like that?"

"They will make you pay, you got no idea," Lizard screamed as blood trickled down his chin, dripping to the floor.

"Perhaps we shall continue, you prefer the whip? Don't worry, I will pull out more teeth, but for now, let's play."

"Wait, please, what can I do to make you stop?" Lizard choked.

"You will make me continue if you cry like a baby, you know, with people like you, it's not fun to take you down fast, it must be dynamic."

"I will tell you everything you want to know if that is what you are after," Lizard sighed, defeated.

"Oh, now we are talking, so basically you are choosing to live by betraying, right?"

"Yes, if you want to call it that."

"But the ones who betray have to be tortured more; you gave me a new idea."

"No, please don't, I am begging you," Lizard shrieked.

"I was kidding, now you better start talking, who is the leader?"

"The leader of what?"

"The leader of the dead fly on the moon. The leader of the cult, you fool."

"What cult?"

Vic grabbed the pliers and moved towards Lizard.

"Wait, please, I will talk."

"Then don't waste my time."

"The leader of the cult goes by the name The Head Of The Dragon. It's a female, the real name of her nobody knows, she is blind but very powerful, I have seen her only once, and since then the fear of her never left me."

"Interesting, tell me everything else you know about her."

"She has one weakness, and that is poetry. When she hears a new poem that she likes, she can be manipulated. She wanted to be a good person, but something turned her into being evil. I suppose her husband, because he left her and never came back. From all that pain, she lost her vision over time and started a cult and promised to make him pay."

"Even more interesting, when can I find her?"

"I don't know where she is, but all I know is that she appears at the ritual only during the eclipse."

"When is the next eclipse?"

"I think it's on May 19th, two months from now."

"Anything else I should know about the poetry, broken-hearted lady?"

"Yes, one more thing, her necklace gives her the power, so if you want to take her down, you'd better cut off her necklace."

"Well, Mr. Lizard, now you are a free man, congratulations!"

"Thank you very much, man, may I know your name?"

"The pleasure is all mine; my name is Fox, and of course, you are not free."

"But I told you everything we had a deal; please don't do this."

Vic smirked and headed for the door, leaving Lizard tied up.

Vic left the castle the same way the woman had escaped. While the wolves were busy tending to the pups, he ran as fast as he could to mount his horse and reach safety. There was no time to look back. Just as he neared his horse, one of the wolves broke loose and came at him, looking furious.

Vic stepped back a few paces and pulled out his torch to scare it away, but the wolf did not retreat. The best defense in that moment was to be ready to strike if the wolf attacked. As it turned out, the wolf was the mother of the pup Vic had held earlier at the window, and her rage came from that. Vic waited several tense minutes, but the wolf never attacked—she only left in silence.

He tried to mount his horse, but the animal was restless, trembling from the fear stirred up by the wolf's fury. So, Vic decided to travel on foot, leading the horse by its reins. Step by step, the long journey toward the Temple of Justice began.

Before he could arrive, dawn was breaking. Exhaustion weighed on him, his eyes heavy, his body drained of energy. He sat down on a nearby rock and fell asleep.

In his dream, he heard birds singing and the river flowing. Then, suddenly, he found himself in another world. He was swimming in red water, the shore far away, and he couldn't bring himself to look back. The waves pushed him forward, but it felt as though he was swimming toward the shore for eternity. Finally, when he reached land, the water turned deep blue.

Curious, he dipped his toe into the water, and instantly it turned red again. In his dream, he thought, *"What the hell is this?"* There was no battle, no sign of life—the sea was deserted. He sat down at the shore, staring at the waves, unable to understand why the water bled red at his touch.

At that moment, a voice thundered from the sky.

"Don't give up hope when there is no hope left."

"Who are you?" Vic asked, looking around for the source.

"I am your voice of the universe."

"What do you mean by: when there is no hope left?"

"You will see when the time comes."

"Why does the water turn red when I touch it?" he asked.

"If you give up hope, you will sell your soul, and if you sell your soul, you will become worthless. Don't become worthless, my child."

"How do you mean sell your soul?"

"Don't fall into the trap of desperation. Many tried, but none of them succeeded. Do not give up hope."

In the dream, dark clouds began to form in the clear sky, and soon heavy rain poured down. Vic sat there in disbelief, drenched and confused. He was jolted awake by a passerby who, thinking Vic was dead, had started poking him with a stick.

When he opened his eyes, his head throbbed with pain, and he was left with more questions than answers. He assured the passerby that everything was fine and there was no need to worry. A moment later, Vic told himself that the dream meant nothing, that he would never lose hope. Whatever it symbolized, he convinced himself there was no reason to dwell on it—at least, that's what he thought.

Vic mounted his horse and continued on to the Temple of Justice. Upon arriving, he exchanged greetings with the guard at the entrance before heading inside. In the main room, only Peter was there, waiting.

"Welcome, my dear, you look like you have seen a ghost. What happened?"

"It's all good. It was just a dream, no need to worry."

"I am here to listen if you want to talk about it."

"No need to talk about it, just a dream that's all."

"As you wish, then, what could you find out about the leader?" Peter asked.

"Yes, but I forgot to loot the place, oh, such a waste."

"You never forget that, I am surprised."

"I am too. I guess I got distracted, but it's not important now. The leader is a blind woman who goes by the name of the head of the dragon. She has a weakness for poetry, and she shows up at the ritual only when it is the eclipse. The next one is on May 19th, as I was told by the lizard."

"I understand. What did you do with the lizard, by the way?"

"I left him to be eaten by the wolves."

"Good choice, now let's talk about the leader, shall we?"

"Please proceed…"

"If she's that soft when it comes to poetry, why don't you take a few days off and draw inspiration from nature? Write a poem—a romantic one, as if you've fallen in love with her. You don't even need to approach her during the ritual. Just read it aloud from the middle of the crowd. That will stir her emotions, and when she's at her softest point, that's when you make your move to take her down. Since you won't be allowed to carry any weapon into the cave, she'll likely want to speak with you after the ritual. That's when you take your chance."

"Since we enter May in a couple of days, that is an amazing idea."

"With her gone, the war is over, and after that, we can throw a feast!"

"Sounds good to me, we can get drunk as well."

"That we will definitely do."

"I will get going now."

"Good luck!"

After leaving the room, Vic mounted his horse and rode to the lake, where he sat to enjoy a moment of peace. He began thinking about what he could write to impress the lady and win her heart—so that, in the end, he could bring her down for the greater good.

The birds sang, spring was in full bloom, and the scent of flowers filled the air. Vic closed his eyes and thought deeply about what it would feel like to fall in love. At first, no inspiration came to him. But after five long hours of meditation, he slipped into a deep state of peace and harmony within his soul.

The words were constructed by themselves; all he had to do was to memorize the entire poem.

Vic opened his eyes and felt a strong feeling while creating those words in his head, as if he could do anything just by putting his mind into something; it felt like nothing was impossible.

Shortly after, he was headed home and rushed to find the ink and a feather pen to write the poem down in order not to forget it. When he finished writing it, he hid it under the pillow until the day that he had to use it. After that, Chris and Otto were surprised about the fact that he did not greet them but rushed to write something. He apologized and explained everything, they understood it and did not bother him.

He left the house and decided to walk into town, since he had been absent for some time. Going on foot felt right—he wanted to feel the streets beneath him, see the familiar faces of the locals, and pass by the shops and stalls that reminded him of home.

When he arrived, he noticed a woman in need of help, though no one else seemed to care about her troubles. Her name was Sophie. She had been searching for her son for ten years and had never lost hope. She claimed he had been taken away to be trained as a warrior and forced to fight in a distant land.

Her voice was frail, and her expression carried an irreparable sorrow. You could see her soul shattered into pieces, and it was impossible to imagine the weight of what she had endured for a decade. When Vic approached her, she poured out her story in detail— what she remembered firsthand, and what she had gathered from the whispers and rumors of others.

"From what I can see, there is so much pain in you. What can I do to help?" Vic asked.

Sophie's gaze did not leave the ground.

"My son, they took my only child. It has been ten years so far. His name is Theo, and he must be fifteen years old now."

"Who took him? You must tell me everything you know in order to find him. I have a bit more than I week because I must return, due to the work that I have to do here."

"They took him to fight, to become a warrior."

"Who are they, Lady? The world is wide and long, the name means nothing if you don't provide me with more details"

"I was holding his hand, we were walking to go to buy him a present for his birthday when two men dressed in white with the blue straps took him and ran away, I heard rumors that they work for some kind of cult and somebody mentioned the stars they use him to become a warrior due to his strength that he had as a child, stronger than all the kids his age."

"Lady, I know where he is, he is not that far, I am just fearing that maybe by now they convinced him that what he does is the best thing to do, you understand me?"

Sophie began to sob.

"Oh, after all these years, somebody is willing to help"

"Just calm down, everything will be all right, you will see your son again. I will attend the ritual, but I can't promise that he has not changed. I will do my best to convince him to come home, I give you my word."

"It would mean a world to me, like every mother's love for her child; I would be thankful for the rest of my life."

"I understand, please be patient like you have been until now. I have to go now. I will do my best to see what I can do about Theo."

Days passed in the most beautiful month of the year, and the 19th of May was getting closer and closer. Vic spent his time going on quests such as finding the missing sheep of a farmer, collecting crops for a disabled lady, and helping people around town to get by more easily. Those humane acts made him feel more valuable as a person and brought him a sense of accomplishment at the end of the day.

On May 16th, he went for a walk and sat down by the river. His mind was occupied with thoughts of varying range and depth. He began asking himself why this world is so filled with evil and hate. How is it that good people are always the ones who end up hurt, or worse? Where is the sense of justice, and what could we do to make everything better? Perhaps we should all start with ourselves. These thoughts had captured him before, but this time they weighed on him more heavily, just days before he was meant to perform two acts on the same day.

As the river flowed, he gazed at the stones and watched fish swim by. He decided to jump in for a swim, since it always helped him release the pressure in his mind. All those questions he had asked himself seemed to disappear temporarily in the water.

After the swim, he did not want to go home. Instead, he chose to spend the night in the woods alone to feel his connection with nature. He stayed there for three days, roaming around and eating fruits he found, watching wild animals from a distance, and feeling both free and troubled at the same time.

On the morning of May 19th, he was ready. He ran home, grabbed his poem, told his friends he would return in a couple of days, mounted his horse, and rode straight to the cave to be ready for the ritual.

Chapter Five: Another Realm

As the cultists were all inside waiting for the leader, the head of the dragon, everyone was feeling somewhat high expectations out of this eclipse, as if it was supposed to bring them some kind of power, or even a reward for their dedication. Vic thought to himself, "Fools, you waste your time in believing the old tales and summoning demons, you will never know what life is about," as they all were forming a circle by holding hands.

Vic joined them, and one of the members lit the fireplace with a torch. At that moment, the head of the dragon appeared and positioned herself in front of the fire. Vic thought for a moment, maybe he could just push her into flames and finish the job, but decided to approach with the poem.

After the eclipse, as the head of the dragon was about to leave, Vic closed his eyes and remembered every word of the poem. At that moment, his heart was beating fast, and he was not sure if he should do it. After a deep breath, he just started:

Oh, the precious flower in the spring

Why love hurts like a scorpion's sting?

Why your love was hurt at all?

Why, when we fly, we just fall?

Oh, your beauty, so soft like the snow

Where is that one who let you go?

Where is the love that you once felt?

Where is the hand that you once held?

Hey, now, don't you cry for that, all is in vain

Don't forget to stand up and forget the pain

You are young, free, and full of life

One day, you will be somebody's wife

Right then, she grew pale, and her legs started to shake from emotions she could not stand, but was held and helped by two members. She started to cry out loud, and her heart was filled with joy at the same time, but with sorrow as well. After she calmed down, she decided to ask who created such a beautiful poem.

Vic from the crowd said, "It was me. I wrote these words just for you."

She was overwhelmed and told him to wait for him outside after the ritual. Vic agreed. After half an hour, Vic was approached by several members to congratulate him on a beautiful poem, but many of the members got jealous because they never got the chance to say a word to the leader, nor had they had the chance of her asking anyone to talk to her. From a distance, Vic's attention was caught by a member who was taller than everyone else, and somehow, he thought that maybe that could be Theo. After all, he promised Sophie that he would try to bring him home, since he was short on time, and soon, he had to talk with the leader. He had to act fast and effective in order to achieve both goals without overthinking and hesitation, so he decided to approach.

"Stars be upon you, brother; may I ask your name?"

"Stars be upon you too; my name is Theo, and yours?"

"No time for a long talk here. I will be sincere with you, what I am about to do is for the best of us all; there is no place for you here. Sophie waited for you for a full decade, and she is out on the streets looking for you and asking for help from strangers to find you. They took you since you were a child, and you are not aware of what they are doing to you, filling your mind with nonsense and toxic beliefs. I don't know you at all, and what have you become from being here, but trust me when I tell you, if I only got the chance to see my mother once more, I would give everything; the choice is yours."

A solitary tear rolled down Theo's cheek.

"How do you think I can escape? I thought they killed her that day. I remember that she took me to buy me a present for my birthday. I missed her ever since"

"Good boy, now listen to me very carefully. Follow the members and be the last one on the row, improvise, and find a way to be the last one. I will call my friend who can control the animals and lead a furious attack on all of them, but in the meantime, I have to deal with the leader. Just trust me, and you will be free."

"I understand, but what if you don't succeed?"

"I always do."

As they were preparing to leave one by one, Vic stood by the fire and waited until the end was near. With his eyes closed, he was hoping that Theo would find a reason to postpone his exit. He was being called and told the members that he would exit after he finishes with the cleaning of the stones and putting down the fireplaces. It was not his obligation, but he just wanted to buy some time. Vic opened his eyes, and the one before Theo was being suspicions about him, but Vic intervened by telling him to go because he had to talk with the leader. Theo managed to exit the last one, and Vic signaled him by nodding that all would be good and it's going according to the plan. When Vic exited the cave, the leader was waiting for him, and she started expressing her gratitude for the poem.

"In my entire life, I was not gifted a poem like yours. How come you wrote it in the most captivating way possible?" she asked.

"There is a first time for everything."

"How long have you been a member?"

"Long enough to realize what it takes to get to your heart. "

"My heart is broken, but you mended it. You made me believe in feeling again. I never thought my heart could feel anything again at all."

"Then why did you choose to become evil?" Vic asked.

"How do you mean?" she asked through pursed lips.

"Are you aware that this war broke off because of you?"

"I wanted revenge; it did not come out of the blue. I was abandoned by sorrow and agony, and I lost my vision."

Vic noticed her necklace gleaming in the light.

"Perhaps, you made the wrong choices so far."

"Or I was done wrong? How come a poet like you can't see the depth of the sorrow? Doesn't art come from sadness?"

She left Vic speechless.

"Now, what would you do if you were in my shoes? What would you decide? To strike or not to strike? Or to remain calm after everything that has happened?"

"We all do what we must at some point, but sometimes it is not up to us to choose the fate of others; we cannot base one fact or a situation, and from that, create chaos, don't you think?"

"What did I do to deserve all this? I just followed one rule that kept my heart beating."

"I suppose that rule was to destroy everything that you once held so close, prove me wrong!"

She was left speechless.

"Now, we are walking on the edge. What would you do if you were me? I made a lot of wrong choices too, even though I am a poet, an artist, and a fighter, somebody who never gives up."

"Hope cannot be bought in the streets; it must be driven by a force inside us."

"Then why don't you find it? Why have you never tried that? Instead, you split the black magic spell between two nations. How did it make you feel? Proud? Fueled with more hate and rage? For what? For something that was done to you? Don't you think bad things happen to us all? We all suffer from something and somebody throughout our lives, but not all of us do what you did."

Vic's words again left her speechless.

"Now listen to me very carefully, lady, you have two options here:

To hand over that necklace of yours and to sign the treaty.

To be eliminated here for the good of the entire Europe, since you brought this hell onto earth, and to hell it shall go with you!"

"But I thought that maybe there would be another way to resolve this?"

"Not in this lifetime, lady, the poetry was just a trap to drag you outside."

"I will sign it," she stated as she handed over the necklace.

"Good choice, now I will get your signature right now, and I would never like to see you again."

She began to sob.

"I will respect your opinion," she sobbed as she signed.

As Vic mounted his horse, he did not feel any emotion at all. He said what he had to say, what he felt like should have been said. He rushed the horse to spring in order to catch up with the members and hoped that Theo was the last one on the line of the members.

As the horse was sprinting, Vic could not see or hear any sign of the members, and at that moment, his only hope was Oni. Oni spread its wings, and the location of the members was revealed. They were going north up the hill, and Vic felt sorry for rushing his horse to run, but time was of the essence. Once again, he had to rush, and finally, he caught up with the members as they were all singing a strange song with a high-pitched voice.

Vic and his horse could not be heard from a hundred meters away. In the distance, Theo could be recognized, being the tallest among them. As Vic approached, he reached out from the right side of the horse and pulled Theo up, seating him on the back. Theo had to hold on tightly as they galloped down the hill. The others soon realized he was missing, but by then it was too late to stop them.

Vic and Theo escaped, though Vic insisted the horse should rest after its earlier sprint. Theo remained quiet, uncertain how Sophie would react to seeing him after a decade. Vic did not ask questions either, knowing his promise was only to return the boy to his mother, not to interfere in the story. After half an hour, they continued their journey. When they arrived, they dismounted and walked for about five minutes into the town. Vic wanted to care for the horse, ensuring it was fed and not overworked in the coming days.

As they drew nearer, about twenty meters from Sophia, Vic told Theo, "Now, be strong."

When she saw him, she burst into tears. She could not believe she was seeing her son after ten years. Her sorrowful expression vanished, replaced by joy and love. It felt to her as though the entire world had been placed before her eyes. Citizens gazed at her, and many gathered to see what was happening. Her cries of joy carried through the streets, and they, too, shared in her happiness. After a decade, she had finally been reunited with her son.

She wept for an hour, while Vic stood aside, watching both her and the faces of the citizens. He marveled at how a single act could bring such happiness to a life. At last, when she had calmed a little, she was able to speak.

Sophie ran and took Theo in her arms.

"My son, my Theo, my light of the sun, my everything in life, you are finally here. I missed you so much every day and every night, every moment since they took you."

"I missed you too, Mother, but I thought it was the end for my life; they poisoned my mind into thinking that life was not more than that."

"My son, life is always what you want it to be, at least now you are here with me."

"And I will be, Mother, from now on. You don't need to worry anymore, my savior here made up my mind to escape with him and to come back home to you."

Sophie turned to Vic.

"I am sorry, Victor. From the flow of emotions, I could not thank you properly. There are no words that I could express my gratitude towards you, you brought home my Theo, now my life has a meaning. I will never forget this act of kindness from you."

"It's my pleasure to see you two happy and together. It was nothing, I just grabbed him and brought him home finally, and the war will be over soon, so we can all sleep in peace now," Vic replied.

"You really are a legend, and you will be remembered as one! Mark my words!" Sophie cried.

"Hah! Consider them marked, I don't tend to be a legend of any kind, I just act as I see fit, and my actions are based on my emotions and judging the situation correctly. I am no hero or a legend, I am just a simple man who loves to help people in need and to take down those who destroy our lives and our future."

"I couldn't agree more with you there. But still, thank you again for everything."

"It's my pleasure. Now, Theo, you take good care of your mother; you owe her in some way for a decade, and never ever leave her side. I should go now."

Sophie and Theo both chimed, "Until we meet again."

While Vic was going home, his heart was filled with joy and happiness. Again, every good deed that he did made him feel like he mattered in this world. He just smiled inside and said to himself, "I should get drunk with my friends tonight, maybe we should call Oni to drink with us too, so that we could watch him do silly things and fly like a drunk raven." But even though he had to go to the Temple of Justice in the morning, he decided to get drunk with friends, and there was nothing that could stop him from doing that. As he was walking back home, he started to sing and be happy like everyone should be. Upon arriving home, he opened the door, and his friends were asleep.

Vic thought for a moment they must be exhausted from helping the wounded ones all day, every day, so how could I get drunk alone now? He whispered to himself.

Maybe a drink or two wouldn't have done much harm, but once he started, he couldn't stop. After the second, then the third, he lost count altogether. The first kick of alcohol had lifted his mood, but it soon spiraled into a bad situation. He drank until he couldn't drink any more, and then came the vomiting and the pain that spread through his whole body. It felt like endless agony, and as dawn approached, he couldn't even get up.

Luckily, Chris woke first and sensed something was wrong. He went to Vic's room and found him completely wasted. Chris said nothing, unaware that Vic was supposed to attend the treaty, a meeting of great importance for both countries.

Vic eventually fell asleep and didn't wake until just before sunset. He had missed the treaty. The man who had brought peace between the two nations had been asleep through the event. When he woke, his head felt as heavy as an elephant. He couldn't focus, couldn't orient himself, couldn't even pull himself together. The overjoy of achieving two great goals had been over-celebrated — or rather, over-drunk.

Later that evening, he managed to get up and drank plenty of water. Chris and Otto just looked at him and remarked, "That's what we call a proper celebration."

Vic only smiled and stepped outside. Before leaving, he explained that he had to go to the Temple of Justice to see how it had gone, even though all he truly wanted was to lie down and wait for the hangover to pass.

As he promised himself that he would not use his horse for a couple of days, he rented Otto's horse without asking, but the horse did not recognize him and several times tried to push him off its back. Because of that, Vic struggled to make it to the Temple of Justice, but managed somehow. When he arrived, the member at the front door, instead of greeting him, was just surprised to see him in that state and was staring constantly.

Vic just said, "Hey, man, I know."

After passing the entry, he walked through the corridor and arrived at the main room. There were all three leaders along with Eddie, and they were celebrating the success that peace had come, and the war was over. When they saw Vic, they were surprised as well, but mostly happy to see him.

"Victor, our legend, our pride of the country, you are late," Peter cried with open arms.

"I know, I just wanted to see how it went, and from what I can see now, we made it."

"You made it, Victor; you are the honored one," Jakob cheered.

"Oh, come on, people, I just did what was right, what I had to do, don't overexaggerate this," Vic mumbled, avoiding eye contact.

"I heard that you became a poet as well, am I right?" Anthony asked.

"As it seems, I did. It was just a trap to lure her out of the cave and to get to talk to her, so tell me, did you mention me this morning at the celebration or…?"

"Of course, we did, but you missed the ceremony. As far as I can see, judging from your state, you had way too many drinks, I suppose," Peter replied.

"Obviously, I wanted to celebrate with my friends, but they were asleep, so I celebrated alone. I could not come here in the evening, so I had to wait for dawn."

"Why not? This is your home too, we are all like a family, and you are more than welcome to stay here for as long as you need or want to."

"Thank you, it means a lot to me. I will consider the offer."

Eddie stood and approached Victor.

"It's always a pleasure to see you, Victor. I could not be happier that you made it. You brought peace into our lands, and for that I am sincerely thankful." Eddie thanked Victor warmly, shaking his hand.

"And so let there be peace for everyone. It's my pleasure, Eddie. I think I should go now. I just wanted to see how it went."

"Wait, we have something for you," Jakob started as he rummaged through a small metal box and retrieved an item. "This is just a sign of gratitude from us. You may have this medallion, and may it bring you only the best wishes and fulfilment. It was gifted to me by my father, and it was a legacy in our family for centuries. I gift it to you in the name of glory and respect and everything that you did all these years, for all the roads that you went up and down and for all the sacrifices that you made."

Vic's jaw dropped.

"I don't know what to say, I feel honored, I don't know if I deserve it. After all, it's a legacy from your family, I don't think I can accept it."

"A gift should not be rejected, I am sure you know that. After all, you are a part of the family too, so please accept it as a sign of gratitude."

"Thank you, this means a lot to me," Victor replied as he reached out and accepted it.

"Good, then it's our pleasure."

"I should go now, see you in a couple of days."

As Vic left the Temple of Justice, he mounted Otto's horse. He felt respected, but he thought that perhaps it was overexaggerated due to him being the focus and "the star" of it all. It made him feel somehow as if all of it was not genuine, but he did not bother to overthink it since he was still feeling the hangover. In that moment, he remembered that Leonard could control the animals. Since Otto's horse was restless, he needed Leonard's help, perhaps also a potion for the hangover, why not? Vic whistled three times, but Leonard was not near; the only hope was for Oni to find him.

As Oni spread its wings in search of Leonard, at first it seemed hopeless. But after a long while, Leonard was finally spotted beneath a tree, gathering plants that looked like flowers to use in a new potion. Guided by Oni, Vic followed the road, watching the sky as they passed through forests and near enemy fortresses. He knew those fortresses were too well-guarded to approach, so he chose to avoid them and press on.

After about half an hour of walking, Vic found Leonard beneath an old olive tree. Leonard was muttering to himself.

"It must be a wizard thing," Vic whispered under his breath, and he watched from about twenty meters away to see what he would do next.

Leonard seemed to be searching for a particular type of plant, though even he did not know its name. Vic decided to approach, feeling unwell from the lingering effects of his hangover.

"Leonard, you seem to be in distress and anxious from what I can see," Vic explained as he watched Leonard dart about frantically.

"Oh, yes, for sure. You know when you want to find something so badly and you end up losing yourself in the process of searching for it, does it sound familiar to you by any chance?"

"Ha-ha, you must be playing games with me, or it's another wizard thing?"

"No, my son, what? No games, I am being honest with you, if I wanted to play games, I would have left you to die by a venomous snake that night."

"You are seeking a reward for it, or you are just mentioning it as a fact?"

"None of those, I am just telling you that I am not fooling around."

"In that case, let's just assume I trust you, and besides that, yes, I have found myself in that situation before, maybe way more often than I should have, but in life, you don't get to choose the outcome, you just get to choose your actions. Don't you agree?"

Leonard examined the bushes, searching for the plant.

"I do not agree with you there, my son. Often in life, our actions define the outcome. What is bothering you there? First of all, you look hungover as hell, and besides that, you look like you are fed up with life. Maybe I could give you the potion for the hangover right now, I think I have it with me somewhere, but for the second problem, I don't think you want the potion since it would take you to another world and back."

"Give me the potion for hangover first, and about the other one, we will talk shortly."

"Hold on until I find it, maybe it's here, wait, not this one, not even this one, wait a bit. Hah, I found it. Here," Leonard explained as he handed the potion to Vic.

Vic got a whiff of the potion and gagged. He held his nose and knocked the potion down his throat in one gulp.

"Pew man, it tastes like piss. From what is this made?"

"It's made from plants, of course, there is chamomile, olive leaves, and the rest, I forgot it's in my book."

"Your book, judging from you, I guess you make mistakes in mixing the ingredients pretty often, huh?"

"Ha-ha, Leonard, make a mistake, never! By the way, why are you so arrogant all of a sudden? You know, people that want you to be good cannot tolerate you forever."

"As you said there in your diagnosis, I am fed up with everything, even life, so…"

"So what? Hangover is gone, not even a thank you? You needed me, that's why you came to me, not the other way around, so what?"

Vic was speechless.

"That's what I thought. Now, man the fuck up for once, and learn to behave. You can follow me to my beloved cottage, and there I will prepare the potion for you to open the doors of your soul and to send you via dreams to another life. What you will be experiencing there will stay in your memory for as long as you live, and if you for even once more behave like a child, an arrogant one, I will call the fucking wolves and bears and all the wild animal kingdom to hunt you down, am I being clear?"

"Crystal," Vic growled.

"Now follow me, and shut up!"

Vic followed him for nearly three hours. Leonard's cottage was on the far eastern side of the town, and throughout the journey, Vic did not say a single word. Leonard, on the other hand, spoke constantly, muttering to himself and boasting about his life, his past, the ex-wife who had left him decades ago, and his daughter who had sailed to another part of the world. It was clear that life had not been kind to him.

For Vic, those three hours felt like reading ten books at once. Leonard's rambling jumped from one topic to another, circling endlessly. Vic followed him as faithfully as a dog follows its master, but remained silent, not wanting to make Leonard more irritable than he already was.

When they finally arrived at the cottage, more drama unfolded. Leonard had apparently lost his book and flew into a rage, smashing objects inside his home and cursing life itself, as though Vic were somehow to blame. He searched every corner of the cottage, then began digging outside near a tree. He even climbed the tree, thinking he might have left it there.

After exhausting himself, Leonard rested briefly, only to resume digging with greater frustration. From the roof of the cottage, Vic watched him, curious to see what he would do next. Leonard then wandered to a nearby horse farm, searching like a madman. When he failed to find the book, he even asked permission to search the neighboring houses, which was, of course, refused. Furious, he returned to his cottage and slumped on the porch.

By chance, his hand brushed against his leather bag. The book had been with him all along. "Wizard," Vic muttered under his breath. Leonard burst into a dance of joy, celebrating the discovery. In his excitement, he forgot Vic was even there and carried on with his eccentricities until Vic finally climbed down from the roof to remind him.

"Congratulations, you have found your book!" Vic cheered.

"Hah, yes, I did indeed, it was under the table, I don't recall who put it there. I thought you left. Let's proceed with the potion, shall we...?"

"I knew he was crazy, but this crazy is beyond my imagination," Vic whispered to himself.

"At least you have found it. Of course, let's proceed," Vic announced, joining Leonard.

"Now, let's prepare the potion..."

Leonard read the list of ingredients and hurried to collect everything.

"Now, I have all the ingredients, I think I can make it for you," he explained.

Victor waited patiently as Leonard clattered around, all of the bottles clinking.

"I hope I will not make a mistake and send you God knows where. That would be a chaotic outcome, but listen, I will do my best to take you there. Here, I think that's about it, and the color of the potion is in the right one. I think it should be dark blue. I think you should drink it now, and soon it will make you fall asleep, and you will be there."

"Are you sure you got it? Maybe I should not drink it. Listen, Leonard, I think I should go to see my friends, and then we can meet perhaps another day. What can this potion do to me to make anything better?"

"You know things will be clearer; perhaps you can see what you want the most. The potion will trigger your brain to take you to places beyond your imagination. I am not trying to hurt you or to do anything bad to you, Victor. I am trying to help you, since you need my help. You are overburdening yourself with emotions and worries, and it's eating you alive. You need this to have a better understanding of everything. Trust me, I am not your enemy. I am crazy in my own way, I guess all the wizards are like that, but you should trust me."

"Then, let it take me where it should take me, and let it be what it should be. If you say it that way, you convince me that you don't wish me anything bad, and I am thankful for that. So be it," Vic replied as he lifted the potion to his lips and drank every last drop.

"Now, lie down, you will fall asleep soon. When you want to wake up, you will know how."

"Wish me luck."

"You are lucky without that, but good luck."

As he was falling asleep, he could hear a loud ringing in his ears, a rising heartbeat, followed by heavy sweating, and his legs were shaking.

Leonard was near him, and if needed, he could wake him in a state of emergency. Vic fell asleep and travelled through the air at an insanely high speed. He woke in another realm where the air felt different, the gravity was lower, and everything was slower than in real life.

Vic tried to open his eyes in the dream, but when he reached his face, they were already open. Everything he was looking at seemed real. To be absolutely sure, he touched the ground, the stones, and every solid object nearby. It all felt real. Since he had woken in the middle of nowhere, he kept walking until he saw strange creatures he could not explain.

They were not hostile at all. They looked frightening at first, but they were harmless, like pets. As he continued, reality struck harder. In the distance, Vic noticed a gathering of people. As he came closer, he realized they looked different. They had four eyes, their ears were no more than small dots, their heads were smaller than human heads, their fingers were short and dull, and they stood almost twice the height of an ordinary man.

Their language was incomprehensible, and Vic could not understand a single word. They seemed to use water for everything, as though it were the most important element in their world. Their water was purple. It tasted like normal water but gave enormous energy. When Vic wanted to drink more, someone nearby stopped him. Drinking too much caused chaos, and this was a realm of absolute peace. There were no wars, no murders, no arguments. Nobody killed animals for food; instead, they fed on blue plants, while the green ones were toxic.

Vic learned all this by observing their behavior. Though he could not speak their language, he did not give up and kept gathering information, trying to understand why he was there. He soon realized he was not the only human in the realm. While walking, he spotted a young woman and ran towards her. From a distance, he saw her studying the strange foliage, especially the huge leaves hanging from the white trees. These trees bore grey leaves and fruit at the tips. The locals called the fruit "kaskinimini," and anyone who ate it became instantly joyful, dancing as if there were no tomorrow.

Vic did not want to taste it yet. He only wished to speak to the girl, but she was too busy laughing and dancing under its influence. Unsure how long the effect would last, he decided to wait and investigate further until she came back to her senses. While moving on, he was bitten by a strange fly the size of a human hand. The bite caused intense pain, and he screamed, unable to find peace for half an hour. At that moment, he wanted to give up and find a way to wake, but as the pain began to ease, the girl returned to her senses, and he rushed to talk to her, even though she was running from him.

"Hey, wait, please wait, I need to talk to you, don't run away, I just need to know where we are," Vic gasped.

"No, I don't want to talk to you. I don't know you. Get away from me, leave me alone," she cried as she ran, trying to escape.

Vic sped to a sprint and tackled her.

"I just want to talk. Calm down, I am confused too," he explained as he wrestled her, trying to subdue her.

"Why did you tackle me? They will attack you now."

"I just want to talk, just calm down and tell them that it's all fine, please, I just need answers, nothing more."

She spoke in a language that they understood, and they backed off.

"What do you want to talk about?" she asked.

"Who are you? Why are you here? Who are those people? Where are we?"

"My name is Ingrida; I came here probably the same way you did: by drinking the potion."

"I am Victor, by the way, but why did you drink the potion? Why were you seeking this place?"

"Well, I wanted to see my sister who passed away years ago, and the wizard told me that I could probably see her here, you know. But I got here, and it feels like an eternity. I could not find a way to wake up whatsoever."

"What? You could not find a way to wake up? What am I supposed to do now? To spend my life stuck in a loop here forever?"

"Maybe, we are not the only humans here, perhaps there is a way to wake up, maybe we will find it out. I hope one day you will."

"One day! Are you insane? We need to find out how to wake up right now. Oh, Leonard, I will kill you when I wake up. Remember this!"

"Leonard, no way! That's the wizard who made me the potion!"

"Impossible, when was that? How is that possible?"

"Well, we must be connected by fate then? I think I saw you in my dreams in real life, I mean, before I ended up here, you were running from me constantly."

Snippets of the same dream flashed before Vic's eyes.

"Wait, I had the same dream, but I never got to see the face of the girl who was running away from me."

"This is getting interesting. What do you suggest we do now?"

"I don't know, perhaps we should continue to explore or to think deep. Maybe if we get into conflict with them, we could wake up, since the brain does not let you die in the dream."

"Wow, I did not know that before. Where did you find that out?"

"In my dreams. It's a normal thing, I suppose."

"Let's try it. We should attack them at the same time, so that if we wake up, we wake up the same time, and if we wake up, I will find you."

"Find me, what for?"

"To have a talk, perhaps we could get back here again."

"Thank you, but I can do that without you. We should attack them."

"Then, let's do it."

After engaging them in combat, they exited the dream the same way they had entered. It worked. Ingrida woke back in reality, but far from home. She remembered falling asleep in Leonard's cottage and found herself in the depths of the Alps, surrounded by snow.

Vic woke in his hometown in Bavaria. He, too, remembered entering the dream at Leonard's cottage, yet he was surprised to find himself somewhere else. Everything felt different. Vic did not feel that this was actual life. He thought it might be a dream within a dream and that this was only the first portal to wakefulness. He began searching for clues to wake up. He looked for people, for anyone, but had no luck.

Vic wondered whether repeating the same actions might wake them both, but he was also worried about Ingrida because there was no sign of her anywhere. He called for Oni, but there was no Oni in the sky. He called for his horse, but there was no horse in sight. He even tried to hurt himself by smashing his head against a tree, but he felt no pain. In that moment, he was certain this was a dream. Vic became desperate and resolved to find a way to wake up. When he did, he wanted to beat Leonard up. On second thought, Leonard might have been right.

From a distance, down the hill, Vic noticed a man and a woman and decided to approach. He could not be sure who they were, but as he drew closer, tears began to stream down his face. In front of him were his parents, holding hands and smiling. Vic fell to his knees, unable to believe his eyes. He felt the urge to cry, but crying in that realm was impossible.

"Father, Mom, is that you? Is this really you?" Victor asked, his hand cupping his mouth as he approached them.

"Victor, my son, you have grown so tall, you look amazing," Lara exclaimed as she reached out to stroke Victor's face, but stopped herself.

"Son, I am proud of you; you should know that," Thomas added.

"How come you are here? You haven't aged a bit since I saw you last time." Vic asked.

"We ended up here, it's another realm, you know, but once we pass two millennials here, then we move to another realm, that's what we were told," Thomas explained.

"Told by who? How is this even possible? What about the rest? Where are the rest of the people?" Victor's questions were never-ending.

"We are alone here, we don't know about anyone else. This place is limited," Lara explained.

"How do you mean limited?"

"There are borders that you cannot cross. We tried everything."

"We were told that we need five keys to unlock the gate and get to another realm. Each key has a symbol on it (earth, fire, air, water, and spirit), which can be found in real life in different places; those are called the keys of life," Thomas added.

"Who told you, Father, Mom? Who communicated with you?" Vic looked from Thomas to Lara, completely bewildered.

"The voice from the sky, can't you hear it? It's singing the song of liberation of the spirits," Thomas explained.

"I can't hear it, Father, what liberations? Of whose spirits?"

"Victor, the answers lie within you, not around you. You should know that," Lara reassured as she reached out to place a hand on his chest.

"What answers, Mom? What are you talking about? You two are making me confused." Vic's head felt as though it was going to explode.

"Find the keys and come back again so that we can unlock the door that will set us free," Thomas urged.

"I will try to find the keys, but I think I deserve answers, and I am doing the best I can to find and take down the ones who eliminated you both."

"Eliminated? No, my boy, we are alive. Can't you see?" Thomas explained as he reached out and touched his shoulder.

"Can't you feel my hand, Victor?"

"No, I can't. Because you are not alive, this is a dream in another realm, but don't worry, I will do what you are asking, and I will come back," Vic replied, disoriented now.

"Take care, my son, and be good. We always remember you as a good boy," Lara whispered tenderly.

"Thank you, Mom. I will. Does any of you know how to wake up in the realm?"

"I think that the one who put you here can wake you up by calling your soul to return back," Thomas explained.

"How will he know when the time is? How do I tell him?"

"You just don't, that's the point. He will do it by himself. Perhaps, there is one alternative way to wake up; you need to find the door to the depths of the soul, its location is shown by the signs on the road down the hill," Thomas pointed in the direction that Victor needed to go. "When you open the door, since it's unlocked, you just need to jump. It will trigger the soul to return to your body."

"I understand, I'd better get going then. I love you both, and I'll see you as soon as I retrieve the keys."

"We love you, too, son. Take care," Lara and Thomas's voices echoed as they waved him off.

Vic rushed down the hill as fast as he could, desperate to wake up. He still could not believe he had seen his parents. He was happy and sad at the same time. As he searched for clues and signs along the way, there was no luck at all. The fields were empty, the grass had grown tall, and his feet felt heavy. Every step was painful, yet he refused to give up, knowing Leonard was as unreliable as ever.

Vic searched and searched, but still found nothing. Perhaps Thomas had meant "signs" in a different sense. Vic tried to focus harder, wondering what it could mean and where the door might be.

Growing tired, he lay down on the ground and looked at the sky. There, arrows were drawn across the heavens, pointing a long way ahead, with the finish line circled. The map to the door was written above him. Smiling, Vic got to his feet and continued along the road.

At one moment, the day turned into night, and the arrows vanished. He was only at the beginning of his search. All of a sudden, he stopped and muttered to himself, "What now?" As the night slowly passed, the only things visible in the sky were the stars. In that realm, the stars hung much closer than in reality, close enough to frighten anyone who looked at them.

Vic decided to lie back and gaze at them. He began naming the stars, counting them one by one, just to let the time pass. Then strange animal voices echoed from the distance, sounds unlike anything he had heard before. They rose and fell like a melody, perfectly in sync, shifting through notes like a song. He admired both the stars above and the voices around him, and joy began to grow in his heart.

At that moment, Vic felt something pulling him from the ground, dragging him away with the same speed that had first carried him into the dream. He passed through everything at enormous speed and rose into the clouds once more. As he broke through them, his heartbeat quickened, and in that instant, he opened his eyes. He had woken. Leonard was staring at him with surprise in his eyes.

"Victor, what happened to you? You look pale, like you have seen a ghost. I had to pull your soul back to your body because I was scared, you know?"

"You pulled me right when you were not supposed to. I was gazing at the stars and hearing the sounds of animals there. I was feeling happy," Victor snapped.

"Hm, that's not good, you know, if you felt happy and your happiness was rising in another realm, that means that your soul wanted you to stay there, that's why you are pale. Because you nearly died."

"Oh, so you kind of saved my life. Knowing how reliable you are, I could have been dead so far. So thank you very much, you know," Vic sneered.

"Well, to be honest, I kind of felt sleepy, but a raven could not let me sleep, constantly crying with a heartbreaking sound."

"Oni, saved my life, obviously, see I told you that you were unreliable."

"I know, but tell me, what did you see? Where did you go? You were supposed to go to two realms, am I right?"

"Ha-ha, you are right, but you sent me unprepared, and then you pulled me out. Thanks to my raven, if Oni did not sense my danger, you would have left me to die there."

"Well, I just…" Leonard stammered.

"You what, Leonard? In the first realm, I met a girl that I saw here in my dreams in this world, and she had the same dreams about me, too. She told me that you had sent her there. Her name is Ingrida. We looked for a way to wake up, and the way to wake up was to get into a fight. You did not tell me any of that, so thank you once again for your help."

"Oh, Ingrida, I might have forgotten who she is, but if I remember, I will let you know. And about waking up, I forgot to tell you that part too, my bad. What else did you see?"

"Of course, you forgot. I am not surprised. When I woke after we got into a fight, I woke in my birthplace and saw my parents. They told me that the place is limited for them and they require five keys, keys of life, in order to be set free."

"Ah, keys of life, did they mention the map for them by any chance?"

"No, they did not mention the map. So, what now? I need to find the map. Where is it?"

"Well, the map has a riddle to solve in order to find it. That's what it says in one of the books I found, but I lost the book a long time ago."

"How could you lose a book of that importance? I mean, I am not surprised, but what can I expect from you anymore? What should I do now? You leave me no choice but to rage."

"Calm down, there is another way. Perhaps you can solve the riddle. I will try to remember the words from the riddle. It's something like 'when the sun lies under the mountains look for…' Wait, I'm trying to remember. There was another phrase after it," Leonard scratched his head, searching his mind for the answer. "Wait, I think I know what it said…"

Victor shook his head, his eyes full of disappointment.

"Ha! I remember now - 'when the sun lies under the mountains, look for the hole to fit the star in, if you find it, knock on the stone five times and the door will open, take the map and leave your sword, it will take you to another world.'"

"Where should I start looking?"

"At the mountains, of course, at the sunset."

"No way, you don't say. I thought I should start looking at the sea," Vic said, rolling his eyes. "Which mountains?"

"I don't know, but wait, there has to be a clue. There are five keys, and we are looking for the map. According to myths, the map should be in the middle and the keys all around it, so perhaps try to wait…" Leonard scampered off to his vast bookcase and skimmed the titles.

"Five elements they must be connected… what if all those elements have to be in one place, in order to reveal the location of the map?" Vic muttered to himself as he thought.

"Yes, you are a… wait. Am I a wizard, or are you? How did you know that?" Leonard asked.

"Just by using the ability to think, I guess."

"Ha-ha, very clever, I remember now, fire comes from the top of the mountain, it is surrounded by water, the wind blows from the south all the time, and the soul who finds the map gets to keep the keys to unlock the door of those waiting for their souls to be free."

"Well, from now, I guess I just need Oni; I'd better get going in my quest to find the keys. Oh, and by the way, thank you."

"Wait, you will need this as well. Take it with you and return it when you find the keys," Leonard explained as he handed Vic a small corked vial.

"What is this? Why would I need it?"

"It's a serum for snake bites; it may come in handy. Good luck, and may you find the keys."

At that moment, Vic left Leonard's cottage and called his horse, ready to begin his journey with the aim of setting his parents' souls free. After about an hour of searching for the mountain, the day turned into a storm the likes of which he had never imagined. The clouds turned black, the sky seemed ready to split apart, rain fell in torrents, thunder roared, and hail began to pound the ground. Vic dismounted and took shelter in a nearby cave.

The storm lasted for a full five hours, covering the land with a layer of ice from the hail. Just before it ended, a voice from the sky called out, "Do not go and look for the keys." Vic ignored it, determined to free his parents' souls. The voice came again, louder this time: "Do not go, it is a trap." His horse grew restless and fearful. When the voice spoke a third time, a bolt of lightning struck the tree beside them, burning it to ash. The warning was clearer now: "If you find the keys and open the door, there will be consequences you cannot imagine. Every hailstone means a soul." Moments later, the sky cleared and the storm was over.

Vic sat in silence, turning the words over in his mind. What could possibly go wrong if he found the keys? What kind of bloodshed could the voice have meant? He considered telling Leonard, but then dismissed the idea. Leonard was too unreliable. Instead, he sent Oni into the sky. But as soon as it rose, the winds hurled it back to the earth, leaving it unable to fly. At that moment, Vic was sure the voice was doing everything it could to stop him from seeking the keys.

He decided to spend the night in the cave and reconsider in the morning. As he lay beside his horse, sleep overtook him. In his dream, he saw a battle led by a man whose evil was written plainly in his eyes. His army crushed all who stood against them, merciless and heartless.

Among the carnage, Vic saw Leonard holding the key. He woke in terror.

Vic began to suspect that Leonard was his true enemy, that the vision of his parents had been nothing more than a trick to lure him into seeking the keys. Perhaps Leonard meant to betray them all and plunge the world into chaos. He reconsidered his suspicion and resolved to stay silent for a day or two. Then an idea came to him. To test both the dream and the warning voice, he would go to Mile and ask him to forge five keys, each with a different symbol. He would then present the false keys to Leonard to see how he reacted.

So, instead of resuming his search for the true keys, Vic turned towards Mile's workshop. When he arrived, he found Mile busy at work with a long line of customers waiting to place or collect their orders. Vic waved to catch his attention, then decided to wait it out at a nearby bar. After several drinks and several hours, his turn finally came. He returned to Miles' workshop and explained exactly what he needed.

"Welcome, Victor, long time no see. How have you been, my friend?"

"Thank you for your concern. I have been good, no complain whatsoever. I was just up and down, from here to faraway lands. How about you?" Vic asked.

"As you saw when you came, pretty busy every day except on Sundays. Hm, I see. No wonder you are an adventurous spirit. How can I help you today?"

"I need the latest sword, throwing knives, the newest axe, and an upgrade with my bow, but I came here to ask you for a favour as well."

"Consider it done when it comes to weapons. What kind of favour?"

"I need you to make five different keys. I will show you each one of them, in order to let you know how they look, from memory."

"Not a problem at all, Victor. For you, anything, my friend, proceed."

"One has a symbol of a tree on it, the second has a symbol of fire, the third has a symbol of water, the fourth has a symbol of wind (air), and the fifth has the symbol of soul," Vic explained as he scribbled each one on a sheet of papyrus.

"Of course, no problem, I will make them, but before that, may I ask what you need them for? I am asking this because this is a very familiar case."

"What do you mean, very familiar case? You heard of this before?" Vic asked, puzzled as to where Mile may have heard this.

"Yes, I did, you need fake ones, I assume? I heard stories that those keys were hidden by the Gods on purpose, and they were never meant to be found. But as you know, there are way too many evil people there, so I would not be surprised that somebody tricked you into going and looking for them. I am telling you this as a friend, I hope you will understand."

"Yes, of course, the fake ones. I just want to test a person who put me through all this, and in the end, if I can prove that he is evil, I will take him down. Because the society does not need people like him. He made me a potion to take me to another realm and tricked me into seeing my dead parents. They requested those keys from me, and thank you for your trust in me. Mile, it means a lot to me."

"I understand, so there is an evil wizard out there, all right, Victor. I will make you the fake keys and consider them done by morning. One more thing, my friend, be careful! Because he will not stop playing tricks on you."

"Thank you, I will be here in the morning. And don't worry, I know him very well and there is no way on earth that he could make up my mind into doing something wrong."

"We have a deal then, see you in the morning."

After leaving Mile's shop, Vic felt the urge to be outside. As soon as he stepped through the door, a soft, calming rain began to fall, and a great sense of peace settled over him. He walked the deserted streets until he reached the road that led down to the river. At the riverbank, he stood for a while, then lay down to feel each drop of rain and listen to the river flowing. He thought about his life and the realm he had visited. "Is this life real?" he asked himself. His heart quickened, and memories from his childhood came back to him, vivid and full of meaning. He passed the night that way, and the rain did not stop until dawn.

When morning came, Vic drank from the river, looked up at the sky, and said, "If there is a God above, lead me to justice." Tired and soaked, he went back to Mile's shop to collect the weapons and the keys he had ordered. When he opened the door, Mile could see he had not slept properly and offered him a room behind the shop to rest. Vic accepted and, without collecting anything, went straight to bed.

He woke in the afternoon feeling refreshed and full of energy. Mile was busy forging a sword for a special customer. Vic collected his weapons and the keys, left one hundred gold coins on Mile's desk and a note that read, "Thank you for everything," then mounted his horse and rode straight for Leonard's cottage.

On the way, he almost ran into mercenaries seeking the bounty on his head, but he avoided conflict and escaped. Just before he reached the cottage, Vic dismounted and slipped behind the bushes, then climbed a tree to watch Leonard without being seen. From his vantage point, he saw Leonard mixing a potion and cursing because he had forgotten something. He looked for the lost item with the usual absent-minded frenzy of a wizard.

Vic wondered how he could prove Leonard was evil. You could not judge a man only by a dream or by rumors. Maybe the voice from the sky was an illusion. He was torn. If the voice was real, how could it keep appearing before decisions that mattered so much? How could everything feel and sound so real? When he had been swimming, the water had turned red, and then the voice spoke to him. Who, then, was this voice?

On the other hand, if Leonard were guilty, why had he saved Vic's life? Perhaps Leonard needed him for a quest. Maybe Leonard was plotting to betray everyone and bring chaos. Vic was unsure. How could he trust even his own senses after seeing his parents and being asked to do something that might destroy lives? Perhaps that too had been an illusion. Doubt gnawed at him. What would Peter, Jakob, and Anthony say if they knew he planned to look for the keys? Would they laugh at him for believing the voice?

Mile had suggested the gods had hidden the keys because they did not want the door opened. What if the door should be opened? What if the voice was right and opening it would cost innocent lives? There had to be an answer, but how could he find it? Should he consult a witch to see his fate, or simply follow his heart? Could following his instincts lead him to the answers he sought?

After an hour of wrestling with his thoughts, Vic decided to talk with Leonard.

"Hello Leonard, how have you been? You look nervous. What did you forget this time, friend?" Vic asked as he strolled into the cottage.

"Welcome, Victor, it's a pleasure to meet you. Oh, I forgot the amount of rose oil drops goes in this potion to make something very interesting and new," Leonard replied as he rummaged through the cupboards.

"Very intriguing, what are you making this time? Of course, if it's not a secret."

"Ha-ha, it's not a secret, of course. It's a potion for seeing a deeper picture of life that I want to use for myself; don't blame a curious old man like me. How have you been? Did you manage to find the keys?"

"I understand. Well, I wish you nothing but luck to make that potion, well, uhm, about the quest, it's kind of complicated."

"Thank you, how do you mean complicated? What happened?"

"Well, I don't know how to tell you this, but I was stopped on my way several times."

"How do you mean stopped? Be open with me, you know I am your friend, tell me everything. After all, you don't have to do this if you don't want to or doubt me in any way."

"Thank you for understanding. Can we perhaps not talk about it?"

"I would like to know what you have been through, that's all."

"I found the map and the keys, but I did not open the door, since a voice from the sky told me not to, because it would create a chaotic impact on the society of the entire world. As far as I could gather info, I found out that the Gods hid those keys on purpose, and the door should never be open."

"Hm, very interesting, let me take a look at the keys for a moment."

Vic handed him the keys.

"Here."

Leonard examined the keys, and his eyes darted back to Victor.

"Do you think I am a fool? Those are fake ones and were made recently. Why are you doing this? You never found the map, did you?"

"I had my reasons not to, you sent me into those realms in order to make me believe in all this, how come you did not go yourself to look for the keys?" Vic snapped.

Leonard became enraged, smashing everything on the table.

"I knew you wouldn't do it; I thought I disabled that voice in you once at for all, but I forgot."

"I knew you were an evil bastard," Vic growled, slowly reaching behind his back for his axe.

"Now, I will take you down!" Leonard shrieked as he lunged at him with his sword.

Vic dodged Leoard's blade, and it got lodged in the wall. As Leonard tugged at it desperately, Vic escaped, closing the door behind him. He lit a match and tossed it.

"Now you rest in peace for good," Vic growled.

As the cottage was in flames and Leonard was inside, Vic waited until everything turned into ashes and wanted to make sure that Leonard was done for good, so he waited for hours there in front of the burning cottage. After several hours, Vic went inside to see if Leonard was there or perhaps not, and he confirmed that he was there. After that, he decided to go somewhere, but he did not know where to go after all that had happened to him lately. Vic took the path to find the cultist that he had long wanted to find, but for that, he needed to consult with the Temple of Justice, and he was not feeling like going there at the moment.

While he was walking the streets of his town, he saw something suspicious in the distance. There was an old lady spreading the rumor of the King's son missing. Vic was very interested to know more about the highly paid job if the King's son were found, but at that moment, somebody took the mission before him — a mercenary that Vic did not want to fight with. He goes by the name Gregor the Terrible, and for heaven's sake, he is terrible.

However, Vic continued his path, walking through the streets, and saw a boy crying in the corner. He approached and asked him why he was crying, and he said that it was about his family. They did not support him in being a writer and told him to get out of the house if he did not join them to be a farmer. Vic then asked the boy where his parents lived and suggested they go there together so that he could try to settle this dispute with them.

As they were walking, the boy explained everything to Vic. He said that he saw inspiration in everything and had written some interesting stories about the wrath of the sea and the power of fire. Usually, the boy claimed that his stories were abstract and did not have an exact line to follow. Vic supported him, and while they were walking further, Vic asked to sit down and listen to the boy, so that he could retell a story he had written, and Vic could say if he liked it or not.

The boy, with a smile on his face and happiness that words could not explain, started to tell one of his stories, which he had named *The Blue Ocean of Mine*:

(This is my sea, this is my motion, I set it all in motion since I wanted to see the waves and the ships sail. All the fish in the sea cannot see what I see. This is a story about me, and I want it to be free.)

Vic asked the boy what his name was. He answered, "My name is Carl." The boy explained that the words came naturally to him and that he frequently woke from sleep in order to write down what had come to his senses. He added that his stories were short and usually consisted of made-up characters and dialogues.

Vic told the boy that he had potential and should never stop following what he loved most, because one day it might be too late to continue something that had been left aside for years or decades. Vic added that if his parents would not support him, he would take him home and pay a teacher to train him in techniques and skills. The boy started to cry again, but this time from joy.

As they approached his parents' home, Vic told him to stay calm and self-confident, because everything would be good in the end, no matter what the outcome of the conversation.

Chapter Six: When Love Hits

Vic was approaching with the kid holding his hand and saw his parents working at the farm. He asked the boy the names of his parents. The boy replied, "My father's name is Ben and my mom is called Elke."

"Mister Ben, may I have a word with you, you as well, Mrs Elke. I am sorry to take up your time since you are working, but I will be short and I am willing to compensate your time."

"Of course, five coins and we can talk!"

Vic handed him five coins "Here."

Ben leaned back and sat in the grass, and Elke joined him.

"What do you want to talk about? I assume about Carl, but you paid, and I will listen."

"Yes, it's about him. I was walking earlier and I saw him crying in the corner of the street. He told me that you want him to become a farmer, is that right?" Vic asked.

"Yes, I want him to become a farmer, that's absolutely right, but he sits all day under the tree and writes nonsense. If it stays that way, he cannot earn anything and cannot help us either."

"Let me ask you a question: what did you want to become when you were a kid? Perhaps now you may have that same passion?"

"Oh, I always wanted to become a blacksmith, and yes, it's my passion so far. Why are you asking?"

"Yes, why are you asking that? What does that have to do with Carl?" Elke asked, her fine lines deepening.

"Well, Carl wants to become a writer, and you both are not supporting him. We can make a deal. I can take you to one of my friends, and you can work at his workshop as an assistant to a blacksmith on one condition: to support your son. Listen, my parents were eliminated when I was a kid, so I had nobody to support me in my life. But every time I see a person in need, I tend to help," Vic explained.

"We are sorry about your parents. You seem like a nice person," Ben and Elke replied.

"Thank you, but being nice is not enough in this life sometimes; action is required."

"Are you serious about your offer? What about my wife? She can't work on the farm alone," Ben asked.

"Then let her be the one who will do the jobs of the house instead of working at the farm, sell your farm since you will make more at this job that I am offering you."

Carl had heard everything and tugged at Ben's sleeve.

"Please do this, Father, so that we can do what we love; both of us should listen to him."

"I cannot believe that you are offering me to work on something that I have always wanted," Ben exclaimed, not entirely certain that this wasn't a dream.

"Life is strange, and sometimes things that happen cannot be understood. But here is your chance to work on what you love, and that goes for Carl, too. I promised him that I would get him a teacher to teach him new styles of writing, and that is on my expense."

"I accept the offer," Ben dropped his shovel and grinned.

"I never saw you this happy before," Elke conceded, her eyes twinkling.

"Now, you start tomorrow morning at nine, don't be late. You can find him in town very easily. In front of his shop, there are always people waiting in line to get their newly purchased tools or weapons. His name is Mile. Tell him that Victor sent you to work there." Vic explained.

"Thank you, Victor, you changed my life; it means the world to me." Ben shook Vic warmly by the hand.

"Thank you from my side as well… Carl, go write you are free now," Elke added.

"May all of you have a wonderful day. I will get going now." Vik beamed before he turned to leave.

As Vic was leaving the area, he knew that he had done the right thing and let a bird fly instead of leaving it with the broken wings. Maybe the kid one day will become very famous and sell many books, who knows, though, Vic. As he was continuing to walk, he could not stop thinking about his visions after he was in those realms, but one thing was worrying him the most, that it was what Peter, Anthony and Jakob thought when he told them about this story and what had happened since it must be somehow connected. All the facts lead to one conclusion: someone must be a traitor, and somebody will do something bad, I can sense it, he thought.

He decided to sit down on the grass and create a strategy about this approach: *If I tell them right away what happened, they will not believe me, who would believe that a wizard can take you to another realm by creating a potion? People are in enough fear as it is, not by telling them tales, because of war and poverty and everything that they go through. So I should just mention that I heard a story about the five keys, and I should wait to see how they will react, and in that way, I will understand the outcome. But wait, what about not mentioning it? Maybe they will mention this first. Now, I just go there and act calm like nothing happened, and that I was just helping people around, perhaps that will be the best approach in this situation,* he decided.

As he was walking and getting closer to his destination and was getting closer, this time there was no guard in front of the door, and something was feeling very strange. He walked carefully and slowly, and thought that maybe they were attacked or ambushed by somebody, so his left hand was touching the sword handle if needed to react. While he was continuing to walk, he saw that there was nobody inside, and when he reached the main room, only Jakob was there, standing alone and reading some letters. He seemed very worried, and something was definitely going on. Vic approached and wanted to know what was happening.

"Jakob, where are the rest of the members? What is going on?" Victor asked, looking around.

"They went to a celebration party at the King's palace. He wanted to thank all of us and show his gratitude. You were invited as well; they sent you an invitation letter to your home. Why did you not attend the party?"

"Oh, for a moment I thought that something bad had happened. I was not home, I was busy," Victor explained.

"Busy with what? If I may ask," Jakob asked.

"How come you did not go? I was busy helping people around, you know, the usual. Nothing special, just took some quests, that's all."

"Quests, you say, huh? I did not go because I did not want to."

"I don't understand. How come you did not want to?"

"I don't want to talk about it. You need anything else perhaps?"

"No, I am sorry that I asked. I will go now," Victor explained as he left.

Jakob continued to read the letters, and while he was reading them, he seemed worried that Vic might find out what was going on. From this, Vic could sense fear in his eyes, but Jakob did not speak another word, and Vic stood there for several minutes trying to understand the essence of the problem. Yet the problem was deeper than it should have been, so Vic reached the point of ignoring the facts and decided not to talk to Jakob anymore about it. Instead, he chose to leave the area, since that felt like the right thing to do at that moment.

Vic left the Temple of Justice and immediately went to the King's castle to attend the party, for one reason only: to talk with Anthony and Peter about Jakob, since something was off. Vic immediately ran towards home to grab the invitation. He did not have time to chat with his friends. When he was close to his house, he saw Chris and Otto busy caring for the elderly people who were in need of food and looking after. Vic just told them, "Keep up the good work, since I must go and find out what is going on."

As they noticed Vic's worried expression, they suggested going with him, but Vic rejected and told them he better go alone, even though they too were invited, no matter the fact that they had been absent for a long time from any mission.

Chapter Six: When Love Hits

Vic grabbed the invitation and ran to the King's castle. Running out of stamina, he spotted a black horse with no owner nearby. He tried to approach, but the horse was restless. He came up with an idea to calm it by petting it slowly before jumping on its back. As the horse grew calmer, Vic explained the urgency while catching his breath from running. At last, the horse settled, and Vic mounted it. Together, they arrived at the King's castle within an hour.

Upon arriving, Vic was greeted by the guards with high respect, and they did not even ask him for the invitation. However, he could not go inside immediately because he had been running and felt he needed a bath. Luckily, the river was close, and before entering, he asked the guards not to lose sight of his gear and horse. They told him not to worry, that neither the gear nor the horse was going anywhere. He jumped into the river, and as he dove beneath the surface, he saw a shiny object at the bottom. It was a golden medallion, which he decided to take and inspect later. When he came out, he dressed and returned to the guards to collect his gear. "I'm ready to enter now," he told them, "and I feel much more refreshing."

Wet and slippery from the water, he stepped into the King's hall. Music was playing, people were dancing, drinking, and enjoying games. The King and his Queen sat in their chairs, watching the feast with admiration. As Vic entered, looking strange and upset, dripping from head to toe, the music stopped. The worst part was that he knew what he was about to say, but he did not do it immediately. Instead, he grabbed a beer mug and poured himself drink after drink until he lost count. Everybody stared at him with strange expressions, but nobody spoke.

The King rose from his chair, ready to ask what was going on, but Vic moved first. Being drunk gave him the courage to speak without hesitation. From across the room, Anthony and Peter grew more worried, knowing that Vic had gone to the Temple of Justice and only Jakob had been there. They feared he was about to cause a scene and bring shame upon them. As Vic staggered, barely able to walk straight, he drained another beer and stepped onto the stage where the musicians had been playing. Now he was at the center of attention, with no fear of what anyone might think or say. He put down the mug and finally prepared to speak. This was only the introduction to what was about to happen next.

"Kings and Queens, and everyone in between, this day is a day of great importance for all of you present here in the King's hall. Some of you know me very well, while the rest of you may only have heard of me. I stand before you because I sense that something is not right. I would rather hear it from you than find out from somebody else," Vic babbled, his voice echoing.

"Your Majesty, please forgive my friend here, he had a bit too much to drink, and all you ladies and gentlemen as well," Peter apologized as he looked at the king.

"I want to say what I have to say," Vic slurred.

The crowd erupted in outrage.

"I deserve it after everything I did for you, I need to know!" Vic cried.

The king held up his hand, and silence fell.

"Let him speak, everybody stays quiet. Victor, please proceed."

"I want to know who among you is the traitor and why Jakob did not attend this party," Vic asked, looking at Anthony and Peter.

Anthony cleared his throat and stepped forward.

Well, my friend, if he did not attend this party, that does not mean that somebody is backstabbing. You are drunk, but since the King allowed you to say what you have to, I, too, want to hear what you have to say. Please, tell us what you have to say."

"I was taken to a realm where I saw my parents, a wizard named Leonard, make a potion for me. Since then, I cannot take those scenes out of my head, and I burned him down in his cottage. I am feeling the guilt because, maybe, I did the wrong thing, but he attacked me first," Victor explained.

"Leonard was another member of the cult, and you were supposed to take him down, but since you are stubborn and do not listen to anybody, what do you expect us to do? Jakob was investigating a scene, and we all know what you did, but we decided to stay quiet until we had the chance to speak about it with you," Peter exclaimed.

"Leonard once tried to fool my Queen, too; he told her that she should drink a potion in order to get well, hence she was ill several moons ago," the King interjected.

"We all knew him as an evil man, so you don't have to worry about it whatsoever," Anthony assured.

"Anything else that is bothering you, Victor? Please share it with us, get it off your chest," the King asked.

"I just feel that I did not do enough, that's all, and sometimes I feel strange since I hear a voice from the sky, sometimes it talks to me," Vic explained as the crowd erupted into gasps.

"Quiet, everybody! The voice from the sky, well, that must be a special feeling since none of us has that privilege to be connected with a higher power. Perhaps you should listen to what it says, and I am sure that you will not make the wrong decision."

Peter tugged at Victor's arm, trying to lead him outside.

"Please, my friend, let's go and talk in private. You are making a fool out of yourself here in front of everybody."

Vic ripped his arm from Peter's clutches.

"Leave me alone! You are to blame for all of this! You, Anthony, and Jakob, too."

Anthony's eyes fell to the floor as shame washed over him.

Peter grabbed Victor's hand as he tried to guide him through the crowd.

"Let's go outside. Now, I said! Excuse us, everybody, he drinks from time to time, but you know he is a good man."

"What do you want? I don't want to talk with you anymore." Vic garbled.

Peter stormed out of the hall, dragging Victor with him.

"You fool, you are making a scene, are you happy now?" he hissed.

"I am happy I made you look like an idiot there, ha-ha," Vic joked.

"If you were not close to me, I would have killed you there," Peter spat.

Vic leaned forward and heaved until he vomited in a bush.

"I feel better, but everything around my head is spinning. What were you saying before? I didn't get it," Vic asked as he stood and wiped his hand with his sleeve.

"I said that you are a fool, and you fooled us all in front of the King and Queen."

"Oh? Well, it's my pleasure then if it's like that," Vic smirked.

"Well done, Victor, well done. I did not expect this from you at all."

"Sometimes it's not about the expectations, sometimes it's about the reality of things you know. Since you think that you know it all, you can't hide things from me anymore. And I don't trust you anymore at all."

"What the hell are you talking about? I treated you as my own son. What things did I, or the rest, keep hidden from you? You were away from us, and you were doing what you thought was the right thing to do. What the hell was I supposed to do?"

"In that case, if you are speaking the truth, then it was my fault and I shouldn't be suspicions at all. But only if you are speaking the truth, since I don't know any more who is lying or not."

"I am speaking the truth; it's not a big deal what you said there. But it was unnecessary, you know that we are not your enemy, and we are doing everything to bring justice to society through you and the rest who fight for it. Perhaps you should rest for a couple of days, and then let's arrange a meeting on Monday morning to discuss the next step."

"What is the next step? Yes, justice, but it doesn't look like I got a bit of it so far."

"Justice does not come through the night, and it does not work how you think it does; it takes years, even decades, and lifetimes to get served. But you know that everything you did so far was for justice, and you felt it, don't act like you did not."

"You are right there, but you did not answer me. What is the next step?" Vic asked.

"The next step we will discuss on Monday, and for now, just go and don't overthink anything. Just go and act like nothing had happened. I will talk with the King and Queen."

"I don't know where to go, I feel bad, and I don't know what to do," Vic explained as he stumbled, clutching his head as it throbbed.

"Just go, and it will pass in a few hours. I need to go inside to have a word with the King," Peter explained as he headed back inside.

Peter approached the King.

"Your majesty, Vic had way too many drinks. Forgive him on my behalf. Sometimes the need for justice kicks him so hard that he loses it. I told him to leave for a couple of days in order to find his peace of mind. Please try to understand."

"It's not him that I am worried about, what worries me lays beyond our imagination. When he finds out about the strikers of his parents, he might send us all to hell, and there will be nothing that we can do about it."

"I am trying my best to keep that hidden for as long as he lives. It was a mistake that we will never forgive ourselves for, you know that."

"I know. That's why I am scared that one day it will come to the surface, but let him be for a while. When he makes a scene the next time, let's just roll on with it, you know? We should act like he is right all the time. Did you tell him that you love him as if he were your son? And stories like that?"

"Of course, I did, by the way, is it possible that he hears the voice from the sky? What do you think?"

"Very much possible since he is a special person and he must be linked with the higher power, so I don't doubt, and if that power rises, we are all doomed."

"Let's hope that it will not end up like that. I will leave you now until we talk next time. Try to enjoy this party."

"We all will try, but let's do our best to keep track of the hidden past."

"I agree, indeed."

After their conversation, Peter went to speak with Anthony and explained everything he had discussed with the King. They went to the balcony to talk in private. Anthony told Peter that Vic would never find out about the mistakes of the past and that they should carry on as though nothing had happened.

Meanwhile, Vic was trying to recover from the beer. He wandered into the woods, searching for a place of peace. Tears rolled down his face as he recalled moments with Leonard, how Leonard had once brewed him a potion to cure a hangover. The sorrow weighed heavily on his soul, crushing him with guilt for burning Leonard down. The thought that Leonard might not have meant to harm him only deepened his sadness.

Vic's path took him to the ruins of the cottage, where the tears did not stop. He wished Leonard were still alive so they could make their wizard jokes again. Falling to his knees, he apologized for what he had done, feeling guilty and ashamed. Pulling himself together, he told himself that perhaps, in another world, he would meet Leonard again and apologies in person. (Little did he know that the future was not so distant.)

Leaving the ruins, Vic walked towards a road that led to a village known for its mysteries and witchcraft. He hoped he might find some answers there. As he entered, he noticed every house looked the same, and every villager wore the same outfit, haircut, and hat. What is even stranger is that each house bore the same symbol on its front door. It felt surreal, almost dreamlike. The sight was breathtaking, and yet unsettling.

At that moment, Vic longed to sneak a glimpse into his future, no matter the cost. Fear lingered, but so did curiosity. Perhaps there was something he needed to know. He did not approach anyone with a direct request, choosing instead to act friendly, almost as if he was simply passing through. The villagers minded their own business, and no one stared at him. It seemed he was welcome there, with no fear of being judged.

Eventually, he decided not to pursue answers in the village and to continue his journey. As he left, he asked a nearby woman for directions back to town. She told him he had strayed far and must return. Not wanting to retrace his steps, Vic chose to take a longer road instead. As the sun set, he fell asleep beneath a giant tree.

In the morning, he was woken by the sound of birds in a nest above him. A white eagle was feeding her chicks. Refreshed, Vic decided to bathe again in the river before heading to town.

On his arrival, he was surprised to see life returning to the people. Children played in the streets, traders bustled in the market, and the town felt alive once more. The darkness and gloom seemed to be lifting. Passing through, Vic spotted Mile working in his shop alongside Ben. The sight filled him with happiness, and he decided to approach.

"Good day to you both, Mile and Ben, how is your day going so far?" Vic asked cheerily.

"Hey there, Vic, welcome. Things are okay, I feel so relieved since Ben started to work here. As you know, the amount of work that is required here now, half of it has been reduced by half since Ben is helping me a lot. I have never seen anybody doing something with so much love as he does. Look at the sword that he is working on, it has so many details crafted to perfection, don't you think?" Mile replied.

"Oh, I love it. I never knew that Ben could reach this stage in a couple of days. If everybody did what they love, the world would be a better place for us," Victor gushed as he examined Ben's artistry.

Ben emerged from the back.

"Hello Victor, I hear you are talking about me."

He laid his hammer down.

"You've got no idea how happy I feel when I leave home to go to work. I kiss my son and wish him good luck with his writing, and hug my wife. While I walk to work, I feel happy like I never did before in my life, and when I finish the work, I feel that I have reached the level of creativity for the day."

"I am so glad to hear all this, Ben. As far as I can see, you are getting along pretty good with Mile there. I told you he is a good person. When it comes to your family, how is Carl's writing going so far? And send my regards to Elke as well."

"Well, Carl is writing and continuing a story that he is working on, it's about the stars and how they are connected. It's all from his imagination, so we will see in the end to publish it, you know. I want to thank you for all this."

"Yeah, he told me about his son. He is a very talented boy, and I offered any kind of help as well to support the boy and to see if his work will see the light anytime in the future," Mile chimed in.

"I must say I am very happy to hear all this. I will pay you both a visit in a month from now so that we can discuss his progress and see you again. I should get going now, I have an important meeting. Stay safe and don't work too much. See you," Vic remarked as he headed back towards the door.

"Take care, Vic, stay safe, until we meet again." Mile and Ben called as they busied themselves with their work once again.

"You two take care, goodbye for now, dear friends, until we meet again"

As Vic left Miles' workplace, he felt very happy and pleased that everything was going so well and with a lot of progress in such a short time that had passed. He recalled the moment when he met Carl as he was walking further through the town, and with so little effort, you could change a person's path and talk them into a better future. Perhaps Vic felt again a sense of accomplishment, and as life was going on, it had its ups and downs, it's the way it is. Not far away, there was a young couple selling fruits in the market. Vic decided to purchase some peaches since he was craving some. Upon taking three peaches, he left them a pretty penny on the table, five golden coins. The couple were in tears from joy. Vic left and continued on his path while enjoying the fresh peaches and their amazing taste. After some time, he decided to go home and talk with his friends, but little did he know they were not there.

When he arrived at home, he saw that the door was open, and everything inside was a mess as if they got robbed or something. Nothing was in its place. He grew concerned and furious upon seeing the scene he wished to never see in his entire life. Most of the furniture was broken, and everything was scattered across the floor. The sword that Vic gave Chris as a present was broken in half. Who would do such things and why? Vic felt an enormous pain in his chest and could not think properly in the moment. Oni was his only chance to find them and to discover what was going on. As Oni spread its wings in the sky, it was behaving strangely, as if fear was captivating it entirely. Screams of pain could be heard from above, and upon locating them, Vic could not believe what he was seeing. Chris and Otto were captured by Gregor the Terrible, that bastard of a mercenary, what he would not do for money.

They were held prisoners at a camp west of the town. The camp was highly guarded, and Vic could not rescue them alone, bearing in mind that Gregor was the most powerful mercenary at that time. He possessed the power of one hundred men, and if approached, he would kill in an instance. Vic felt terrible as he called Oni to land on his right arm. He encouraged it by saying not to worry and that we would find a way to get to the end of this situation. On the other side, he knew there was no point visiting the Temple of Justice since they were full of anger due to what happened at the party. Perhaps Vic could hire some warriors and pay them dearly to join him in this quest that was above his level in any way possible. Being angry, furious, sad, and disappointed at the same time, he left the house and decided to visit Vincenzo's castle.

Vincenzo was a powerful trader on the east side of Vienna. He was the main exporter of olive oil, and since he immigrated from Italy, he had become rich in Austria at the time. Vic decided to pay him a visit and hope for the best outcome of the situation. He hoped that Vincenzo heard about Vic and perhaps that would give him a better chance of renting the warriors, probably some powerful guards as well. Vic called for his horse and sprinted towards Vincenzo's castle, since there was no time to waste, and time was of the essence in this situation. He did not have time to spare his horse this time, but while sprinting, he promised the animal that if he makes the deed, he will let him be for a while. Again, the horse nodded as if he understood what Vic was saying. Upon arriving at the castle, there were five guards guarding the entrance. Vic dismounted his horse and approached.

"Good day to you all, I know that I do not have an appointment with Vincenzo, but is there any chance that you could ask him if he has a little bit of time to meet me?"

"I don't think that he can see you. We cannot let you through, I am afraid," the mightiest guard replied.

"I understand, but it's an emergency and I just want to speak with him, just five minutes, that's all I need," Vic explained, his voice full of urgency.

"I told you once, you cannot get through!" the guard bellowed, which alerted Vincenzo.

"What's wrong down there? You woke me up," Vincenzo called down.

He looked at the guard who had awoken him and added, "You will no longer work for me. I told you once not to wake me up anymore."

"But this guy wants to see you, and he does not have an appointment. I did not mean to wake you up, Sir; you know that I respect you. Please don't let me go, I worked for you for fifteen years, and I cannot afford to lose this job," the guard begged.

"Who wants to see me?" Vincenzo asked, scouring the faces and spotting Vic.

Vitorio, I heard about you. Come through, I am upstairs. We can have a glass of wine or two, and you," . "Vitorio will decide whether you will work here anymore or not."

"Excuse me, guards, I guess that I have an appointment just about now. You heard Vincenzo?" Vic stated as he shoved past the largest into the castle.

The guards all stood there without words.

Vincenzo jumped up and shook Victor's hand.

"Please sit there on the balcony, while I bring the wine so that we can talk, my friend," Vincenzo requested as he went to retrieve a bottle of wine.

"Thank you, Vincenzo, for agreeing to meet me. It is of high importance, and to be honest, an emergency situation that I got into," Vic called out.

Vincenzo reappeared with two glasses and the finest red wine from Italy. He filled each glass to the brim and took a seat across from Victor.

"Vitorio, tell me what you need, but before that, I heard so many things about you. People call you a hero, and the deeds that you did impressed me, even though I am just a trader; it does not mean that I cannot value a good person."

"Thank you for your high opinion of me. But I am not a hero; but what I did, I did it for the sake of justice and the well-being of society, for us all. What I need from you is to lend me, perhaps ten of your warriors, and ten of your guards, because my two friends got kidnapped by Gregor the Terrible and got imprisoned there. I will pay you if you just name your price."

"Oh, Vitorio, you know that I don't need the money, with no hesitation or the need to think twice, I will help you rescue your friend. But I am afraid I cannot come with you since I am not trained to be a warrior; I am just a trader, my friend."

"Thank you so much for this. Whatever you need, you can come to me since I owe you a favor for this."

"No, no, Vitorio. You don't owe me anything, to be honest, just go since you are in a hurry, take those guards at the entrance and on the side of the castle. I will signal the warriors now to join you in this quest."

Vincenzo whistled.

"Let's go, let's go. Now, join Vitorio. You need to go on a rescue mission," he cried as warriors gathered in front of the castle alongside the guards.

Vic waved to Vincenzo and began his quest.

As they were leaving, Vic was leading them, and the rest were marching behind him, singing a song to take down Gregor the Terrible, encouraging each other to gather the strength to go onwards and to never look back. Vic felt hopeful, but at the same time, he was thinking of a way to succeed in this quest, knowing how terrible Gregor was and what he was capable of once he set his mind on something. *Perhaps we could surround him from all sides and somehow take him down,* thought Vic. As they were getting closer to the location, Oni could be heard from the sky, signaling Vic that danger was near and that it would not be easy to succeed. Oni was scared that something might happen to Vic. As soon as Gregor was visible from the eyes of the raven, Gregor was in the yard sharpening his massive sword with two sharp edges. That sword could not be lifted by ten normal men. On the other side, his guards we heavily equipped with the latest spears and shields. They did not ask questions; they attacked on sight.

As Victor was approaching, he had to make a plan with the rest to see how best to attempt this quest. He told the guards to climb onto the cliffs and take down Gregor's men with arrows in stealth mode, since they could not afford to raise the alarm. On the other hand, the warriors and Vic would prepare a trap for Gregor if they could manage it. The plan, as Vic explained, was to place oil jars in one position and lure Gregor there, then set them alight so that he would be on fire. Afterwards, they would all attack him at once, as the fire might slow him down and make him weak. Vic told the guards to give the signal when only Gregor was left. The guards faced no difficulty since they were highly trained in archery and possessed great accuracy. But one of them, who feared he was about to lose his job, was late returning. He had been stealing gold and whatever else he could grab, hiding the loot in a bush nearby and marking it with a red cloth he carried for luck. When he rejoined the group, he claimed he had lost his way. Nobody questioned him further, since there were more important things to deal with.

Vic told the guards to be ready to help if the warriors alone could not take Gregor. They agreed, though a little afraid. Vic and one of the warriors prepared the trap by collection all the oil jars into one position. Then a guard lured Gregor by mocking him and throwing stones. Gregor grew furious and chased him. As Gregor approached the trap, Vic lit an arrow wrapped in cloth and prepared to shoot the jars. But Gregor seized a massive rock and threw it at the guard, missing. The guard tried again to lure him, but was unsuccessful, as Gregor realized what was happening. The guard panicked and whistled for help, but Vic had no plan B. One warrior suggested a different tactic: throw the jars directly at Gregor and then set him alight. Vic thought about it and, although reluctant, he accepted the idea. They moved to engage. Everyone was afraid they would not make it, including Vic. As one warrior picked up a jar, Gregor shot him with his huge crossbow, killing him instantly. The rest froze in fear, but Vic encouraged them, "If we don't make it alive, at least we tried."

Within seconds, while Gregor reloaded, they threw the oil jars. Three failed to break, but the rest burst, covering Gregor in flammable oil. A warrior lit another arrow and fired, and Gregor was set ablaze. Vic told them to wait until the pain slowed him, then attack. Gregor thrashed about, trying to put out the flames, but one unbroken jar exploded from the heat, weakening him further. At once, they charged with swords, spears, axes, and even a great hammer, until Gregor lay helpless on the ground. After the long struggle, they had subdued him. Vic urged them not to kill him but to chain him and bring him to the King, so they could earn the reward and pay the guards and warriors, since Vincenzo did not want payment for his help.

Victor felt relieved and ordered them to bind Gregor, saying it would take one hundred horses to drag him to the King's castle. As the chains were fastened and the horses readied, Vic rushed to free Chris and Otto from the camp. Running through, he saw terrible sights he wished never to see, but his mind was fixed only on rescuing them. He unlocked their cages and, seeing they were unharmed, felt a deep relief. The three of them hurried back to rejoin the others, who were preparing to haul Gregor to the castle. Vic glanced at the fallen guard and felt sorry, though there was nothing he could do. He also worried about how Vincenzo might react when he learnt the truth.

The road to the King's castle was uphill and exhausting. The horses grew tired and needed to rest, unable to bear the load. After three hours, Vic and the others fetched water for the horse and cut grass to feed them, before pressing on. When at last they reached the castle, the formation of the horses was too wide to fit through the gates. They had to change formation, losing another hour. Even then, Gregor hardly fit through the gates due to his size. The King and the Queen were waiting in front of the castle to greet Victor and his men.

"Welcome, Victor. As far as I can see, first of all, you are not drunk and upset anymore, that makes me feel happy for you, you know," the king explained.

"Ha-ha, drunk? I will be, eventually. Perhaps tonight with my friends. I need a beer or two, or until I cannot count them anymore. Time will tell, but I brought you Gregor the Terrible. Does your offer still stand? To pay bounty for him, one thousand golden coins?" Vic asked.

"I see that you brought Gregor the Terrible. Yes, the offer does stand still, but I do not know what to do with him."

"Perhaps make him turn into one of your own warriors, since he does not have a choice."

"Even though, as far as I can see, you severely burned him. But he could be used as a warrior, but it will take me time and effort. And, to be honest, supplies. Even if it succeeds, it's not that easy to feed this beast."

Gregor awoke and looked around.

"You should have killed me, Victor. I would never serve anybody. Once I am free of these chains, I will take you all down, and I will hunt you down, Victor"

"Of course you will. When the King's army surrounds you, you will be as good as dead. So, shut the fuck up, we are having a conversation," Vic cried as one of the guards stepped forward and rapped Gregor around the head, knocking him unconscious again.

The King looked at the guard and beckoned.

"Bring the coins to pay Victor."

"No, those coins are not for me; those are for Vincenzo's warriors and guards. Give the coins to them evenly," Victor clarified.

"How noble of you, Victor. I expected nothing less from you."

"I know my ways, Your majesty. I should get going; I need to meet with Vincenzo to thank him. And afterwards, I want to celebrate the rescue of my friends with my friend, and tomorrow we will see what a new day brings."

"I am happy that you rescued your friends, and please bear in mind that you can count on me, too. You know that."

"I know, but this time I chose another path. Anyhow, thank you. We should get going."

Chapter Six: When Love Hits

As Vic and the guards, along with the warriors, took the path to Vincenzo's house, Chris and Otto went home to save what could be saved from the furniture and to fix the mess in their house until Vic returned. Before they separated, Vic gave ten golden coins to Chris and asked him to purchase three barrels of beer for the rescue celebration in the evening. Chris took the coins and accepted the request. They continued towards Vincenzo's castle, and Vic was feeling terrible for the one that did not make it; little did he know he had no reason to worry about it. When they arrived at Vincenzo's castle, he was standing on the balcony drinking wine. He greeted them with a smile on his face and offered them to stay for a glass or two. However, Vic told him that he had no time, but Vincenzo insisted. Upon deciding to stay, they talked about the mission and how it went. Vic explained everything and told him that one of the guards did not make it. Vincenzo told him not to worry and that the most important segment of the case was that he rescued his friends and captured Gregor the Terrible. Vincenzo told Vic that he could count on him, whatever he needed in the future, and from that moment, they became friends and shook hands firmly. Vic thanked him very much and told him that the guard who nearly lost his job can keep his job as a guard since Vic thinks he is a good man indeed. Vincenzo nodded as a sign of acceptance. In that moment, Vic told him that he had to go and that they would meet in the future, perhaps for a celebration, not when they needed something, added Vic. As he was leaving the castle, he arrived in front of it and told the guard that he was an employee and had no reason to worry. The guard was very happy and told Vic, "Thank you for your decision." (However, the guard still wanted that loot and had a plan to go retrieve it.)

Vic left the area and arrived home. Upon arriving, he saw that the mess from before had turned into a decent interior and that it could be characterized as a normal house. They all sat down and talked as the sunset was at its peak, drinking beer and talking like friends do. They all got drunk pretty fast and went outside for a talk. While they were talking, they were loud and could be heard by the neighbors. Vic was yelling, "We took the Gregor down; he is missing the crown."

Some of them joined for a beer or two until there was no beer left. They slept outside and woke up the next morning, not remembering anything from the night. Vic was having a terrible headache and could not think properly. Otto was still sleeping in a tree with his right leg hanging down. Chris slept on a chair outside, and some of the neighbors who joined were on the grass in the yard. One by one, they woke up by midday, and none of them could remember. Vic went to the river for a refreshing swim, hoping the hangover could pass. While he was swimming, he thought about Leonard again and deep inside his heart, he was missing the poor old wizard. When he got out of the water, he felt a little bit better, but the hangover was still an ongoing process to recover from.

He went back to the house and saw that the neighbors were gone. Chris was preparing a soup while Otto was lying in the yard, complaining about a massive headache. Vic did not talk much but instead decided to eat the soup. After eating, he felt even better and told them he wanted to go to the town to purchase some supplies since, after the incident, the house was nearly empty. As he was walking through the streets, before entering the store, he saw a gathering in the market and was intrigued to know what was going on. As Vic approached, there was a family who had moved from London. A man named Richard was known for his business, owning several construction companies. He left London and moved to Vienna, hoping to expand. Vic did not approach him, of course, but was curious to know what was happening. Richard's wife, Anna, was a lady of high class. She approached Richard, looking different from the women of Vienna. She looked like a classic lady from London, with her Victorian-style clothing. As they walked, the locals showed them the way around. Vic continued his path and did not intervene since he had no need. Little that he know what was going to happen.

While he was walking, he saw a girl from a distance, not knowing she was the daughter of Richard and Anna. She looked like an angel, and Vic immediately fell in love at first sight. He did not know what to do and was totally captivated by the feelings. He acted like he needed to do something, but hesitated to approach. Instead, he decided to write her a love letter. He was feeling the butterflies in his stomach and could not stop thinking about her, yet he wanted badly to know her name. He asked the locals, but nobody knew.

At that moment, her mother called out, and the name struck him like lightning: "Emily, come here, darling, we are going to see our new home," said Anna.

Victor disappeared from the scene and went uphill to sit under an olive tree in order to captive his feelings immediately by writing her a letter. He did not know where to start or what to write, since he had never fallen in love before, but he wrote what his heart was saying.

Dear Emily,

I know that I am a stranger to you, and perhaps in London, things are different; people approach differently. But I just want to let you know that in my entire life, I have never fallen in love before, and I don't know what to do. You look like an angel that has fallen from the sky. Maybe you were intended to fall on another planet, but here you are in my town. I never thought that this would happen to me, but I cannot take you out of my head. I saw millions of flowers during my entire life, but a flower like you I have never seen, since you are the most beautiful angel in the entire universe. Please do not let this fire go out.

After finishing the letter, Vic did not like it and tore it out, aiming to write another one. But he did not know how to write a love letter, and he did not know who to ask to help him. He thought to himself, *If I ask Chris and Otto, they will make fun of me, and I will end up being embarrassed.* The next move was to go and find a solution to this. Vic decided to wait and calm down before he could write another letter to her, since he wanted so badly to send it to her to express his feelings and emotions that were bursting into flames inside his heart. Perhaps something romantic, he thought, would make her interested. *Let's give it another try*, Vic whispered to himself.

Dear Emily,

Among all the roses, you are the most beautiful one. All the love that I feel for you cannot be expressed with words. There are not enough pages that I could write that could describe my feelings towards you. My heart is on fire since the moment I saw you today. I cannot stop thinking about you, and I keep recalling your face.

Vic tore the page again, thinking it was pathetic and she would not like it. He thought that perhaps this letter thing was not a good move. He went home and tried to act normal, but it was obvious to Chris and Otto that something was going on.

"Vic, you okay there, friend? Something is up with you, you know that," Chris started.

"You don't say. I am fine, don't worry about me. How have you been doing?" Vic replied.

"I'm okay, I mean, there is nothing much to do now, but no complain so far. Listen, if you want to talk about it, feel free to talk. We are friends, you can trust me."

"From what I can see, our friend, Vic, here looks like he has fallen in love. I never saw him more lost in his entire life. What else could it be, Chris? It's obvious," Otto added.

"Ah, come on, guys, I knew this would happen. Now drop it, and don't make fun of me all day," Vic sighed.

Otto chuckled.

"Ha-Ha, I knew it, I told you, Chris. You mind telling us, Vic, who is the one who captured your heart? Is she somebody we know, perhaps?"

"Let him be for a minute, he looks… Oh, Vic, are you blushing?" Chris bantered.

"Look at him now, now this deserves another celebration," Otto replied.

"I mean, you got it, Otto, but it's more complicated than you think. Her name is Emily, and she moved here from London with her parents. I wanted to write her a love letter, but I can't seem to write one properly. I lack the skills to put the words my words together and sound convincing," Vic explained.

Chris looked at the torn pages scattered across the floor.

"I can see that you have been trying there. Let me think for a moment."

"We need to come up with an idea for this, perhaps to kidnap her, ha-ha, I would love that," Otto joked.

"What are you talking about? That is out of the equation," Vic snapped.

"Shut up for a moment, Otto. Be serious for once in your life. Vic, listen, I came up with an idea. Listen, what about I go there to their house dressed like a cleaner? I will get the tools from the market and offer them a service of cleaning for free so that I can sneak into her room and leave her the letter that we will help you write to her," Chris explained.

"Sounds like a good plan, but I doubt that they don't have their own cleaner in the house," Otto replied.

"Perhaps another role, but just to make it into her room," Chris commented.

"Let me think, because we clearly need a plan here, and I don't know what to think," Vic added.

"Listen, you should write her a letter, and after that, we will decide what to do. I don't know how the girls from London are, and what they like or love. But like any girl, I think that you should be honest with her, write what you feel, and I will personally go there to give her the letter. Perhaps we should spy on her and follow her movements in the town, and once I see the chance, I will hand her the letter," Chris explained.

"Sounds like a good plan. Our friend Victor here is about to smash it," Otto replied with a wicked grin.

"For heaven's sake, Otto, just cut it, man. We are being serious here," Chris stated, rolling his eyes.

"Me too, man, he will smash her eventually," Otto mumbled.

"Then I will write it," Vic snapped as he shot Otto a scornful look.

"Sorry, friend, I will shut my mouth now. But I am happy for you, you know that," Otto replied, looking down at his feet.

"Now just be honest, and write what your heart is telling you," Chris said as he placed a reassuring hand on Victor's shoulder.

"I will do my best then," Vic replied as he listened to his heart and began to write.

Dear Emily,

I am writing to you for the reason that I fell in love with you since the moment I saw you today in the town. I know that you probably used to romantic letters in London, but I just want to let you know that I would love to express my emotions for you in person. If you are interested, please write me back.

Chapter Six: When Love Hits

Sincerely Victor

"What do you think?" Victor asked as he thrust the letter into his hands and patiently waited for his reaction.

After he had finished, Chris tutted and shook his head.

"No, man, this is not good at all. I mean, you could try, but I don't think that she would reply at all. Let me go to town tomorrow, and I will try to talk to her."

"But I cannot wait until tomorrow, I will not be able to sleep at all."

"Oh, it's definitely love then, huh?"

"Obviously it is. Let's go now. I will call Oni to find out about her location, and you talk to her."

"Why me? You are supposed to talk to her, not me."

"But I..." Victor stammered.

"But what?"

"I am afraid that I might freeze in the moment and become speechless, man," Vic sighed.

"Just take several beers before doing the talking, and you will be fine."

"I will smell of alcohol and she will think the worst of me."

"With or without her, you will drink. Just be who you are, you don't have to avoid something just because you fear what she might think."

"We have a deal then, let's go now."

Chapter Seven: A New Home

As they left the house, Otto wanted to join too, but was rejected by Vic, since he might make a scene and make Vic mad. Vic called Oni to reveal the location of Emily, and after a while, it was discovered that she lived next to Vincenzo's castle. Upon finding out, Vic did feel relieved; perhaps he could do something like putting out a good word there. But Vic hesitated to ask Vincenzo for another favour, and instead thought it might be a good idea to go to him as a friend and during the conversation, he could mention what was bothering him. Anyhow, those were only Vic's thoughts.

As they were waiting to see what to do, Chris asked Vic, "Should we knock on their door, or do you want another approach?"

"Let's go home," Vic said.

From there, they went home, and Vic locked himself in his room, thinking all that night until morning, when he fell asleep from exhaustion. Vic woke up afternoon and went outside to go to the town, hoping to see Emily by accident. As he was walking, he felt the urge to say something if he saw her, but what, he was not sure yet.

Upon arriving, he saw Vincenzo angry at a worker who had spilt an entire sack of olives on the ground, and Vic decided to intervene in the situation, hoping for a chance to mention what was on his mind. As he was approaching, there she was, walking alone in a red dress that suited her perfectly. Vic froze in the moment. He did not know what to, less what to say. The moment that Emily saw Vic from a distance, she smiled. Her smile rushed every drop of blood in Vic's body, and he was in disbelief at what was going on. In the next moment, he was approached by Vincenzo, who became calm after seeing Vic, that how much respect he had for him.

"Vitorio, Vitorio, my good friend. I am glad to see you. How are you doing?" Vincenzo asked.

"Vincenzo, likewise, my friend. I don't know, to be honest, how to say what I feel."

"What's bothering you? Perhaps I could help," Vincenzo trailed off as he spotted Richard and Anna in the distance. "Richard, please come to meet a hero," he cried.

"No, no, please don't, Vincenzo. You don't understand, don't do this to me," Victor begged.

"It's all right, Vitorio, I know him, we work together now. They came from London, moved here, and now they are part of us, you know," Vincenzo reassured.

All color drained from Victor's face as he prayed to the universe that it would open and swallow him whole.

Richard approached and shook both Vincenzo and Vic's hands.

"Hello, young boy, my name is Richard. I came here with my wife, Anna, and my daughter, Emily. It's a pleasure to meet you, Victor. Vincenzo told me so much about you, to be honest, I am impressed."

"The pleasure is all mine, Sir. Welcome to Vienna, and may you succeed in whatever you are hoping for," Victor replied.

"Anna, meet Victor; he is of high importance here," Richard explained to Anna.

"It's a pleasure to meet you, Victor," Anna explained as she shook Victor's hand with a smile.

"The pleasure is all mine, nice to meet you too," he replied.

"See my friends, this is Vitorio, I guy I told you about. I have a high respect for him, and by the way, where is Emily? Anna, go and look for her, she should meet Vitorio," Vincenzo gushed.

Vic snuck to Vincenzo's side and whispered, "Please don't do this to me, you don't understand, trust me."

"She will like you, I'm sure of it," Vincenzo assured.

"There she is, my beautiful, well-mannered daughter Emily. Come, love, you should meet Victor," Richard waved Emily over.

Vic was hoping that this was all a horrible dream and that he would wake up soon.

"Hello, Father. Who should I meet…?" Emily trailed off as she locked eyes with Victor, the color draining from her rosy cheeks.

Vic was white as a sheet, too.

"Now I understand what is going on here, Vitorio," Vincenzo announced as he watched the pair frozen in time, gazing into each other's eyes.

"I think I do too," Richard replied.

"For goodness's sake, they are in love," Anna exclaimed.

Emily and Vic were both standing speechless at the sight of each other.

Why don't we all organize a dinner tonight at my castle and let the young love birds have a chat? What do you say, Richard? Perhaps, Vitorio and Emily could have a time of rest before they meet again tonight, since we put them in an unpleasant situation?" Vincenzo proposed.

"Of course, my friend, how about ten o'clock tonight?" Richard replied.

"We got a deal, my friend," Vincenzo grinned.

Although all Victor could think was, 'What the hell is happening,' he accepted the invitation.

"I will be there, see you all tonight."

As he was leaving, he could not believe what was going on. His heart was filled with joy and love, but on the other side, the amount of embarrassment was even higher than he could ever imagine. At that moment, he sprinted towards his house so that he could tell Chris the news. Everything came up to that moment when he was getting ready to officially talk with Emily. This was a moment of extreme importance for Vic. When he opened the door, he explained everything to Chris in the tiniest details possible. Chris told him to remain calm and that, obviously, Emily had fallen in love at first sight, too. He encouraged Vic to stay calm there tonight and to speak only when asked to, not to reveal for whom he works and what he does. Instead, he told him to say he does something different.

Vic did not like that suggestion and told Chris that he is not ashamed of what he does; he takes down bad people, and that is nothing to be ashamed of. But instead, Vic added that Vincenzo will cover that topic. As they were talking, everything was overheard by Otto, though this time he did not speak a word. Vic was preparing to get ready for attending the dinner and decided not to wear anything formal, and even if he wanted to, he had no such clothes. He brushed his hair, put on a red leather jacket, and went on his way to Vincenzo's castle. It was fifteen minutes to ten o'clock, but he did not rush. He intended to be a bit late, not to meet them in front of the castle. He left the house and went on foot. During the time he was walking, he was constantly thinking about Emily and hoping that everything would go well. Little did he know that she was madly in love with him, too.

Upon arriving, they were already there. When Vic approached, he was greeted by the guards, and they made way for him to pass through. As he was entering, Vincenzo got out of the house to greet him and open the door for him.

"Vitorio, my friend, welcome. This way, please."

"Good evening, everybody. Sorry, I am a bit late," Vic explained as he looked around at everyone.

"Good evening, Victor," Richard greeted him.

Vic's gaze drifted to Emily. He tried to pull himself together while trying to gather the strength to speak to her, but tripped over the table.

Vincenzo helped him steady himself and brushed him down, leading him over to Emily.

"You okay, my friend? My goodness, I cannot believe this," Vincenzo giggled.

Vic's hand trembled, but he held it out and shook Emily's.

"Hello," he managed to gasp.

"H… Hello," Emily stuttered.

"Vittorio, sit, my dear friend, let's have some wine. I can see that this is a bit tense, but don't worry, everything will be all right," Vincenzo reassured as he gestured towards an empty seat.

"Victor, is it true that you did so many good deeds, as people say?" Richard asked.

"Well, apparently, there might be some truth in what they say, Sir," Vic replied.

"Hm, I understand. How noble of you, don't you think, Anna, dear?"

"Yes, indeed, I think that is very noble of Victor." Anne nodded.

"Vitorio, he saved a lot of children from forced labour, too, you know?" Vincenzo interjected.

"Well, that is something that deserves to raise a glass for," Richard replied as he raised his glass. "Cheers."

"Cheers," everyone chimed back.

"I might consider letting you talk with Emily alone one day in that case. But until then, you will need to prove your intentions with her," Richard explained.

"I respect your decision, and I am okay with you considering that option, Sir," Vic replied.

"Perhaps it's a bit early for that, Richard," Anna interrupted.

"We will discuss it in private, dear," Richard replied, tapping her arm lightly.

"Richard, my friend, you don't have to rush with decision-making, yet. Let it go naturally," Vincenzo chimed in.

"I agree, but my daughter has never been with anybody so far."

"Who says I did, for that matter?" Vic replied.

Silence followed for a moment.

"Richard, how about we discuss business now and leave this love thing to develop as it should? Perhaps it's the best decision not to intervene between them. Like it or not, they are in love with each other, and there is nothing that anybody can do, even if they want to. So, tell me, what do you think? Should we link our businesses together and make it easy for the society to get at least the essentials, since you know poverty is becoming more and more of a problem?" Vincenzo asserted.

"On that matter, I couldn't agree less when it comes to love. But business here, as far as I can see, is done differently than it's done in London. Perhaps there are several reasons for that, but I would like to my part of the work in order to help those in need since we both know that you and I do not need to get the income from poor people," Richard replied.

"Well, that is what I call a business partner, right there. Cheers to that for the future."

"For the future," everyone cried.

"Well, it's getting late, and we should get going; we have an important day tomorrow. Emily starts to learn the local language, and she is excited about it. Aren't you darling?" Richard asked Emily.

"Yes, Father, I am indeed."

"We wish you a good night, and until we meet next time. Victor, it was a pleasure."

"The pleasure is likewise, Sir. I should get going, too," Vic began to make his way to the door.

Vincenzo placed a hand on his arm. "You stay, Vitorio. I want to talk with you about something, friend."

As Vincenzo led Anna, Richard and Emily to the door, Victor's gaze never left Emily.

Once at the entrance of the castle, Vincenzo murmured, "Richard, what can I do for you to let Emily meet Vitorio tomorrow? I can guarantee for him."

"Vincenzo, my friend, don't put me in that position because I cannot do that. I hope you can understand," Richard replied.

"I do, my friend, I just wanted to ask, that's all."

"Good night, and thank you for your hospitality. It was a pleasure."

"The pleasure is all mine, my friend," Vincenzo replied as he closed the door and hurried back up the stairs.

"Vitorio, my friend, I tried, but Richard is being typical, you know. Hopefully, he will let you meet her alone in the future," Vincenzo gasped as he reached Victor.

"I don't know, even though I am in love with her, I think that maybe I do not deserve her," Vic replied.

"Oh, Vitorio, don't say that, my friend. Of course, you deserve her, you are a good man, the best that I know so far. What are you talking about?"

"Thank you, but she might not be safe with me since I always put myself in trouble and things don't go as they should."

"Life is cruel, my friend, but you deserve to be happy. I will try to convince Richard again, don't worry about it at all."

"Thank you, it means a lot to me. I should get going now, friend."

"All right then, Vittorio, let me escort you to the gates," Vincenzo replied, following him.

"Thank you, have a good night and thank you for everything."

"It's no problem, Vitorio, rest until we meet again."

Chapter Seven: A New Home

As he was leaving and walking through the night, he looked at the sky and hoped for the best outcome of the situation he found himself in. However, there was too much on his mind at that moment, so he felt overwhelmed. With a lot going on, he could not focus on anything. His thoughts were all over the place, and the most dominate one was, *"What if I hurt her?"* Starting with only one *what if*, it led to millions of following situations in his mind. *What if one day I hurt he unintentionally and make her cry, breaking her gentle heart into pieces, making her regret every decision she made?*

He sat on a rock nearby, since he could not take those thoughts anymore, but they had just started. *What if somebody hurts her and I am not there to protect her? What am I supposed to do in that kind of situation?* His thoughts continued to make him feel that he was not the right one for her. But his emotions only continued to grow, and he had no control over them. On the other hand, we were ready to go for it, since his heart was telling him to, but his mind was rejecting the heart's request. He carried on towards home, eager to fall asleep from the exhaustion of so many thoughts. When he arrived, he simply opened the door and went to bed, entering another dream and another experience that would haunt him for a long time.

In his dream, he found himself in the middle of nowhere, blood on his hands, unable to speak, move, or feel anything. He was trapped in a sleep paralysis that lasted the entire night until midday the next day. When he came back to his senses, he started to move the tips of

279

his fingers, then slowly tried to recover from that agony and immobility. After some time, he was finally able to get out of bed. The effects of everything were terrible, from a massive headache to dizziness and lack of focus, along with a loss of orientation. The main question on his mind was, *"Whose blood was on my hands?"* He feared the worst, that something bad would happen to Emily if they ended up together. At that moment, Vic decided not to follow his heart and perhaps to disappear for a while, which led him to absolute isolation — but that only worsened everything, mostly for Emily.

Vic decided not to tell anybody about his plane. He left the house before sunset and headed north. The horse was constantly upset and tried to kick him off the saddle, as if it were some kind of sign. Vic ignored the horse, grew nervous, and finally let it go back. The horse sprinted home while Vic continued his journey on foot. After three days of walking with no rest, hunger began to kick in as a sign of starvation. He did not care much until he fell on the ground. The next morning, when he woke up, he found five apples next to his arm. He ate two of them and kept the rest, but the question remained: who left them there? Little did he know that a higher power had been beside him all the time.

It took him nine days and nights to reach his destination, the Alps. Upon arriving, he entered a cave and isolated himself for seven months, living like a primitive. His aim was to forget Emily and return with no emotions whatsoever. But he did not know that Chris and

Otto were worried to death, Vincenzo was searching for him everywhere, and Emily was crying and fearing the worse. If he had known all that, would he still have taken this path? Who knows…

After all that fuss just to escape society and isolate himself, seven months later, he looked exactly like a primitive, with a grown beard, poor hygiene, illness, and mental frustration. When he finally arrived home, he found Otto asking around for him. He was unrecognizable, and upon knocking on the door, Otto saw him from a distance and cried out:

"Go away, we do not have anything to give to a beggar. We are looking for our friend," Otto screamed as he saw a disheveled man.

Vic didn't move a muscle; his will collapsed, and a river of tears began to flow.

Otto came running over to the window.

"I told you to go away. Wait, Vic, is that you?"

Vic choked on every breath, unable to respond.

Otto flung the door open and guided him inside to a seat.

"Come on inside, what the hell happened to you?"

Chris arrived home, exhausted from searching for Victor all day.

"Why is the door open, Otto?" he huffed.

"He came back, look at him. I did not recognize him," Otto explained.

"Vic, is that you? Why did you do this to us, man?" Chris asked as he began to cry.

Otto could no longer hold back his tears either.

"I am sorry, friends, I made a bad decision for which I am sorry now, but I was trying to forget her," Vic gasped finally.

"And did you succeed in that? It does not work like that, man," Chris scowled.

"How do you know about that? How does it work or not?" Vic barked.

"Just calm down, guys, please, at least he is home now," Otto pleaded.

"How the hell can I calm down? He is not aware of what he did to us, to Vincenzo, to Emily and her parents. We thought that you were dead, man! How can you not understand that some things have consequences, Victor? And you always do the opposite of what you are supposed to do. You thought that disappearing for seven months could do you any good? Are you happy now?" Chris ranted.

"Enough, man, you are making this even worse," Otto snarled.

"How can I make it better, then? What am I supposed to do? To expect the worst at any given situation here, if you want to disappear, do it now and never come back, so that at least we do not have to worry about you, since you do not care at all. But guess what? We do care, because you are our friend," Chris screamed as he got up and left, slamming the front door behind him.

"He is upset, Vic. And I do not blame him, to be honest. He is right, you know?" Otto explained.

Vic was lost for words at the trauma that he had caused.

Otto handed him a plate full of food and a cup full to the brim.

"Here, eat and drink water. You need a good rest. Tomorrow I will take you to the barber; we need to make you look good. You look like a wizard, man."

"Thank you, and forgive me for this," Vic replied, smiling weakly.

"There is nothing to forgive, but at least next time let us know, man. We need to fix your appearance tomorrow and let Vincenzo know that you came back. Perhaps you should inform Emily, too. She is worried sick."

"I don't know what to do anymore, man. I feel like I let you all down."

"Don't say that, just rest for now. Tomorrow is a new day, into new victories."

As Vic was lying on his bed, he felt that he had let them all down, and the feeling of guilt started to eat him from the inside. His eyes were filled with sorrow and pain that could not be expressed; everything felt like it was a never-ending agony. His fear was how they would react and what they would say after seeing him after seven months. Will they respect him like they did before? All those thoughts and the rest kept him gazing at the ceiling all that night.

As it seems, Vic was not ready to face the consequences of his disappearance, and not caring about the people who genuinely cared about him. This just put another problem to deal with. As the night was progressing, he recalled all those nights that he slept in the cave and talked with himself, drawing on the wall and howling like wolves do. Everything that he tried to do was just to forget Emily, but in the end, he did not succeed; it just made matters worse.

When he was trying to close his eyes, he was faced with the recalling of the thunderstorm and remembered that he had enjoyed watching it all night. That picturesque color when the thunder strikes in the ground, that's why he trained his eyes to stay awake all night. Among the other things he did was drawing on the stones of the cave, pictures resembling what the ones who took down his parents would look like from memory. While he was gazing at the ceiling, a couple of tears rolled down his face when he recalled that particular memory, due to the pain and sadness that it brought with it to the core.

The next emotional moment was when he kept recalling the voice from the sky, telling him to go home, several hundred times during the time that he was there. Again, he did not listen. When the dawn was ready, he knew he needed a good sleep, and going like this among people was unacceptable. He was a man who was highly respected in the society, and his reputation could not be ruined, at least not to go out like that and in that condition.

When Chris arrived home, he saw Otto upset, standing next to the window, and asked him what was going on. He responded by saying that Vic is in a very bad condition and he needs help, perhaps to call a doctor or something. Chris denied the request, saying that he is fine, he just made a bad choice, and added that if he is asleep, let him sleep.

Sometime later that day, in the afternoon hours, Vic woke up and decided to face his fate. Otto had already made an appointment to take him to the barber to fix his appearance. Luckily, the barber was next door, so there was no need to make a long run for it. Vic gathered the strength to go and, upon getting a haircut and cutting off his beard. When he saw himself, he could not recognize himself at all, and it felt like something new, at least a small step to live among society, like before.

Moments later, Chris arrived to see him at home, and after a few seconds he hugged him and cried with joy, recognizing him friend again. He apologized for his behavior and asked him not to leave like that again. Vic promised not to. After a short time, they all went together to Vincenzo's castle. While they were walking, Vic was in constant fear and asking himself all the time if he was mad at him, and if Emily would be there too, and how it would be a heartbreaking moment to see her like that.

In front of the castle, as usual, the guards were there. Vincenzo was on the balcony, and from the moment he saw Vic, he immediately ran downstairs towards the entrance gate to greet him.

"Guys, I am scared what will he tell me? What if he is angry?" Victor explained frantically, pacing.

"Take it easy, Vic, if he was angry, he would not rush to come downstairs, he would stay there," Chris replied, trying to calm Victor.

"I think you are right there, Chris," Otto replied.

The door soared open, and Vincenzo came bounding out.

"Vitorio, my friend, where the hell have you been? We have been looking for you everywhere, man. You made us all worry. Come on inside, let's talk," Vincenzo cried as he hugged Vic firmly.

"Thank you for having us, Mr. Vincenzo. I am honored to be here," Chris said politely.

"It's my pleasure, friends, come on inside," Vincenzo led them inside. "Make yourselves at home, friends, I will go to bring wine," he gestured towards the sofas as he vanished into the wine cellar.

"I am scared that some critics will be thrown at me very roughly. I am afraid," Vic whispered.

"You should be, man, you deserve it. I hope that you know that," Chris hissed.

"Let him be, man. I think you made your point several times; it's not the end of the world, you know," Otto pleaded.

"Well, it's not, but behavior like that cannot be tolerated, you should know that," Chris replied viciously.

"You cannot be tolerated sometimes, since you are so prideful and selfish most of the time. But we tolerate you just because you are our friend," Otto spat.

"Great compliments, thank you," Chris replied through a false grin.

Vincenzo reappeared with three bottles.

"Here I am, friends," he filled each of their cups to the brim. "Here is some of the finest wine, friends, enjoy. My kitchen staff prepared a meal for you, so enjoy. We are expecting guests by the way, Vitorio here will be very happy to see somebody."

Vic's skin prickled as his heart began to race.

"Vincenzo's friend, please don't," he croaked.

"Vitorio, you remember what you said to me when we called her
_"

"Vincenzo, please, you don't understand," Victor wailed

"Well, I guess that I understand now pretty good."

"As you wish, my friend. I'd better drink some wine before she
arrives, since I do not know her reaction," Vic replied as he drank
down every last drop of wine in his cup.

"You will know pretty soon, but before that, Vitorio, why did you
disappear on all of us, man? We were worried about you, and I even
sent an army to look for you, my friend. What made you do it? You
did upset us all. I hope that you are aware of that now."

"Um, I mean, it's true that I made a bad decision, Vincenzo. But
I was captivated by the negative thoughts, and I thought about the
worst-case scenarios in my head, such as: I do not deserve her, what if
I hurt her, and things like that. I simply wanted to disappear for some
time in order to forget her."

"I understand, but you could have discussed it with your friends
and me, perhaps. We are here to help you always."

"He doesn't care about that; the decisions he makes, he makes
them alone. And he thinks that he is right all the time," Chris spat.

"I told you to cut it, man, you can't seem to listen. They are having a conversation here, in case you don't see that, perhaps you don't understand that as well…" Otto barked.

Chris bit his tongue and swallowed his words this time.

"Take it easy, guys, best friends do not fight. Vitorio, did you manage to forget her?" Vincenzo asked.

"I worsened the situation, and of course, I could not, as it seems that is impossible."

"It is impossible indeed, but it's true love as well. Tell me, Vic, what did you do for those seven months? Anything interesting at all?"

"I did isolate myself and drew on the stones inside, talked to myself pretty often, heard the voice from the sky again, I was nearly going insane."

"A voice from the sky, you say? Interesting, tell me more about this voice."

"Well, it speaks to me sometimes, often when there is something important to decide. When I need it the most, basically."

"Yeah, right, as if you ever did care for what it says," Chris scoffed.

"Enough!" Otto roared as he stood up, ready to strike.

"You want to fight me, let's do it and let's do it now," Chris growled as he jumped to his feet.

Vincenzo jumped between them, his hands raised.

"Calm down, guys. Otto, my friend, Chris, here is very upset about what Vitorio did. Give him a couple of days to calm down, and everything will be as it was."

"I hope so, because if he continues like this, there will be hell to pay," Otto replied as he returned to his seat.

"Vitorio, explain the voice from the sky in depth. How does it feel?" Vincenzo asked.

"It does not feel like a God or something. It's more like a spiritual guide or, as some say protective angel from the sky. Perhaps it's something to guide me during hard times, you know?"

"I understand, Vitorio. Oh, our guests arrived. Wait here, friends, I will be back soon."

"Oh no, what should I do now? How will she react?"

"Perhaps throw yourself out of the window to escape, that is what you wanted after all," Chris sniped.

"Good one, Chris. Perhaps I will throw you out of the window. How about that?" Vic replied, glaring at him.

"Ha-ha, classic," Otto chuckled.

"Here, my dear friends, our Vitorio has arrived, as you can see," Vincenzo called out.

Emily ran towards Vic and hugged him tight, soaking his chest in her tears.

"Why did you leave me, my love? I thought something bad had happened to you. I missed you every day."

"Emily, my rose, forgive me, please, for what I did," Victor whimpered, his own tears stinging his cheeks.

"See, Anna darling, I told you they cannot live without each other," Richard whispered to Anna.

"Let's celebrate, our dear friends. It's a night to remember," Vincenzo cried, throwing his hands in the air.

"Welcome back, Victor. We missed you," Anna and Richard cooed.

"Thank you, Sir," Victor replied with a smile.

"Forgive me, my love," Vic whispered in Emily's ear as he hugged her tight.

"You are forgiven, my love, but please do not leave us again. I cannot imagine another day without you. I missed you so much, you have no idea, my love." Emily replied, pulling away to look into Vic's deep, dark eyes.

"I missed you too, so much." He sobbed.

"See how cute they look together; she will leave us soon, Anna darling," Richard murmured.

"How do you mean leave us soon?" Anna asked, glancing over at the happy couple.

"They will live together pretty soon."

"Our dear friends, perhaps we should call a priest now?" Vincenzo announced.

Richard guffawed.

"Ha-ha, good one, isn't it a bit early for that?"

"I am just kidding, but look at them, my eyes are becoming teary."

"I have never seen my friend this happy since I knew him," Otto added.

"I can relate to that, to be honest," Chris agreed.

"Finally, you said something that makes sense," Otto replied.

"Ha-ha, at least I said it."

Richard considered asking Victor about his disappearance, but bit his tongue so as to not ruin a tender moment.

As they were all having one of the most beautiful nights, everything was going smoothly and with a true sensation of having a feast. Vic was focused on Emily and could not take his eyes off her, while on the other hand, Vincenzo was having a deep conversation with Richard about the meaning of life, both of them being drunk. In the meantime, Anna was admiring the new couple, Chris and Otto were fighting over silly things that did not matter at all.

They all celebrated until dawn, and everybody fell asleep in the positions where they were. When the morning came, Vincenzo was woken up by the guards, who were having a hard time fighting a lynx. Upon waking, Vincenzo went downstairs to see what was going on. As it seemed, the lynx was just roaming around and wanting to mess with people. Vincenzo ordered the guards not to kill it; instead, they should put it in a cage, and so they did what they were told.

Vincenzo, after that, went back to sleep in his sleeping room. After lying down, some time passed, and he felt so tired that shortly after, he entered the REM phase that took him into a dream that would be engraved for the rest of his life in his memory. In his dream, he found himself in the middle of a dark forest where a strong wind was blowing. He could not stand on his feet without holding onto something. The wind blew so hard that the trees started to fall, and their roots would break. His thoughts were racing, and he could not find a solution. In the dream, he saw somebody from a distance but could not approach until the wind slowed its speed. As it seemed, what he saw in the distance was the soul of his mother, Maria.

Vincenzo never spoke about his mother to anybody else whatsoever, but he was very close to her. She always took care of him until her last days. She had a message for him, but the message was not clear, as Vincenzo would not let go of the tree due to the wind. The dream felt so real and powerful. Upon waking, Vincenzo was admiring Vic and Emily, who were asleep while hugging each other. The happiness in his heart could not be measured. After some moments, Vincenzo took a cold bath and went to rest on the balcony. While he was sitting and enjoying the beautiful view, he thought about the dream he had had earlier, and his eyes were filled with tears. His tears were from sadness and from missing his mother so much that he could hardly live with the fact that she is no longer alive.

In that moment, Emily woke up, and Vincenzo overheard what she told Vic while he was sleeping: "My love, my darling, I want every day of my life to spend with you and never to let you go. Please do not disappear on me and the ones who love you." And after that, she kissed him on the forehead.

Vincenzo, at that moment, got up and told her, "We will not let Vic disappear again."

Moments later, one by one, all were awake, and everyone was having a headache from the previous night's alcohol. Chris went for a swim in the river, while Otto was looking for a way to get through the hangover state. Vic was still hugging Emily, while on the other side, Richard and Anna were doing the same.

Vic asked Richard if he could take Emily for a walk, and he responded, "Yes, of course."

Vic got up and went out of the castle while holding her hand. He told her that he wanted to go for a walk with her through the town. While they were walking, Emily felt proud and happy that this was finally happening after everything. Vic, on the other side, could not believe it was happening, since he always thought it would be very hard to end up with her.

"My love, have I ever told you?" Vic started.

Emily turned and looked at him innocently.

"Told me what, darling?"

"That I love you more than life itself, my love."

"I love you too, my love," Emily replied, blushing.

"We should start to live together, what do you think? I would purchase a small place for us in a village. And then, from time to time, we can visit my friends and your family."

"I would love that, my love, since living together would strengthen our love, but you need to ask my parents first."

"I will ask them; you don't have to worry about it. I am sure that they will have nothing against it whatsoever."

"And what if they do?" Emily asked.

"Then I will steal you and run off with you far away from here."

Emily giggled.

"Ha-ha, my darling, don't be ridiculous, you would not do that."

"Of course I would do that, darling, isn't love all for being next to each other?"

"It is, but you cannot kidnap me and run off with me."

"Would you mind?"

"Hm, love, you are making me go crazy for you," Emily purred, gripping Victor's arm tighter.

"Well, that we have in common, I would say."

"We have a lot in common, I would say as well."

"Such as…"

"Our love for each other, the fact that we care for the ones we love, the fact that we do not tolerate injustice, and such."

"I did not know that you have a rebel soul, darling," Vic replied, gob smacked.

"Now you do, my love."

"You see that tower over there, that is the highest one?"

"I can see it, of course. What about it?"

"I jumped from it and landed on a cornfield."

"Really, love? I would love to try that."

"Ha-ha, I would never let you do that, my love."

"Why not?"

"Because it is dangerous and it requires a lot of practice."

"Can I ask you something?"

"Anything"

"What do you do for work?"

Vic considered his answer before replying.

"I rescue the ones who are in need, and I get paid for that, along with the other missions."

"Other mission doing what?"

"Well, for starters, there are missions when you need to find clues about something, in order to gain the full knowledge of what happened in a particular situation. And after that, you pursue what you are meant to."

"I understand love, but do you have to do anything bad in the meantime?"

"By anything bad, you mean…?"

"Never mind, let's act like I never asked."

Vic was speechless, in shock from Emily's directness, but thankful that she did not pry any more than she had.

Emily spotted a shop and pointed.

"Look, there is a shop for chocolates, should we get some?"

"Of course, my darling, let's go."

"Do you often eat chocolate, love?"

"Sometimes, but not that often. What about you?"

"I prefer it on a daily basis, to be honest, along with a cup of tea."

"I understand, my love; they say the right amount of it is healthy for you."

"It is indeed, here, love, take it," Emily replied, breaking off a piece and handing it to Vic.

Vic popped it into his mouth and was in heaven.

"Mm, darling, it is delicious. I like it."

"I like it, too. Should we head back now? Because they might get worried, I think."

"Of course, we should go back, you are right," Vic replied, turning back towards the house.

"I will speak to my parents about us moving in together, and the next time we meet, I will let you know. Can we do it like that?"

"Absolutely, we can, darling."

While they were heading back, Vic felt the freedom with Emily; he saw a friend and a soulmate in her, and he was thinking to himself while they were walking back that with her, he could talk about anything without hesitation. Vic felt that he was the luckiest man alive and that she was a gift from the universe to him. On the other hand, he was worried about what he should do about the situation with the Temple of Justice and how to let them know that he wanted to resign from the organization and no longer work for them. Vic had in mind to open a small store where he could sell food and supplies just to have a peaceful and simple life with Emily, to create a family and to be left alone by troubles of the outside world.

When they arrived, Richard was looking at the new couple with a smile on his face, as well as Anna. Vic hugged Emily so hard before they parted and whispered in her ear, "I love you."

She replied with "I love you, too, darling."

As they left, Vic greeted Vincenzo from afar and thanked him for everything. He replied, "It's no problem, Vitorio, just don't disappear on us again."

Vic told him that he would not, and then he went home. While he was walking towards his home, he saw a couple fighting in the street and did not want to intervene. He decided to bypass that situation and go directly home to sleep.

When he arrived and opened the door, Chris was preparing dinner, while Otto was writing something. Vic went to bed, and shortly after that, he fell asleep. In his REM phase, he entered a dream. In his dream, he found himself flying a golden dragon above Europe, while Europe was at war. At that moment, he felt scared because of the fact that he was scared of heights, and the other point that he was not aware of was that he was not aware of the fact that he was dreaming. Europe was falling apart, and there was nothing that the dragon could do without Vic's orders. He felt disoriented and did not know who was fighting whom. Shortly after that, the voice from the sky was heard, and it was saying, "Go east, go east."

Poor Vic was afraid to go east, but listened to the voice. While the dragon was flying, Vic felt a sensation of freedom; somehow, he felt that the dragon would not let him fall, and this was meant to be.

When he arrived above Eastern Europe, the voice from the sky could be heard saying, "Lower the position and order the dragon to burn their forces."

Vic did as the Voice told him to do, but after that, Vic yelled, "What now?"

As he was ordering the dragon to go up in the sky again, the voice said, "Now, land the dragon."

Vic had no idea how to land a dragon, since he never rode one in real life. He asked the voice, "How do I land a dragon?"

The voice answered by saying, "Tell him to land."

Vic did so, and the dragon landed in a safe place in the western parts of the Alps.

Vic landed successfully and felt relieved at that moment in a dream. The dragon flew off, and in that moment, an avalanche from the southern side of the mountains was preparing to fall, due to the fact that he felt the shaking of the land from underneath. Vic started to run but got run over by the snow, and in that moment, he woke up sweaty. At the same time, he was feeling that he had the best dream of his life ever. At that moment, Chris and Otto were asleep, and Vic decided to go outside to look at the moon.

When he went outside, he took a barrel of beer with him, and after ten beers, he came up with an idea to ask for three wishes directed to the moon. He expressed his wishes in the following manner: Dear Moon, that you shine in the sky, that you light our way and our paths of life. I ask you for only three things and nothing more. One: I want to marry Emily. Two: I want to have kids with her. And three: I want to avenge my parents. If you grant me those wishes, I will stay loyal to you and pray to you every night at this time.

While the dawn was ready to start a new day, Vic was thinking about starting a life with Emily as soon as possible, so he was getting ready to search for a small house to purchase and then to move in together. But first, he wanted to find one in the village, not in town. Since his decision was made, he decided to do it and to surprise Emily. On his quest to find the perfect place, he started by mounting his horse and heading north to the village that was not very inhabited, to see if someone would sell the land. He wanted something to start with, at least, because it would take a long time to build a house from scratch.

While he was on his journey, he saw a perfect place to live. Not far from Vienna, and everything was not that far from the city. He dismounted his horse and went to a bar to drink some beers because he was feeling happy and everything seemed to go as planned. He opened the door and was welcome by the owner of the bar, who goes by the name of Adrian, even though the place was crowded.

"Welcome, stranger here," Adrian greeted as he gestured towards an empty chair.

"My name is Victor, thank you for your hospitality," Vic replied as he took the empty seat at the table.

"You are most welcome here, Victor. What would you like to drink?"

"A big beer, please. On second guess, make it two."

"Wait a bit, Victor, since we are crowded today," Adrian replied as he rushed over to a customer who had been waiting before Vic had arrived.

"No problem at all, as long as it takes."

"So, what brings you here, Victor?" Adrian asked when he eventually returned.

"I saw the beautiful nature here while I was travelling, and I thought to stop by."

"Here, enjoy your beers," Anthony said as he placed two wooden cups filled with beer on the table. "Ah, I see so you like nature, huh?"

"Don't we all? Of course, I do." Victor took a gulp from one of the cups. "Hm, this is a good beer that you got there."

"Well, not all of us like to see what nature gave us with the same eyes, you know? And thank you, I try to do my best in producing a high-quality beer."

"Well, I can assure you that you are doing a good job."

"Thank you, I own this place, but I don't do much, you know, since my son fell ill. I just pour some beers during the day, and the ones who work for me do most of the work."

"I am sorry to hear about your son. It's a nice place that you got here"

"Anything else I can help you with, young man?"

"Well, I am looking to purchase a small piece of land with the possibility of having a decent house on it. I would not mind if the house needs some repairs, you know?"

"Oh, that sounds really nice. I suppose you are moving with your significant other, am I right?"

"You are totally right there."

Adrian thought for a moment.

"Well, you see that small house there? With wooded fences all around it? That one is for sale if you are interested. I can call Hilda, she wants to sell it since she wants to move to France," Adrian explained as he pointed at a small house on the west side of the bar.

"I see it, I like it from the first view. You can call her, of course. I hope you will not have to go far to call her if she is not home."

"Oh, no worries, she is a guest here every day… Hilda!"

"What do you want? Can't you see I am dancing and having fun?" Hilda shouted.

"Come here, you crazy women, this gentleman is interested in purchasing your land with the house."

"Oh, here I come, Adrian, one moment," Hilda huffed as she walked over to Victor's table.

"Meet Victor, he is from Vienna, interested in moving here. I will leave you two to talk business now. I have to go see my son."

"Thank you, I appreciate your help," Victor exclaimed as Adrian left.

"Hello Victor, how are you? What brings you here?" Hilda asked.

"The beautiful nature, I would like to see your house from the outside and inside, and then we can talk about the price."

"No problem, let's go," Hilda said as she led the way to the house.

When they arrived, Vic stood and examined the house for a moment.

"It has an interesting, yet simple style. It's not too small, but not too big either," he finally commented.

Hilda opened the door and led Victor in.

"As you can see, here is the living room, on the left is the kitchen, and it has two bedrooms, along with a small room that I used for painting."

"I like how it's compact, yet it has plenty of space. It needs some renovations from what I can see, but that's not a big job. Tell me, Hilda, how much would you sell it for?"

"My starting price would be fifty thousand golden coins."

"Isn't that too pricy, don't you think?" Vic replied as he tried to calculate how much gold he would have left.

"How much would you pay, because I would use the money to start a new life in France?"

"What if I offer you thirty-five thousand and we seal the deal?"

"Forty thousand, we seal the deal?"

Vic took a moment to consider and eventually replied, "Deal then, forty it is."

"Great, the house is yours."

"Meet me tonight at my current house so that you can receive your payment, because I need to tell my friends that I bought a new home for my future wife and me."

"Let me know where it is and I will be there."

Vic grabbed a map and scribbled for a couple of minutes.

"Here at this location," Vic replied as he handed her a map.

"See you tonight."

As he was running in a sprint to his home, his mind was filled with dopamine, as if he were the happiest he had ever been in his entire life. Everything that he always wanted in life was in front of him, but life took him on another path, and everything had changed for him. At that moment, it started to rain heavily; every drop felt like a blessing, and he was enjoying himself as he was running through the rain. Before he arrived home, he felt like things he wanted to do he had to do them in a rush since he did not have time to argue with his friend about how and why and how come.

When he opened the door and pushed it, Chris was preparing dinner while Otto was reading a book. Vic went to his room and picked up a big box of coins; there were approximately fifty thousand golden coins. The problem was that the box was heavy and he could not carry it alone. He asked Otto to help him, and there was no time to explain what he needed the coins for, since those coins were his, and Chris and Otto had theirs in their room. So, there was no need to justify the reason for spending his own money. Otto did not ask him for anything, just helped him to carry the wooden box outside, while Chris did intervene by asking what was the purpose of this. But Vic just answered by saying, "I am moving."

Chris continued to argue, but there was not enough time for Vic to answer his questions.

Moments later, Hilda arrived with two big leather bags to divide the coins separately, so the horse could carry them in balance. She did not stay for long; she just greeted Vic. Meanwhile, Otto went inside to continue reading the book, but he burst into tears, since he knew that he would miss his friend very much, and there was nothing that he could do. But on the other side, he was just happy for Victor and

Emily, that they would move together and they would be happy, being a true friend and valuing their happiness. Hilda went with the money and congratulated Vic for purchasing a new house, and wished him all the best. Vic, on the other side, wished her the best, too, and wished that she would find everything that she was looking for in France.

Everything was going according to the plan, but Vic felt a little bit sad because of not explaining to his friends and decided in the moment to have a talk with Chris and Otto before going to meet Vincenzo and then to tell Emily and her parents next. As Chris was making the dinner, he was furious and telling Otto that they did not deserve this kind of behavior, and Vic owed at least an explanation for all this. While Vic overheard their conversation, he decided to approach softly and calm down the situation, since he felt deep in his heart that those two were his friends since he was a kid, and he would never forget them or leave them behind.

"Chris, can we have a conversation? I need to have a talk with you and Otto. It is important and kind of urgent. Even though I think that both of you know what is going on."

"Of course, thank god you decided to talk about it at least, before running away again."

"I am not going to run away, my friend. I am about to move. I just want to talk with you two about it."

"Please sit, Vic. And Chris, we shall talk about it as friends, not like we are arguing or something," Otto insisted.

"I agree with you there," Chris replied as they all sat.

"Listen, both of you, I have loved you since we were kids. Since we became friends, unfortunately, in a place that we should not have met, but it is how it is, and we cannot change a thing. I love you two with all my heart and soul, and I would give my life for you, but I am moving with Emily. And to be honest, I will not be far from you, you will visit us, and we will visit you," Vic explained.

I understand, and I am happy for you. What makes me happier is the fact that you are willing to visit us, but don't think that we have anything against it. I just thought that you would at least talk to us before moving," Chris sneered.

"He is talking to us, Chris, let him tell us what he has to say, and after that we can answer, man. We should take this easy, even though it is not easy at all, because we were like a family," Otto urged.

"Sometimes I can get mad, but let's never forget that he rescued us, and without him we would now be dead," Chris admitted.

"It is not about that, and I don't want to take any credit for it. I just want to talk about this moving situation, since it is of high importance to me. I want you both to understand that the both of you, tomorrow, will find yourselves a partner, and when you, Chris or you,

Otto, fall in love someday in the future, that does not mean that you are leaving your friend behind. Because friends are there for life." Vic exclaimed.

"I understand you completely, and I do not have anything against your decision, but do not forget us. Come here from time to time, but I think that there will be trouble with those at the Temple of Justice since they will get mad, not us," Otto replied.

"They can get mad as long as they want; there is nothing that we can do about that," Chris commented.

"Perhaps we should expect a visit from them since it has been quite a long time since we last met them. But, we should be ready in this case," Vic replied.

"What do you suggest that we do in case they come to us?" Otto asked.

"I suggest we take a soft approach in the beginning by explaining that we want to resign and follow a different path in our lives. If they come again a few times, then we should see about the next step, but I don't think that they will attack at all or anything similar whatsoever," Vic considered.

"We shall see about that…" Chris whispered.

"Indeed, I must go now, friends. I have two more places to be; we shall meet soon. Bye for now."

"Take care and good luck," Chris and Otto cried, and Vic headed out the door.

As Vic was leaving his house, in which he had spent most of his life, he started to feel a sense of nostalgia the exact moment he set foot out of the front porch. Every memory that he had with his friend started to appear in his mind, every laughter and tear, every word that they said and that he said too. It was very difficult for him to cope with this emotion, but he suppressed the tears from coming out of his eyes, since he was on his way to visit Vincenzo and to tell him about the good news that he was moving in with Emily in his newly purchased home. In the meantime, Oni was circling around Vic from above as if it was sensing that Vic was upset and sad.

After a few moments, Vic sat down on a stone that was on his left side and started to think about what would happen if any of the leaders came to hunt him down, or do anything bad to Emily or to Chris and Otto. His thoughts overtook him and left him to worry for a long time. After approximately two hours, he stood up and told himself, "I would protect my love and my friends with everything that I can, and I will never let anything bad happen to them."

He continued to walk and was imagining the future moments with Emily and how happy he would feel to visit his friends from time to time, and vice versa.

His heart was filled with joy and sadness at the same time; perhaps, this was another level of awakening for Vic. As he was getting closer to Vincenzo's castle, a sense of bravery was rushing through his veins, because he knew that he would always support and love him for who he is and just the way he is. Upon arriving at the castle, Vic was greeted by the guards and welcomed in a warm manner. While he was walking, Vincenzo was not on the balcony due to the weather being harsh and windy. Vic knocked on the front door, and Vincenzo's voice could be heard as he said, "Come in."

When Vic opened the door, and Vincenzo saw who it was, he rushed to greet him.

"Vitorio, it's such a pleasure to see you, my friend. Come, let's sit and have a talk."

"It's a pleasure likewise, my friend. How have you been?"

Vic and Vincenzo moved to the lounge and sat.

"Vitorio, I have not been feeling good lately. To be honest with you, I feel a bit ill and dreams are haunting me every night."

"What kind of dreams are we talking about, my friend? Since I have the same problem from time to time. To be honest, sometimes I feel like I am cursed; I do not know why."

"Cursed, no, my friend. You are not. Well, I just keep having the same dream over and over for more than a few weeks, and I do not understand why it is happening to me. In that dream, I found myself trapped in a room filled with snakes, but the moment one of them bites me, I wake up. I find it very hard to believe that not every night I get bitten by the same one. Sometimes, I can feel the venom rushing to my brain in my dream, imagine that Vitorio."

"Very strange indeed, snakes in a dream represent enemies as far as I know. And knowing that you are bitten by different ones, that would mean that you have a lot of enemies that want to hurt you in different ways. But, I want you to know that your enemies are my enemies as well, my dear friend."

"Hm, I see. Well, they can try, and we shall see how it will end. Thank you, Vitorio, it is the same for me, you know that, right? So, tell me, what have you been up to lately? How is your significant other?"

"I couldn't agree more with you there. Well, that's why I came to pay you a visit. I purchased a house in a village from a lady who wants to move to France. I plan to move in with Emily. After that, I was in a rush and I wanted to leave as soon as possible. But I felt guilty for not explaining myself to my friends, so I had a deep talk with them. I feel like I dropped a big stone off my shoulder by talking with them about it. And, of course, Chris got mad at first, but later he understood that we would see each other, of course. On the other hand, Otto was full of understanding and always by my side, to be honest, not that Chris is not, but Otto is a different character."

"Let's raise a glass to this Vitorio. Wait a moment, let me bring the wine," Vincenzo called as he disappeared into the wine cellar.

Vic looked at the pictures on the wall. An old drawing drew his attention - he wondered if he should mention it and decided against it.

Vincenzo reappeared with a bottle of vintage wine.

"Vitorio, we shall celebrate your very important phase in life." Vincenzo filled their cups. "Your life will change from now on, in my opinion, since it will take another path."

Victor raised his glass, "Cheers to the bright future! How do you mean another path?"

"Cheers to the bright future! I mean that you will be a family man now, you will focus on other things in life, rather than completing quests and doing other people's business, you know? Life will take you through another journey; perhaps you will become a husband in the near future and a father, so your life will be different."

"I guess that you are absolutely right there, but that is, I am afraid distant future. Because I need to come up with a plan to figure out how I will provide for my family, that part of my life must change."

"How are you going to take that approach, since you know what those you worked for are capable of?"

"That is the main problem, because if I get in trouble, Emily will be in trouble as well. Perhaps the best way would be to ignore them until they decide to stop reaching out to me."

"I will be here whatever you need, but bear in mind that those people are not to be taken for granted."

"I know that. I am afraid that is a part of me that I often don't pay attention to, even if I know that they can do very bad things."

"What are your plans for your main income? Perhaps I could offer you something?"

"I have no plans for the moment. I was thinking of using the leftover gold that I own until I figure something out. What do you have in mind? It would be my great pleasure to work for you."

"I understand, maybe you could transport my cargoes twice a week, and I will pay you pretty good since we are friends."

"I would love to do that, you mean just from point A to point B, and that's it?"

"Yes, I mean, I do not need somebody to drive a carriage, but I am willing to give you that part of the job, and it's the easiest one."

"I understand, then I will be glad to accept it."

"Cheers to the new life."

"To the new life! By the way, could you tell me what we would do if they attacked? Any plans that you would suggest?"

"I think that they will not attack anybody in that way. First, they warn you several times, and then they strike, but I am afraid that there is not much that we can do since they are unpredictable, as you know."

"I am afraid that you are right there, but I will be ready. Perhaps I could pay them a visit in the near future to explain to them about my situation and that I would like to resign."

"I am afraid that they will not grant you that request. Once you are in, there is no going back. But what fears me even more is that Chris and Otto were involved too, so if they strike, they strike you all."

"I am very aware of that, unfortunately, but I will see what I can do in a week from now. Because I will try to set things straight with them, but to continue to do their dirty work does not come into consideration."

"I agree with you there, but be careful because you never know how they will react after not seeing you for a long time. Act like nothing has changed in your life, and if they immediately start to talk about the next quest that they have in mind, just cut the cord and tell them why you are there."

"I will do that, thank you, my friend. This means a lot to me. I should get going now, because I want to go to Emily and tell her that

I purchased a new home. Of course, a serious conversation must be held with Richard and Anna as well before moving with Emily."

"I wish you luck, though you do not need it. She will move sooner than you think, Vitorio. Stay safe, and whatever you need, I am here."

"Thank you, Vincenzo. I will let you know in case something happens. Until we meet again."

As he was leaving Vincenzo's castle, he did not go directly to Emily's house, which was next door; instead, he decided to think about all this near the lake in the opposite direction. As he was walking, his mind was filled with *what-ifs*; it was hard to cope with all that pressure, and his mind was over occupied with every possible way of imagining the worst-case scenarios. After a while, Vic tried to calm down, but there was nothing that could help him. "Perhaps a swim will do," he whispered to himself, but later he realized that if he jumped in the water, it would not be nice of him to go all wet to Emily's house.

Everything felt upside down just by a stream of thoughts that captivated him so deeply. Instead of going to where he was aiming, he decided to go to his newly purchased home alone. While he was doing so, he thought that it would be better to delay that plan and rest for a while; perhaps in the morning, things would be better, and his mind would stop suffering.

As he was walking, he stumbled upon an old lady who was screaming in despair after falling under a horse. Nobody seemed to care about her or even try to help her, but Vic did. He whistled for his horse to come, and when it was there, he tied up the fallen horse's front legs with the saddle's hook on his horse in order to move the fallen one from the legs of the poor lady. He succeeded in doing so for the reason that his horse was bigger and stronger than the one that had an incident. However, the lady was in need of a doctor, and Vic had to find one fast, but that day was a very lucky day for the lady, because at that exact moment, a doctor with his wife was passing by in a carriage on their way home. The doctor stopped and took the lady to treat her.

Vic continued his story and looked at the bar he had previously gone to, where he met Hilda. With a high desire to drink, he chose not to, because he was trying to prepare himself for a serious relationship, and such a lifestyle would not be appropriate for his future. As he was fighting to avoid the temptation, his brain wanted beer, but his heart did not let him have any. In a desperate state, he went home and focused on tidying things a bit. He started by cleaning the floor and the entire walls, then he rested for a bit and continued by cleaning every area of his new house. Exhausted from hours of work, Vic fell asleep on the bed, hugged a pillow, and imagined that the pillow was Emily.

As he was entering the REM Phase and entering a dream, he found himself in a beautiful field covered with flowers and Emily was approaching him from a distance, wearing a white wedding dress. She smiled and ran towards Vic to hug him, but slowly, blood started to drip from her belly. As Vic was trying to stop the bleeding, he was stabbed in the back in his dream, and immediately woke up in the middle of the night, as the brain wakes the body up in case of death. Vic woke up in sweat and tears, attempted to go back to sleep again and to relax, but until dawn, he just gazed at the ceiling and spent several hours thinking of running away again because he feared the worst.

As the dawn arrived, Vic got out of his bed and went into the woods to chop some wood. He intended to fix some parts of the house and to make some furniture. That day, he worked so hard the entire day and fell asleep on the porch of the house by sunset. He woke up around midnight and was confused because he did not know what to do the entire night. Instead of wasting the entire night again, he was tempted to go to the bar and drink, but on second thought, he did not go; it was a split-second decision.

Vic went inside the house and spent the entire night doing small repairs around the house and throwing away what he saw as useless. As the morning was on its way, he went outside to wait for the dawn, sat on his chair and watched the night slowly turning into morning. "What now?" he whispered.

At that moment, he remembered the boy named Carl and thought that it would be great to go visit Mile's store and ask Ben how Carl is doing. Vic whistled for his horse and went directly to Miles' store. Mile was busy with work as always, while Ben was making an axe for a customer. As Vic was approaching, he was greeted with honor by both of them.

"Victor, welcome. It's been a long time, my friend. How are you doing? Let me just put this axe to cool down so that we can talk for a bit," Ben called over to Vic as he finished and took the axe to cool down.

"Welcome, Victor, it's nice to see you. I will be with you in five minutes. I am in the middle of something," Mile advised.

"Take your time, Mile. It's no rush. Ben, hello there, I am fine, thank you. I can see that you look good yourself, and every time I see you, you look happier than ever."

"That's because I do what I love, thanks to you, my friend," Ben explained, grinning.

"Don't mention it, that was the least I could do. How is Carl doing? How is his writing coming along? I remembered this morning that's why I came, and of course to see you, too."

"Thank you very much for asking. I appreciate it. Carl is about to finish his first novel, which is about a kid who lost everything at his young age, but it's kind of a long story. Perhaps you can join us tonight for dinner, and we could talk."

"Lovely, I would love that to be honest. So, at what time should I arrive?" Vic asked.

"Eight is good for you?"

"It is perfect, see you tonight, then."

"See you," Ben called as he headed out the back to continue working on the axe.

"Hello Victor, sorry I was busy. How are you doing? How can I help you, my friend?" Mile asked as he rushed over.

"Hey, Mile, I am doing fine, thanks for asking. Oh, I just came to pay you two a visit, that's all."

"Anytime, you are more than welcome. I don't mean to be rude, but I have got to get back to work," Mile explained as he looked back at the counter.

"It's all right, no worries. I have places to be, too. See you, bye for now."

At that moment, when Vic left them, he felt the urge to do something from all those emotions that were being held captive inside his soul. He just could not wait to reach Ben's house in the evening and see where Carl was with his process. But his heart was racing as if it was trying to tell him something.

Vic just stood as he was looking at the view of the city and all those people passing by him, as if he had frozen in time. Everything that he wanted was to tell Emily how much he loves her, and all those emotions were suffocating him at that moment, but he knew that if he did that, there was no turning back and that everything would change in a split second. Nothing was of more importance than what he was feeling at that moment, and again, everything in front of him seemed useless in comparison to his emotions.

In his mind, he imagined his approach to Richard and Anna, but he could not stop thinking about those "what ifs." Moments later, he came back to his senses and just started to walk slowly, while millions of thoughts were attacking his brain. He decided not to run or sprint, even taking the horse was out of consideration. He just wanted to take things slowly and to think five hundred times before the decision was made.

It took him two hours to reach the destination, and there he was in front of their house. It was approximately eleven o'clock, before noon. Vic just stood there and thought to himself, *"Here I go, this is my destiny, and everything will go as smoothly as it should. You got this, Vitorio."* He smiled with a childish smile, remembering that only Vincenzo calls him like that.

But moments before he was about to enter, tears rolled down his cheeks, and he remembered every moment, every second, like flashbacks since the day that he saw Emily for the first time. While on tears, he smiled again when he remembered how Vincenzo introduced him to her and how he was emotional and tried to ignore all those feelings. Again, he whispered to himself, "You got this, you can do it." In that moment, Richard opened the door, and Vic froze.

"Victor, such a nice surprise to see you here. For how long have you been standing there? Is everything okay?" Richard asked.

Victor just stood there frozen, unsure of what words to say.

"Come on in, Victor, let's have a talk. Please, you seem worried," Richard suggested as he approached.

"I came to talk with you and Anna. I am so sorry that I was standing there; I could not manage to calm down my thoughts. Please accept my apology."

"Why are you apologizing? It's okay, come on in, it's a pleasure to have you here."

As Victor stepped through the door, the stress began to boil his brain.

"Thank you, it's a pleasure, to be honest."

"Please be seated, Victor. Anna darling, bring us something to drink." Richard gestured towards the chaise longue.

"It's okay, I decided not to drink alcohol anymore, just water, please."

"What has gotten into you, man? You seem different from when we met last. You sure you are okay?" Richard asked.

"Yes, I am. I just decided to change some things in my life for the better."

"I do not understand. What does alcohol have to do with it? You were not the type of person to drink every day, were you? Darling Anna, where is Emily?"

"Wait, my love, I will be there soon. Emily went to purchase something, I do not know what," Anna called from the kitchen as she prepared lunch.

"I understand, darling. Victor, what is new with you apart from drinking and letting it go?" Richard asked, turning his attention back to Vic.

"I did not drink every day, Sir, but when I did drink, I usually overdrank, so I hope you understand me."

"I do, of course, no problem there, but you seem in distress. I still cannot believe that you are okay."

"Here, darling. I brought you both cold drinks. Welcome, Victor, it's a pleasure to see you. How are you, dear?" Anna interrupted as she appeared with two glasses.

"Hello, Mrs. Anna. Thank you, I am doing fine. The pleasure is all mine," Vic replied.

"Anna, darling, let us know when you see Emily coming. This will surprise her," Richard asked.

"Of course, I will, my love," she replied as she headed back towards the kitchen.

"What else is new with you, Victor? Please feel free to talk about it, since, as you know, we are your family now," Richard asked, turning his attention back to Victor.

"To be honest, Sir, I do not know where to start. Since I want to get it off my shoulders, but it took me some time to gather the courage to appear here, I am in absolute fear because some people whom I worked for might do something dangerous, and I would never let anything bad happen to Emily."

"I understand. How dangerous are we talking?" Richard asked, leaning in.

"Strikers dangerous," Vic whispered.

The color drained from Richard's face.

"Oh my, Victor. Tell me you are joking!"

A plate shattered in the kitchen.

"Oh, dear god!" Anna gasped.

"I should get going, please forgive me. Tell Emily that I died or something. Please, Sir and Madam Anna, don't blame me because I never knew that I would fall in love, and to be honest, I never believed in love. I never imagined being in love, and I was never with anyone before," Victor explained as he stood and turned to leave.

"Calm down, Victor, please. There is a solution for everything. I will write a letter to one of my good friends, and you too shall move together, perhaps in France. But even if you wanted to escape love, you cannot. Trust me, everything that is meant to be, it will be, like it or not, it's the law of the universe," Richard reassured.

A solitary tear rolled down Vic's cheek.

"Thank you, sir," he replied, his voice trembling.

"I told you, we are your family now," Richard replied as he crossed to Victor and pulled him into a hug.

"Richard, dear, tell Victor to wipe off those tears. Emily is coming," Anne cried, poking her head out of the kitchen.

"Oh, lovely. Victor, don't let her know about this, not now. I will make something up," Richard pleaded.

Victor had no words; his whole being had frozen.

The scene that welcomed her was unbelievable. As Emily flew through the door, she saw Victor standing with eyes full of tears.

"Father, Mother, what is going on? Love, why are you crying? What happened?" she cried as she ran to Vic.

"Don't worry, my dear, those are the tears of joy. Victor here bought a house and wants you to live with him," Richard explained.

Vic's jaw dropped.

"That is true, my love."

"Oh, darling, this is the best day of my life," Emily screeched as she hugged Vic tight.

"We congratulate you, dear. Don't forget us, visit us sometimes," Anna added.

"Of course, I will, Mother. We are a family now," Emily replied cheerfully, pulling Anna close.

"This deserves a toast. Anna, could you bring us some wine? Victor, will you please drink, too?" Richard insisted.

"No, Sir, I stopped drinking, I cannot."

"Oh, come on, love, a glass or two will not kill you," Emily implored, that twinkling of her eyes tempting him.

"All right then, but only a glass."

"A glass, more or less, it does not matter because this is a big reason to celebrate, not every day one purchases a house." Richard filled everyone's glasses and raised his own. "Cheers to the future and family bond."

"Cheers! To the future and family bond," Vic cheered.

Emily looked deeply into Vic's eyes lovingly.

"My love, you are everything that I have dreamt of."

Vic met her eyes with that macho gaze that made her feel safe.

"You are, too, my everything. I cannot describe the emotions that I have for you."

"Victor, I must leave soon. I am afraid I have a meeting with Vincenzo about a business, but I will be back in three hours, I think," Richard advised.

"Oh, I promised Ben that I would visit them, I forgot."

"Who is Ben?" Emily asked.

"Ben, my love, is a friend of mine, whom I had to convince to let his child pursue the dream of becoming a writer," Vic explained.

"I see, my love, perhaps I could come with you?"

"Of course you can, darling, you are more than welcome. We will go on foot, it will take us a while, but we will get there. What do you think?"

"Yes, love." Emily jumped for joy. "I can't wait to meet that child. I love children so much."

"My darling Emily, as far as I can see, after that meeting, you will go with the love of your life to see your new home, am I right?" Anna asked.

"I am sorry to interrupt, but I think that you are right. Those two are made for each other. I am in a hurry, see you," Richard explained as he threw on his jacket and headed for the door.

"Bye for now, say hello to Vincenzo," Vic, Anna and Emily called after him.

"Madame Anna, it's up to Emily to decide, and with your permission, she can spend the night in our house," Vic declared.

"Spend the night!? Excuse yourself, did you purchase it for us to live there for one night or to live there for the rest of the time, my love?" Emily scoffed.

"Oh, my darling, it's our home for the rest of the time, but we have to get married first."

Emily blushed and thought for a moment.

"Married? Then let's get married."

"Oh my, that was faster than the speed of light," Anna exclaimed as she clutched her chest.

"Love, we should talk with Richard about this first, my darling," Vic stated.

"My father has nothing against us getting married, can't you see that?"

"There are some manners and traditions, my darling."

"Emily, my light of the sun, my everything, one does not rush this. You will get married when the time comes, sooner than you can imagine," Anna advised.

"But I cannot wait, I want to live with the love of my life," Emily replied, desperate for her life with Victor to begin.

"You will, you will be moving soon, I do not see what the problem here is?"

"But Mother, I love him; can't you see that? Can't you see my love?" Emily pleaded as she looked at Vic.

"Of course, my love, but sometimes you cannot rush things like that. Perhaps we should get going; they must be waiting for us," Vic replied as he stroked her hand.

"Let's go, we will talk during our journey."

"We have to go, see you, Mrs. Anna."

"Stay safe, see you two," Anna called after them as they headed out.

As they were leaving, Vic took her hand and they were walking like the two sweethearts who were connected with each other tightly with heart and soul. Vic could not believe that all this was happening, and he started to forget about those *"what ifs"* that were draining him. Emily was flying with happiness and could not wait to move in and live with him. While they were walking, Emily stopped and could not hold back her desire to ask.

"My love, I want to ask you something."

Vic stopped.

"Of course, my love, anything you want in this world."

"Have you ever been with a girl before?" Emily asked through fluttered eyelashes.

"No, my darling, never. Have you ever been with a boy before?" Vic asked, his face as red as a rose.

"No, I have not. So, you never had a kiss?"

"How could I ever have a kiss when I have never been with a girl before?"

"I wonder what it feels like. Have you ever thought about it?"

"I did every night before sleeping, hugging the pillow and thinking about you, since the first time I saw you, even when I disappeared."

"Me too, my love, since we met the first time. I love you more than you know."

Blood rushes to his brain, and butterflies start moving in his stomach as she faces him, centimeters away from a kiss. She closed her eyes and stood there desperately waiting for a kiss as Oni could be heard from the sky giving signals to Vic that it was the right moment. Vic closed his eyes as well and kissed her.

They both got the feeling that they were flying and hugged each other tight for several minutes, thinking about nothing and feeling the moment. They continued to walk and did not talk at all, since both minds were in synchronization, but somehow silence was louder than every word possible in the universe.

After all that silence, they arrived the Ben's house, as it seemed that they were waiting for Vic since the candles were lit in front of the house. Vic approached and knocked on the door.

"Come in, Victor, we were expecting you," Ben called.

"Good evening, friends," Victor replied, opening the door and stepping inside with Emily at his side.

"Good evening, welcome to my humble house," Ben greeted Emily.

"Ben, my friend, let me introduce you to my significant other. This is Emily. My love, Emily, this is Ben, my friend," Vic explained, gesturing from Ben to Emily and vice versa.

"I am honored to meet you, Emily, please be seated… Elke, my love, where are you? Come down, our guests have arrived," Ben called to Elke, who was upstairs with Carl.

Carl bolted down the stairs.

"Victor, you arrived!" he exclaimed as he hugged him warmly.

"Such a lovely family. So, this is Carl that you told me about," Emily asked Victor.

"Yes, isn't he such a sweetheart? Our future famous writer."

"Well, nice to meet you, Mister Little Writer," Emily said as she shook Carl's hand.

"Please be seated all, we have a lot to celebrate tonight as far as I can see," Ben explained as he gestured at the table.

Elke appeared at the bottom of the stairs.

"Good evening and welcome, Victor, long time no see. It's a pleasure to have you here."

"Thank you, Mrs. Elke, the pleasure is mine. Let me introduce you to my significant other, Emily," Vic replied.

"Emily, it's a pleasure," Elke explained as she reached out and squeezed Emily's hand.

"Likewise, Mrs. Elke," Emily beamed.

"Please be seated at once; we cannot hold a conversation while standing," Ben urged.

Vic chuckled.

"Ha-ha, Ben, that sense of humor"

Once everyone was seated, Ben began.

"I would like to congratulate you, new and beautiful couple that you are. Miss Emily, we met Victor via little Carl here. I am not sure if you are familiar with the story." Ben looked to Emily.

"Thank you, I just know how you met, not the entire story."

"Well, let me tell you then. Carl was crying when Victor met him, and Victor came here with him. We were working around the house, and Vic convinced me to let him write and pursue his dream. By the way, he made me pursue my dream to become a blacksmith, so here I am now, happier than ever, all thanks to him."

"Impressive, to be honest, my hero and the hero of our city," Emily replied, beaming at Carl.

"Oh, come on with the hero thing," Vic sighed, rolling his eyes.

"He is my hero, I am nearly finishing my first book, people," Carl cut in.

"Well, that is what I want to know, little man. Tell us what it is about?"

"Well, I cannot tell you much; I want it to be a surprise," Carl explained, glancing over at Ben.

"Tell them, my son, who are you going to tell if not your hero?" Ben shrugged.

"Okay then, Papa, I will. It is a story about a little boy who got lost in the woods and did not escape for a full decade and was raised by wolves, but comes in contact with humans and returns to the woods."

"I would return too," Vic butted in, causing everyone to collapse in laughter.

Carl cleared his throat and continued.

"And then it becomes sad because people are afraid of him and think that he is some kind of prehistoric man, and they start to hunt him down. But the wolves do not let anybody come close to him."

"See, Ben, I told you, your son is a born writer. Carl, little man, I am so proud of you," Vic explained, tears rolling down his cheeks as he remembered how he and Carl met.

"Thank you, Victor, because you showed me that I could believe in myself," Carl replied, also remembering and crying.

"Let's raise a glass to the bright future and success. Elke, could you bring us some wine, please, my love?" Ben interjected.

"Of course, I will, darling," Elke replied, pushing her chair back and gliding to the kitchen to grab another bottle.

"We cannot drink anymore, Ben. I stopped drinking, please, man," Vic explained, holding his hand over his glass.

"It's not every day that we celebrate this kind of success, my love," Emily said, tugging Vic's hand away from the cup.

"Let's do it then. I mean, I am nearly drunk to be honest," Vic declared.

"Aren't we all, for that matter," Ben replied.

"I am not. I want to get drunk, too," Carl nagged.

"You will my soon when you grow up, stick to the writing for now," Ben assured.

"Good luck to the new writer here!" Vic cried as he raised his glass.

Vic's toast was met with 'cheers' and the clink of glasses in return.

"Emily, you tell us. How did you meet Victor?" Ben asked.

It was not long after we moved here to Vienna. That day, my father and Victor's friend Vincenzo met to discuss about business partnership that they are currently still doing, and Vincenzo gathered us all to meet him. The moment I saw him, I knew that he was the love of my life, and that I wanted to spend the rest of my life with him. I looked in his eyes that day and felt that kind of strange feeling, you know? After that, we just both were reconnected by the universe and the rest is just a long story," Emily explained.

"Impressive, what a story! Love at first sight, those are the best," Ben replied.

"I agree too, since Ben and I had a similar love story, too," Elke chimed in, reminiscing and smiling at Ben.

"Really! Well, I did not see that coming to be honest," Vic scoffed.

"Yes, to be honest, it was similar, but we were very young," Ben advised.

"Tell us how you two met, please!" Emily squealed excitedly.

"Perhaps another time, you know," Ben replied, glancing from Emily to Carl.

"I understand, another time it is then!"

"Dear Ben, Elke, and you, little sweet Carl, we should really get going. I can't wait to show Emily our house," Vic explained as he pushed his chair back to stand.

"It's all right, no problem there. It was a pleasure to have you here. Come by sometimes," Ben replied as he crossed the room to the door.

"You three come by sometimes, too." Vic smiled as he looked at the family's faces.

"We certainly will when we find the time," Ben replied.

"Until we meet next time, dear friends," Vic called back as he took Emily by the arm.

Chapter Eight: Love Hits To The Core

As Vic and Emily were leaving, it was nearly midnight, and the new moon was clear and visible in the sky. Vic stood and looked at the moon, remembering those three wished that he had asked, hoping that they were on the right track to get fulfilled. On the other side, Emily was holding his hand very tight and skipped with joy as she walked and could not wait to see the newly purchased house. As they were approaching, Vic hoped that she would just take a look at the house and he would walk her home afterwards, but things did not go as planned. As Vic opened the door, they both entered. In those moments, Vic was struggling to find the candles because of the feeling of being half drunk, but managed somehow. After that, he lit up the oil candles, only two out of four, aiming to create a romantic atmosphere. Emily was impressed by how Vic cleaned up and repaired the house, but she did not care much for it to be fancy or rich. Her dream was not to own a castle or to be wealthy; she just wanted to be happy with Victor.

In those moments, she was imagining living in that house until they grew old together, getting married, having children, everything was like a split-second wish. While Vic, on the other side, looked at her without uttering a single word, just admiring her and saying to himself, "I must be very lucky to have her."

At that moment, there were no words. They both looked into each other's eyes as they were slowly walking closer. Vic kissed her, and Emily kissed him harder. As they were kissing, Vic put his arms around her waist while Emily slowly put her hands on his shoulders as they began to kiss more passionate. They moved around the living room. Vic tripped over the bedclothes on the bed where Emily wanted so badly to be the first night. She even considered asking him, but she could not resist the temptation and started to undress him.

"What are you doing, my love?" Vic gasped as he jumped backwards.

"You are the love of my life, and I want this right now. I can feel it, can't you feel it too?" Emily asked.

"Feel what? Are you out of your mind? Imagine what your parents will say, we must get married first. I think that you know that already."

"As if I or you would tell them. After all, why does it matter what others think? You are the love of my life, my first and last love. I want everything with you, married or not. What difference does it make? It's not like God will punish us for loving each other, and after all, since when did you become religious?" Emily asked with a smirk.

Vic laughed nervously.

"Ha-ha, I would not tell them, you are being silly, my love. I want everything with you, but I don't know… and no, I am not religious, I am just telling you that we live in an era where making love is a "sin" before marriage. Not like people don't do it before, but I am just saying…"

"Then what is the problem? You ruined the moment; we would be flying now. Fuck what people say or think, and fuck all the rules. We will get married, I am sure of it, and if you want, we can get married right now. We don't need a priest or somebody else to give us a proper marriage; we can do it by ourselves," Emily snapped.

Vic paused for a moment.

"We would be the first couple in the entire world to do that. So let's get married then, do we need a special dress or something? What's the plan?" he asked.

"Just stand up, silly. We will make those classic vows. Shall we?" Emily replied, dragging Vic to his feet.

Vic stood and ran his fingers through his hair so as to neaten it.

"We are gathered here before you all…" Vic began.

Oni's call could be heard from the sky, and he landed on the windowsill, which made Victor snicker.

"Why are you laughing?" Emily asked.

"Look at it, it's making fun of us," Vic giggled.

Emily looked at Oni and rolled her eyes.

"Oh, dear god. Let it not interrupt you, this bird for sure has a deep sense of humor."

"We are gathered here as me, Victor and my lovely future Bride, Emily, will get married with Oni the Raven over there by the window as a witness, our best Bird (Man)-"

Vic fell about laughing, unable to take it seriously, while Emily couldn't stop staring at Oni, chuckling.

Vic composed himself and continued.

"Ladies and gentlemen, and the bird, as the moon is our witness too, we are getting married right now; every laughter from now on is punishable hardly."

"In this night, do you take me to be your loyal bride, until death do us part in good and bad, poor and rich?" Emily asked.

"I do," Vic replied.

"Good answer!" Emily quipped with a wink.

Vic began roaring with laughter again, unable to contain it.

"Excuse me, please, we shall continue," Vic explained, clearing his throat. "Emily, will you take me to be your future husband, to be loyal and very good for you in every moment. In good and bad and worse, I love you, just say yes," Vic's eyes darted as he searched his mind for the correct words.

"Yes, I do!"

"Since our bird cannot talk, I guess I can kiss the bride now," Vic explained before leaning in and kissing Emily tenderly.

"Now we are married, we shall proceed," she asked as she clung to him with her arms around his neck.

"No, wait! That fast? I mean, are you sure about it?"

"I am my love; we are married now, that is what you said, right? After getting married."

"I know my love, but I never did it before, and it's kind of strange for me."

"I did not either. What is there to be strange? Just enjoy the moment, we are a couple now. Don't act like you do not know what to do."

As they continued to kiss passionately, Vic was the one to accidentally bite her lip, which made her feel the fire of love. For a moment, they stopped kissing and stared into each other's eyes while Emily was looking at Vic with so much love and burning passion.

On the other side, Vic felt like he was about to fly from happiness. Emily stole a kiss at that moment, and they both lay down on the bed. Afterwards, Emily started to undress Vic, and he was convinced that it was the moment she took off his shirt and started to touch his chest, feeling his heartbeat made her synchronize her emotions with passion. Vic did not spare her but continued to kiss her and proceeded to her neck. Upon kissing her neck, it made her very wild, to the point of making a very seductive sound. Afterwards, Vic's heartbeat started to rise, and he started to touch her leg, and moved his hand further. She became vulnerable and was about to give in. Moments later, the fire erupted when they both started to make love for the first time in their lives. Two bodies were like one. Emily was at her peak when Vic saw her face; he was about to reach his top momentum, too. As they both were done, it started the phase of cuddling for hours and staring again. As they were hugging each other in the same position, they fell asleep. After ten hours, they woke up, and Emily was the one to wake up first. She prepared breakfast for Vic and brought it to bed. They both ate and then dressed up to go for a walk. They wanted to let everybody know that they got married. As they left the house, Emily was impressed by what a beautiful day it was.

"Look, love! How the sky is clear and how the sun is bright just like our love," Vic gushed as he stood in awe of it.

Emily smirked as she gripped Victor's hand a little tighter.

"You're a hopeless romantic, aren't you? Our love is brighter than the sun, so you try better next time."

"Everything seems like a dream. I still cannot believe that we are married. By the way, have you seen our best bird anywhere?" Vic asked, looking around for Oni.

"It is a dream indeed, but we are the main protagonists in it. Oni, I do not know, it must be somewhere nearby."

"Maybe it became jealous and left me forever," Vic replied, still scanning the sky and trees for any sign of him.

Emily giggled.

"Ha-ha, there is a high possibility for that to happen, so I think that you are right."

Just then, Oni could be heard cawing from the sky. Vic looked to his right, and he flew towards him, landing on his right arm.

"Oh, since when do you speak English, you little smarty?" Vic asked as he stroked Oni's head with his finger.

"Sometimes, I think that Oni understand what we say, what if it can spy?"

Vic grinning, gazing at the bird.

"You troublemaker, are you a spy or are you our best bird?"

Oni nodded his head from left to right as if replying, and Emily let out a chortle.

"I told you this raven is a special one; it must be sent from the Gods," Vic explained as he looked back at Emily.

"There is a high possibility for that as well."

"I believe so, darling. What should we do now? I believe that the best thing to do would be to walk through the town, and perhaps we should visit Chris and Otto, and let them know the news."

"I agree with you there, my love, but we should visit my parents too. And afterwards, we will let Vincenzo know as well."

"Perfect, so let's head for a walk, while we are on our way to visit my friends."

"Let's go," Emily replied, tugging Vic's arm to lead him forwards.

While they were walking and holding hands together, they drew people's attention, as if they were the most beautiful couple in Vienna. People who were passing by were staring at them, while Vic and Emily did not react at all; they knew that they were only walking, nothing more, with no additional intention. Some people recognized Vic and greeted him, while the rest were just curious about Emily. There were also looks of jealousy in the male population since Emily was genuinely beautiful and they wanted her for themselves, but nobody could or had the bravery to say anything due to knowing how powerful and what Vic was capable of.

Moments later, Vic and Emily were greeted by Miles and Ben, but they did not have the time to talk due to having so much work to do. Vic greeted them from a distance, and they both smiled. It could be seen and felt that both of them were happy to see each other walk together, especially Ben, not that Mile was not happy, but he was an introvert and kept things to himself. While passing through the town further, they were admired by the elder population as if they made them recall their youth. At that moment, Vic asked Emily if they should head to Chris and Otto, and she said they should. Upon arriving, from a distance, Chris could be seen chopping wood, and Otto was the one who was carrying it, stacking it at a place. Vic thought that it would not be the best moment to visit them, but of course, they approached.

"Look who is being a hard worker. Hello there, my friends."

"Hello there and welcome, it's a nice surprise to see you both. I did not expect such a surprise," Chris grinned.

"It is your pleasure to be here, but perhaps we came at the wrong moment since you are working," Vic replied.

"Greetings, Chris. It's a pleasure to see you," Emily greeted with a smile.

"Greetings, Emily, you look good together and happy as well. No, Vic, it's all fine, don't worry about it. We were about to take a break, so no worries. Come in."

Otto appeared from behind the house, sweat pouring from his brow as he had just finished stacking wood.

"Look who is here, welcome you both. Wow, what a pleasure. I am so happy to see you two together."

"The pleasure is all ours," Emily and Vic cooed.

"Sit down, please," Chris requested, gesturing at the chunks of wood.

They all took a seat, basking in the sun.

"My friends, welcome. Should I bring some beer for you, or do you prefer something else?" Otto asked.

"No, my friend, water would be fine," Vic replied.

"Water? How come? Are you ill or something?" Chris asked, looking at Vic as if he had gone completely mad.

"No, my friend, I am not ill. I just don't want to drink anymore," Vic replied.

"Somebody is becoming a real family man, huh?" Otto grinned.

"Tell us, dear friends, what is new with you? How have you been?" Chris asked.

"We got married last night," Emily blurted, excited to share the news.

"Married, you can't be serious, where are our invitations?" Otto asked through a frown.

"Hold your horses now, both of you. We got married alone. Oni was our best bird," Vic explained.

"Ha-Ha, I knew that bird will never leave your side," Chris chuckled.

"Well, I am happy for the both of you, but how did you get married without a priest? I do not understand," Otto asked.

"Well, we did not need the priest; we did it by ourselves, the vows and everything," Vic explained.

"This is the first time in my life that I have heard that some couple got married all by themselves. To be honest, I am impressed and a bit disappointed, because you should have called us. Let's say tomorrow I get married and I don't invite anybody, not even Otto, how would he feel?" Chris asked.

"He is right, my love," Emily explained as she looked at Vic and thought for a moment.

"My sincere apology to the both of you. We did not think this through; it was all about the volcano of emotions that we have for each other, and it somehow took us further, so we did it," Emily explained, looking at Chris.

"No need to apologies, but I have an idea and you will love it, I think…" Chris began.

"Let's hear it, please!" Vic replied.

"What if I go and invite Emily's parents, Vincenzo, Mile, Ben with his family, some other people that we love and respect, and after all that, I invite the priest and do the proper marriage for both of you. It will be at our expense, because nobody will believe you when you tell them that you got married all by yourselves," Chris explained.

"That sounds like a good idea to be honest, but I cannot decide alone," Emily looked back at Victor. "What do you think about this, my love? Should we do it or just continue as it is?"

"To be honest, I do not know what to say. That is so generous of you two, but after all, it is not about money, it's just that we did get married," Vic replied.

"I am sorry for interrupting, but I think that Chris is right. After all, you are our best friend, and you deserve a proper marriage, my friend. In the end, we will not live a thousand years, so I think that you should accept this offer from us. We will have a little celebration, with a total of twenty to thirty people. Chris will organize and call people. You two stay here with me until the evening that we make it happen, what do you say?" Otto asked.

"Do you want this, my love?" Vic asked, looking to Emily.

"I do, I think both of them are right."

"I should get going. If you need to rest, both of you go to sleep, because in the evening we will drink and celebrate until the late hours, perhaps until dawn," Chris advised.

"Off you go, now. Chris, while they sleep, I will go to purchase all the food and drinks needed for this special night. And Chris, don't forget to find the musicians," Otto replied.

"Don't worry, I got this," Chris replied before standing up.

"I should get going too, now you have a good rest. See you tonight."

Chris and Otto both set about getting everything organized.

"Emily, my love, I feel like this is our day and may it be the best day of our lives, my darling. Should we head to sleep?" Vic said, stroking Emily's hand gently.

"It will be perfect, I am sure of it. We should sleep, because we have a long night before us," she replied, squeezing his hand back.

As Vic and Emily went to sleep, they soon entered a state of dreaming. Each having a different dream. Vic had the same dream, about Emily wearing the white wedding dress and bleeding from her stomach, while Emily had a dream that she was looking at Vic with red eye pupils, which made her scared, and she ran away from him.

While they were sleeping, Chris first went to Emily's parents and let them know. Next, he went to Richard, who, upon hearing the news, became emotional and started to cry, since he did not expect that this would happen so soon. Anna, on the other side, was in a state of shock and rushed to hug Richard.

While they both were crying from the joy that they felt, Chris told them that he must hurry to invite Vincenzo and the rest, and that their arrival was expected at eight o'clock in the evening. Chris then went next door to invite Vincenzo, who was chilling on the balcony. Upon arrival, the guards let him pass, and Chris remembered that he and Otto were rescued by the guards and, in that moment, decided that he should invite them as well. Vincenzo asked Chris what was going on since he had heard Richard and Anna cry out loud. Chris told him that Victor and Emily were getting married tonight, and he was invited to the wedding along with his warriors and guards.

Upon hearing this, Vincenzo yelled, "My god, Vitorio is getting married? Everybody on alert to start having the best night of our lives!"

Chris told him that he was in a hurry to invite the others and asked one of the guards if he could do a small favor and find a priest to get them married. The guard answered, "Of course, I will go right now."

Chris mounted on his horse and went to town to invite Mile and Ben. While he was on his way, the horse grew tired, and Chris did not want to waste any time. He went on foot, sprinting towards Miles' shop, and upon arriving, he was struggling to catch his breath. Both Miles and Ben got worried since they thought that something bad had happened, but Chris told them, "Tonight, both of you, with your families, come to our home. Vic and Emily are getting married. Come at eight o'clock."

Ben and Mile could not believe this. Mile closed the shop and told Ben to go home and get ready. Chris was trying to remember if he had left somebody without an invitation and could not remember, but instead, he called Oni to see if there was somebody that they should invite. Oni did not react, and Chris went home to rest because he became very tired from running around all day.

On the other side, Otto arrived in town and purchased a lot of food and drinks, but one horse could not carry it all, so he decided to whistle for Vic's horse and bring the food and drinks with two horses. He managed it somehow, but it was a massive weight for the horses, and he had to unload them three times and feed them.

,Otto grew tired, but did not give up. Of course, he managed it, arrived home, set the tables, and decorated the place all by himself, while Vic and Emily were still asleep, and Chris fell asleep moments after. It was five o'clock and everything was set and ready. Otto decided to rest on a chair, and moments later, he fell asleep.

He entered a dream, and in his dream, he was in a black carriage with two people, exiting it, right at that moment, thunder struck the carriage, and they escaped. Otto woke up from the sound of the thunder in the dream, and it was seven and a half. He then did not pay much attention to the dream, went to wash up and to wake up the new couple, along with Chris.

Vic was tired from the sleep and more tired from the dream, while Emily was confused due to her dream, but they both decided not to pay attention to their dreams as well. Chris, upon waking up, was ready for the celebration and remembered that he had forgotten to call the musicians. It was a chaotic situation upon realizing, and he said to himself, "Oni, you drunk raven, how could I rely on you?" Vic decided to have a small talk with Chris and Otto moments before the guests arrived.

"Chris and Otto, I just want to let you know that you two will be my best men in this celebration of ours."

"It was accepted, am I right?" Chris asked.

"Of course you are, I just wanted to let you both know."

Otto fell into Vic's arms and began to cry.

"Thank you, this is true friendship, I am so happy for both of you."

"It is my pleasure and honor to have you both, I think that you should know that," Vic replied.

"The pleasure is all ours, we shall start to greet our first guest now," Chris and Otto replied as they saw Anna and Richard approaching, the first to arrive naturally.

"Greeting our friends, it is a special day for us all; what a decoration, who made all this happen so fast?" Richard asked.

"Welcome, Sir, it is indeed a special day. My friends made it all happen," Vic replied.

Emily bolted towards her parents and hugged them both.

"Mom, Father, this is the happiest day of my life. Thank you for supporting us. I love you both with all my heart."

"We love you too, darling. Of course, we will support you, because love is the most important thing in our lives," Richard replied, his eyes full of tears.

"It is the happiest day of my life, thank you from the bottom of my heart," Emily replied.

"You are our sunshine, let us greet the groom, darling" Richard pulled Victor in for a hug.

"Thank you, Sir. It's a pleasant surprise," Vic explained, a little taken aback by Richard's affection.

"Take good care of my daughter, will you?"

"I will, Sir, I will protect her with all my power."

"Emily, my love…" Anna's voice cracked, and she couldn't muster anything else as the tears would not stop flowing.

Vic looked over at Emily and Anna, and his eyes, too, filled with tears.

"Oh lord, this is getting tense," Richard exclaimed.

"Please be seated. I know it's emotional, but all of this is from joy, so it is justified," Otto tried to butt in.

"Shut up, let them enjoy the moment," Chris replied, elbowing Otto gently in the side.

Otto was speechless due to being winded.

"I wish you two the best together, and may love and respect build your future together," Anna exclaimed, hugging Victor.

"I could not agree more, darling," Richard interjected.

"Here they are, the rest of the guests," Chris declared as he noticed Vincenzo and the other guests arriving.

Vincenzo sauntered over elegantly.

"Vitorio, is it true that you are getting married, my friend, or am I imagining all this?" Vincenzo asked.

"Vincenzo, my friend, I am indeed. Thank you for coming. Without you, it would not make any sense."

"What about us? We are nobody to you, huh?" Chris asked Otto with raised eyebrows.

"Don't do this on my wedding day, you know that without his help, you two would not be here today. So please, show some respect, because I never loved him more than I love you, or I never love you more than I love him," Vic replied sincerely.

"Wise words there, my friends. I am so happy for you, may you two have a long, happy life together and in some years from now have a kid," Vincenzo explained as he hugged Victor.

"Thank you, my dear friend."

As they continued to talk, everybody got seated. The priest arrived two hours later. In the meantime, there was still no sight of Mile and Ben with his family. Vic started to worry, but moments later, they showed up. It made Vic so happy; they greeted each other, and right after, when they were all seated, the situation grew more tense, to the point that they were having a bit too much to drink, including Vic.

After greeting Mile and Ben with his family, Vic went to Emily and signaled the priest that they were ready, but at that moment, a black carriage showed up and but nobody from inside got out. Vic felt like a sword was cutting through his heart, and immediately felt that it must be one of those three or some other member; he wanted the land to open and to make him disappear in those moments.

He did not know what to think, and Vincenzo immediately understood, along with Richard, looking at Vic, while worrying. Vincenzo's guards and warriors were ready to strike, but Vincenzo signaled them to stay still. After a while, the carriage left, and the celebration continued, but Vic knew that deep inside, it was not a good sign.

He did not know what to do or how to react. Vincenzo got up and told him in private that everything would be all right. Vic worriedly replied, "I hope so, my friend, but if they strike, I will strike too."

As the moments passed, Vic was trying to be relaxed, but deep inside, it was freaking him out. Emily did not know what was going on, since she was madly in love. As the priest was getting ready to marry them and proceed with the celebration, the moment he got up, musicians showed up, everybody was cheering and reacting in that moment, knowing that there would be music and the atmosphere would be on fire.

The priest sat down, and everybody started to dance and sing along while somebody drank beer, somebody wine. It was a night to remember. After three hours of dancing and celebrating, there was finally time for the main procedure. The priest got up, and they all gathered as he started.

"Brothers and Sisters, we are gathered here for the marriage ceremony of Emily and Victor. I would ask for some attention and silence from you all, please, so that we shall proceed," the priest began as he looked around the room.

Everyone excitedly took their seats.

"Go on, sorry I got carried away with drinking, my friend Vitorio is getting married," Vincenzo called out.

"The ceremony of marriage brings two people together, to promise to each other the life in good and bad moments, as we all know this is a bond that cannot be broken until death do them part, it is one of the most important things in life since our existence. So before I proceed, if anybody has anything to say about this marriage, please state it now, or be forever silent."

You could have heard a pin drop, that it how silent it was.

"This will take hours. Cut to the chase, please!" Vincenzo slurred.

The priest didn't even look at Vincenzo and continued.

"So, I should start with the vows. Victor, do you take Emily to be your loyal and truthful wife in good and bad, in hard times of sorrow and in moments of joy until death separates you?"

"I do," Vic replied.

"Emily, do you take Victor to be your loyal and truthful husband in good and bad, in hard times of sorrow, and in moments of joy, until death separates you?" the priest continued.

"I do," Emily replied eagerly.

"I now pronounce you Husband and Wife, Victor, you may kiss your bride."

Vic leant in and kissed Emily, who was shaking from head to toe with happiness.

As they experienced the official kiss, her parents, along with Vic's friends, Vincenzo, and literally everybody else, were in tears of joy; the music was the most intense, and they were all dancing together, pretty drunk. Vincenzo was among the happiest ones and could not believe that this was happening. It all felt like a dream to him, seeing Vic and Emily having their moments, and everybody around; it was all unexpected and fast.

"How could this be? My friend, Vitorio, is getting married," he whispered to himself as all the flashbacks from his youth resurfaced in his head when he saw his uncle Pietro getting married.

It was a nostalgic moment for him. "What a moment," he whispered to himself. Vincenzo, soon after that, felt the tears falling down his cheeks and approached Vic and Emily to be the first one to congratulate them. As he was approaching, Chris was looking at him with a sense of jealousy, while Otto was just being happy without any ill-centered thought. While Vincenzo was approaching, Vic caught the expression that Chris had and somehow knew that it would cause tensions, since he knew how Chris behaved in these kinds of situations, but there was nothing that he could do at the moment.

Until it escalated, but in the other direction.

Vincenzo ran over and grabbed Vic by the shoulders.

"Vitorio and Emily, you two love birds got married. Is this a dream, my friend?"

"Vincenzo, my friend, without you all we would not have the best wedding celebration ever," Vic replied, pulling Vincenzo into a hug.

"May the Lord be with you all, since this is the best wedding that I have ever seen in my entire life," the priest cried as he swiped tears from his eyes.

"I guess that everybody at some point is about to cry. This is history right there, kids should learn in school about this," Emily declared.

"And I should write a book myself, calling it "The Romance of Victor and Emily," Vincenzo chimed in, grinning from ear to ear.

"You should indeed, include us all and everything that we went through," Vic added.

"Let's raise a glass, all of you, since this conversation, I am afraid that it will last for days," Richard cried, lifting his glass.

"Ha-Ha, I think it should, Sir, indeed," Vic chuckled.

Otto approached Vic and Emily.

"May you two be happy for eternity, I wish from the bottom of my heart. I wish you two the best. This is for you from me, it's just a small gift with a letter inside," Otto said as he handed Vic a letter.

Vic pulled Otto into a hug.

"Thank you, my dear friend. I cannot wait to read it, Otto. I am very thankful for everything that you did."

"It is my pleasure, we should raise a glass indeed, as Richard said. Come on, everybody."

"Cheers to Victor and Emily, may their love last forever and ever, and may this night be the beginning of lasting love." Everyone cried, glasses raised.

"May I say something?" Chris asked, stepping forward.

"Please go ahead, Chris, my friend," Vic replied.

"I know sometimes I can cause scenes for everybody, and they are unpleasant…" Chris started, his voice beginning to tremble. "…but I always loved you as my brother, and I want you to know that I wish you nothing but happiness and love. Sometimes my tongue is sharp, but I apologies in front of you all, and may you two be happy and treat each other with love and respect. Cheers." Chris raised his glass as tears flowed down his face.

Vic beamed and threw his arms around Chris.

"Aw, Chris, my friend, thanks you for those beautiful words. I love you two like my brothers, and you will always be my friends. I am happy to have you all in my life, every one of you, but let's not forget that without you all this night would not this perfect."

Vincenzo beckoned to Vic.

"Vitorio, just to let you know that before the dawn, I have a gift for you," he whispered.

"Vincenzo, my dear friend, haven't you done too much already? It was not necessary."

"It is just a symbol, nothing too much, do not worry about it."

"Thank you so much, I appreciate it like always," Vic replied.

"We all do have something for the lovebirds, I guess," Richard chimed in.

Emily clinked her glass to get the crowd's attention.

Ladies and gentlemen, I am sorry to interrupt your conversations, but I want to let you all know that we have a young writer among us, and I think that he deserves the attention. Please welcome our boy, Carl, here. There is something that he wants to share with us."

"Oh, no…" Carl replied, his face flushing scarlet.

"Go, my son, you are a little special guest, let them know how it all started, my boy. Share with us all what you are working on," Ben shouted.

"Father, I am shy to talk," Carl muttered back.

"Go, my darling, you got this. I have faith in you."

Carl stepped forward sheepishly, looking at his feet.

"Victor and Emily, I wish you the best in life and may you be happy together forever…" Carl took a deep breath as he looked up at the sea of faces. "My name is Carl, and it all started when Victor made it possible for me to pursue my passion in life. It is a long story, but it is all thanks to him and to my parents. I believe that every one of us

364

should do what they love and what makes them happy. For me personally, it is writing. I want to let you all know that I finished my first book, it is a story of a man and wolves, and it is a gift to Victor, my hero and the one who made all this happen."

Tears of joy poured from Carl's eyes as he ran to Vic and hugged him.

Applause and cheers filled the room.

"Thank you, little friend. I cannot wait to read it. We will do everything that we can to let the world know about your book and the ones that will come after this one. Well done, Carl," Vic praised, tousling Carl's hair.

Ben wiped the tears from his face and pulled Elke in close.

"My love, our son made it. Is this true, or am I dreaming?"

"It seems like a dream, I cannot believe it, nor are there any words to express this happiness," Elke replied.

"Everybody, it is time to dance and drink. Let's celebrate, because there are a lot of reasons to do so," Vic cried.

Love was in the air indeed. Vic grabbed Emily, and they started to dance, making the atmosphere more lively and catchy. As they danced, they both started to drink like there was no tomorrow. Emily, after the third drink, started to feel the alcohol kicking in, and it made her more in the mood. She whispered in Vic's ear, "If only you knew what I want to do to you tonight."

Vic started to laugh and immediately imagined in his mind how it would look, looking at her with sparkly eyes. He replied, "If I knew it, then it would have no point. You will let me know, won't you?" She just smiled and blushed as they continued to dance.

Soon after, Vincenzo joined, holding a bottle of wine and drinking from it pretty fast. He started to jump around and dance like a pirate. The expression in his eyes was so powerful that it could move a mountain. As the rest were motivated to dance as well, they all formed a circle and started to enjoy the moment. Little Carl secretly stole a beer and hid to drink it. He drank it fast and then stole another. Upon exiting the corner of the kitchen where he was hiding, the alcohol got to him so fast. Ben noticed it and laughed; he decided not to criticise his son, since this was a once-in-a-lifetime celebration.

In those moments, Carl started to walk towards the crowd, but could not walk properly and was losing his balance. Vic noticed it and grabbed his hand, inviting him to dance, telling him through a joke, "You did try it, didn't you, little sneaky boy?"

Carl started to smile and did not answer because he wanted to enjoy the moment. After Carl joined, Ben and Elke started to dance too, while Mile was the only one sitting and looking at them all having fun. In his mind, he was missing something that he did not prefer to talk to anyone about. Deep inside, he was missing his wife, whom he had lost many years ago. Ben tried to make him dance, but it was an unsuccessful attempt.

Upon feeling the sense of nostalgia, Mile was the first one to leave the celebration. He left a note on the table and, on top of the note, a brand-new handcrafted axe for Vic. Anna and Richard, on the other hand, were dancing with Emily and trying to keep her in balance due to her overdrinking from joy, but did not notice anything unusual in her because she was overflowing with emotions. At that moment, Anna felt a little bit of sadness in her heart because she would not get to see her daughter every day. It was hard for her to let her go that fast. Vic was looking at them dance while he was having a few drinks with Vincenzo, Otto and Chris. As Mile was leaving, he did feel regret and came back; at least he wanted Vic to let him know that he wished to leave. As he was approaching, Ben just took a few steps back and did not intervene.

Mile approached Vic, placing a hand on his shoulder.

"Victor, I just want to congratulate you and your bride, Emily. May you have the best time of your lives. I feel like I should get going, my dear friend."

"Mile, why leave so soon? Is everything as it should be?" Vic asked.

"It is, of course, all is good. I just feel like I should go because I feel tired, and I had a very long day. Sincere apologies, I hope you can understand. I left something for you at the table. It is just a symbolic gift for you," Mile replied, gesturing towards the table.

"Oh, Mile, there was no need for that. I did notice that you did not dance and barely had a drink. I do not want to get into details, but I do hope that you are all right."

"I am, do not worry about it. Dancing is not really my thing, and I do not prefer drinking, so thank you for such a beautiful celebration."

Mile hugged Vic goodbye and waved at the rest on his way out.

Vic watched him leave, searching his mind for reasons for Mile's strange behavior.

He spotted Ben and approached him.

"Ben, what is happening with Mile? Do you have any idea what might be going on? He seems a little off," he asked.

"To be honest, I do not know because he never shares anything with me in particular. God forbid, he talks about his personal life, all I know is that I heard rumors that he lost his wife, Antonia, a few years ago. There are a lot of versions of the story, and I do not know which one is true," Ben replied.

All happiness drained from Vic's face for a moment.

"I understand now. I never thought that Mile would be the type of person who would smile or be talkative, but in this case, there is something deeper that is making him sad; however, there is nothing that we can do about it. I wish there was."

"To be honest, I know how it feels because I work with him every day, but there is absolutely nothing that can be done. It is better to leave it as it is, and not to mention this to him."

"I agree with you there."

Suddenly, Emily came tumbling into Vic, holding his chest to steady herself.

"My darling, you know the world is spinning around me. It feels good, but I feel strange," she babbled.

Vic pulled her closer and chuckled.

"Ha-ha, Emily, my love, that is because you had way too many drinks. This is only the first phase; the upcoming ones are not that good."

"What do you mean by the first phase? What is next?" she asked as she tried to stop herself from wobbling.

"You will see in no time, my love. The same world that is spinning right now will start to crumble in the upcoming hours."

"Oh, dear lord, what should I do in that case?" Emily asked, clutching her face melodramatically.

"Do your best to keep calm and wait for it since it cannot be avoided."

"Will do, my love. Have you seen the mead by any chance? I cannot see properly, my vision is blurry," Emily asked as she squinted and looked around.

"It is down the hall, left. Be careful while you walk, you might trip and fall."

Chris overheard and came over, trying to guide Emily by the arm to a nearby chair.

"Emily, sit down, please. You are drunk. Victor, do not let her do this; she will fall ill. It is her first time being drunk."

"I am afraid it is a little too late for that; there is nothing that I can do," Vic explained.

"At least you could stop her from drinking more," Chris replied, scowling at him.

"There has to be a first time for everything; her being drunk is not a problem at all. There are other things that worry me."

Chris was lost for words at Vic's flippancy and just stared.

As the night was progressing, nobody wanted it to end, but dawn was getting closer. Everyone except Vic had far too many drinks, and one by one, they all fell asleep. Richard and Anna were in the left corner of the living room, lying on the couch, Anna holding his hand while he snored. In the right corner of the same room, Ben and his family were sleeping, while Carl was vomiting outside. Chris and Otto were fighting not to sleep, but eventually they fell asleep too, pretty soon. Vincenzo was outside, looking at the sky while he was lying down on the grass. Vic took Emily to their room while she was fighting the alcohol in her system. In those moments, she had reached the peak phase of being drunk, meaning that she was in intense pain. Vic tried to talk to her, but she was not able to do anything, and all she wanted was for the effects to pass away. As the dawn was at its peak, Vic went outside and left Emily there, while she was entering the state of sleeping. Lucky for her, until she wakes up, she will not have to worry about the aftermath of alcohol.

Vincenzo heard somebody stepping outside and, with a tired voice, he asked, "Vitorio, is that you?"

"It is me, my friend. How are you feeling? You drunk too?" Vic replied as he crossed the grass to sit next to Vincenzo.

"Not that drunk, Vitorio. I feel happy, you know, there are no words that would describe how I feel. It's all about caring for somebody, and then when they are happy, you are happy too for them." Vincenzo grinned.

"It usually should be that way between people who build strong relations. Oh man, I cannot believe that I got married, but something worries me deep inside. I hope that everything goes as it should," Vic replied, looking up at the stars.

"Do not worry, my friend. I will do the best that I can to keep you all safe. Perhaps you should consider leaving this place and start a new life with Emily."

"I should, but I cannot leave you behind. What about Chris, Otto, and Emily's parents?"

"Do not worry about me or them. In the end, everybody lives their own lives. You do not owe anything to anyone; you should seek your happiness. What about moving for a couple of years and then coming back after all this is settled down?"

"I do not know, because Richard offered to help us move to France. But what if something bad happens to Chris or Otto, or to you, even though you have your own guards and warriors? You never know what could happen," Vic replied, nibbling his lip as he thought of all the potential for chaos.

I understand your point, but again, if you keep worrying about other people and putting yourself in last place, you will end up having no dreams in the end, because your life will not be in the first place, and you will constantly live for others. If not for you, do it for Emily.

Just go, and, of course, I am able to come to visit you from time to time, sometimes alone and sometimes with everybody."

"Thank you dearly, my friend. I will consider your offer. It would mean the world to me if Emily were safe, you know? Because if something happens to her, I'd rather be dead."

"Nothing will happen, my friend. Come here, lie down on the grass next to me and let's gaze at the stars. They say every star has a special power. Perhaps it is your time to choose your star and make a wish, you know, it may come true eventually."

Vic lay back in the grass, gazing at the sky in wonder.

"Ah, the stars, the moon, and the sun, aren't they magnificent? What a pity that the dawn is close, and we have only a little time to watch the perfection of what nature gave to us. If we only valued it more."

Vincenzo let his head drop back into the grass to stargaze with Vic.

"I wish people would think like us more often. The world would be a better place for us all, but anyhow, it is what it is. You see that star up north?"

"I do see it; it is shiny and beautiful, full of something mystical, I guess, since it's different from the rest."

"Well done, there. They say it is the star of a rebirth and spiritual progress. The ancient nations believed it. Even Odin himself, even though he was not into stars, said he preferred a different sense of spirituality."

"The Nordic Mythology is very rich and powerful, yet there is too much to learn from it. I did not know that you were into that kind of mythology. I thought you preferred the Roman one."

Vincenzo chuckled.

"Ha-ha, Roman mythology is full of drama and things that I do not like, but they had their own pros and cons as well."

"I guess then this star is my favorite and I shall make a wish."

"From here to Valhalla, you should have your wish granted then."

Vic closed his eyes and made a wish.

"Valhalla, you say, what a perfect way to express the heavens," Vic replied.

"Let's not talk about this in front of anyone. You know how Christianity has its domination here."

"Of course, it is between us. I think that I might fall asleep here, Vincenzo. I do not know about you," Vic yawned.

"Of course, sleep well. Eventually, I will fall asleep, too. Pretty soon as well."

"Sleep tight, I hope nobody will wake us up."

"We will see…"

As Vic was closing his eyes from tiredness, he was slowly entering a state of dreaming. Shortly after, he entered another realm. In his dream, he was seeing fjords and the never-ending ocean from the bird's perspective. While he was flying, he soon became aware that it was a dream, and as he was getting the grip of his senses, he was able to control this lucid dream. Everything around him felt pure and beautiful. He was looking around and trying to call for Oni, but Oni was never to be found in his dream. While flying, he saw dark clouds from a distance and did not want to avoid them.

Instead, he went straight through the clouds to feel the rain and see the thunder. Little did he know that it would not be fun at all. Upon entering the dark clouds, his position started to shift from left to right as he was being tilted by another force. The clouds felt heavy and unbearable while the rain was about to form and fall. Vic tried to escape those dark clouds, but the force was too strong and it could not let him go.

As the rain started to fall, every drop felt like a burden on his shoulders, and he started to feel pain, the intense pain that words could not express. Soon after, the thunder started raging around him, which made it even harder for him to resist. Every strike had a sensation of burning to the core. Vic, from pain, started to cry, and in that state of mind, he even began to beg for it to end. Not very long after, a voice from the sky was heard, saying, "There are always two ways in life to choose, either this one, or the one that you felt good about before you decided to enter the dark."

Vic was confused and in intense pain. Upon hearing the voice, he could barely answer, but managed to utter some words, "Please, make it stop. I did not want this," he replied.

The voice insisted on convincing Vic that it was right, "Now, as I will let you go, remember that you always can choose between darkness and the light."

The voice disappeared, and Vic was woken up by a farmer nearby who was relocating his cattle, while Vincenzo was still in a deep sleep. Vic opened his eyes and felt a terrible pain in his head and chest; he could not seem to shake the sensation of the dream. It left him speechless. He just stayed there, lying down on the grass, while Vincenzo was about to wake up. Vic was thinking that maybe the voice from the sky could be right. *But on the other hand, everything in life gives you a choice, but sometimes you have no choice,* he whispered to himself.

Vincenzo opened his eyes and looked to his right, seeing Vic still there.

"Vitorio, how was your sleep? I had a terrible dream, by the way, I am glad I woke up."

"You are not the only one, for that matter. I had a pretty bad nightmare myself," Vic replied, staring at the clouds.

"Well, if you want, you can tell me what it was about."

"Of course, I will share it with you. It was all perfect in the moment, I was flying and enjoying it, and all of a sudden I saw dark clouds and out of curiosity I wanted to feel the rain and thunder, you know? It tortured me to the core, but that is not all, because I heard a voice from the sky, telling me that I can always choose between good and bad. I am so glad that I woke up because I was in terrible pain," Vic explained.

"Oh, Vitorio, that voice from the sky is haunting you to the core. It must mean something; it is not just an imagination, you know? Perhaps you should be careful when you choose a path in your life, and always think twice before you choose, since everything can have its own symbolism."

"I understand, but sometimes life leaves you with no choice, you know."

"I understand what you are referring to, but please be careful, because now it is expected of you. You are a husband now, and one day you will become a father."

"You are right, to be honest. I have no argument there, whatsoever. What about your dream? You want to share it with me?" Vic asked.

"Thank you. Well, I had a dream in which I saw a beast roaring at night, and it was a bloodthirsty one, human alike, but stronger and faster. To my surprise, it did not do me any wrong. It just looked at me as if it knew me somehow, with those deep red eyes and long hair, dressed in black."

Emily emerged from the house looking disheveled.

"My darling, why are you lying on the grass?" she called out.

"Emily, my love, how are you feeling today?" Vic asked, lifting his head to look at her.

Emily clutched her head.

"You were right. I feel barely alive, having a terrible headache, and everything around me is making me nervous. I even argued with Chris. Vincenzo, is that you?"

"It is me, Emily, yes. Drink some water, it will help you," Vincenzo replied.

Vic returned to staring at the clouds.

Memories of his moments with Leonard flashed through his mind.

"Oh, how I wish Leonard was here. What a mistake I made, I will never forgive myself…"

"Who is Leonard, my love?" Emily asked innocently.

"Was…" Vic replied.

Emily's jaw dropped.

"Oh… then there is nothing that you can do. Listen, love, I am about to go for a swim in the river; hopefully it will help me recover a bit."

"Go for it, my love, it certainly will… Wait, why did you argue with Chris?" Vic asked as he propped himself up on his elbows to look at Emily.

"Because he was annoying me with his 'I told you not to drink and such' speech."

"But he was right, my love, sometimes you have to listen to people who wish you good."

"Just leave me alone, you two. It was my wedding night, and I wanted to drink," Emily replied, rolling her eyes and turning to go.

"As you say, my darling. If you ask me, you can drink day and night," Vic called to Emily as she strutted off into the trees.

"Well, she really got some temper there…" Vincenzo said after some time.

"She is in love; I do not blame her, bless her soul. She is my love, so as a man I try my best to understand her."

"She is so lucky to have you, my friend. You are full of understanding and respect."

"Thank you, my friend. Could you please continue to talk about that dream of yours? It sounds interesting and pretty strange."

"Oh, as I was saying, wait, I forgot most of it now. I just remember that it was a creature, human-like, as I told you, and it did not do me any harm. But I had the feeling that it recognized me somehow, as if it wanted to tell me something. I am not sure."

"Did it remind you of somebody?" Vic asked.

"Yes. It did indeed, but I saw deep sadness in those eyes. He was looking for somebody, three people in particular, and he was seeking revenge."

"I see, perhaps that dream of yours must mean something deep as well. Should we get up and see what the rest are doing? Or perhaps we should let them wake up by their own."

"I do not know, but we will see about the dream. Let them sleep, they sure need it," Vincenzo replied as he lay his head back in the grass and let his eyes flutter closed.

As the day was progressing, nobody woke up before noon; the first one to wake up was Chris, who got out of the house and had a terrible headache. Following Chris was Ben, and then, one by one, around four o'clock, everybody was at their own homes.

Vic did not want to wait for Emily, but he was the only one to start cleaning his house. It was a mess inside and outside, and it took him five hours to tidy up the place. As he grew tired, he sat on the chair and started to worry about Emily. The moment that he was thinking about her, there she was at the door. She was still nervous, so he decided not to bug her. As she was still having a hard time recovering, Emily just went straight to bed, still having a deep hangover. Vic chose based on his feelings that maybe it would be best to go for a walk, since he also needed a break.

As he was leaving the house, Emily asked him, "Where are you going, my love?"

Vic answered, "Just for a walk, I will be home before sunset."

Vic left the house and went out. While walking, he felt strange, and somehow, he was being haunted by the dream that he had that morning; he was not being haunted only by his dream, but by Vincenzo's dream as well. Vic thought for a moment that maybe it could have some meaning, but he was not able to figure it out for sure.

As he was continuing through the narrow street, he thought he saw something, something like a shadow. He did not hesitate to move further, and there it was again: a black shadow of somebody or something. Vic decided to sprint, hoping that he could catch it somehow, but the shadow was faster than anybody could even imagine.

In that moment, Vic felt scared, as if he was having a moment of intuition that something was about to happen, but he was not sure what or when. Being scared and cautions, he started to think that maybe it was time to pay a visit to the Temple of Justice. But then, he stopped walking and thought for a moment about whether it was a terrible idea to do so.

Right then, a noise from above the building was heard. A big piece of wood was about to fall. Vic took a swift moment and backed up several steps as the piece of wood fell on the ground. He looked up and there it was again, the shadow. He decided to move along, but this time with extreme caution since he started to figure out that something was chasing him.

Perhaps it was the creature from Vincenzo's dream; he then proceeded by entering the center of the town, where there were a lot of people, perhaps there he would get a better look at the shadow, hoping that the shadow would not hurt civilians. As he was walking through the crowd, several parts of metal and wood fell again from above. Vic got furious even though nobody was hurt, and he decided to run after the shadow, jumping through the market tables and climbing through everything that he could. He just wanted to know where this shadow would lead him.

As Vic was sprinting, he crashed into a lady's little shop and destroyed her entire place. All the fruits and vegetables were on the floor; he did not have the time to stop and apologies to her, but only said "sorry" as he was running. But as it seems, he could not catch the shadow and was left with more questions than answers. In that moment, he stopped to catch his breath as his heart was racing.

He saw the clear sunset and remembered that he had told Emily that he would be home by then. Vic could not sprint anymore, so he just stole a horse nearby and did not care much as he mounted on that horse and rushed to get home. Upon arriving, he saw a black carriage again. He got very mad and rushed the horse to follow the carriage, but one horse against six could not match the speed.

He was about to explode inside as he was looking at the carriage disappear in the distance. He left the horse and got home. Upon opening the door, he saw Emily sitting by the table, half-naked, waiting for Vic. He reacted with a surprised look on his face and understood what was about to happen.

As he approached, his heart was on fire, but this time it was racing from pleasure. As they both started to kiss passionately, Vic grabbed her by the hips and positioned her on the table, and there they were, two souls burning by their unlimited love for each other. As they were making love, Emily was reaching her peak, and Vic was looking at her with that sharp edge in his eyes. Both were sweaty and on the limit of heart rate, as Vic was about to reach his peak, she held him tight, grabbed him strong, and everything else was left to time. They both lay down on the bed and hugged each other tight. But Emily could not hold her tongue.

"Are you mad, my love? I can see in your face that something is not right."

Victor paused for a moment.

"Maybe it is too soon, my love. It feels like you wanted to secure me for yourself for the rest of our lives, but that was a very bad move."

Emily couldn't utter a response.

"A married couple should make decisions together, not alone and not in this manner, you know? Because maybe I was not ready, but on the other hand, I have a very high understanding of you, and I do not blame you a bit," Vic explained.

"It was not a selfish act if that is what you are referring to. I just wanted us to have a baby, that is all," Emily whispered, unable to meet his eye.

"But it's our first day of marriage, isn't it a bit absurd to rush things that fast?" Vic asked.

"I mean, I don't know, but I just felt it. It was stronger than me, maybe it won't work, so there you go, you will get your wish granted," Emily explained as she glanced at Vic.

"What wish? What are you talking about? Do you think that I do not want us to grow into a family?"

"Judging by your behavior, I do not think that it is your priority at this moment," Emily snapped.

Vic frowned.

"How can you be so selfish, Emily? The first day of marriage, and you act like a little child, you know life is not about having everything that you want right now. Everything takes time, and you do not care what others think; you just do what you think is right. Starting with arguing with people and now this, I do not understand how you plan to progress in your future if you continue to behave like this."

"You may be right. It was my mistake, but I did it out of love. I swear that I did not have bad intentions. Sometimes, I feel that I might lose you, so those feelings do not let me have my peace of mind," she explained as she looked at the floor.

"How on earth do you think that you can lose me? That would only happen if I die or somebody kills me, you think that I would leave or such?"

"Maybe the love that you have for me, eventually, can fade away."

"Nonsense, Emily, you are talking nonsense. From the moment I saw you, I knew that you would be the one that I would give my love and my everything to, for as long as I live and beyond," Vic gushed.

Emily pulled Vic into a firm hug.

"My darling, I love you. Please forgive me for being suspicions."

"I love you more, and it's not a big deal now, my love. But please, next time, if there is something that is troubling you, just let me know. There is nothing in this world that we cannot fix together, you know, that's what love is about, and it should be that way. Otherwise, we would not be together just for the sake of being married and having kids, because there would be no point."

"So, you are not mad after all? What if I get pregnant?"

"In that case, I would work day and night to give our kid what I did not have as a child, and what kind of husband or father I would be if I got mad over such things?"

Victor left Emily speechless once more.

"I think I need some air. Excuse me, my love, there is too much going on. I have to clear my mind if that is okay with you," Vic asked as he stood up.

"Go, but don't come late, please. I will be missing you," Emily replied, planting a kiss on his cheek.

As Vic was leaving, he opened the door and went outside. But he could not believe what he was seeing. From the distance Eddie was approaching, Vic's heart started to race; he did not have any weapon by his side and was not prepared. Of course, he did not expect this to happen, so as Eddie was getting closer, Vic was fearing that it would be a bloodbath.

But to his surprise, Eddie lowered his hands and told him, "Do not worry, I am here just to talk."

Vic felt a little ease, but still feared that something bad would happen. Eddie explained that he had nothing to do with this and that Anthony had planned all this, starting from the black carriage.

As Vic was trying to believe him, but he asked, "Can we please talk? Because I have a lot of questions to ask?"

Eddie answered, "If there is somebody in your home, please do not leave them out of your sight. We should talk here," Eddie said.

"What do you suggest I do in this case? What are they planning? Why are they following me? What do they want from me?" Vic asked, his head in pieces.

Slow down, Victor. I will explain everything to you. Just please, don't pressure yourself. I tried to talk with him, but it seems they want to shake your world. A lot of time has passed since you did not show up, nor Chris or Otto. All of you are on their list, my friend. I have nothing to do with this. I did this on my own because I believe that you are a good and honest man. I could not stand back and see them take you all down."

"What do you mean, take us all down? What the fuck are you talking about? What did I ever do wrong to them?"

"You broke the promise. You were supposed to stay loyal to them until the end. Have you forgotten your oath? Just trust me, I can arrange an escape for you all before dawn."

"I am not scared of anybody. I will not escape or run from anybody if they want to face me like real men, so let it be. But if they are cowards and will stab me in the back, that is their problem, not mine. I was loyal and I did everything they asked from me, but I decided not to work for them anymore." Victor explained plainly.

"But you did not even tell them that. I suppose it's too late now. If you do not want my help, then do as you wish; I will not force you. But there will be consequences beyond your imagination, because I know what they are capable of doing."

"Let there be, what it must be. I will say it again, and I hate to repeat myself, I am not afraid of anybody, let them come to me if they are as strong as they think they are."

"I understand. Do you have any further questions? Or should I go? Because, as far as I can see, I am not welcome."

Emily heard their voices and poked her head out of the door.

"Victor, my love, is everything all right? Who are you talking to? Invite the man inside, please. It's getting cold outside now."

"It's okay, my love. It's a friend of mine, we used to work together. We are just catching up. I will be home soon, love you," Victor called.

"All right then, darling, as you say. I love you more, my love," Emily called back as she disappeared back inside the house.

"For god's sake, Victor, do it for her. I did not know that you got married, but just trust me," Eddie begged.

Vic thought for a moment.

"What can I do, Eddie? If all that you are saying is true, do you think that they will not find me wherever I go?"

"I know, but it should not be like this. I always respected you, you were a kid when I found you…" Eddie's voice began to tremble. "It would kill me if something happens to you."

"Well, it will kill me, too. I will do my best to defend myself; perhaps I will take them down before they take me down."

Eddie searched the trees for shadows.

"I should go before they catch me, because I am risking my life here. I will try to talk to them, but there is no chance on earth that Anthony will listen. By the way, just to let you know, Peter is on your side along with Jakob, but Anthony is manipulating them both."

"That son of a bitch, I knew that he was evil from the beginning. I cannot leave Emily alone, but if I can, I will manage to hire guards and warriors to protect her. She will be mad at me, because she does not know any of this."

"I will arrange her protection, if you want. At least let me do that, so you can go and talk to them. What do you say?" Eddie asked.

"When can you make it happen? I accept your offer because I have no other choice."

"In two hours from now, you'd better explain all this to her. I am leaving now. Take your weapons with you once you leave. See you soon," Eddie explained as he set off running.

"Do it as fast as you can. I will be inside, talking to her," Vic called after him.

Vic opened the door and was thinking of a way to explain all this to Emily, but was captivated by the fear. Because of all these unexpected events, he could not think straight and was confused, but that did not stop him from approaching her in the most romantic manner. Since her heart was pure and the love that she had for him was gentle. Vic asked her how she was feeling, and she replied, "I have never felt happier in my entire life."

In that moment, he was not sure if he should smile or cry, and decided to remain calm for a while and to act like nothing was wrong. But holding it all back was suffocating him. "What do you think if we move somewhere, my love?" he asked her with a calm voice.

"Where would we go, my love?" she answered.

"Perhaps somewhere far away," he said.

Emily was confused at that moment and did not know what was going on. She did not take his question seriously and continued to look at him, imagining their future together, how they would go through the streets of Vienna with their small child, and how people would admire them even more.

In her imagination, she also saw other girls being jealous of her and looking at Vic with envy. She did not talk at all, but continued to look at him. Moments later, she told him, "I love you, and I will love you for the rest of my life and beyond."

In that moment, Vic's eyes started to shed tears one by one; his heart was racing once again. Emily thought that his tears were those of joy; little did she know that those tears were from fear and sadness, and for everything that was yet to come. Moments later, they both continued as if nothing had happened, and everything seemed normal to Emily.

However, when Eddie arrived, along with ten guards. In that moment, Emily knew that something was not right. Just as Eddie knocked on the door, she started to question Vic about what was going on.

"What is this, Victor? What the hell is happening? Is this the reason you did not want kids now with me?" Emily asked, desperate for answers.

Just at that moment, Eddie rapped on the door.

"Can I come in?" he called.

"Come on in, stranger. Of course, maybe you will explain to me what the fuck is going on here?" Emily cried out, "Since I do not know anything, perhaps my husband here thinks that I should not know?" she hissed, her glare fixed on Victor.

Eddie stepped into the house.

"Calm down, please, Mrs. Emily. I will explain everything to you," he reassured Emily as he called back to the guards. "Please guard the house."

Vic approached.

"Eddie, thank you. At least now I can go in peace and talk with Anthony. Hopefully, he will understand, and if you have to leave, go, because Emily will be safe here as long as the guards are here. So please, explain everything to her," he pleaded.

"You are not going anywhere, my love, until you and only you explain what is going on," Emily interjected.

Vic was frantic.

"There is no time, my love. I wish I could. I did try, but I could not tell you."

"You fucking stay here and talk right now!" Emily yelled.

"Emily, please calm down. Victor used to work for some dangerous men. I work for them too, and I chose to help him out," Eddie explained.

Emily frowned.

"But he told me that he helped people and did not do anything bad or hurt anybody. Didn't you, my love?" she replied as she shot Vic a hurt look.

"I am afraid it is a little more complicated than that. You see, the thing is that Victor used to take down bad people for money, and those bad people were connected to even more worse people that you could never imagine. So, I suggest you stay still until he goes to see if there is something that we can do to stop this madness," Eddie explained.

"What the hell are you talking about? My love did not kill anybody! Victor, please tell me that this is not true? Please tell me that?" Emily looked to Victor with wide, pained eyes.

Vic sighed.

"It is true, Emily. Please forgive me, I never thought this would happen. But I promise you, I will do my best to make things right, I swear."

Tears tumbled down Emily's cheeks.

"What if they hurt me, Victor? What if I am pregnant and they hurt our baby? Who would take the blame? Does my father know about this?"

"He does. He offered to help so that we could move to France together, but I did not know how to explain all this to you. Even though I wanted to, badly."

Eddie cut in, his hand on his head.

"Victor, I wish I knew this before, man. You are on the path to becoming a father? It should not be like this, I think you should go if Emily has nothing against it."

Emily looked away.

"Do as you want, both of you. If I die, I will still love you, Victor, even in another world. Just go and try not to get us in trouble, please."

"You will not die, darling. Do not ever say that, my love," Victor replied, his heart full of sorrow, knowing that he had hurt Emily.

"Go now, Victor. I will stay here with her and guard her in case anything happens." Eddie instructed as he took a seat at the table.

Chapter Nine: I Would Never Hurt My Friend

As Vic was rushing to go, he grabbed his axe and sword, along with the bow and some arrows. He opened the door of the house and went outside. He grabbed a horse by the leash from a guard without any question, mounted the horse and went straight to them. As he was riding the horse, millions of questions rushed through his head. *"What if they kill me, and newly married Emily with a child becomes a widow?"* he thought.

As the night was dark and gloomy, nothing could stop him on his path. He encountered some wolves along the way, but immediately lit up a torch and waved it as he was riding the horse, making the wolves go away. As he was getting closer, lightning struck on his right side and, from the sky, a white circle formed.

Right at that moment, the voice from the sky could be heard, saying: "Do not get in, go back."

Victor could not help but ignore the voice and just told himself, *"You are only in my head, you do not exist,"* he whispered.

Not long after, the voice pressed again, saying, "Run and never look back. If you go in there, the water will turn red."

Vic decided to ignore it again, and before the voice could be heard anymore, the thunder struck three times in a row. Vic dismounted his horse and got closer to the door. As he was about to open it, he felt an intense pain in his chest, and his heartbeat got faster. While not paying attention, he proceeded to move.

As he opened the door, there was nobody inside. This time, nobody greeted him. The corridors were empty walls with not the slightest detail. As he was getting closer to the main room, he saw that some of the walls were damaged, the stairs were half broken, and as he approached the main room, there was nobody inside and nothing inside.

He yelled at that moment, "Anthony, where are you? Is anybody here?"

He could only hear his echo, nothing more. As he climbed and then jumped to pass through the stairs that were missing in order to reach their places, he could hear a sneaky voice around him. He grabbed his axe and was ready to strike if needed. Moments passed, and the steps would only be heard from around him. He held to his axe with a strong grip, and Anthony spoke, saying, "You were the strongest one of us all. Where have you been until now?"

Vic did not feel scared; all that he wanted was to get the chance to explain everything. Instead of answering, he remained silent and was hoping that Anthony would show up so that they could talk.

Anthony then spoke again, "What do you think will happen now, Victor?"

Vic then grabbed his bow and took an arrow, pointing in the direction of the steps. In that moment, he shot an arrow, and Anthony said, "Ha-ha, you think you can scare me, I can sense your anger."

Vic then replied, "Just show up, I mean you no harm."

Anthony stopped moving at that moment and requested that Vic put down his weapons if he wanted to talk. Vic resisted for a moment and then did as he asked. Soon after, Anthony showed up, Vic was shocked to see that he was missing an arm and his left eye. As he was approaching, Vic stood still.

"Look at me, Victor, what do you see in me now?"

Vic looked him up and down.

"A desperate man, somebody that I cannot recognize anymore. What the hell happened to you?" he asked.

"We were ambushed while you were god knows where. How about that, Legendary Victor? How about your promise to us? You left us crippled," Anthony snapped.

"I am so sorry to hear about this. Where are Peter and Jakob? Don't get into promises now because life is unpredictable, and some things in life just change as we progress further in life."

"Like what? What made you turn your back on us? May I know, or is it a secret of yours, perhaps like many others?" Anthony sputtered.

When did I hold secrets from you? Why are you trying to make me feel that I am the one to blame, when you know very well that is not the case? In fact, it has always been you who has been hiding things from me since the beginning and continues to do so."

Anthony took two steps closer to Vic so that they were face-to-face.

"Listen to me, you little prick. We gave you the chance to get your life together, you came here seeking our help, not the other way around. So you better listen to me, or I will chop you up into pieces," he roared as he pointed his finger in Victor's face.

Vic bit his tongue for a moment, knowing that if he didn't, he would lose it.

"Tell me what you have to say," he finally replied.

"What is the reason that you left? Speak right now, I said!" Anthony cried, his spittle raining in Vic's face.

"I fell in love, got married, and I have a child on the way," Vic replied earnestly.

"And what do you think will happen now?" Anthony asked.

"Maybe we could find a solution. Perhaps we could agree on some kind of compromise here," Vic proposed, searching for some sign of the Anthony he used to know.

"You want me to show you some mercy? Are you hearing yourself right now? Are you a little girl, or are you a grown man? This is not a farm where you can leave because you fell in love and changed your life's path. This was the most powerful organization of serving justice to those who could only dream about having justice served in their lives. We risked everything in hopes that you would fucking show up; we did not want to beg you to come. Haven't you seen the black carriage, or did you just decide to ignore it and act like nothing had happened throughout all these years? Everything that we did for you, do you not feel a little ashamed? Look at me, what do I look like right now? A fucking crippled person! I lost everything because of you. You were our best one, and we all relied on you," Anthony sighed. "You left us no choice, Victor."

"Calm down, Anthony. We will figure something out. What do you want me to do, man?"

Anthony's face contorted.

"'Man?' You are calling me man? We did not go to school together, 'mate.' Shame on you, Victor, and even more shame on us because we trusted you."

"What the fuck do you want me to do?" Vic roared, losing his temper and slamming his axe into the table, sending splinters and planks of wood flying. "Tell me right the fuck now, because I must know, lives are at stake now!"

Anthony took a step back.

"There is only one way out of this: take it or leave it. If you want your legendary friend to live, your wife and the baby in her belly, you must take down the one who is responsible for this mayhem."

"Who might that be? It would not be a problem for me to accomplish this last mission, just tell me who it is, so that we can settle this up."

"His name is Vincenzo, he lives in a castle."

Vic's eyes widened.

"Stop right there, you want me to eliminate Vincenzo? Are we talking about the Italian businessman who moved here from Italy?"

"Yes, that one, you know him?" Anthony asked.

Vic remembered himself and let any sign of his love for Vincenzo drain from his face.

"No, I really don't. I just saw him two or three times in town, but I never had a chance to meet him; he did not strike me as someone who could be capable of doing all this. What is the reason behind all this, Anthony? Or perhaps, it is another secret of yours."

"It is not a secret anymore. I eliminated his wife, Emilia, many years ago because I wanted her only for myself. I was jealous of her beauty and soul. I saw her with him, and I wanted to take her from him. So, the sins of my past caught up with me."

"Oh, that is why... I mean, what the hell, man? How could you be so mean and lusty?" Vic cried.

"I was young and in love, so what I did I do not justify now. But I used to think that it was justified back then. Vincenzo sent five hundred men to take us down, and as you can see, he succeeded."

"I understand. But where the hell did he manage to get all those men? I do not understand half of this story that you are telling."

"The best part of all this is that you do not know him. Trust me."

"At this point, I do not know you. For god's sake, Anthony, you eliminated the love of his life. What did you expect? Perhaps for him to be friends with you?!"

You have eight months to finish the mission; otherwise, there will be consequences that you cannot reverse. And trust me, this time I am giving you more than enough time for all this. I wanted to chop you into pieces because you turned your back on us, but I decided to cool down for the sake of the respect that I always had for you. Do I make myself clear, Victor?"

"Crystal…" Vic whispered, his eyes full of hate.

"Not get lost from my sight. Just go, because I am not glad to see you right now," Anthony requested as he turned from Victor.

Vic left the half-ruined building and could not believe what he heard. While he was walking, the only destination that he wanted to reach as soon as possible was Vincenzo's castle. The moment that he left, he felt a sense of relief that Anthony had given him an eight-month period for this to be done.

But how could Vic do that to his dear friend Vincenzo? He would rather die than hurt him, but there were eight months ahead of him to figure this out. As Vic began to sprint, he forgot that horses exist; he forgot everything. The only thing that he wanted was to talk to Vincenzo, but it was a great distance to reach by sprinting. But Victor did not stop, even though his heart was racing and he grew tired.

As he was slowing down, he started to think about the various solutions to this situation. He knew that time was of the essence to reach the castle, but at least Emily, Chris and Otto, for now, were safe. So, after having that thought, he decided not to sprint anymore. Whenever he reached the castle, Vincenzo would open the door, uncaring of what time it was. Vic thought for a moment that perhaps finding somebody who looks like him would be a good idea. But what was bugging him the most was the question of how Vincenzo would react to all of this? Maybe he would get mad, maybe he will be furious. Or perhaps, he wants to take down Anthony with his own bare hands.

Vic, deep inside him, knew that Vincenzo would never put his, Emily's, or anybody else's life at risk due to the respect that he has for them. Vic continued his journey and stumbled upon a passenger on horseback, stopped him and asked to borrow his horse. He offered that the price would be two hundred golden coins, along with the explanation that it was a serious and urgent matter. But to his luck, the passenger was deaf, and Vic did not have the nerves to waste more time explaining.

He continued to walk further towards his destination. As the clouds were turning grey and the rain was preparing, Vic thought that this would make it even harder because of the exhaustion, but he could not afford to give up or to stop. At a certain point, his mind was occupied by millions of thoughts, and he was desperately trying to find a solution before he reached the castle.

He thought that if he could maybe think of something, all this chaos would be over, and finally they could all live in peace after all, but little did he know, there was no peace, not between Anthony and Vincenzo. Vic moved on and was halfway to his destination, soaked in water as the rain continued to fall, followed by a strong storm and wind, while the thunder was raging on the earth. He was out of energy and fell down on his knees, looking at the sky and hoping for an answer from the universe.

"Just a sign, I beg you," he said with teary eyes.

Soon after, the voice from the sky could be heard again, saying: "Do not sell your soul, because you will never get it back."

Vic got nervous and did not understand what the voice was referring to, and got angry with the voice, following with his answer, "What the hell are you talking about? I would never sell my soul. I just want this nightmare to end."

There was no further voice from that point. And Vic did not know what was going to happen. Hours passed, and he walked with no energy in his body and even less in his mind, but he managed to reach the castle after six hard hours of walking. Upon arriving, the rainbow could be seen, and the sun was drying all that rain on him. He could barely stand on foot, and with a low voice, he was calling, "Vincenzo, Vincenzo, I need to talk to you."

As the guards saw Vic in that state, all of them rushed to grab him and take him inside. He looked like a dying person. One of the guards yelled to call Vincenzo, but he was asleep. When there was no answer, he went inside, rushing, and woke him up. When Vincenzo saw Vic in that state, he could not believe his eyes, while worrying badly.

"Vitorio, what the hell happened? Did somebody die, god forbid?" Vincenzo cried, sitting up in bed.

Victor's legs gave way, and he collapsed onto the chaise longue next to Vincenzo.

"Vin... we need... to ta... talk," he gasped.

"Give him some water, for God's sake, and food too. Vitorio, be patient, we will talk, my friend, you need to recover first."

"Should I go to his house to see if Emily is fine? His friends, too," one of the guards asked.

"Guards, gather up!" Vincenzo bellowed as they rushed towards the living room. "Listen to me now, six of you sprint your horses towards his house and check up on Emily, while the rest of you sprint towards the house of Chris and Otto, go right now!"

"They are fine, we need to talk about Anthony," Vic panted.

"What! What did you say? Or I may have heard that one wrong," he asks, shocked, before turning to call out to his guards. "Guards! Stop! Don't go anywhere." He turned to Vic again, "You know that son of a bitch! Out of respect and love for you, I will give you half an hour to recover, but we really need to talk!" Vincenzo screamed.

"It is not my fault. He wants you dead, and I would never let anything happen to you," Vic wheezed.

He tried to grasp Vincenzo's shoulder, but his hand fell like a lead balloon.

"We will talk. I need to think now, I will be on the balcony. You need rest and recover. Don't forget to eat and drink some water."

As Vincenzo was reaching his balcony, every flashback, every second with Emilia was rushing through his memory. Every tear and every smile, everything that was suppressed for years. He could not understand how Victor knew Anthony, but was patient enough to wait and find out. Tears were forming in his eyes, and soon after, one by one, rolled down his cheeks, remembering how he saw her dead on the floor.

He started to smash the chairs on the balcony and to curse the day that Anthony saw them and did what he did. Vincenzo, at that moment, just yelled on the top of his lungs: "God damn you, Anthony, I will chop you off and feed you to the pigs, you lusty, greedy son of a bitch."

His hands were shaking, and his heartbeat was on fire; he could not stop the rage. Even the guards became scared and could not utter a word. Vincenzo waited for those thirty minutes to pass, as every minute seemed like a year to him. He managed to control his anger and slowly went back to Victor to have this deep conversation, hoping that the bond that they have will never break.

As he was slowly approaching, Vic had gathered a bit of his strength. "Vitorio, now could we talk? Let's start from the beginning. How do you know Anthony? Be specific and tell me every detail, you know that I am your friend and I will always be."

"When I escaped the orphanage with Chris and Otto, we went to them, and I became one of them. I worked for them until I fell in love. Anthony, Jakob and Peter were the heads of the organization, and I trusted them until I started to smell something fishy and everything was clear. But it was a little too late, we brought justice to the people who needed it the most, we took down bad people and got paid for doing so," Victor recalled.

Vincenzo tutted.

"Vitorio, I did not ask you to explain the surrounding story; I asked you to tell me how you know him. Do you know what he did to me?"

"Yes, I know, that's why I came here."

"Then tell me, how do you know him?" Vincenzo pleaded.

"I guess that I do not know him at all."

"Exactly! So, what did he tell you? I suppose you went there to meet them?"

Vic sat up a little.

"Could we talk like friends? I have a feeling that you want to choke me with questions like that."

"I am sorry, Vitorio, you are right there. Please forgive my fury, I know that you are not the one to blame here, you just want to make sure that the ones you love remain safe."

"Including you, who, in this case, is the most wanted one," Vic added.

"Me? How come me? That prick thinks that he can take me down. If he is so brave and dangerous, why doesn't he come and face me?" Vincenzo asked, the rage boiling up inside him.

"Vincenzo, he wants me to kill you; if not, he will take down Emily, Chris and Otto, too."

Upon hearing this, the guards unsheathed their weapons and moved closer.

"Is that so? And what did you decide…" he trailed off as he saw his guards and turned to them. "What the hell do you think you are doing? Lower your weapons," he snapped before turning back to Vic. "Vitorio, tell me everything that he told you, and we will think of something."

"I am tired of everything. I should have never got married, I should have never dragged Emily into this or my friend, or you," Vic sighed.

Vincenzo grabbed Vic by the shoulders.

"Don't say all of that, just try to remain calm as much as you can because everything has a solution, and it is not as dark as you think. If you need more time, take your time. When you are ready, tell me everything in detail so that we can come up with something together."

Vic held his head, trying to make sense of everything that was going on.

I do not need any more time. He just gave me eight months to do it and threatened that he would take down Emily and my friends. But I think that Emily is pregnant and I do not know what to do. I would never let anybody hurt her or you, Chris and Otto. Oh God… this is madness."

"I wish that we were under different circumstances to celebrate you becoming a father, if you want to do it-" He cut himself off again as he saw his guards standing alert. "Just lower your weapons, I said!" Vincenzo tried to comfort Vic whilst batting his guards back.

"I would never do such a thing, Vincenzo. You know how much I respect you, you are like a brother to me," Vic explained as he held Vincenzo's arm.

Vincenzo's eyes filled with tears; he could no longer hold himself together.

"I know Vitorio, you are too, but Anthony has to pay. We need to come up with a plan. I will leave myself, without any guard or warrior, just to protect Emily and tell your friend to come and live here until we finish this."

"They are protected already."

"By who?" Vincenzo asked

"Eddie brought guards for me. I trust him," Vic explained.

"Who is Eddie now? Everything here is unpredictable. If you don't tell me everything, how am I supposed to help you?"

"Eddie is somebody I used to work with; he is a member just like I was. He found me after we escaped the orphanage."

"And do you think that you can trust him?" Vincenzo asked.

"I am not sure, but he sounded convincing, because he did not have to tell me anything about Anthony whatsoever, and yet he made sure that Emily would be safe. So, at this point, I trust him; I do not see any reason not to. But do not take this as my final answer, since I only trust you, my friends, and Emily," Vic explained.

"I see, so what is the plan then?"

"What do you suggest?"

"I suggest that whenever I get the first chance, I take him down!"

"What about the rest?"

"You mean those other two, Jakob and Peter?"

"Yes, those two as well, since all of them are connected."

"Vitorio, one by one, my friend, one by one."

"And how do you intend to do it, if I may ask?"

"I will not, you will."

Vic raised an eyebrow, impressed by Vincenzo's strategizing.

"I see, so reverse plan, huh? Should I go alone, or may I borrow your army again?"

"We should wait a bit and then make a plan. I will ask you one more time, do you trust this guy, Eddie, or should I worry?"

"I am not sure. I am telling you, I do not know how to answer this question. As long as Emily is safe, I have nothing to worry."

"I see, my friend. You should go to her now and let this all rest for a while. I will come to you to have a talk about the upcoming plan. Do we have a deal?" Vincenzo asked

"We have a deal. Can I borrow one of your horses? I cannot walk anymore."

"Do not ask, just take the damn horse!" Vincenzo cried.

He left the castle and mounted on a big, black, muscular horse, riding it to the house. While he was riding the horse, his mind was occupied with this plan about Anthony; little did he know that Anthony was somebody who was at the end of the list. Vic felt a bit of relief since he had sorted out this situation with Vincenzo, but that did not make him feel entirely sure about it, fearing that this act would trigger other ones in a row, like a chain reaction.

Vic became sad and depressed; he was on the verge of not having the will to live anymore, but could not give up this fight for the sake of love for his friends, Emily, his unborn child, and Vincenzo. But he could not save anyone, but he would die trying. Soon after, he was getting closer to his home and out of nowhere, again, rain started to fall. Vic grew tired of the rain and started to suspect that it must have a hidden meaning, but could not pay that much attention due to the fact that he could not wait to talk to Emily and to at least let her know that they would be safe for the upcoming eight months.

On the other side, he was captivated by the feeling and fear of what she might say and how she would react to all this, having in mind that she would still be angry and mad about this situation. Upon arriving, he saw that the guards were surrounding his home. In that moment, he knew that Emily would be safe inside. He dismounted the horse that he had borrowed and opened the door. She was sitting at the dining room table alone, and there was somebody in the kitchen preparing food.

Vic did not ask her who it was, since he thought that it would be Eddie. In that moment, he went to Emily to hug her, but when he saw who it was in the kitchen, he grew pale and his legs started to shake.

Emily asked him, "What is the matter, my love? The fine gentleman there, preparing us dinner, is your uncle Peter. I did not know that you had an uncle, my love. He made sure that we would be safe, my darling, so I do not worry anymore. Have you been to Vincenzo lately? Peter asked about him; they are friends, too."

Vic could not recover from this scene, seeing Peter in his kitchen with his pregnant wife there. With guards outside the house, he felt like he was being trapped inside his own house, and he was hoping that Eddie was not eliminated because if he was, Vic could never forgive himself. Peter greeted Victor with a smile on his face, a wicked smile of an evil man.

"Victor, my favorite nephew, it's been a while since I have seen you. How have you been? I came by to say hello. You did not invite me to your wedding. What a shame!"

"Uncle Peter, I thought you were in Italy for your meeting there. How come you are here?" Victor asked so as not to provoke suspicion from Emily.

Peter stood and drifted over to Vic.

"Oh, Victor, I came just for you when I heard that you got married. What kind of an uncle would I be if I didn't come to congratulate my own nephew?" he asked through gritted teeth.

"Of course, dear uncle..." Vic replied as he reached for his sword.

Peter stood a little closer to Emily, who had her back to them, and dragged his finger across his throat, indicating that she would be dead if Vic tried anything.

Vic released his grip on the sword and sat at the table.

"So, can I stay for the night? Aren't you going to eat? I made a delicious dish for us," Peter continued.

Vic's head fell into his hands.

"I am not hungry."

Emily floated over and placed her hand on Vic's shoulder.

"How come, my love? You haven't eaten all day. Don't let your uncle's food go to vain, darling. After all, he came all this way for you, for us."

Vic lifted his head.

"Uncle Peter, may we go for a walk outside? I want to show you my plans for the business, Emily cannot know because I want to surprise her."

414

"Of course, my nephew, how can we not? Lead the way."

As Vic was leading the way toward the door, Peter held a tight grip on his knife and pulled the front door closed.

"What the hell is this? Since when do you do these kinds of tricks? How could you come to my house, you bastard! What do you want?" Vic whispered.

"Do you want her to live, Victor? Or perhaps she should have the same destiny as Eddie?" Peter hissed.

"You son of a bitch, you did not! How could you? Eddie was like a son to you."

"You were as well. Perhaps you want to join him in death, don't you?"

"I cannot believe that you could be such an evil man, Peter. I trusted you, I did everything that you asked all those years, and now you come to my house and threaten me? Don't you feel any shame, or perhaps empathy?" Vic asked as he searched Peter's eyes for the man he once knew.

"We are all cold-hearted people who work in the darkness to see the day. Don't you think?" Peter replied with a wicked grin on his face.

"You are one sick bastard who has no emotions and enjoys making people suffer, don't you think?"

"You have always been good with words, perhaps better with actions. But I am so sorry, my dear, there's only one way out of this."

"What might that be? Let me guess, to eliminate somebody?"

"Exactly! See how smart you are, you know what to do. I want you to eliminate Jakob," Peter beamed.

Vic couldn't help but laugh.

"Ha-ha, what the hell is going on here? This makes no fucking sense at all. Why the hell do you want him dead now?"

"Well, it is kind of complicated, but I have no time to explain. And I am kind of short with my patience, so you'd better decide quickly."

"And what then, what after I do it, you will ask me to eliminate Anthony, too?"

"Probably. You know how it goes, it's not your first day at the job," Peter replied as he balanced his finger on the edge of the knife.

"And what if I cut your head right the fuck now?" Vic asked.

Peter turned to meet Vic's gaze.

"The guards have an order to kill on sight if something happens to me, so say goodbye to Emily. Of course, they will not kill you because I told them so. If you take me down, you will be left alive to suffer for the rest of your miserable life."

"You pathetic, ill bastard! How could you be this evil? Where is Jakob? You want me to go right now? Or can this drama of yours wait?" Victor spat.

"He is at your friend's house doing the same thing as me. You see, Victor, sometimes in life you cannot know what the consequences are until you realize that you have been playing with."

"Oh, dear god! What did I do to deserve this?!" Vic proclaimed, looking to the sky, as though searching for answers.

Peter chuckled.

"There is no god that could save you right now, Victor. You'd better run to see your friends; perhaps they are still alive."

Vic shook his head violently.

"I cannot do it, I cannot leave Emily. I just can't. My life is over, but trust me, yours will be too, pretty soon!"

"Ha-ha, you can be so funny sometimes, you know that? It's up to you; the clock is ticking. You can save your lovely wife, after all, I hear that she is pregnant. Perhaps if you get there in time, you can save your friends too, you know, so we all win."

"And when I get back, you ask me to take down Anthony, and then what? You finally leave me alone, right?"

Peter grinned, "Very clever, but not so fast, Victor. After that, the final mission is to take down Vincenzo."

"Is this a joke? Am I dreaming all this? What the fuck did Vincenzo do to you?"

"Well, to be honest, I loved Emilia, too."

"Let me guess, Jakob did as well?"

Peter clapped

"Bravo! Victor, you finally solved the riddle. You get bonus points for that one. I promise that I will not touch a single hair on Emily's head."

"You are all sick bastards. I knew you were sick, but not like this. I will go and trust that you will not touch Emily. But if you even try, I swear to you, I will chop you into pieces," Victor whispered malevolently.

"We have a deal. Take down Jakob, take his medallion as proof, and come back to me."

With deep sorrow and fear in his heart, he left the house, mounted on the black, muscular horse and went straight to the house of his friends to try to solve this situation. Which, as it seems, had become so complicated that one could not understand it at all.

Vic hoped that Emily would be safe, but in his mind, he could not find a way to take down Jakob, since he knew deep inside that Jakob would come up with a different story, and it would be a never-ending back and forth, since all three of them hated each other very much.

Vic was trying to think, but he could not control all the situations at once and could not rely on any of them at all. Before he arrived, he came up with an idea to act like he did not know anything and to try to convince Jakob to give him his medallion and to show it to Peter, hoping that at least Jakob would fall for that strategy, since Vic could not afford to lose anybody that he loved.

Oh, how he wished that he could take down all three of them at the same time and end this nightmare, but little did he know what would happen next.

As Vic was getting closer to his friend's house, of course, from a distance, he could see guards, and he was very familiar with what was to come. As he dismounted his horse and opened the door, Chris and Otto were tied up and helpless, while Jakob was sitting, having a drink in the living room. Jakob greeted him and started to smile.

"Victor, long time no see? Don't mind them, we could not negotiate, so I needed some peace, you know? As an old man, you don't have much patience or nerves. I hope that you will understand. How have you been? I found out that you got married and your wife is pregnant. Well, congratulations. I wish I had brought you a gift at least."

Vic feigned happiness.

"I missed you, Jakob! You were always my favorite one of all of you three. Yes, I got married and she is pregnant, thank you. I wish we had met under different circumstances."

"Was I really your favorite, or are you trying to fool me?" Jakob asked as he studied Vic's face, uncertain of his intentions.

"You were, Sir, I mean it. I always trusted you, and I always doubted Anthony and Peter."

"Well, I might believe you, so I guess you know what I want you to do?"

"Of course, Sir, to eliminate them, am I right?"

"Well done, Victor. You have always been my favorite member as well. But you have to go now if you want your friends to live."

As Vic looked at Chris and Otto sitting there, hopeless and unable to save themselves, he recalled the moment when they were captured by Gregor the Terrible, hoping deep down that there was a solution.

"Sir, the thing is that Peter is keeping my wife, Anthony, and perhaps her parents hostage. You are doing that with my friends. The only way that I could do this is by taking your medallion and taking down Peter."

Jakob's eyes narrowed.

"My medallion, why? What good will it do to you?" he asked skeptically.

"That medallion would prove to Peter that I took you down, and I will take my chances to take him down and come back to you," Vic explained.

Jakob paused.

"Hm, let me think for a moment. Maybe you could be right."

"Please, Sir, do not make this any harder than it should be. Just hand over the medallion, you should be aware that I must take the guards down too, and as you can see, I am alone."

"If I can trust you, I can send my guards to take down his guards," Jakob offered.

"What about you, Sir? Do you think that it is a good idea? What if Anthony is looking for you?" Vic asked.

Jakob stood and walked over to Vic.

"You are right, now I can trust you. Take half the guards; I will let six of them come with you. And take the medallion," Jakob explained as he handed Vic the medallion.

"Let's go fast!" Vic demanded as the guards sprinted towards their horses.

"Now listen up, all six of you! My wife is inside the house, and all of the guards are outside. When you hear me whistle, you will strike, you get it? When I whistle, Peter is done for good, do you understand?" Vic shouted to the guards.

"Understood, Sir," they replied in unison.

As Vic and the guards were getting closer to his house, deep inside, he was hoping that he got this, and perhaps with another strategy, he could take down Anthony and Peter. But all this was suffocating him to the point of going insane. As they were getting closer to the house, Vic told the guards to lie low and not to make a sound. He instructed them to dismount their horses and to go on foot from there, as he wanted to make it look as if he were alone.

When Vic opened the door, Emily had no idea what was going on and was having dinner with Peter. Vic tried to act normal and relaxed, but deep inside, he was feeling that every cell of his body was on fire. He greeted them, acting as if everything was fine and there was absolutely nothing to worry about. Starting with Emily, hugging her and kissing her softly, while his heartbeat was faster than any bird in the sky. And then Peter, of course.

"Uncle Peter, how are you? I brought you something special since you travelled all this distance to come and visit us," Vic beamed as he placed the medallion on the table.

Peter picked the medallion up and examined it in the light.

"Oh, Victor, my nephew, how generous of you! I wanted one like this all my life, thank you. My dear, may your uncle hug you?"

"Of course, dear Uncle Peter," Vic replied with a smirk on his face.

Chapter Ten: Never Forget What You Have Become

As Peter approached, thinking that Jakob was taken down for real, Vic used that moment, one in a million, to reach for the knife on the table and put it through Peter's heart. Upon doing so, he whistled, and Jakob's guards rushed to take down Peter's guards. Vic left Emily inside, screaming, and grabbed his sword to help the guards take down the other ones.

As he was doing that, Vic felt the rage in his heart along with the unbelievable feeling of what was happening. As the guards did not speak a word, Vic could not resist going back and taking Peter's medallion, while Emily was screaming and crying, yelling at him: "You killed your own uncle? How could you!"

Vic just looked at her and replied, "He was a striker, my darling, not my uncle."

Emily was in shock, but Vic could not explain anything to her at that moment, since time was of the essence. He went outside and was trying to figure out what to do next. He asked the guards to guard Emily because he was on Jakob's side. They accepted his request in a naïve manner.

At that moment, Vic mounted again the black, muscular horse, and while he was on his way to his friend's house, he whistled for Oni. When Oni landed on his right arm, Vic wrote a small note and attached it to Oni's left foot craws, told Oni to take it to Vincenzo, and released the raven into the sky.

Vic continued to sprint the horse towards the house, and upon arriving, he saw that there were no guards outside. He thought in the moment that perhaps the guards would be inside. As he opened the door, there was nobody inside. Vic could not believe this; millions of unanswered questions were rushing through his head. Immediately, in that moment, he rushed back to his house, understanding that he had been played; they made a fool out of him.

In the meantime, Vincenzo received the note and read it:

"Vincenzo, please send some warriors to my home, it's urgent. – Vitorio."

Vincenzo did not wait a single second and did as Victor requested. When Vic was getting closer to his house, he saw from a distance that the guards were there and felt relieved that Emily would be inside. Upon arriving and opening the door, Emily was indeed inside, still crying. Vic approached her slowly, but she was still angry and hard to communicate with.

"Darling, it is not what you think. Please, listen to me. You have to," Vic pleaded.

"Leave me alone! I should have never trusted you, loved you, or even thought about you. How could I be so stupid? Oh god, how was I so naïve to love a striker?" Emily wailed.

"Emily, my darling, please don't break my heart. It is not what you think, just please let me explain it to you. He wanted to kill you; they all do. Only Vincenzo is our friend, along with Chris and Otto," Vic implored.

"You killed your uncle. How evil are you? I loved you, I am pregnant with your child!" Emily shrieked erratically.

"He is not my fucking uncle, can you understand that for once!" Vic roared with the ferocity of a lion.

Emily turned and walked slowly towards Vic.

"Then who was he? I do not know anymore who is who and who does what! What the hell is going on? I should have known this from the beginning, because this love was too good to be true. You know that as well, all the best things in life last for only a few blinks and heartbeats."

Vic fell to his knees in disbelief at the madness that had unfolded.

"I guess you are right; you should go to your parents and move to France. I will try to save my friends and live a miserable life," Vic replied, his voice as flat and defeated.

Emily looked at Vic, her eyes filling with tears. As the tears rolled down her face, she knelt and hugged him tight.

"But I love you and I will love you for the rest of my life. I would rather die than live my life without you."

Vic took her hand in his.

"Then just trust me, and listen to me, so that you will not make a mistake."

"I will listen. Now, explain to me, who wants you, your friends, and me dead?" she asked.

Vic sighed.

"Well, one is dead now for sure. But there are two of them left, and once they are taken care of, I think we should be safe."

Emily grabbed Vic's face.

"Then what are you waiting for? Go and hunt them down like rabbits."

Vic's face fell from her hands; he could not bear to look her in the eye.

"I wish it was that easy, my love. I am waiting for Vincenzo to send us his warriors to guard you so that I can go and hunt them down."

Emily leaned back and sat on the floor, her arms hugging her legs.

"Well, let's wait then."

"That is the wisest thing to do right now. I just hope that Chris and Otto are safe."

Hours passed, but there was no sight of Vincenzo's warriors. Vic began to worry madly, while hugging Emily and hoping that all this would come to an end. There was no sight of Anthony or Jakob whatsoever. Emily soon fell asleep, and Vic went outside, just waiting and hoping for those warriors to show up.

As dawn was getting closer, Jakob's guards fell asleep, and Vic kept hoping for at least a sign. As the new way was being prepared, one of the warriors came running badly injured, and Vic rushed to him to ask what the hell had happened.

As he approached, he was barely alive and uttered, "They killed us. I escaped. It was a man named Mile." The warrior, after saying his name, just looked at the sky and died.

Vic could not believe all this. He thought that it would be impossible for Mile to do this, and why on earth would he do that? As it seems, Emilia was wanted by him too; perhaps that's why he left the wedding first. It could never cross his mind that Mile could do this. Vic could not believe it at all.

After some time, he did not know what he should do in this situation. In his mind, he was worrying badly about everyone and did not know where to go first, but at least Emily was there. Soon after, some steps could be heard from outside. Vic was not sure if it was Anthony, Peter or even Mile. Vic held onto his weapons very tight, in his left hand the axe and on the right side the sword.

Vic told Emily to stay behind him and hoped that nobody would hurt Emily. While the steps could be heard approaching, there was a knock on the door. Vic remained silent and proceeded with caution as the door handle was moved and the door was opened.

Mile stood in the doorway, his shadow almost enveloping the room.

"Victor, may I come in?"

Vic's back straightened as his grip on his weapons tightened.

"Mile, what do you want? Is it true that you murdered all those people?" he asked, dreading the answer that Mile would give.

Mile strode in, "Let me explain myself, there is an explanation for this."

Vic took a step back.

"I do not think that you can justify this, Mile. It never crossed my mind that you could do this…"

Mile took another step forward.

"Please, Victor, I have to explain this to you, because I do not wish you any harm. I was just hoping if we could come to an agreement together since we are friends, you know."

Vic stood his ground this time.

"Mile, you are not my friend anymore, and I do not want any kind of agreement with you. Can't you see that I cannot trust anybody? All of you have betrayed me. I do not know if I am alive or dead."

Fear overtook Emily, and she began to shake uncontrollably.

"I never wanted it to be like this, Victor. I never wished you anything bad, I swear. I just want you to take down Vincenzo."

Vic lunged forward, completely enraged.

"For fucks sake! The entire Europe wants him down. What the hell is going on? Can't you understand that he should take you all down one by one like rabbits? Emilia was the one who lost her life here, and why? For all the lust that you and the rest had and all the jealousy? Shame on you all! You better get out of my house before I attack you," Vic screeched as Emily began to cry.

"Or I attack you! There is not the slightest chance in this world that I am leaving this house without you promising me that you will take him down," Mile wailed, malice in his tone.

"I will promise you one thing if you do not leave this house. It is up to you if you want to leave dead or alive," Vic snarled, now face to face with Mile.

"If you put it like that, then we should settle this outside since I don't want to make your wife more upset than she already is," Mile snarled, glancing at Emily bitterly.

As they were both leaving, Vic locked Emily in the house, and they went outside to fight. At that moment, Oni intervened by harassing Mile and attacking him on his face. He was vulnerable and could not defend himself that easily, since Oni would never give up. But it was the first time that Oni had done such a thing.

Vic did not want to attack Mile in an unfair manner and whistled for Oni to cut its harassing behavior. It hardly let go. As they both grabbed their weapons, Vic was trying to at least let him know it should not be this way, but Mile was persistent because, as it seemed, they all blamed Vincenzo, and Vic could never betray him.

As Mile was getting ready to strike with his sword, Vic held a tight grip on his axe, and when Mile did strike, Vic blocked the attack and, with the other hand, punched him in the face as hard as he could. While Mile was pushed back from the punch, he got mad and angry and began to rage.

As Vic was trying to control and block his attacks, there was a moment to take him down instantly with a spin, cutting into his chest.

As he was lying on the ground bleeding, Vic did not feel any kind of regret and did not feel bad for him.

In that moment, he uttered his last words, "Vic… Victor, I never wanted it to end like this, I… I just…" Right then, his soul had left his body.

Vic, feeling angry about everything that was going on, went inside the house to Emily, while she was crying and screaming. Vic had a lot of pressure in his mind already and could not bear even more, but there was nothing that he could do to make Emily calm down.

As hours passed and the new day arrived, he was just sitting in the corner of the house, thinking about what the hell he had done in life to deserve all this. Thinking and thinking, he could not find an answer. Emily had fallen asleep on the floor, and her face was pale. There was nothing that could be done, since Vic could not afford to risk her life and leave the house.

As the morning sun was shining through the windows, Vic was feeling tired and could not postpone the urge to sleep any more. Emily was still asleep. He got up with the little energy left in him and just walked in circles in order to stay awake, but that did not last more than five hours. Emily had woken up in the meantime, and she realized that her dream had nothing to do with the agony of the reality that they were in.

After some moments, she asked Vic, "My love, how long will this last?"

He replied, "Until I take down those two sons of bitches."

As the moments passed, Vic sat on the floor and collapsed on the floor soon after, entering a state of dream. In his dream, he woke up surrounded by wolves in the forest, but to his surprise, the wolves, instead of attacking him, were protecting him. Vic tried to figure out who they were protecting him from, but was unable to see in the distance since it was dark and gloomy.

At that moment, bats started to fly above him, and they were heading south. The wolves were being cautious and protective at any given chance. He just sat down on the ground and, as if he was waiting for somebody or something to happen, until he was awoken by a knock on the door.

When he woke up, he immediately grabbed his axe, but behind the door, when he heard the voice, his face, strangely but surely, uplifted in a smile. It was Vincenzo with the rest of his warriors; he had decided to come personally to Vic's home in order to protect Emily so that Vic could go and save his friends.

Vincenzo's fist pounded on the door with the strength of Thor's hammer. "Vitorio, open up, it's me! Where are the rest of my warriors, and where are my guards? For God's sake, I did send them!"

Vic shouted as he approached the door, "Hold up, I am coming to unlock the door."

Vic couldn't help but throw his arms around Vincenzo and squeeze him tightly at the sight of him.

"Welcome and thank you, my friend. The rest are dead, killed by Mile."

Vincenzo's jaw dropped. "Mile? You cannot be serious? How is he involved in this?"

Vic shook his head, still in disbelief, "For the same reason as the rest. Imagine that."

"Dear lord, this is madness, indeed. But I think that we do not have much time to talk. I suggest you go and save your friends; hopefully, that snake has not done anything bad to them."

Vic placed his hands on Vincenzo's shoulders as if placing all of the responsibility he felt onto him, "Please, guard Emily with your life until I come back. I can do this alone."

"Vitorio, I will come with you; we can do this together. At least I will help you take down some guards, and we will interrogate Jakob."

Vic's eye narrowed "You really wish to come with me, Vincenzo? Why? I never took you for a direct combat type of person. I guess there is nothing that can surprise me at this moment."

Vincenzo pulled Victor towards the door "This is not the time to talk, Vitorio, we need to rush to save your friends."

As they both left the house mounted on their horses, Vic offered Vincenzo his sword, but he rejected it. As it seems, he had his own that he never talked about, took it from the guard who always had it in his possession, and gave orders to the guards to protect Emily with their lives.

While they were sprinting their horses, Vic could not believe that they were going to do this together. On the other side, he was afraid that something bad might happen to Emily. As they were riding on their horses, they did not speak much, but were focused on arriving and executing this mission as best as they could.

Upon arriving, they stopped, dismounted their horses, and left them in the distance and continued on foot. Vic stopped for a minute and asked Vincenzo, "What is the plan?"

He told him that it would be best if he went inside alone and tried to convince Jakob that both Peter and Anthony are dead, and to see how the situation would escalate. Vincenzo asked Vic to signal by whistling when it is all good, and to signal by yelling "attack" if something goes wrong.

Vic proceeded and tried to act all tough, and that he did indeed take them down, but little did he know what he would see inside the house of his friends. Upon approaching, there were two guards outside acting like they were guarding the house. When they saw Vic, they did not react or attack. Vic felt strange in that moment, and he thought to himself, perhaps Jakob is inside, and Chris and Otto are fine.

As he was approaching further and was getting closer to the door, his heart started to race. He did not pay attention to that sign and opened the door. What he saw inside cut him in half; he fell down on his knees and turned pale as tears fell like rain.

There he was, Chris, dead on the floor. Vic could not gather the strength to yell "attack." He just started screaming, "Chris, no!" In that moment, Vincenzo knew what was happening and immediately rushed to take down one guard, attacking him and quickly taking him down, while he crippled the second one, grabbed him by his throat and began to interrogate him.

There were flames in Vincenzo's eyes as he spat, "Speak, you son of a bitch! Who did this?"

The guard whimpered fearfully, "It was Jakob. Please, don't kill me, I have nothing to do with this!"

"Where is Otto, where is Anthony?"

"Anthony, I don't know. Jakob took Otto to a cave."

The ground shook as Vincenzo screamed, "Which cave? Speak right now! Or I will cut you into pieces!"

"Please don't kill me, I don't know, they did not tell me anything. There was somebody else with them!" the guard pleaded as his eyes filled with tears.

Vincenzo felt only anger as he continued to probe, "Who else was with them?"

"Two older people with black hoods!" the guard blurted

While Vic was going through the agony of his life, seeing his best friend dead on the floor, he overheard the conversation of Vincenzo and the guard, and from the depths of his memory, instantly knew that those two older men were the ones who had eliminated his parents. He was about to die from sadness; his tears would not stop, and this was killing him from the inside out.

As he was looking at the dead body of his friend, he could not forgive himself for not saving him. The blame and the sadness embraced together, creating a deeper feeling of agony. In those moments, he was trying to utter some words but could hardly speak. After some moments, he just said a single sentence: "Chris, my friend, I will avenge you, I promise you that."

In his mind, the phrase, "Please forgive me," was on repeat. He could not move as Vincenzo knocked down the guard and went inside to help Vic get up, because they both could not afford to waste any time. As Vincenzo was approaching, he saw Chris and could not believe his eyes. Tears started to fall as he was grabbing Vic by the shoulder to lift him up.

Vincenzo's voice shook as he tried to fight back tears, as he needed to be strong, "Vitorio, this is not your fault, my friend. We need to go, there is no time! At least we can try to save Otto. Come on, get up now. You can never surrender, remember? There is no falling down."

Vic could not utter a single word; every word that he tried to say gripped his throat into a tighter chokehold.

Vincenzo continued to ramble, desperate for some sort of response "Come on now, be strong. We cannot lose him as well. We need to run after those bastards and chop them like wood, one by one!"

Vic's voice was as flat as a gravestone when he was eventually able to reply, "I cannot, I failed my friend. I would be better off dead, I am no good to anybody…"

"Come on now, Vitorio, I do not know you to be like that. You are a hero, and will remain a hero for the rest of eternity! There was nothing that you could do; they will pay dearly for this!" Vincenzo swore vengefully.

Vic was dead behind his eyes. "I was supposed to guard them with my life, to have them in my life until we all die from old age. I let him down; he is dead now."

"We need to go, there is nothing that we can do now. Come on now!" Vincenzo snapped.

As they left the house and were heading out of the house, Vic could not walk, but Vincenzo kept holding him by the shoulder, and they walked together. But Vincenzo did not know the location of this cave, and their only hope was Oni. But since Vic could not call Oni, there was nothing that they could do, except roam around, hoping that they would find the cave by accident.

Vincenzo tried to convince Vic to whistle, but Vic was still in a state of shock. As they walked together for two hours, Vincenzo stole a horse from a nearby farmer and gave him twenty golden coins for it. He explained that they needed the horse urgently. The farmer did not hesitate and gave them the horse.

In that moment, Vincenzo carried Vic and put him on the horse's back while he was walking in front of the horse, trying to find this cave. After seven hours, finally, Vic came back to his senses and asked Vincenzo, "Where are we going?"

Vincenzo knew that Vic had temporarily forgotten what had happened, and it would be best not to answer where exactly they were going. As they were continuing their path, Vincenzo began to feel tired and could not walk anymore. He was about to ask Vic to call for Oni, but from a distance, Vincenzo saw another scene that should not have been seen.

In the depths of the forest, there he was hanging from the tree. Vincenzo turned pale and was trying to hold back his tears, but Vic, upon seeing his face, just sprinted the horse, and as the horse approached the scene, Vincenzo fell on his knees, and Vic immediately fell unconsciousness when he saw Otto dead, hanging from the tree.

Vincenzo could not gather the force to get up and pick Vic up once again. He was looking at the ground as the tears were falling and just said, "Dear lord, if you exist, give me the strength to get up, to unsee what I saw, so that I can help those who need my help the most one last time."

Moments later, Vincenzo could not gather the strength to get up, but was crawling to Vic, and when he reached him with the help of the horse leash, he got up somehow, and tried to carry Vic. But upon trying, he fell once, twice and then a third time again. While lying down on the ground, he started to pray again, "Dear lord, if you really exist, do not let me fail my friend."

After some time, he did the best that he could to lift Vic up to the horse's back and made it. After that, he fell again due to the crippled feelings and the agony that he was going through, along with the lack of energy. In that moment, he just rolled over on his back, looked at the sky and just said, "Thank you."

As Vic was on the horse's back, and Vincenzo was down on the ground, helpless and hopeless, Vincenzo heard footsteps approaching them and was trying from the top of his lungs to call for help. As it seemed, there was a mercenary that was passing by, and when he saw them, upon approaching, he figured out that Vic was unconsciousness and Vincenzo was barely holding on to life.

He asked Vincenzo for fifty golden coins to take them home. Vincenzo told him, "Take it all, just take us." The mercenary took all the coins, lifted Vincenzo and put him next to Vic. He walked the horse and left them in front of Vic's house, where the guards rushed to grab them both and take them inside.

When Emily saw Vic in that state, she began to scream, making things even worse, and on the other side, the two guards were taking care of Vincenzo, giving him water and helping him to regain his strength. As the sunset could be seen from the windows, Vincenzo fell asleep, and Vic came back to life.

Everything was still blurred at the edges for Vic when he saw Emily and asked, "My darling, why are you crying? What happened? Did anybody die?"

Emily stroked his hair as she reassured, "No, my love, nobody died. It's just... I have never seen you like this before."

"What do you mean, like this? Don't mind me, darling..." Vic's voice faltered, the words dissolving before they fully formed "Oh, I fought an endless battle, I will be all right, my love... I just have a feeling that I just had a bad dream. Have you seen Chris and Otto by any chance?"

Emily drew in a sharp breath, her chest tightening as if the air itself had turned heavy.

"Weren't you supposed to save them with Vincenzo? That's why you went there, didn't you?"

Seconds stretched and folded in on themselves as Vic tried to remember.

"I do not remember, darling. Where is Vincenzo?" he eventually replied.

"He is asleep, he's completely exhausted. I don't know what happened, but something does not feel right..." Emily explained as she searched Vic's absent eyes for answers.

Vic's brows furrowed as he looked around, disoriented, and he began to get up, "I don't understand. Why can I not remember, Emily? I need to speak to Vincenzo."

Emily caressed Vic's face, guiding his head back down to the pillow "Let him be, don't wake him up now. You two must have gone through a lot, so you'd better save the conversation for the morning."

Soon after, Vic closed his eyes and entered a dream. In his dream, he was alone in a cornfield that seemed like an endless labyrinth. As he was walking and walking for eternity, he met Chris, who was lying down on the ground and playing. In the dreams, Chris was a kid, and Vic, upon seeing him, asked, "Chris, why are you a kid, man? Where are we?"

Chris answered, "I do not know about you, but I am in another world."

Vic felt confused and could not understand what was going on, along with the fact that he was not aware that it was a dream. Moments later, Vic found himself by the river and saw Otto running down the riverbed, again as a kid. In that moment, Vic was awoken by Oni, who was making weird noises and flying in circles around his house. As he woke up, he saw Emily next to him and told her that he had a strange dream about Chris and Otto and that they were kids, but Emily was in tears.

Vic's eyes were filled with worry "Why are you crying, my love? What happened?"

The tears continued to flood Emily's eyes and roll down her cheeks as she sighed, "Victor, the sooner you accept the reality, the better for you."

Vic's concern turned to frustration as he barked, "What do you mean, Emily? I am asking you why are you crying? Answer me!"

The anger in Vic's voice shocked Emily, and the tears stopped flowing in an instant.

As she wiped the tears from her cheeks and cleared her throat, Emily explained, "Last night you did not make it, both of you."

Vincenzo emerged from the shadows "Vitorio, we failed them."

Vic's gaze darted to Vincenzo, and he paused before asking, "What do you mean we failed them?"

Vincenzo hung his head "They are dead, my friend. Killed by those two, along with the ones who eliminated your parents."

In those moments in Vic's head, everything came back as a flashback, starting from when he was a kid and until the night before. There were no tears to cry at that moment; his eyes were sore, and the urge to cry would not stop. After hours of silence, Vincenzo spoke.

"There must be a way out of this madness, I am sure of it!" Vincenzo proclaimed, determined as ever, but apprehensive as he moved towards the window, hoping he may find the solution somewhere in the storm.

Emily broke the silence, "I always heard my grandmother saying that…"

She trailed off, staring into space, longing to recall the stories from her childhood she once knew so well.

Once she had remembered her grandmother's tales, she continued, "There is a cave in Romania and inside lives a monster, alike to humans and can turn a human into a Vampire."

Vincenzo turned from the window to meet Emily's gaze as he recalled, "My Nonna spoke about that as well; perhaps it might be true. She said that the monster there would be free if offered another soul."

Emily almost didn't want to know the answer as she asked, "What do you mean 'another soul?'"

Vincenzo looked away from Emily and back to the rain as he solemnly explained, "Like selling your soul to get the power of a ten hundred men, or the speed of light, or senses that no man could think were possible."

Emily clutched her chest in shock as she exclaimed, "Oh, dear lord! That sounds like something from the books!"

Vincenzo's brow furrowed and his fist tightened as he snarled, "Perhaps I should give it a try, I have nothing to lose... I want to avenge Chris and Otto!"

Vic had heard enough and finally lifted his head from his hands. "No, I will go."

Emily and Vincenzo turned to face him as Vic continued, "You two stay here, and once I come back, I will do what I have to do."

Vincenzo's eyes pleaded as concern for Vic consumed him, "Can I at least come with you? Together we are stronger, my friend."

"No, this time you cannot," Vic replied firmly as he went to Vincenzo's side at the window, watching the lightning dance in the sky.

Vic met Vincenzo's stare as he earnestly explained, "My only remaining friend, I need you alive. I may not make it out of the cave… If I don't return alive in four moons, take care of Emily and take care of my child as if it is your own. There is enough gold for you two to survive for at least twenty years. The gold is located-"

Vincenzo was no longer able to suppress his emotions and concerns about what may be as cut Vic off, crying, "Stop it now, Vitorio! Don't speak nonsense, you will come back. I am sure of it!"

As he was feeling devastated and had no idea what would happen, Victor could not stop. He knew that his friends were gone and there was nothing that he could do, but on the other hand, he could not believe that they were dead. As he was getting up and started to leave the house, he looked one more time at Vincenzo and Emily, and with that sad expression on his face, he went out, mounted on the horse and went on his journey to Romania.

He knew that it would take him a lot of time to reach the destination, but there was nothing else left to do at that point. His heart was filled with sorrow, and he knew that sorrow would never pass. But at least he was willing to turn into a monster just to avenge them and the rest. As he was riding his horse, he was feeling that the world was collapsing around him, and all the weight of the world was on his shoulders.

Besides that, he took all the blame, thinking that he could have saved them, but he was being selfish and focusing on Emily, although that was not true at all in reality. But in his mind it was. He told himself, "How could you leave your friends behind?" with a low voice that was dying inside. In his journey, the first four days, he could not sleep; he was just riding his horse until the horse could not go any further.

On the fifth day, he fell asleep on a big rock. Upon waking up, he felt an intense pain in his chest, but he did not want to pay attention to it. He mounted on his horse and continued his path. That day it was windy, and the wind was so fast that it made the horse stop. Victor knew that there was nothing that he could do to change the weather, so he decided to stop and find a place that would not be affected by the wind.

After three hours of searching in an unfamiliar territory, he found a cave. Upon getting there, he chose to go and gather the food for the horse. So he did, but the pain that the wind caused him hurt him deep into his bones for a week. Just like that, with a broken heart and soul, Victor continued through mountains and fields, crossing lakes and rivers, villages and towns. Through pain, blood, mud, and all the harsh weather, just to get to Romania.

As he was still going, he thought that he was getting closer, but he was roughly halfway there. He did not know this until he decided to reach out to the first person he met. But when that happened, he hesitated to ask and just continued on his path. Two months had passed, and he had barely eaten five times during that time. He had lost weight and looked like a starving man, not because he could not find the food, but because of the pain that he was feeling in his soul. As he continued the journey, he stumbled upon a witch called Nora. As she was approaching him, Victor wanted to ignore her and not engage in communication with her, but she insisted.

As she was approaching, she was holding a book in her right hand. "You look like you need help. What if I can offer you something that you cannot refuse?" she said

Victor was doing his best to ignore her and continue on his path as she insisted again, "There is a way to fix your sadness. I can see what is killing you inside. I have something that you might want," she added.

He just continued again, while feeling that the horse was weakening. In that moment, Victor knew that it was time to let the horse rest and that perhaps it would be a great idea to lie down to rest as well, he thought. But as he was sitting on the ground, Nora opened her book and started to read the lines that Victor would never forget in his entire life.

The moment that she opened the book, thunder struck, and she started to read:

"All who lost their will to live must come up this hill,

Up this hill I call you, I will show you what to do,

Where they go up this way, there will be hell to pay."

She closed the book and looked at Victor with a strange look in her eyes.

He wanted to talk but did not have any idea where to start, but as the time was passing and she was standing there, the silence broke. "May I know what it is that you have to offer me?" he asked her.

As she was feeling happy that he had finally spoken, her voice started to feel like it was cut into pieces because she was talking so fast. "I can offer you a map that will take you half the time, shorter than you would this way," she said.

Victor was a bit surprised, thinking of how she would know where he was headed to. "And that map of yours, lady, where does it lead?" he asked in a sarcastic way.

"It leads to the place that you want the most," she replied with a sense of confidence in her voice.

And as he was thinking that the conversation with her was a waste of time, he just replied, "Where do you think I am headed to?"

Nora just showed him on the map and said, "Here, right here, where men go to turn into monsters," showing him the location of the cave.

In that moment, she definitely had his attention, and he could not believe that she could know such a thing. Surprised, he asked her, "What do you want in return for this map?"

As Nora was preparing to answer again, another lightning strike struck nearby, and she replied, "I just want you to be what destiny wants you to be."

"How do you know all this?" he said while looking at the sky, which was a mixture of white and grey clouds.

As she was opening her book again, she was interrupted by him, "No, please do not read anymore. I have no energy to listen to the things that I cannot understand right now. You have already been too much for me," he stated with a sense of tiredness in his voice.

"But at least let me prove it to you that I was sent by the Gods to guide you," she requested, just another chance from him, as she did not want to let go without convincing Victor to take the map with him on his journey.

Moments later, after thinking for a while, he decided to continue on his path without the map. As he got up from the ground, he just told her, "Farewell, I should go now."

As Nora was looking at him leave, she understood that there was nothing that she could do at that moment, since she could not force him to take that map with him. Victor continued his path and did not even bother to think about the conversation that they had.

But he did not make it very far. He collapsed on the ground, as everything caught up with him, starting from sadness, agony, tiredness and starvation. As he was lying down on the ground looking at the sky again, he could not help but ask for help. As he was lying down hopelessly, he called Nora and told her to give him the map and to gather some food for him, since he did not have any energy left in his body and even less in his soul.

Nora did not hesitate to go as fast as she could to bring some food for him and to help him regain his strength. She did not take long to do so, and as soon as she arrived, she fed him. With a sad expression on her face, she told him, "I know how it feels to lose those that you loved the most. I myself lost my daughter," she confessed, as her eyes were tearing up.

Vic could not say anything in that moment and was recalling everything that he had gone through all that time, but little did he know that Nora was Emilia's mother. After five hours, Vic had recovered and was feeling that he was ready to continue his path, but he could not stop thinking about the scenes that he had seen that had completely killed his soul.

While he was looking at the distance, he took a deep breath and made a promise to himself by claiming, "I will make it, and I will turn into a monster. The blood of my friends will not be in vain. I will hunt down Anthony and Jakob, along with those two who eliminated my parents."

Upon hearing this, Nora felt a cold shivering through her heart and could not help but ask him, "Are we talking about the same sons of a bitches?"

Vic was surprised to hear that and did not understand, but chose to ask her, "The same in what way, and how do you know them?"

She just looked at him for a moment and was not sure whether to say or not to say it, but as she confirmed his suspicion as she mumbled, "What about Peter?"

Vic was in shock to hear that and, with wide eyes, asked her, "How come you know them? Is this a dream? Peter? I killed him."

Things were getting clearer for her now, and she knew that this was destined to be. But as her head was falling down, she said with a broken heart, "Emilia was my daughter."

In that moment, Vic's blood was boiling, and everything made sense. As he closed his eyes, he firmly told her, "I am sorry for what you had to go through. I would have never betrayed my friends, so I chose this path."

"I know, I am sure of it. It is pretty obvious," she claimed.

"Now I should go. Thank you for everything, and bear in mind that she will be avenged along with the rest," he told her with such self-confidence.

As he mounted on his horse and continued his path, he felt more secure in some sense because of the conversation that he had with Nora. Although it still felt unbelievable to him, he knew that life was unpredictable and that anything could happen. In that moment, he was feeling sure that the map was real and there was no doubt about it, so he chose to follow the road according to it.

As he was continuing on his journey, his thoughts were focused on the monster in the cave and what the chances were of him becoming one.

"Perhaps, many have tried and failed," he said to himself with no hope at all.

Moments later, Vic heard the voice of wolves howling nearby. While the horse got scared, he dismounted and chose to stay still while petting the horse and trying to keep calm. As the wolves continued, he decided to find a better place than being in the middle of the field. As he walked holding the leash tightly, a bear's roar was heard from the opposite side, and Vic thought to himself, "What's next, now a dragon throwing flames all around?"

He reacted quickly, mounting the horse again in the hope of escaping as fast as they could. Luckily, they managed to escape, and Vic was glad that there was no trouble from the hungry wolves and a raging bear. At the end of that day, while the dawn was getting closer, Vic saw a rather unusual sight from a distance; it looked like a sandstorm early in the morning. There was nowhere to hide, and the most panicking question that he asked himself was, "What if the horse does not make it?"

Saying it with a sad sensation in his voice, he did not know what to do. There was no shelter nearby, and it seemed like the end of their journey. But to his luck, the sandstorm did not approach, and it was just a slight hallucination from being exhausted. Days passed, turning into weeks and months, and the journey felt like it was a never-ending path to the destination.

But after five months, Vic arrived at the destination. The beauty of nature captivated him, but he could not feel joy or happiness of any kind due to the sadness that was all around his heart like a thousand piles of spider's nest. He dismounted his horse and left it there, but looked back at it with deep emotions, before he chose to proceed alone and told the horse, "Thank you for bringing me here," while petting it.

Vic decided to sit for a moment and think about his approach. But, deep down, he knew that either he would make it out of the cave as a monster or not make it out at all. Above the cave, there was the monster's castle, and the castle looked nothing like an ordinary castle.

As the sunset was slowly turning into night, Vic started to walk downhill towards the cave.

As he got closer, the small rocks almost tripped him up, and he decided to go inside only with his sword, but little did he know that his sword was made of silver. As he was walking through the tiny tunnels of the cave, bats were leaving the cave. He could not feel any kind of fear, nor was he frightened of what the monster might do, but instead, he was self-confident, and in his mind, there was nobody who could stop him at that point.

As the tunnels were almost over and he was entering the cave, he started to notice a large number of skeletons. At that moment, he said to himself, with irony in his tone, "So I am the next one, huh?"

As more bats flew above him in the direction of exiting the cave, he continued until a scream could be heard. The scream was so loud and powerful that the stones began to shake. Only then did he know that he was there, and either it was the end or the new beginning. As Vic tried to look everywhere around him in order to discover the location of the monster, the monster found him first.

"Many have tried, and they all failed, as you can see. Welcome to my dungeon," he warned him.

Vic pulled out his sword, and it made the monster disappear, which made Vic ask, "Why?"

But soon after, he could hear his voice saying, "If you want to talk, get the silver out of my sight," the monster requested.

"So that you can kill me faster?" Vic stated.

As the monster was hiding in the shadows of the cave and walking around, he claimed, "Many came here, and in all of them, I smelled only fear and desperation, but you are nothing like them. When you stepped foot here, you only carried hope. It's about time we got introduced, don't you think?"

Vic could understand bits of what he was saying but not all of it, and proceeded by stating, "All I want is the power to avenge those who murdered my friends and my parents. I am not sure if my wife will make it either. I guess you know my name, but I do not know yours."

"Oh, that is how far you will go? Is that so?" he said.

Vic, feeling that he was making a fool out of himself, answered, "I would die for the ones I love."

"Is that so, Victor? What if you are already dead?" he said.

"Does it look like I am not?" Vic ironically asked.

As he was approaching slowly and his hands were reaching Vic's chest, he warned him by opening a small wound, and as the blood was dripping, he said, "If you want to have the power of a two hundred men, you must be ready for it. So, are you ready to become a vampire?"

"I am ready. What are your requirements?" asked Vic.

He answered with an evil smile, "Requirements? I help you, you free me."

"Are you that bored of living? You must be very old," Vic asked.

Looking at him, he just answered, "You have no idea."

"What is the price for freedom for you? Is the price for vengeance for me?" Vic told him.

With a surprised expression on his face, he replied, "It is indeed. Shall we proceed?"

"We shall," he answered.

As he was looking at Vic, he knew that this was one in a million chance, perhaps the only chance to get through all those years to set him free. While all the bats had left the cave, the monster said, "I have a name, and it is Valor," as he was getting ready to cut into his arm with his fangs. As he looked at him, he asked, "Are you ready for this? There is no turning back."

Vic, with complete determination, answered, "Yes, I am."

Then, his blood dropped, soon to fill the cup. Vic did not feel any kind of fear, and in his eyes, you could only see hope, since this was his last hope for getting that power, even though it meant the end of him pretty soon. As the cup was getting full, he approached.

"May this give you what you want, and set me free after all these centuries," proclaimed Valor while raising the glass.

"How long do I have?" asked Victor.

"As long as you can resist the temptation of blood yourself," answered Valor.

"But you did not tell me this in the beginning," asked Vic, a look of surprise flashing on his face.

"There is a lot that has not been told, or done. Give it some time. Drink now," ordered Valor.

"To hell with you and your tricks, Valor," he said with an angry tone in his voice.

"Drink now or else I will personally take you to hell myself," insisted Valor.

As Victor was raising the cup closer to his lips, he closed his eyes and saw Chris and Otto, as they were smiling and greeting him from an unknown place. Victor drank the blood from the cup, and it was the worst thing that he had tasted in his entire life. But his hope was very high as he asked Valor, "What now?"

Chapter Ten: Never Forget What You Have Become

He answered, "Now, I welcome you to the world of immortals. As you go, you will see for yourself."

In that moment, Valor left Victor there, waiting for the effects, as Victor collapsed to the ground. As Valor was waiting for the dawn to be set free and to be mortal again, he had a smile on his face, since it seemed he had gotten bored with the immortal life. As the dawn was starting to be visible and moments later the sun was up. Valor, upon seeing and feeling the transformation, just continued to walk out of the cave and into the woods while singing, "I am free! I am free! This is the new me, no darkness, no more eternal night, let the sun shine so bright."

Valor was feeling like a kid again, embracing the moment of life, and recalling every moment while he was mortal a long time ago. On the other side, Vic had not awakened yet; he was in deep body shock from the process of transformation. As hours passed and the night was getting closer, Vic finally woke up. Upon opening his eyes, he felt something strange, but he did not know what it was until he started to get up. Upon starting to get up, both his hands did what he could not have ever imagined in his wildest dreams.

Upon touching and a bit of squishing the stones in the cave, while he was getting up, the stones shattered into tiny pieces. He said in that moment, "Interesting, this could be useful soon."

After getting up, Vic felt a burn around the neck and smoke was coming out from the wound, as silver was not something that a vampire could wear. He took it out, wrapped it with a cloth, and put it in his bag. While he was looking at the surrounding area, he noticed something rather unusual. His sense of hearing became stronger, and he could hear the spiders making their webs, only by focusing.

Upon hearing the spider making its web, Victor began to understand that this was it. He started to walk around the cave and was eager to figure out everything when it came to the transformation. He put his focus on hearing again and wanted to test the area of length. When he found out that it was unlimited, Vic was impressed.

In that moment, he realized that he could avenge them all if he just focused. In that moment, he wanted to hear Emily's voice and to see if it was possible. Just like that, upon focusing, he managed to do so. He overheard her conversation with Vincenzo about him and how much she wanted him home. Upon hearing, Vic felt very happy and calm knowing that she was doing just fine.

Moments later, as he was exiting the cave and seeing the mountains on the other side, and the woods again, another sense was enhanced; it was sight. He could see everything from kilometers away. All this left him speechless, and he could not believe that it was real, until, while walking, he felt the pull of hunger and hardly resisted.

Chapter Ten: Never Forget What You Have Become

While a lady was passing by, Vic saw the veins in her neck and they were somehow highlighted with red color, and he saw the veins pulsate, raising the heartbeat and making him feel hungrier. When she saw him, his eyes turned red, and she ran in terror. Vic continued his journey, and as he was walking, bats started to follow him, hundreds of them forming a big circle about him.

He did not understand what was going on and tried to call Oni, but Oni was nowhere to be found since he did not recognize Vic anymore. Vic tried several times, but it was unsuccessful. Moments later, Vic thought for a moment, "If I have all their powers, there must be something to speed things up."

While walking, he remembered that coming into contact with the sun could be deadly, so Vic started to run, and after some meters of running, his body reached the speed of light. As the bats were following him, in a matter of seconds, he passed the distance that it had taken him weeks to pass as a mortal.

After doing it once more time he was home, and at that moment, he whispered, "Valor was right, this is a hell of a power."

As he was ready to open the door, the voice from the sky spoke, "I told you not to sell your soul, now pay the price," and thousands of thunder struck the area around him, making his entrance in the house dramatic, but way too scary, especially for Emily's sensitive heart.

461

Vic opened the door and got in. As soon as Vincenzo saw him, he could not believe his eyes. And when Emily turned around upon seeing him, she ran into his arms just like a small kid.

"My love, you came back! Thank goodness," she said while hugging him.

"Of course, my darling, here I am. Now, it's time to hunt," he said with confidence.

Vincenzo interrupted their conversation by saying, "That's fast, Vitorio. You have not even told us yet how your journey was, and if you made it, and such," Vincenzo claimed.

"There is nothing to talk about. I need to avenge my friend right now, before the dawn arrives," Vic stated while focusing on his superhuman vision and hearing.

"Go, my love, you know I will support you in whatever you do," Emily stated while looking him in the eyes and touching his shoulders.

"Now listen very carefully to me, both of you. No matter what, you cannot leave the house," Vic requested from them as he was trying to find Jakob's location.

"Where is that son of a bitch," he whispered while anger started to captivate him, and his blood was boiling, making him angry and furious as the fangs were visible for the first time. Upon seeing this, Emily backed off, and Vincenzo stood in shock as they could not believe their eyes. But they were witnessing something that they used to believe was only a tale.

As Vic was struggling to find Jakob in his visions, Emily wanted to approach him, but a force upon finding the location in his mind was released, causing the house to shake like it was an earthquake. Emily and Vincenzo were in deep fear and did not know what to expect next. But as Vic knew where Jakob was, with no words or sign, he left the exact same moment, running with the speed of light to the hidden house in the woods east of Vienna.

Upon arriving, Vic smashed the door, and there he was, Jakob, with ten guards around him. Vic did not wait a single second and took down the guards in a matter of blink of an eye. Upon sucking the blood of the last guard, Vic felt his powers enhanced, and with an evil smile on his face, approached slowly towards Jakob.

"What is it, Jakob? You look like you've seen a ghost. Did you think that I would not find you?" Vic said with a sense of joy in his voice.

"Impossible! This cannot be," Jakob stated while he was taking some steps back.

"As you can see, it can be. Now, we should have a little talk, don't you think?" Vic requested.

"Wait, Victor! Please, do not do something that you might regret," he stated.

"There is no time for regret now. Regret went to sleep, and it might never wake up," Vic exclaimed.

"After all these years, you told me that I was always your favorite, please do not do this," Jakob begged as he was shaken with fear.

"Favorite, you say, when I was mortal, I did everything that you asked me to, I even went against myself, I followed every rule, and you murdered the ones I loved the most. What do you call this? Is it justice or is it betrayal?" Vic asked.

"What do you want me to do?" Jakob asked.

"I want you to accept your fate," Vic requested.

"What fate? What are you talking about?" Jakob asked, surprisingly.

"Why are you acting like a fool, Jakob? You know what you did and why I'm here," Vic asked him while taking further steps towards.

"Please stop, you don't have to do this, Victor. We can make a deal, perhaps, or come to an agreement. We always come up with something," Jakob requested while fear was shaking him.

"Not this time, not in this lifetime," Vic stated.

While Jakob was fearing for his life, he felt that those moments would be the last. But at that point, Vic did not want to send him to his maker that fast and decided to play things differently by requesting the names of his parents' strikers. As he approached and as Jakob was fearing the worst, Vic asked him, "If you tell me who eliminated my parents, I will spare your life."

Jakob, upon hearing this, knew that if he talked, there would be no force in this universe that could save him, and he would rather not be dead. In that moment, he decided to answer desperately, "I do not know, I wish I knew."

After hearing this, Vic became furious, and his rage began to grow. As the dawn was getting closer, he did not have much time. As he took the last step towards him, Jakob was pushed to the wall with no way out.

"Any last words before I do what I have to do?" Vic asked him with a calm voice and a cold look.

"To hell with you," Jakob answered as he knew what would happen.

"There we shall meet then. This is for Chris and Otto, and may their souls rest in peace. But I hope you burn in hell where you belong," Vic told him as he took his life with a bite on his neck.

As the blood was spilling on the floor and Jakob was having his last moment, Vic looked at him and recalled every moment since he set foot in the Temple of Justice for the first time. He did not feel anything, cold as ice; he stood there and was about to leave before the dawn. He went out of there, sprinted back to his home, and got there at the speed of light.

Upon arriving, he knew that all day he must stay hidden from the sunlight, and when Emily and Vincenzo saw him after he opened the door and got inside, they knew that it would be better not to say anything. As Vic was sitting down on the chair, he thought to himself, "I need to find Anthony, and I will make him talk about those who took the lives of my parents."

Moments passed, and Vincenzo was gazing through the window, thinking about this, looking at Emily as they both feared what Vic might do next. Vincenzo was not sure if it would be wise to talk or not, but he wanted so badly to ask him, "How would you live with this curse?"

He had been wondering about it since he saw him transform, and understood things even further after he came back from Romania.

Moments later, by accident, Oni came to the window and was first seen by Vincenzo. When Vic saw it, he stood up and wanted to get closer, but when it saw Vic, it flew away in fear. Vic got back to his chair in despair and feeling very bad, but deep inside, he understood that it was the right thing to do. But ever since he had turned into a monster, he couldn't help but wonder, "How long will Emily and Vincenzo stay by me like this?"

Things started to change drastically; nothing was as before. Vincenzo started to distance himself and to feel fear and sadness at seeing his friend as a monster. While on the other side, Emily still loved Vic, but she knew that he was not the same, and was praying for her child to be well and away from them both.

But she did not want to show that emotion out of fear as she stood there in the corner of the living room, waiting to see what would happen next. As the day was passing, all three of them were silent, and Vincenzo chose to break the silence.

While he was slowly approaching towards Vic, "Vitorio, my friend, I think that I should get going now since your powers can protect you and Emily," he stated.

Vic looked at him with a smile. "As you wish, my friend, as you wish," he answered with a cold tone to his voice.

Emily interrupted the conversation as she got up from the corner of the room. "My love, I am hungry. I should get to the town to purchase some food, please," she requested.

"No, darling, not while they hunt us. I cannot let you go until dark, stay still until then," he ordered her.

"Perhaps I could bring you some food," said Vincenzo while looking at Emily.

That would be amazing," she answered with a smile on her face.

Vincenzo left that moment and went to purchase some food for her, while she was sitting there with Vic, exchanging no words. Half an hour had passed, and Vincenzo came back with the food, left it on the table, and was about to leave for his castle. Before he left, he just looked at Vic and told him, "Good luck, my dearest friend, may you achieve what you want."

Vic did not answer and just looked away as if he were made of stone. Emily sat at the table and was preparing her meal while Vic was looking at her and was thinking of a way to break the silence. Moments later, he spoke.

"My love, do you not love me anymore?" he asked her with no emotion in his voice.

"Can't you see what you have become? How do you see our future like this?" she said as her voice was trembling and her hands were shaking, fearing that he might react with anger.

"I never wanted to hurt you; all I ever wanted was to have a happy life," he stated as he was getting closer to her.

Her heart was beating faster as he was approaching. "What are you doing, my love?" she asked.

"I want to feel your touch, like before. I want to feel loved," he requested.

As she was vulnerable and not sure what to do, she kissed him as tears rolled down her cheeks.

"I love you," she told him in the saddest way.

Vic understood everything and chose not to speak, not to react and to back off. He went to his room and locked himself up as regret started to hit his broken heart. As the sunset was preparing, Vic knew that it was time to hunt down Anthony. That was the only thing on his mind that was of importance. Since he understood that neither Emily nor Vincenzo liked what he had become.

Vic was looking at Emily and feeling guilty, but deep inside, he knew the reason for turning into a vampire. Now, as the clock was ticking and as the darkness was ready to cover the land, Vic could sense bats coming his way. He knew that it was time to go, but he at least wanted to let Emily know that this time, he would not return until he found Anthony. And upon finding him, he was hoping that perhaps he would find those two as well.

As Vic got up and looked at Emily, he chose not to approach, but rather to tell her something from a distance. With a cold look in his eyes and a burning fire in his soul, he looked at her and caught her attention.

"My love, I have to go. I do not know when I will be back or if I will be back at all. In three moons from now, if I do not return, name our child after my father if it's a boy, or after my mother if it's a girl," Vic requested.

As tears formed in her eyes and her face turned pale, she replied, "How do you think I am supposed to live without you? All those moments that we had? It seems like they passed so fast. What should I tell our child when he or she grows up and asks about you?" she asked as she collapsed to the floor, crying out loud.

Vic stood there, and those words hit him deep inside, shattering his heart into pieces as he hardly spoke. "It is better like this than to risk you, our kid, and Vincenzo too," Vic concluded.

"Do what you have to do, but never forget that I will love you for eternity," Emily proclaimed.

"As long as I live and the sun sets, the moon is bright and the stars are in the sky, remember that for this love, I am ready to die," Vic told her as he was getting ready to hunt down Anthony.

"Do not think that I do not feel the same. But is this all? All in vain?" Emily asked him while she was feeling deep inside that this love would never end.

"Nothing is in vain when it is done from love. Forgive me for everything, I need to go," he told her as he was opening the door and leaving.

"Don't you want to touch my belly and feel your child, since I do not know if you will ever make it?" Emily asked as her soul was shattering.

"With the power that I have, I can see my child but not ever feel it. It's a boy," he told her.

"I guess your powers are beyond imagination, then. Thank you for letting me know, darling," she answered.

"I will make sure that you will be safe for the rest of your life, along with our child, even though it should not have been like this," Vic concluded.

"Go now, make them pay for what they did and come back, please. I will love you just the way you are, even like this, and we can still be the same," Emily proclaimed.

No, darling, this is not the life that you want," he answered calmly.

As he was leaving the house, he looked at Emily for the last time, opened the door and sprinted just to get as far away as he could. When he reached the mountains up high, he started to focus and search for Anthony. Upon focusing, Anthony was nowhere to be found, and Vic started to think that perhaps he had fled the country and escaped somewhere far away beyond the reach that Vic could see.

In that moment, he felt furious, and the rage in his heart could not be stopped. He yelled from the top of his lungs, and all the birds from the mountains flew away upon hearing his rage. Moments later, as the moon was full in the sky, he started to look for Valor. He wanted to ask him some questions before the third day of being a vampire ended. But Vic knew that this curse would stay with him forever since he did not resist the temptation when he took down Jakob by biting his neck, or perhaps it works in a different way.

Vic wanted to at least try, but upon re-thinking, he decided to leave Valor alone and to continue looking for Anthony. As the night was progressing, Vic travelled at the speed of light everywhere he could without stopping in order to find him, but he was nowhere to be found.

As the night was about to end, he sprinted towards the closest cave nearby, where he entered moments before the sun was about to rise. But he was not alone inside the cave, and there were some mercenaries inside who, upon looking at him, would not dare to say a word or to do anything at all.

Vic, upon seeing this, decided not to engage in action but instead acted like there was nobody inside. The mercenaries were not brave enough to leave the cave, since they feared for their own lives. As Vic was sitting on a stone and thinking about various ways to find Anthony, everyone else present in the cave remained silent along with him.

Moments later, he decided to break the silence. "You can leave if you want. I am here to escape the sun. I am no threat to you," he proclaimed.

One by one, they started to step back slowly and headed to the exit of the cave. As they left, Vic remained alone and was waiting for the sunset, but that day he felt like the sunset was never to come, since the thoughts in his head were attacking him every second, and there was no way that he could get to calm down.

Again, he could not resist the rage and started to yell, and the cave was shaking as if it was haunted by the fear of his rage. Finally, the sunset was there, and this time, Vic could not accept the fact that he could not find Anthony. He started to search for him, even sending thousands of bats in every direction possible to go and search for him, but there was no luck. It seemed as if Anthony had disappeared.

And just like that, day by day, hidden from the sun, night by night, searching in vain, he could not stop for the entire two months, and the agony was killing him from the inside, as he could not let this fight die. He was not ready to give up, as days passed and nights were usually only for hunting, our protagonist got used to living a life of a vampire, a lonely, cursed life of being a blood sucking monster that led him nowhere and made him colder than the stone.

One morning, as he was entering the cave, something in his heart had woken up. Upon focusing, the focus took him to Emily. Upon seeing her with his enhanced vision, he saw that he had become a father, still cold but deep inside, he knew that it was something that, in the end, was worth fighting for. He decided not to go there and to intervene in their happiness, since she had moved back to her parents and her life was better off without him. He just closed his eyes and hoped that she would remain happy for the rest of her life.

As he was sitting on a stone inside the cave, out of curiosity, he wanted to see what Vincenzo was up to. Upon focusing again, he saw him at the same balcony, drinking wine with a sad expression on his face. Vic asked himself, "Would this sadness in his eyes have anything to do with me?"

He could not help but sprint to Vincenzo and ask him some questions, but upon sprinting, he was stopped by the sun and came into short contact with the sunshine. His skin started to burn, but as he took some steps back, it regenerated. As it seemed, he had forgotten that it was morning. He got back inside the cave and decided to wait until sunset, and perhaps then he could go and visit Vincenzo, since there was nothing else that he could do, since the hunt for Anthony was a failure.

Chapter Ten: Never Forget What You Have Become

That day, as Vic was roaming around the cave, memories came back to his mind like a flashback of everything that he had experienced in life since he was a child. Memories of childhood and the terror that he saw when he lost his parents crashed into him. He was about to cry, but he could not, as if all the tears were finished and there was not a single drop left.

As the memories continued, and took him to the time that he had spent in the orphanage, remembering Chris and Otto, and how they escaped, it broke his heart into a million pieces. Again, there were no tears left.

Vic could not take it anymore and started to crush the stones inside the cave as he was feeling this curse deep inside that was eating his soul, that he had sold it to the devil, in order to seek vengeance. Hours passed, and he could not wait for the sunset to come, so he could find some peace in having a conversation with Vincenzo.

But on the other hand, he feared that Vincenzo would not be happy to see him, and in his mind, Vic asked himself, "What have I become? Is this the life that I wanted?"

As the time to go was getting closer, he was surprised to hear Oni's voice. It was a moment of joy as he slowly headed to the exit of the cave, walking slowly and with caution in order not to scare the raven. There it was, standing on an olive branch, looking directly at Vic.

475

As he approached, Oni was not afraid anymore, and it flew directly to his right shoulder. In that moment, Vic started to pet it and feel its wings, which he had missed for a long time. As he was petting his beloved raven, Vic spoke with a soft voice, "My friend, my old friend since my childhood, you have not forsaken me!"

Oni, as if he understood his words, nodded its head, showing confirmation. Oni spread its wings and flew in the sky as Vic sprinted towards Vincenzo, who was still on the balcony, drinking wine and having that same sad expression on his face. As Vic showed up on the balcony, upside down as a bat, Vincenzo looked at him with that sad expression, but it transformed into a smile instantly.

"Vitorio, my friend! Long time no see, how have you been? I missed you madly, as it seems the emotions in you have not changed," Vincenzo concluded.

"Oh, my dear friend, how I wish I were mortal. To hell with Anthony and the rest," Vic proclaimed.

"You know, Vitorio, life is not about avenging the ones you lose. Sometimes life is about living with the pain that others cause us and moving on," Vincenzo stated.

"I wish I had known that a long time ago, my life would have taken another path. Perhaps I would be in France with Emily and my son right now," Vic said with a shaking voice and sad expression.

476

"Perhaps all of us would, those who made it alive and those who did not," Vincenzo said while he was about to break down and cry.

"There is no going back from what I have become. Emily is better off without me, and you as well," Vic concluded.

As Vincenzo got up from his chair, he looked at the distance, "Look at these stars in the sky, their number is unknown, but you know what is known?" he asked.

"What are you referring to?" Vic asked with a surprising look, eager to hear the answer.

"The number of happy moments, and the moments that become happy memories, and you live to recall them," Vincenzo said as he broke down in tears.

As Vic was feeling his sadness, he could not help but say, "I tried my best. I let you all down from time to time. Forgive me for all my mistakes, since I never meant to hurt the ones I love," Vic requested.

"You did not hurt us, my friend. But you did hurt yourself the most by doing this," Vincenzo claimed.

While he was feeling the sad truth, Vic answered, "I have nothing else to lose now. I tried to do what I could do, and even if it takes me an eternity, I will hunt down that bastard."

"What will happen after you find him? I will be dead from age, perhaps Emily too; your son will grow up without a father. What will you do then?" Vincenzo asked.

As those words were breaking Vic down, he answered, "Perhaps from time to time I will come to see them in the middle of the night while they sleep. I know that, like this, I am not able to give them my love."

"As you wish, my dearest friend. But remember that in our hearts you will forever be the same no matter how much you think that we do not love you as we did before," Vincenzo stated.

As Vic was feeling a little bit at ease but still broken inside, "I do not know anymore what I am or what I will become. Perhaps, from the ashes I became and to the ashes I will return," he answered.

"We will all go there, and perhaps we will or will not return. But how we live here? That should matter," Vincenzo proclaimed.

"You are right, my friend. I will see you from time to time. Stay safe," Vic said before he disappeared into the darkness.

As Vic could not bear to hear about it anymore, he decided to go and hide in the shadows. That night, he continued his hunt until dawn, raging over the mountains and crossing the lakes and the rivers, looking for Anthony, who was still nowhere to be found.

He asked hundreds of people and offered them all the gold that he had, just to find a clue about his location, but all of that was in vain, too, since nobody had seen Anthony in a long time, and a lot of them did not even know who he was.

The next day, Vic spent all the time in the cave brainstorming about what he would do next in order to find him. As the day was reaching its end, Vic had an idea that could help him reach his goal. As he reached the town, he acted like a normal person, trying to hide his vampire traits as he went from place to place, seeking mercenaries and offering them a price that they could not resist, just for a clue about where Anthony might be.

After informing half the town, he was often faced with the question, "Why don't you find him by yourself?" to which he always answered with the same answer by saying, "If I could find him, I would not look for your help."

That night, Vic spent all the time that he had before dawn, just to convince them to find at least something that could help, giving each of them ten golden coins as a guarantee for the big prize. As the dawn was getting closer, Vic decided to escape the place and go back to his cave, where he spends his days. The nights in the upcoming eleven months were not anything different from those so far, searching and searching without any kind of clue or info about where Anthony might be.

Until Thomas, his son, on the morning of May, had his first birthday. That morning, Vic was focusing on his enhanced vision as he was every day to see Emily and his child and from time to time. He would check on Vincenzo as well.

As the day was starting, they were all gathered at the Richards' house and celebrated the birthday of little Thomas. While Vic could not approach, deep inside, he hoped that he would see them up close by sunset. That day, Vic was in agony and in the worst possible feelings of being a father and not being able to cherish one of the most important days of being one.

He cursed the night that he had become a vampire. Every day was getting harder and harder for him to live with it. Nights were even harder and heavier to carry with his broken heart, covered with spiders web and toxic blood. As the sunset was at its peak, in a matter of minutes, right before the last moment before the sun went down, Vic, with the speed of light, travelled to Richard's house and for the first time, he could see little Thomas from close, gazing through the window without being noticed by them. The fear did not let him get closer, and he did not want to be seen by his son in the state that he was.

Richard and Anna were playing with Thomas as Emily was gazing through the other window on the other side of the house, while Vincenzo was sitting on the chair and looking at them playing. In those moments, Vic was closely looking at his son and started saying to himself, "Oh my dear boy, how I wish that I could hug you right now and be there for you. If you only knew."

As Vic could not control his emotions and accidentally stepped on the branch that shattered and made noise, Richard became alert and got up to get out of the house to see who was making that noise.

Vic instantly disappeared and went inside his cave. Upon arriving in his cave, Vic felt the sadness that he had never felt in his entire life before, of being a father and a husband and not being able to share the happiness that he wanted and fought for. As days and nights passed and weeks turned into months, Vic could neither reach his goal nor gather the courage to meet his son.

One night in July, Vic decided to go to Vincenzo's castle once more, perhaps to ask him some questions. As he was focusing on seeing where Vincenzo was, upon finding out, it did not surprise him that he was, of course, at his balcony drinking wine with the exact same sad expressing on his face.

Before he decided to travel at the speed of light, Vic came up with the idea of stealing some high-quality wine from the basement of the church and bringing it to Vincenzo as a gift. Vic, as a vampire, entered the church and was in deep pain from seeing the crucifixes. He barely made it in and hardly got out, but managed to steal the wine, and exited the church with a feeling that he would not enter again.

Upon arriving at Vincenzo's balcony, his wounds from the church had healed. He looked at Vincenzo with a soft smile while holding a bottle of wine and saying, "My friend, I brought some gifts this time."

Vincenzo, upon seeing him, felt happy and no longer had that sad expression "Oh Vitorio, welcome and thank you for the wine. Where did you get it?" Vincenzo asked.

"Oh, I stole it, of course, at the church. But I will never get inside one ever again," Vis proclaimed

"Ha-ha, still that same friend that I once knew, with the same sense of humor. This is a feeling that I missed for a long time," Vincenzo answered.

"As it seems some things never change, my friend," he added with a genuine smile on his face.

As Vincenzo was opening a bottle of wine that Vic had brought him, he asked, "What is it that brought you to see your old friend?" he asked.

Vic was gazing in the distance before he answered, as he needed some time to formulate the answer. "You know, my friend, I went to see Emily and my little son, Thomas. I cried and died inside knowing that I will not be able to raise my son, so I came here to ask you to take care of them in case they need anything," Vic requested.

While Vincenzo was about to break down emotionally, he answered with a calm voice, "Do not put this burden on me. It is harder than you know, my friend. You know I will always be there for them, but it kills me that you cannot gather the courage to face your fears and approach your child. Emily does not hate you, nor do her parents, and little Thomas would be the happiest kid in the world to see his father. While you wait, we grow older, my friend," Vincenzo answered with tears in his eyes.

Vic could not find the words for a while, but decided to break the silence by claiming, "What can I offer to my child, all night roaming and all day hiding from the sun? How can he live with that? Aren't you aware of what I am now? What would you do if you were me?"

"Well, at least you can meet your son; you would not be the first one, nor the last one, to be a vampire parent. I am sure, since I was skeptical about this and my Nona's tales, but as it seems it was all true," Vincenzo stated as he was trying to convince Vic.

"If you continue to do this, years will pass, and it will be harder for your child to accept you as he grows. At least take it as advice if you will not listen to me in the end," Vincenzo suggested.

"I will do it then," Vic claimed with a strong tone in his voice, suggesting that he was strong enough to do it.

Vincenzo got up from his chair, drank all the wine from the glass, and told him, "There is the friend that I know."

In that moment, Vic disappeared without saying goodbye, while Vincenzo was left with an empty glass of wine and said, "Vampires."

Before he uttered the words, Vic had arrived in his cave, and since it was too late to go to meet his son, he decided that he would wait for the next sunset. Since it was the middle of the night, Vic could not spend the night in the cave, but decided to appear in the town among people.

This time, he did not seek mercenaries or Anthony at all. In his mind, all that was present was the next sunset and meeting his son, so whatever the consequences might be, he was not afraid at all.

Upon entering the town, there were a few people roaming, some alcoholics and some mercenaries who were out of golden coins, since they could not complete any missions so far. Vic activated the enhanced vision and saw that there was nothing going on; people were only there to spend some time with the broken ones. While he was approaching, there was a mercenary who went by the name of Martin. He was sitting on the ground and holding tight to his sword as Vic was approaching.

"What brought you here all alone, young boy?" Vic asked him.

"The sad reality of the world that I live in," Martin answered.

"How come it is that sad for you?" He asked him as he was sitting beside him.

As Martin was putting his sword into the ground, he asked, "Why did you decide to approach me?"

"Does it bother you? If it does, I will leave," Vic stated.

"Not in the slightest," he replied with a voice where Vic could sense hope.

"What broke your world, if I may know?" Vic asked.

As Martin wanted to answer so badly, he just said, "Life."

In that moment, Vic was getting up, ready to go, but he added, "Life kills us all, but don't give up."

Martin got up as well and stopped Vic by saying, "My mother was killed by somebody named Anthony."

When Vic heard this, his eyes turned red, fangs grew, and he turned into a monster. He grabbed Martin by the throat and asked, "Where the hell is that bastard? I have been looking for him for a long time. Tell me where he is!"

Martin was fighting to catch his breath as his face turned red from the grip and was hoping that Vic would let go as he was trying to speak. Moments later, Vic cooled down and let him out of his grip, to which Martin said, "If I knew, I would kill him myself."

Vic understood that he had made a mistake by raging and thinking that Martin knew, but instead of further raging, he decided to calm down. "Forgive me for how I acted; that son of a bitch killed my two best friends, and I want him dead. I thought that you knew where he was," Vic said

"What are you, man? You nearly killed me," Martin asked.

"I am a monster now, who is looking for him every night and thinking how to find him every day," Vic said.

"I guess you are not the only one who wants him dead, at least that will motivate you more," Martin said as he was still trying to recover.

Vic looked at the distance and noticed that dawn was near "I should go now. If you find him, I will find you," he claimed

Do not kill me the next time you see me," Martin requested.

As Vic disappeared in front of his eyes, Martin only then knew that he was a vampire, a fact that made him feel at ease because of hoping that the revenge that he wanted would come faster than he thought. But, on the other side, he felt fearful because of the fact that he had no idea what Vic was capable of.

Seconds before the dawn, Vic arrived at his cave. The moment that he arrived, he started smashing stones and everything closer to him. The fact that Anthony was mentioned made him go mad. All day he could not find inner peace, and everything seemed impossible, since he was starting to lose hope after all the time that he had been searching for him.

As that day was about to end and the sunset was at its peak, Vic without focusing on his enhanced vision, went with the speed of light to Richard's house, only to find out that Emily and Thomas were not there.

He started to worry madly and was starting to question himself, "Where might they be?"

In that moment he went to Vincenzo's castle, but they were not there either. Only then he decided to focus on his powers, only to find out that they were at his house. He immediately went there and looked through the window.

As Emily was sitting in the living room and Thomas was walking through the house, Vic felt the love that he thought that he had once lost. But before he decided to finally meet his son, Emily spoke.

"Thomas darling, don't touch your father's favorite bow," as she was dying inside to see Vic again.

"This is the home where me and your father build our dreams, love," Emily told him before she started to cry.

As Thomas was trying to speak, he was too little to utter other words than "Mama" and "look."

In those moments, Vic felt mortal again. From looking through the window, he went to the front door and opened it. As Emily was already seconds away from crying when Vic opened the door and she saw him, tears down her cheeks felt like rain from the sky.

Vic rushed to hug her while she was in disbelief. As they both had their moment, little Thomas uttered the word "dada" for the first time. In that moment, Vic grabbed him and kissed him while smiling and feeling the joy that he had never felt in his entire life.

Emily could not believe her eyes after all this time; she was thinking that this was all a dream, and little Thomas knew without being told who his father was. Moments later, Emily broke the silence.

"My darling, the love of my life, I have been waiting for you for a long time. Our son is a year and three months. Finally, you met him," she told him as tears would not stop falling.

"I never knew that you would accept me like this. Little did I know that Thomas would know it, too. I guess that I was wrong," Vic told her while being confused.

"When did I tell you that I would not accept you like you are, and like what have you become? The loneliness killed me each day and night. I was hoping to see you every day," Emily claimed.

"I was afraid of what you, our son, and even your parents might think of me," Vic told her as he was holding Thomas.

As Emily was approaching to kiss Vic, she stated, "As you can see, we missed you badly," she said as she came closer and kissed him while he held Thomas.

"You never gave up on our love, did you, my darling?" Vic asked her.

"Not even after death, my love, my everything. You know that I love you more than life, and that love has only expanded since we had our son," Emily answered as Thomas was constantly gazing at his father.

"How would I stay like this, a ghost in the night and a hidden in the day?" Vic asked her.

At least stay for a while. Until dawn, since you cannot be present for long," Emily requested.

After Vic played with Thomas for an hour and Thomas fell asleep from exhaustion, he was looking at his son sleeping and feeling the joy that he had never felt before, not like this. In those moments, Emily came to the door and watched them close to each other, and in her mind, there was only one thing.

She thought to herself, "What if I could only have this night with the love of my life?"

As she was approaching Vic, he knew where this would lead, and they both went to the living room, leaving little Thomas sleeping. As

Vic and Emily started to kiss with the flame of passion like never before, Emily felt loved once again. On the other hand, Vic felt her love and devotion no matter what they had gone through.

As he was captivated by the passion, he started to undress her and to make her feel the flames of love. As they got to the point of making love, Emily felt something strange, and it was not like before, since Vic had the strength of a monster, but still the same emotion. As Emily was surrendering to the flames of love, Vic was the one who made her fly from the passion, which led to her being pregnant again.

In those moments, as the dawn was nearing, Vic had to rush towards the cave. He remembered that in his own house, he could stay hidden from the sun as well. With a sense of relief and happiness, he got out of bed and covered the windows with pieces of wood that were saved in the room for work in the house.

He went back to bed and hugged Emily so tight while having the feeling that he never wanted to let go. Soon after, Thomas woke up and came into their bed, tucking himself in the middle of them. Vic, after seeing and feeling it, started to feel mortal again.

When the day arrived, Emily woke up first and went to the town to purchase food for her and for Thomas, while Vic was playing inside the house with his son. When Emily arrived, she started to prepare them a meal, and they spent the entire day together in the house as a happy family. Vic was making Thomas laugh while they were playing, and Emily was the one to join them from time to time. As the sunset was getting ready, she feared that Vic might go and leave them, and God knows when he would come back. But little did she know that Vic spent months enjoying their life together, and as Thomas started to speak, he got used to this life with his parents.

As days and nights passed, Vic got used to this life and felt the acceptance of Emily and Thomas every day and every night. Even Richard and Anna visited them, and not a word was spoken by them about his state. They showed the same amount of respect. Vic was finally happy, Emily was again pregnant, and Thomas was a happy child around his parent.

As weeks passed, Vic, during the night, decided to help people around, and sometimes he would be paid, while on the other side, Emily would contribute to her family business by assisting her father and helping him organize the workers. As days passed and nights were so long without Vic there, Emily was feeling alive again, having the love of her life beside her every day.

As weeks turned into months, Vic had forgotten about Anthony, and his life path had changed almost totally. He knew that during the day he could not get out, and that Emily made sure that nobody would know about his presence, apart from her parents and Vincenzo. On the other hand, she also accepted the fact that he would be absent during the nights, and before dawn, he would sneak up to hug her moments before she would have to wake up. Just like that, days passed fast and nights even faster.

One night, Vic decided not to be absent, and instead, he stayed with Emily and started a deep conversation with her. As she was thinking that he would go as usual, Vic approached her with a smile on his face before he could ask her.

"My love, is this real or am I just dreaming?" he asked her while his eyes were sparkling.

"I am not sure yet. Perhaps you could give me more time to understand that it might be real," she answered as she was feeling the warmth of his love.

"Come here, you little love of mine, before I crush you with kisses." He grabbed her before he smothered her with kisses.

"Oh, stop it, darling, you will wake up Thomas. He got tired today from playing," she claimed.

"You know me. I have no control over myself, especially when I see those eyes of yours," Vic told her as he was touching her hair and looking her deep into her eyes.

As she was trying to escape from his grip, she requested, "Stop it, will you? Before you convince me that it is not a dream, my darling."

"Dream or reality, this is us, this is love. I do not know how long it will last, but as long as it does, I will be here with you. Right in your arms," Vic told her while he was making her tickle and laugh.

You, little devil. I always loved you just the way you are," she told him, while she could not make him stop teasing her.

Just when nothing and nobody could separate their happiness. But one night, when somebody was banging at their door in the middle of the night, Vic immediately got out of the bed, told Emily to look after Thomas. As he was getting closer to the door, upon opening the door, there he was, Vincenzo, wounded and bleeding, he could hardly speak or more.

Vic brought him to the living room, even though he had no idea what was going on. While Vincenzo was bleeding, Emily rushed to him to start treating his wounds. Vic wanted to ask what the hell was going on, but resisted until Vincenzo would feel less pain. While Vic was burning inside out to get to know who had done this to him, Vincenzo was the one who spoke first.

"Vitorio, he found me and burned down my castle," Vincenzo claimed as he could hardly speak.

"Was it who I think it was?" Vic asked, about to rage in a matter of seconds.

"No, it was Oliver, his son," Vincenzo answered.

"Like son like father, huh?" Vic stated.

"Just be careful since you have no idea what you will be facing," Vincenzo warned him.

It could not be worse than what I faced so far. Emily, please find a doctor as soon as you can. I can't afford to lose Vincenzo as well. In the meantime, try to suppress his wounds, I must go," Vic ordered before he left.

As he disappeared in the night, in front of Vincenzo's castle, he saw chaos and a destructive sight that would haunt him forever. Upon approaching, his anger and rage turned into another dimension as he slayed Oliver's army one by one, in a matter of seconds, until there was none left.

The thirst for blood made him even more thirsty as he approached the last ones standing, and there he was, Oliver. All alone, vulnerable in those moments. Vic approached him as his eyes were red, and from his mouth, blood was dripping. Oliver did not fear at all since he knew that his father would soon show up.

As Oliver did not move a muscle in those moments, Anthony showed up, and when Vic reached to grab him, aiming to chop him to pieces, Vic was ambushed from the nets above and chains underneath and was trapped beyond hope. As Anthony was laughing from a distance with his evil smile, Vic could not move or do anything. Then, Anthony spoke.

"Finally, I got you, even though I always thought that I will never manage to," he said with a wicked look in his eyes as he was holding the crucifix in his hands.

Oliver interrupted by saying, "It was a trap when you saved me, Victor. How foolish of you."

"I always wanted to kill you myself, Victor, but I never believed that I could," Anthony claimed.

"Tell him how you enjoyed while you killed his friends, Father. Tell him!" Oliver requested

"Oh, when I killed Chris, I loved it. I felt like a king. And when I hanged Otto? I felt like a Viceroy," Anthony spoke with pride as Oliver was having an evil smile.

"How long do you both think that this will last? Once I get to you, even hell will reject your souls."

Victor told them while being trapped.

"Oh, let's not forget Vincenzo. I left him alive just for you to see him like that," claimed Anthony.

"Father, soon there will be dawn, we shall leave him melt, shall we?" Oliver asked.

"We shall, my son, we shall for sure. And little does he know what will happen next. Oh, how I will slay his wife and son," Anthony threatened.

"Oh yes, Father. For the glory, for our victory, and for the souls of Peter and Jakob," Oliver added,

Go on, try to lay a hand on them and you shall see what will be waiting for you," Victor added.

As they left him and the dawn was nearing, Victor could not move a muscle. But, he chose not to show his weakness and not to yell in despair. Instead, he remained calm, and he deeply knew that there would not be a force in this world that would be able to hurt Emily or Thomas or Vincenzo whatsoever.

But he was getting ready for his end, and there was nothing that he could do to stop the power of the sun, as he understood that there would be no way out. As the sun was getting up right at dawn, Victor had accepted his fate, and deep inside, he was hoping that in this form or another, he would come back and make them pay.

While he was moments away from his end, the sun had already started to melt him, and he was screaming in intense pain as his body was burning. Just when his body had turned into nearly a skeleton, there was a fool from the woods named Marcus who did what he did to bring him back to life.

When Marcus saw Victor's body, all burned from the sun, he knew that it was no ordinary corpse. He dragged Victor's body deep inside a cave hidden in the woods and placed it on the stone. Marcus started to act crazy and to look for clues as to what might have occurred in this situation. As he was moving, he cut his hand by accident, and a drop of blood fell into Vic's mouth. Seconds later, Vic's body started to regenerate, and Marcus, upon seeing this, was more afraid than alive.

"Oh dear God, who are you? What have I done?" asked Victor, who could still not move, but he looked like he had not been burned at all.

Moments later, Marcus escaped the cave and ran for his life, while it took some time for Victor to resurrect just from an accidental drop of blood.

When he came to his senses, Victor remembered what had happened and opened his eyes once again, while he was getting ready to go and seek justice that could not die at that dawn.

www.ingramcontent.com/pod-product-compliance
Lightning Source LLC
Chambersburg PA
CBHW032047020426
42335CB00011B/219